Praise for the novels of Lisa Plumley

PERFECT SWITCH

"There's a rising star on the romantic comedy scene, and her name is Lisa Plumley! She delivers great characters, plenty of laughs and a delicious love story. I give *Perfect Switch* a perfect 10!"
—*New York Times* best-seller Vicki Lewis Thompson

"*Perfect Switch* is so much fun to read, you will not put it down until the last page is turned. The story is witty, original, tender and sizzles with chemistry. It is a romantic comedy you do NOT want to miss."
—*Old Book Barn Gazette*

PERFECT TOGETHER

"*Perfect Together* is a perfectly spontaneous, perfectly fun, fish-out-of-water splash!"
—Stephanie Bond, author of *I Think I Love You*

"Engaging, well-developed protagonists and an abundance of appealing secondary characters. . . . This effervescent and heartwarming comedy will appeal to fans of Rachel Gibson and Elizabeth Bevarly."
—*Library Journal*

"Lisa Plumley is a comedic buried treasure! Screwball comedy with sizzle, *Perfect Together* blends laugh-out-loud antics and touching romance."
—*Romantic Times BOOKclub*

"Plumley's humor sparkles in this thoroughly engaging tale about what's real and what isn't."
—*Booklist* (starred review)

"Plumley is becoming a master at blending silly and poignant. She hits all the marks with *Perfect Together!*"
—*The Oakland Press*

RECONSIDERING RILEY

"Lisa Plumley creates charming characters. Her books are a delight!"
—*USA Today* best-selling author Rachel Gibson

Lisa Plumley

Once Upon A Christmas

ZEBRA BOOKS
KENSINGTON PUBLISHING CORP.
www.kensingtonbooks.com

ZEBRA BOOKS are published by

Kensington Publishing Corp.
850 Third Avenue
New York, NY 10022

All Kensington titles, imprints and distributed lines are available at special quantity discounts for bulk purchases for sales promotion, premiums, fund-raising, educational, or institutional use.

Special book excerpts or customized printings can also be created to fit specific needs. For details, write or phone the office of the Kensington Special Sales Manager: Attn. Special Sales Department. Kensington Publishing Corp., 850 Third Avenue, New York, NY 10022. Phone: 1-800-221-2647.

Zebra and the Z logo Reg. U.S. Pat. & TM Off.

ISBN 0-8217-7860-9

First Printing: October 2005
10 9 8 7 6 5 4 3 2 1

Printed in the United States of America

For John, with love

CONTENTS

MISTLETOE
AND HOLLY

One

It should have been a perfectly romantic evening. The lighting was soft, the music was seductive, the wine was cold. Even the weather had cooperated, in the form of a late-autumn Arizona rainstorm that thrummed on the roof with a hypnotic rhythm. It was the kind of night that invited snuggling up together and forgetting the rest of the world existed.

And it would have been that kind of night, had everything gone according to Holly Aldridge's plan. Instead, things had started going downhill from the moment her boyfriend Brad came home to the cozy Craftsman-style bungalow they shared, swearing and dripping rainwater on the foyer tile. He stripped off his wet suit jacket and, tugging at his tie, came toward her in the darkness.

"Power go out?"

"Nooo."

"Then what's with all the candles, Holly? I can hardly see a thing in here," he complained, finally whipping off his tie with a last irritable tug.

He's had a hard day, Holly told herself. *Be nice to him.*

She patted the sofa cushion. "Mood lighting. You'll get used to it in a minute. Come sit by me."

He did, first catching hold of her feet and swinging her legs up on the coffee table to make more room. So much for her seductive pose. She leaned into him and lay her head on the rain-dampened curve of his shoulder. "Tough day?"

Brad dropped his head back and sighed, staring up at the ceiling. "Yeah, you could say that."

"Sorry," she murmured, turning her head to glance up at him. Even wet and grouchy he looked good, like a glossy sort of Young Republican poster boy—not a single dark hair deviated from its prescribed course. Holly admitted to no one but herself Brad was more skilled with styling gel than she was.

She didn't want to ask about his day and be treated to an hour-long discourse on the impossibility of practicing medicine on a bunch of patients who—as Brad put it—wouldn't recognize common sense if it fell on their heads. Once he got started on that, things would really go awry. So she slid a little closer and started undoing his top shirt button.

"Holly."

Buttons two and three down. He was always telling her how he was tired of making the first move. Tonight would be different. She moved lower and tackled button number four.

"Holly." This time Brad caught her wrists in his hands, as though she'd maul him if unrestrained. "Give me a little time to decompress, okay? It's been a long day."

"Okay, sure."

He let go of her wrists and pulled the ends of his shirt together again. Paradise lost.

"How about a drink, then?" Holly asked brightly. She filled two wineglasses with rosé and handed him one.

He drained his glass, then set it on the glass-topped wrought-iron coffee table with a thunk that set the tabletop ringing, completely bypassing the coasters he usually insisted on using. Holly frowned. Either Brad was very, very thirsty or his mood was even worse than she'd thought.

She splashed more rosé in his glass, hoping it was the former. When Brad finally looked at her, fixing her with what she immediately recognized as his I'm-serious-as-Hell look, Holly knew it was the latter.

"I'm sorry, Holly," he said, now looking everywhere but at her. "Really sorry. But I just can't do this anymore. You and me . . . it's not working. Things just aren't right for me."

Cold trickled down her spine. Of course things were right. She'd planned everything, down to his favorite ratatouille simmering on the stove, down to the CDs she'd programmed on the stereo, down to the perfume the tastefully made-up woman at the Estée Lauder counter had assured Holly was "irresistible, dear."

She wouldn't have gone to such trouble for a doomed relationship, would she?

"What do you mean?" Her voice sounded faraway, broken. She finished off her wine for fortification and glanced at him. Any second now he'd come out with some clichéd line like, "I need some space, that's all," and she'd nod wisely and tell him she'd been thinking exactly the same thing about herself, wasn't that funny, ha ha. And then she'd brain him with the wine bottle and boot him out into the rain.

"I—" He spread out his arms in a choreographed sort of helpless gesture, careful not to actually touch her. "I've got to get away for a while, do some thinking. I guess I just need some space, that's all."

Oh, God. "Brad, I—" Her lower lip trembled and her chin wobbled. She would *not* cry, she wouldn't. Holly poured more rosé and gulped it down. "I . . . that's funny, 'cause I was just thinking the same thing."

Her croaked statement lacked a certain conviction, but it was the best she could do under the circumstances.

He pressed both hands to his thighs and pushed up from the sofa. "I knew you'd understand," he said, ruffling her hair as he passed by.

So much for her carefully arranged, seductive hairstyle.

"Mmmm, what's that great smell?" he went on, looking brisk and assured. *Whew,* his expression said. *Glad that's over with!* Brad hated scenes. "Mind if I eat before I pack up? I'm starving."

"It's ratatouille," she replied numbly. "Help yourself."

"Help yourself? You actually said to him, 'Gee, Brad, help yourself'? Oh, Holly."

Feeling miserable, Holly slumped further in the corner of

her kitchen banquette. She rested her cheek against its soft yellow upholstery.

"Quit shaking your head at me, Clarissa. Come on, it wasn't as dumb as it sounds. It just popped out. I couldn't help it."

"Uh-huh."

"It was supposed to sound cosmopolitan. 'Sure, darling, of course we can still be friends,' something like that. You know. And I didn't say, 'gee,' either," Holly added indignantly. "Geez, you're supposed to be my friend! What am I supposed to do now?"

Clarissa gave her a sympathetic look. "Sorry. I didn't realize Brad the Bad meant so much to you."

"Ha, ha." With a sigh Holly wrapped one arm around her upraised knees and reached for her cup of cappuccino—courtesy of the espresso machine Brad had left behind. She'd need to drink a gallon of the stuff to feel awake after what she'd been through. Maybe two gallons. In fact, maybe she should just skip a step and gnaw on the coffee beans. The wine she'd drunk last night had been a mistake, especially when followed by a can of Brad's orphaned beer and a vodka chaser. She didn't know what she'd been thinking.

"I feel like such an idiot. I didn't even see it coming. How could I have been so blind?"

"You weren't blind, he was stupid," Clarissa replied loyally. "What kind of cheesy line is that anyway?" She flipped her long pale hair over her shoulders and pantomimed a Brad-like stance, both hands on her hips with her chest thrust forward. "'Babe, I need my space.' Didn't that line go out about the same time lava lamps did?"

Holly managed a brief smile. Clarissa was right. Brad's reasons for ending their relationship were weak, but the fact of the matter was, he didn't really need an excuse. He only needed to be gone for it to be over, and he was.

She was alone. All alone. Completely, utterly alone. The holidays were on their way, and she'd be alone then, too. Thanksgiving for one. A solo Christmas. A blue Christmas. A blue, blue, blue, blue Christmas.

Lord, she sounded pathetic. Poor me. Pity party. *Get a grip already,* Holly commanded herself. *You've got a good job, good friends, a good life. Where's your self-respect?*

"Anyway, I have a plan," she announced.

Clarissa grinned. "Somehow, I thought you would."

"What's funny? In case you haven't noticed, this could be considered a tragic moment in my life, here." She picked up a pen and opened her day planner, trying to ignore her friend's skeptical expression. "Okay. Brad and I have been together for a little over a year now. No problems until last night."

"Really? That's amazing."

"You're turning into a cynic."

Clarissa carried both coffee cups to the sink. Prompted by Holly's meaningful glance at the brown-ringed mugs, she turned on the tap and gave each one a cursory swish. "No, really. Didn't the two of you ever argue? About anything?"

"Nope."

"Hmmph." Clarissa grabbed a cinnamon-raisin bagel from the basket on the kitchen table and settled back on the other banquette, picking out the raisins with her long red manicured fingernails. She popped a raisin in her mouth, then another. "I've got to be honest here, Holly Berry. That's abnormal."

"It's true," Holly insisted, printing one last note in her day planner. "Maybe we didn't argue because we were so well-suited for each other."

"Well-suited? Did we warp back into the dark ages when I wasn't looking? What are you talking about, well-suited? I don't think arranged marriages are happening anymore."

"Very funny." Ticking off each similarity on her fingers, Holly said, "Brad and I are the same age. We went to the same schools. Both of us grew up here. We've got the same goals—"

"Career, career, and . . . career?" Clarissa suggested.

"No, I mean life goals. Like we both want a family." Or at least Brad hadn't actively discouraged her on those few occasions when she'd talked about having children together someday. Holly tilted her head sideways, thinking. There had to be more things they had in common. "We're even the same height," she announced triumphantly.

Twirling the remains of her bagel on one finger, Clarissa asked, "Really? I always thought Brad was taller than you."

"I slouched," Holly admitted. They both grinned. Meanly. "But all the right elements were there, and I'm not just going to let this pass me by. I'm practically thirty—"

"Nearly dead," Clarissa broke in, nodding and grinning.

"—and it's time I settled down."

Clarissa shook her head. "You've got to be the most settled-down person I know. You've got a retirement plan. You've got coordinated bath towels, for crying out loud. Even my mother doesn't have towels that match."

Holly's towels did match. Down to the washcloths, they were all a suitably masculine burgundy color, the only one she and Brad had both liked.

"There's more to life than decorating," Holly said, ignoring Clarissa's raised eyebrows. "Besides, Brad and I had a good relationship. Maybe we were taking each other for granted, maybe some of the spark went out of things, but I think we had something worth saving."

Clarissa looked doubtful. Well, let her, Holly thought rebelliously. It wasn't *Clarissa's* love life that had taken a nose dive. Clarissa had been happily married for three years now. She could afford to take the high moral ground.

Squinting at the notes she'd penned neatly in her day planner, Holly went on. "Anyway, my theory is what we've got here is a fear of commitment. I think Brad and I just got so close it scared him."

"I guess so. Maybe."

"Your enthusiasm is too much for me," Holly muttered wryly. She gathered her convictions again. "It's like I said. Maybe Brad and I were taking each other for granted and got caught in a rut, or something."

She hoped her reasoning sounded more convincing to Clarissa than it suddenly did to her. Last night, lying in bed alone, it had all made perfect sense. Unfortunately, Holly hadn't come up with any better interpretations since then.

Her feelings, her love life, her pride were at stake. Her life didn't *feel* like it was supposed to anymore, and she couldn't bear to sit back and do nothing at all about it.

"I mean, Brad didn't actually say we were through," she said, "not in so many words . . ."

Clarissa gaped at her. "Oh, geez, tell me you don't mean what I think you mean—"

Holly nodded, smiling with renewed hope at the notes she'd made. Her plan. Just looking at it made her feel a little better.

"You guessed it. I'm going to win Brad back. I've already got it all planned out. And I'll need your help to do it."

Clarissa smacked her palm against her forehead. "Lord help us. That's just what I was afraid of."

Sam McKenzie had always loved the last day of school. His final act as a student each year had been to haul everything out of his locker and cram it in a backpack for the trip home—where it would sit, untouched, until September. Now, as the college English professor he'd become, things weren't much different.

Sure, these days it was his desk he emptied out, and his things were going in a battered old box instead of a backpack. But as he wedged the last file folder beneath his weighty American Literature text, Sam doubted he'd crack a book again before January rolled around.

For much of the semester, he'd been filling in for Professor Alvarez, who—until this week—had been on maternity leave. Now that she was back, Sam had cut his own semester short to turn her students over to her again.

The decision left him at loose ends, with no classes to teach until winter term—not that he minded very much. Somebody had needed to fill in for Lupe, so Sam had volunteered. They were friends, and he'd never been on the tenure track, anyway. He didn't much care about impressing the faculty. All he cared about was teaching.

Okay, teaching *and* his family. Which explained why Sam was leaving Tucson for a couple of months, headed back to his hometown of Saguaro Vista, where a temporary job with his dad's construction company waited.

Working for McKenzie & Sons was something Sam tried to do on a regular basis, especially now that his father's arthritis was kicking up more often. He liked working with his hands, liked mixing it up with the carpenters and roofers and bricklayers. They reminded him of where he'd come from and what was *real* . . . as did the inevitable get-a-haircut-and-get-a-real-man's-job lecture from his father that was the price of admission. Until after the holidays, Sam would belong to that world again. Just as soon as he said good-bye to this one.

He hefted the box in his arms. "Okay, I'm outta here."

Malcolm Jeffries, campus advisor for returning students and Sam's officemate for the past semester, sniffed vaguely but didn't bother to look up. He'd made his disapproval of what he called Sam's "unorthodox teaching methods" plain from the start, and Malcolm was nothing if not unvarying in his opinions. It had made for a bumpy partnership.

Today, not even Malcolm's standardized-test-approach to life could get to Sam. "Hey, have a good rest of the semester," he told Malcolm with a grin. "See you next year."

The grunt he received in response could have meant anything. Optimistically decoding the sound as, "You, too," Sam turned toward the door and all but ran into one of his students, Jillian Hall.

Affectionately known to the student body as Jiggly Jillie, Jillie lived up to her nickname and then some. Even when standing still, Jillie's blond froth of permed curls, combined with the twirl of her short skirt and the sway of her breasts beneath her T-shirt, somehow gave the impression of perpetual motion. It was quite a phenomenon.

"Professor McKenzie, I'm so glad you're still here," she said breathlessly. "I wanted to talk to you about my research paper."

She watched him so earnestly, it looked as if her wide blue eyes might cross at any second. Sam shoved all jiggly thoughts aside and assumed a more professorial demeanor.

"Sure, Jillie. What's on your mind?"

"Well, there must have been some kinda mistake on my research paper. I can't have gotten a D," she wailed, holding up a stack of typed pages for him to see. "If I don't do better than that in this class, my financial aid is history!"

Sam took the papers she waved at him. He recognized them all right—it had taken him four aspirin and several cups of coffee to finish reading and grading those few pages of freshman composition.

"What happened to your paper on the use of lab animals in cosmetics testing—the one you outlined for me?" he asked gently. "You had some very good ideas for that. It could have been a good position paper, like we discussed in class."

Jillie ducked her head and thrust her lower lip forward. The gesture would have looked more at home on a four-year-old than the twenty-four-year-old single mother of two toddlers Sam knew her to be.

"I thought you'd like this better." She fiddled uncomfortably with her pink-polished fingernails. "It's more serious. I thought you'd be impressed."

"Hearing your own ideas would impress me the most. The best papers come when you really care about your subject, Jillie. Maybe I'm wrong, but I'm not sure global warming is something near and dear to your heart."

Sam glanced meaningfully at her paper. Touching her shoulder, he added, "Environmentalism is a worthy subject, but I don't think you had time to research this properly, and—"

Her eyes filled with tears. "You're just like Mr. Jeffries!" she accused, darting a narrow-eyed glance at Sam's officemate. "He doesn't think I belong in college. Him and all those tests he does say I was meant to be a cosmetologist and that's what I ought to stay." Her tearful gaze swung around to Sam again. "You're no better, are you? You two don't want people like me here at all."

Temporarily setting down his box, Sam shook his head. Hell, *he* was "people like Jillie," a guy who'd spent high school screwing around and the years afterward getting in one scrape after another. He was twenty-three before he finally worked up the guts to walk into the college admissions office. Even then he'd half expected to get laughed out of the place. He remembered what it was like to sweat over the placement tests, the first few papers, the exams.

Besides, he'd rather die than be lumped in the same tight-assed category as Malcolm Jeffries.

"Tell you what." Sam nodded toward his box of books and files. "My grade sheets are still in there. I've got to drop them off to Professor Alvarez by five o'clock, but I think I could see my way clear to writing in a C for your research paper—"

"Really?" Jillie interrupted, sniffling.

Sam nodded.

"Oh, professor, you don't know what this means to me!" She hugged herself, bobbing in a happy jig.

"Hold on," he said sternly, one hand upraised. "There's a catch. I want you to rewrite your paper. You can redo global warming—and put some hard research into it this time—but it would be a shame to waste all the work you've already put into your cosmetics testing idea."

Jillie stopped jiggling. She glanced sideways, biting her lower lip. "Oh, I guess you're right. Okay."

"I know I'm right." Shuffling through his files, Sam tore off a slip of paper and wrote his address on it. "You've got my phone number. Call me if you get stuck." He handed Jillie the paper. "Otherwise, you can drop off your paper to me no later than Friday. I'm leaving town after that."

She clutched the scrap of paper like a lifeline. "Thanks, thank you so much. You'll have it by Friday, I promise."

Her smile widened as she turned to go. Sam picked up his box again, watching her. Halfway down the hall, Jillie paused.

"You won't regret this, professor! Thanks!"

Sam wanted to believe she was right. Something warned him otherwise. Some niggling doubt in the back of his mind told him he might regret his decision very much. Then he realized it wasn't intuition at all. It was the sight of Malcolm Jeffries' gloating face peering at him through his open office door.

"I'll have your butt in a sling for this, McKenzie," his office-mate said with a sneer. "I always knew you were a lousy teacher, and now I've got proof. You just wait. Your little arrangement with Jiggly is going to blow up in your face like your worst nightmare."

Sam glanced at him, making a little tsk-tsk sound. "Gotta watch those mixed metaphors, Malcolm," he said.

Then he was off to enjoy the next few months, academia-free—*and*, more importantly, Malcolm-free.

* * *

Two days after the romantic dinner that wasn't, Holly's conviction that she and Brad belonged together hadn't wavered. This was despite a minor setback that occurred when she came home to find Brad sneaking out of the house, his arms laden with the cappuccino maker and both stereo speakers.

"Hey, those are mine!" She hurried up the front walk as fast as her two-inch heels and double burden of briefcase and gym bag would allow, meeting Brad just outside the front door.

"Huh?"

He craned his neck sideways and peered at her through his glasses in that adorably owlish way he had. His eyes looked greener than ever, Holly noticed before steeling her resolve.

However appealing Brad might look, she wasn't about to let him demolish their stereo system, even for the short time they were going to be apart.

"Oh, it's just you, Holly." He looked surprised. "I, uh . . . didn't think you'd be home yet."

She tapped the nearest speaker. Her new manicure—one of Clarissa's contributions to The Plan—gleamed richly in the sunlight. Brad hated sloppy-looking women. "These are mine, remember?"

"The *stereo* is yours, Holly. These speakers belong to me," he reminded her as he headed down the sidewalk toward his car.

Holly pivoted on the welcome mat and followed him, kicking aside dried bougainvillea leaves with every step. She could always tell when Thanksgiving was on its way, because the first serious cold snap wreaked havoc on her yard. Soon, she'd camouflage the bougainvillea's crispy vines with a few cheerful strings of Christmas lights, but in the meantime she had a boyfriend to reclaim.

Prompted by that reminder, Holly pursued Brad to his car. She needed to move things along before she found herself stringing lights, roasting chestnuts, *and* trimming the tree all alone.

"I'm pretty sure those *speakers* are mine, too," she said.

He sighed. "You blew your tinny little speakers the day after we moved in together. Remember?"

"Oh, yeah." Some passing spiteful impulse made her lean against the door of his red BMW while she watched him load up his things. He slammed the trunk shut, noticed she was still there, and yanked her away from the car. He even looked cute when he scowled.

"Christ, Holly. I just waxed it."

I'll bet. "Ooops," she said. The damn car got more stroking than she ever had, it occurred to her.

"What are you doing here, anyway?" he asked accusingly, glancing at his watch. "It's only . . . oh. You're right on time, I guess. I didn't realize it had gotten so late already."

Holly propped her hands on her hips. She turned her body toward him in a friendly way so the neighbors wouldn't guess they were anything less than blissfully happy together. Temporarily. "What are you talking about?"

"Well, it's 6:30, isn't it?" Brad rummaged around in his pants pocket and came up with his car keys a few seconds later.

Holly could tell from his expression this cryptic explanation was supposed to mean something to her, but for the life of her she couldn't figure out what. "So what?"

To his credit, he looked almost sorry to have brought up the whole subject. "So you're a little predictable, that's what. You leave work at 5:15 every weekday. Afterward you go to the gym for an hour—if it's Monday, Wednesday, or Friday—then home. They could set clocks by you, you're so unspontaneous."

"I am not!" Holly protested, but he was warming to his subject now, she could tell.

He nodded at the neatly folded paper bag sticking out of her gym bag. "Your lunch, right? I'll bet it was a turkey sandwich on wheat—"

"This is dumb."

"—with brown mustard and lettuce on the side. Tomato juice to drink, with a bendy straw. And a green apple."

"It was a red apple," Holly shot back.

"I'm leaving." He opened the car door, slid inside, and revved the engine. She rapped on the window.

He pressed the button that rolled it down. "Let's not make this any harder than it has to be," he said. "I'm not trying to hurt you, you know. I just can't deal with all this right now. I told you, I need some space."

Was it just her, or was his regretful expression a little at odds with the way he kept impatiently revving the car's engine?

"Sure." *Predictable*, he'd said. *Unspontaneous*. "I understand." When she got done with her plan, Brad wouldn't know what hit him. "I just wanted to tell you, I need your house keys back."

He grinned. Then he laughed. She felt like kicking him.

"What for?" He twisted his key ring to release his set of house keys. He dropped them, warm from his fingers, in her palm. "You've found another roommate already?"

Predict this, Holly thought. "As a matter of fact, I have. And *he's* moving in this weekend. See ya'."

Nothing like a little competition to enliven the game, she told herself. Didn't every man want what he couldn't have?

Tempting as it was, she didn't even linger to savor the sight of Brad's mouth hanging open in surprise. She couldn't—she had to get busy finding that new roommate.

"I told you, I'm not interested in having a roommate."

Easing his pickup truck into the early morning traffic that streamed into town, Sam McKenzie glanced away from the road long enough to be sure his cousin Clarissa was listening to him. She wasn't. Oh, she was nodding her head, all right, but he'd known Clarissa since they were both four feet tall—long enough to realize that with her, a nod didn't necessarily indicate agreement. Sam sighed.

"I'm only in town until after the holidays, then I'm back to Tucson. I'm sure your friend Holly is terrific, but I'm not in the market for a roommate. I like to live alone."

Beside him across the wide bench seat, Clarissa snorted.

"Is that why you're staying with your folks, because you like to be alone? You know I love you like a brother, Sam, but I've got to be honest, here. That's truly pathetic."

"Don't hold back. Tell me what you really think."

She hit him in the shoulder, a punch probably aimed at his upper arm but sent awry by the bouncing of his old truck.

"Ouch! Does David know he's married to such a bruiser?"

"My husband doesn't give me any reason to punch him," Clarissa returned archly. "Unlike my knot-headed cousin. Besides, I barely touched you."

She twisted in the seat, nearly crushing the sack of bargain-priced Christmas wrapping paper Sam's mother had left in his truck yesterday. He grabbed it, then deposited it in a safer spot, beside the six cans of cranberry sauce and packets of instant turkey gravy she'd also purchased.

Turning his attention to the road again, Sam automatically scanned the streets and buildings around them. Everything looked the same as it ever did in Saguaro Vista, the same as it had since he'd been a kid steering a bike down Main Street instead of his pickup. The old adobe buildings looked a little more worn, and now there were strip malls sprouting up like weeds at the edges of town, but all in all it was nice to come back to. Comforting.

His mouthy cousin was anything but.

"Anyway, the only time you're alone is when you're between girlfriends," she was saying, sounding so primly sure of herself he couldn't stand it.

"I've never lived with any of them, either," he protested, but Clarissa overrode him, giving Sam a look that allowed no argument.

"I'm not asking you to marry Holly, for God's sake! She's got a boyfriend she's dead-set on already, though I can't imagine why."

Clarissa gazed out the passenger-side window, the very picture of nonchalance. Sam didn't buy her act for a minute. This roommate thing mattered a lot to her, or she wouldn't have been nagging him about it for the past two days.

"This boyfriend doesn't object to her having a male roommate?" Either the guy was very, very sure of himself—and her—or he was just plain stupid.

"Well, technically they're separated." She must have sensed him weakening, because Clarissa smiled and moved in for the kill. "Come on. Do it as a favor to me, if nothing else. I know! Consider it an early Christmas present."

"Ha. I *know* you, remember? You'll still expect a boatload of gifts under the tree."

"Naturally." She grinned. "But you'll be one ahead, won't you? That's got to count for something. And all *before* Thanksgiving, too."

Considering it, Sam jerked the truck to a stop in the mesquite-shaded parking lot of the Downtown Grill. He still didn't want a roommate. "Nope."

"What?"

Clearly, she couldn't believe he was refusing her.

"Bah, humbug," he said for emphasis. "You'll have to wait until Christmas morning for your presents, just like all the rest of the kids."

She snorted, not the least bit deterred by his Scrooge impression. Snapping open her seat belt, Clarissa gave him a no-nonsense look. "Listen. I just want the people I care about to be happy, that's all. If your answer's still no after you meet Holly, then I'll drop the whole thing, okay?"

Sam stared at her suspiciously. Maybe it was because she'd worn him down, or maybe it was just because he was starving and wanted their conversation to end. Whatever the reason, he found himself nodding.

"Fine. I'll meet your damn friend."

"Great!"

Clarissa hopped out of the truck. She came around to Sam's side to meet him. Apparently undaunted despite the fact he'd used his best, most grumbly, feet-dragging tone, she grabbed his arm and swept him along beside her toward the Downtown Grill.

"There's Holly's car right over there," she said, her wave indicating a white convertible parked a few feet away. "She must be inside waiting for us right now."

Sam stopped walking. "Did it never occur to you I might say no?"

"Nah." Clarissa stepped back to let him open the door for her, offering him a self-satisfied smile. "I usually get what I want."

With an answering grin, Sam ushered her through the door. "Must run in the family," he said. "So do I."

Two

All right. Maybe it was just a *teensy* bit juvenile to try to make Brad jealous, Holly admitted to herself as she sat alone in a cracked leather booth at the Downtown Grill waiting for Clarissa to meet her for breakfast. Granted, she'd been provoked into her boast about a roommate she didn't have yet. And her decision had certainly been a spontaneous one, which was some consolation to her bruised ego. Still, she was almost starting to regret the way those words had just popped out of her mouth.

"Hey, Holly Berry!"

Clarissa's voice, loud enough even to carry over the din of the restaurant, yanked Holly out of her worries. Glancing up, she saw her friend wending nearer between the rows of customer-filled booths.

She wasn't alone. There was a man with her. Tall and shaggy-haired, dressed in paint-splattered Levis and a white T-shirt, he somehow managed to look both friendly and slightly disreputable at the same time. He didn't seem familiar, but then Holly had been working such long hours she'd fallen out of touch with many of the people in town.

"I've solved your roommate problem!" Clarissa announced gaily when she'd reached the table. She waved one arm in the general direction of the man beside her. "Holly Aldridge, meet Samuel McKenzie."

"Sam," he corrected. "Clarissa's told me all about you."

His smile was so inviting that, despite her better judgment, Holly smiled back at him.

"I hope everything she said was good," Holly said, accepting the handshake he offered.

His palm was calloused but clean, and big, like the rest of him. She felt his gaze sweep over her, from the collar of her black suit jacket downward and back again. His appreciative expression took her by surprise. How long had it been since Brad had looked at her like that? Since any man had looked at her like that?

Too long.

"Every bit of it was good," he assured her. "It's nice to meet you."

He actually sounded as if he meant it. Holly gave herself a mental shake and withdrew her hand, watching as Sam and Clarissa settled themselves in the opposite side of the booth.

He was the answer to her roommate problem? Okay, so Sam was pretty attractive in a relaxed, just-rolled-out-of-bed sort of way, but by the looks of him Holly doubted he even had a job, much less the means to pay half her mortgage payment each month.

She slid the hot water and tea she'd already ordered for Clarissa over to her friend, along with a curious glance.

Clarissa ignored Holly's questioning look. Uncharacteristically, she remained absolutely silent as she fussed with her tea. In fact, Holly noticed, her lips were pressed tightly together, like a child zipping her lips to keep a secret. Something was definitely up.

"Clarissa says you're looking for a roommate," Sam said, filling the silence at their table.

He turned over the thick white porcelain cup in front of him and settled it in its saucer. Like magic, a pink-skirted waitress appeared and filled it with coffee. Holly wondered absently if Sam got service like that every place he went. She decided he probably did.

"Yes, I am. My last roommate just moved out." Why had

she called Brad her roommate? "And I've been looking for someone to, um, replace him."

Sam nodded. Clarissa snickered and dunked a teabag in her cup with far more interest than the Earl Grey required. She looked like the cat who ate the canary. Holly frowned.

"Is it a house or an apartment?" Sam asked.

As though pulled by his voice, she looked at him again. He had nice eyes, too—clear blue beneath a pile of sandy-colored hair. Hair that looked *way* too straightforward to have been gelled or moussed or fussed with the way Brad's always was.

"It's a house. One of those old bungalows downtown," she replied. Why wasn't Clarissa saying anything?

"Those Craftsman-style bungalows near Spring Street?"

She nodded, surprised he was familiar with the architectural movement that had spawned row after row of houses downtown in the first decades of the century. Hers was one of the few examples of the style that remained unchanged. Many had been demolished to make way for shops and newer stucco houses.

"Those are great houses," he was saying. "Ahead of their time, I think. It's too bad there are so few left now."

"Holly's renovating hers," Clarissa chimed in. "It's going to be beautiful."

"Tell me about it."

Sam handed her a leather-bound copy of the Downtown Grill's menu as though the motion was the most natural thing in the world. As though they'd shared meals together forever.

Holly blinked. *Get real*, she ordered herself, pushing that wild thought out of her mind. She couldn't really be interested in him, could she? Muscle-bound laborers had never been her type. She wanted a man with a future, a man with intelligence and wit, a man who thought beyond his next conquest . . . a man like Brad.

Besides, a guy like Sam probably favored leggy blondes in spandex, not sensible redheads in Chanel-knockoff business suits. Holly put down the menu without opening it.

"I'm still looking for a contractor to handle the bulk of the renovation," she told him. "There are parts I can do myself, but I'd like to get an expert's input, too."

Sam raised an eyebrow at Clarissa, giving her an odd look. "What a coincidence," he remarked. To Holly, he said, "I know a little about whole-house renovation. I'd love to have a look at it sometime."

"Sure."

The waitress, pen and pad in hand, chose that moment to take their order. Holly declined anything but her coffee, but Clarissa and Sam both ordered plates of the Grill's special pecan pancakes, his with a double side of bacon. Scooping up their menus, the waitress went on her gum-snapping way toward the restaurant's kitchen.

"Sam's doing some work for my uncle's construction company," Clarissa explained. "He's one of the 'and sons' in McKenzie & Sons."

At least this potential roommate Clarissa had found for her was employed. "Do you like it?" Holly asked.

"I like the work. It's absorbing, doing a job just right, seeing a vision come to life. Done well, renovation is demanding, but creative." Sam's eyes met hers. "Besides, I'm very good with my hands."

Very good echoed in her head as her gaze flew to his hands. Her mouth went dry. Had he meant to say those words that way, so . . . *loaded* with erotic meaning? Surely it was only her imagination.

"I could give you a demonstration." He leaned against the booth again, his shoulders nearly reaching the top of it. "How about tonight? Say, 6:30?"

"Tonight?" For a few confused seconds, Holly actually thought he was proposing some sort of illicit meeting, some personal presentation of those hands' promised abilities. One glance at Sam dispelled that illusion, however. He was asking to see her house, nothing more.

Before she could reply, Clarissa said, "You sound just like your dad, Sam. Straight down to business." Turning to Holly, she added, "My uncle Joe has got to be the most single-minded guy in town."

How she was supposed to react to *that* statement, Holly had no idea. Then the significance of Clarissa's words dawned on her. Sam McKenzie was Clarissa's "little cousin Sam."

Funny how she'd never mentioned that in this case, at least, "little" meant he was a couple of years younger. Sam was most definitely not the Little League-sized relative Holly had always assumed him to be. She glared at Clarissa and silently mouthed, "I'll get you for this."

With feigned innocence, Clarissa raised her eyebrows. *Who, me?* her expression asked.

"That's why I thought Sam would make such a perfect roommate for you, Holly," she said. "He's dependable"— Holly couldn't decipher the look that passed between the two cousins—"great with old houses, and he'll only be in town for the next couple of months."

"Through the holidays?" Holly asked.

"Until next semester starts," Sam explained, going on to describe his work as an English professor at the university in Tucson.

Holly was surprised—they definitely hadn't had professors like Sam when *she* was a student at the University of Arizona. She'd bet his students loved him.

A few minutes later the waitress slid two enormous plates of pecan pancakes on the table, followed by an aromatic pile of bacon she set in front of Sam, along with the bill. Holly's stomach rumbled as the sugary smell of maple syrup reached her.

Sam swallowed a bite of pancake, speared another with his fork, and held it out to her. "Want a bite?"

She couldn't imagine doing anything so intimate as eating from his fork, Sam guiding the bite of food into her mouth as Clarissa and the whole world looked on. Brad would have been appalled by the very idea, had she ever suggested it to him.

With Sam on the other end of the fork, though, the idea had a new appeal. Some small, hidden part of her *wanted* to try it, urged her to try it. Holly considered it as, spellbound, she watched an amber drop of maple syrup gather on the tip of his fork tines, tremble, then drip slowly to join the butter and syrup puddle on Sam's plate.

Oh, boy. She was really losing it. This whole debacle with Brad had clearly sent her around the bend.

Sam raised his eyebrows. "It's delicious. Do you want to try some?"

Holly shook her head. "Um, no, thanks. I already ate breakfast," she managed to say.

"Anyway, Holly Berry, wouldn't it be perfect if Sam moved in with you? I mean, as your roommate, of course," Clarissa said with a wicked grin. "Aren't you expecting your, ah, *former* roommate to move back in by the new year anyway?"

Naturally, she meant Brad. "Maybe even sooner," Holly felt compelled to say. "In fact, I'm starting to rethink this whole idea of finding a temporary roommate altogether."

Clarissa looked stricken. "But that's not what you *planned*," she said. "I think Sam here would really help with your *plan*, don't you?"

Her emphasis on the word *plan* left little doubt what she was referring to: Holly's plan to win back Brad. A broad wink or two would have made their resemblance to Lucy and Ethel complete.

Sam cleared his throat. They both looked at him. "Isn't that up to Holly?" he asked mildly.

Holly liked him better already. She smiled. "Sam's right," she said, gathering up her day planner, purse, and car keys. "And I'm going to be late for work if I don't get out of here."

"It's Saturday! You're not taking the day off?" Clarissa asked, looking appalled.

"And leave my inbox full of work?" Holly shook her head.

The office was always quietest on weekends. She'd get tons of work done and be that much further ahead by Monday. Besides, Thursday was Thanksgiving. She wanted to make up for the productivity she'd lose during the holiday.

"Oh, right—what was I thinking?" Clarissa smacked her forehead with the heel of her hand. "You probably only put in *sixty* hours last week, huh?"

Okay, so Holly would be the first to admit she was ambitious. What was wrong with that?

There'd been a time when Clarissa had put in just as much overtime as Holly did. They'd become friends over deli-delivered sandwiches, eaten long past five o'clock in one of their adjoining office cubicles. Once she'd married David, Clarissa had decided she was happy where she was, but Holly still yearned for an office of her own and the title that went with it.

"You've got to stop and smell the roses sometime, you know," Clarissa warned. "Life's passing you by."

"There's no need to be so dire," Holly said, feeling exasperated. "Once I make senior-level accountant, I'll have plenty of time to stop and smell the roses."

Clarissa's expression said she'd believe *that* when she saw it. Holly sighed and let go of their old argument. She couldn't explain what drove her to work more and more hours, to achieve yet another of her ever-multiplying goals. She only knew her efforts hadn't quite measured up. Not yet.

"We're firing up the barbecue later," Sam said, calling her back to their conversation. "Clarissa and David and I—sure you don't want to come? It would be great to have you."

Clarissa rolled her eyes. "David saw one of those TV chefs grill a Thanksgiving turkey on his Weber 6000. Now he's dying to try it himself, so we're having a test run this afternoon."

"Sounds tempting," Holly hedged, "but . . ."

"Come on," Sam coaxed with a seductive grin. His voice lowered intimately. "It'll be fun."

He nodded toward the door, as though they'd pick up right there and head outside, just for the fun of it. Holly could picture it: a backyard patio filled with friends, a pitcher filled with sangria . . . her, getting to know Sam.

You'll never get that promotion that way, a voice inside her whispered. *Shut up,* she told it. But the tide was turned.

"I can't. I'm sorry. Thanks for the invitation, though. You guys have fun." She glanced at her watch. "Now I really *am* late. Do you still want to see the house tonight?"

Sam nodded. "I'd love to."

Holly whipped open her day planner. "We agreed on six-thirty, right?"

"I'll be there with bells on," Sam answered. His words called to mind a very interesting image, one Holly refused to contemplate beyond a few seconds. Almost as though he'd guessed what she'd been thinking, he added with a wink, "It's been a pleasure meeting you, Holly."

She fled before he could guess anything more incriminating.

At 6:25 that evening, Sam McKenzie parked his pickup truck in front of Holly's white-framed house at the address Clarissa had given him. The porch light was on, and lamplight shone through both of the curtained front windows. It looked welcoming. Heading up the walk, juggling the things he'd brought, he surveyed the house with approval. It was sturdy, if a little run-down, and it had a character newer houses typically lacked.

Pink geraniums crowded together in the built-in stone planters that flanked the porch steps and filled the air with their spicy scent. The porch itself was clean-swept, adorned with only a *Happy Thanksgiving* welcome mat and a white wood swing that swayed in the breeze. The loud clunk of his boots on the floorboards must have announced his arrival, because just as Sam touched the doorbell, Holly opened the door.

"Hi! You're here."

She sounded surprised. He peered through the aluminum screened door, trying to gauge her reaction. With the light behind her, though, her face was cast in shadow.

"Did you think I wouldn't show?"

"I, ummm . . . well, I guess not." She pushed open the door to let him in. "I mean, I didn't think you *wouldn't*." Holly smiled and rolled her eyes. "That is, you said you would, and I can't imagine anybody who's related to Clarissa saying anything they didn't mean. It must be in the bloodline or something."

He laughed as he moved past her into the house. He'd say one thing for Holly: she definitely had his cousin pegged.

"We're not generally known to be hesitant about things," Sam agreed. One of those things he wasn't hesitant about was Holly. From the moment he'd touched her in the restaurant he'd felt something between them, something hot and intriguing and inevitable. It was that feeling, more than mere architectural curiosity, that had brought him to her house.

Sam turned to face her and saw she was looking at the flat white box in his hand. Nodding at it, Holly sniffed at the savory aroma rising from it.

"Mmmm. I hope that's what I think it is."

"Dinner." He brandished the box that was rapidly heating his left hand. "Pizza, from Angelo's." He handed over the bottle of red wine he'd brought. "And something to drink. I hope you haven't eaten already."

"No—in fact, I just got home from work." Holly motioned with the bottle for Sam to follow her through the wood-framed archway to the kitchen. He did.

"I didn't think I'd be at the office as long as I was," she went on, setting the wine atop the counter. She opened the cupboard and pulled out a pair of plates. "Once I get going, I lose track of time, sometimes."

With a shy smile she reached for the pizza box he'd been balancing on one hand. She slid it gracefully onto the countertop. "I was half afraid you'd get here before I did."

"You're an accountant?" Sam asked, remembering their conversation at the Grill earlier.

"Officially, I'm a controller, but that's just a fancy word for it. I work for the county, like Clarissa."

She went on to describe the people the agency served and the various functions of her office with an enthusiasm Sam might have found unbelievable coming from anyone else. Somehow, it seemed very real coming from Holly. Her words came faster, keeping tempo with her double-speed gestures. She talked about depreciation and budgets with the same zeal his buddies reserved for, say, strip poker or professional football.

She paused. "Why are you smiling like that?"

Sam flipped open the pizza box, stalling for time. "This looks great, doesn't it?"

Holly's inquisitive expression never wavered. He wasn't going to get off the hook that easily.

"You're lucky to have work you love," Sam said, realizing

only as he said it how true those words were. "Even if it is something like *accounting*," he added with a mock shudder.

"Hey! I happen to be very good at what I do."

"I believe you."

She looked skeptical.

Sam went on anyway. "Not everybody is lucky enough to spend their days doing something they love."

She turned her back to the counter and leaned against it, listening, her palms propped on the edge for balance. "Are you?"

He'd walked right into that one. "Until recently, no. Now I am."

He lifted a wedge of pizza from the box and transferred it to a plate, which he handed to Holly. She watched him intently.

"But your teaching helps people," she said. "Do you think that makes a difference?"

Holly took a bite of pizza, then set the plate down again and moved a little closer. Her eyes were green, Sam noticed, green as new spring grass. She expected an answer. He knew it.

Sam wanted to give her one. But standing there so close, close enough to smell the faint muskiness of her perfume, thoughts of work and career planning were the farthest things from his mind.

She seemed different tonight. Why, he couldn't tell for sure. It wasn't her clothes. They were the same kind of lady-lawyer stuff she'd been wearing in the restaurant earlier, a pair of ordinary khaki pants and a plain white shirt. So why was he imagining himself unbuttoning those buttons, revealing the woman underneath? Why was he wondering what Holly would do if he leaned over and kissed her, if he pinned her against the countertop and lost himself in her?

"Sam?"

He'd forgotten what they were discussing. Some smooth talker he was. Sam scrambled for the topic at hand.

"Yeah, I think helping people makes a difference. And for me it was a lot of little things that added up to a job I loved. I didn't plan it that way. Once I'd taken the first step, the rest just followed."

He lifted a slice of pizza for himself, not bothering with a plate, and took a bite. Beneath the toppings, the double cheese and sauce were still hot. Perfect. Sam closed his eyes and savored the first bite. When he opened them again, Holly's curious gaze was still focused on him.

"You're the lucky one," she said. "I don't think anything's ever happened to me that I didn't have to work for." She laughed a little and reached for the wine bottle, pouring them each a glass. "Don't get me wrong—for the most part I've been successful. But I can't imagine just leaving things to chance like that, waiting to see what comes."

"Why not? Sometimes what comes along is exactly what you've been looking for."

Holly shook her head. "I just can't see it."

Sam wondered what kind of failure she'd come up against, what it was that had wrecked her "mostly successful" planning. Whatever it was, it had made her a woman afraid to travel without a roadmap at her side. He didn't know how to explain joyriding to a woman like that.

"You must have pretty detailed plans for your house renovation, then," he remarked, glancing around the kitchen.

A spacious, open-planned room, it was trimmed with the natural woodwork and built-in storage cabinets typical of a Craftsman-era home. It was filled with personal things, too—flowering plants, copper cookware, and a small rectangular table with a banquette that probably wasn't original to the house. Still, it suited her.

"Oh, I do!" Holly said, smiling. "I'll show you." She disappeared around the corner to the living room. She returned a few minutes later, balancing an opened book in her arms.

"See?" She nodded at the opened pages. She moved closer to him, their heads almost touching as they looked at the photographs she'd marked. "It'll look just like this when I'm done."

Her hair brushed his arm. Sam's skin prickled with goose bumps. He couldn't remember when he'd had a response like that to a woman. It felt good. It also felt as if he were seventeen again, trying to hide a surprise erection behind his history textbook.

Grinning to himself, he concentrated instead on the pictures Holly was showing him, squinting at the series of interior and exterior shots of another Craftsman-style house. This one had been gussied up like a museum, with period furniture and hardwood floors you could probably see yourself in.

"It's the most perfect example of the style I could find," Holly said. "What do you think?"

Sam thought it looked like a house that ought to be roped-off so visitors could pass through without messing anything up.

"Well," he equivocated, "this house is in Massachusetts. It would be hard to duplicate the effect out here in the West. What kind of modifications did you have in mind?"

"Modifications?" She looked puzzled. "Like what? This house is perfect."

Sam looked at the photos again, trying to place Holly inside them. Inside that house. He couldn't do it. It looked too stiff. Unapproachable.

"It's too perfect. Maybe that's the problem."

Holly shook her head. "That's ridiculous. It can't be *too* perfect."

"You've got to be able to live in the house, too. This house"—he tapped the photo with his fingers—"wouldn't work in Arizona. The landscaping is all wrong for the climate, for one thing. The chairs look about as comfortable as stadium bleachers, and these bare windows here look nice, but unless all your neighbors live five miles away you're going to want some shutters or blinds for privacy. And—"

Holly snapped the book shut, all but flattening his nose with the pages in the process. Sam felt about as popular as the hunter who shot Bambi's mother.

"Okay," he said quickly, "you don't want me messing around with your design. Understandable. It's perfect. But maybe, just *maybe,* it's not right for this house."

She frowned, drumming her fingertips on the book.

"Renovating a house can be tricky," Sam said. "If you're not careful, it's easy to design the heart, the *you,* right out of it.

Your house has a history. It's had generations of owners. Every one of them touched these walls." Sam reached for her hand and pressed it, warm beneath his, against the white plaster wall. "Every one of them left something here. Now it's your turn."

Beneath his palm, Holly's hand trembled. He brushed his thumb along the edge of hers, downward to her wrist, easing the pressure of his grip in case she wanted to move away. She didn't. Sam moved closer, until they were only inches apart.

She was still, watching him. She was warm, luring him. She was sexy as hell, surprising him. He took the only action that seemed reasonable under the circumstances, and kissed her.

His thoughts were veering into new and dangerous directions by the time Holly ended the kiss.

"Do you always win arguments this way?" she asked, managing to look both hot and bothered, and just plain bothered, as she clutched the book to her chest.

"Nah. Sometimes I need a rebuttal," he murmured, lowering his mouth to hers again. Damn, she felt good. Kissing Holly was like eating chocolate for breakfast—pleasurable, sweet, but probably not very smart.

She dropped the design book on his foot.

"Ow!"

"Ooops, sorry."

She didn't look the least bit repentant. She whipped her hand out from beneath his, then bent to pick up the book and thumped it on the countertop.

"Listen, Lothario. I think we need to get a few things straight."

"Can we wait until my foot quits throbbing? That damn book must weigh at least ten pounds."

She shook her head. "Number one, I didn't invite you over here so you could perform some pizza and wine seduction routine on me. That was a cheap shot—"

"A double deluxe pizza from Angelo's isn't all that cheap," Sam argued. "Have you got any aspirin?" he added, tugging at his boot. If the pain was any indication, he'd lay bets his big toe was broken.

Holly, clearly not a woman to be jollied out of her agenda, cast him a scathing look. "You'll be fine. It's not that heavy a book." She continued talking, ticking off items on her fingers as she went. "Number two, I wanted your opinion on my house renovation, but you just wrecked my whole vision. Have you ever heard of tact?"

"You asked what I thought. I was supposed to lie?"

Shaking her head, she paced to the living room. "How do you ever get any jobs, anyway?" Holly waved the question away. "No, never mind, don't answer that. I think I know."

Carrying his boot, Sam followed her. "What the hell does that mean?"

She faced him. "Oh, come on. I saw how you worked on the waitress this morning at the Downtown Grill, doing that . . . that *smile* thing you do, all oozing charm. I've got to say, it worked like a dream. I'll bet you get great service, don't you?"

"*Oozing charm?* Yuck." He shuddered. "I get jobs because I'm good at what I do. Period."

"Of course, it doesn't hurt when your father's the biggest contractor in Saguaro Vista, does it? Half the town must work for him."

Wham, direct hit. Sam scowled. "You don't know what the hell you're talking about. I do not get hired just because of who my father is. Besides, that's just a temporary job. Most of the year I have a perfectly respectable job in Tucson, remember?"

"Whatever," she said infuriatingly. Then, undaunted, she waggled three fingers at him. "Number three, I happen to have a boyfriend whom—"

"Whom you're separated from?"

"Whom I care about very much," she said staunchly, heading back to the kitchen. Sam followed, stopping beside the refrigerator to massage his injured toe.

Holly picked up a towel, polishing the porcelain sink and backsplash with far more attention than the already-spotless surfaces deserved. She poured more wine, set the bottle down, then picked it up and poured a little more. Carrying the bottle and her glass, she paced back to the living room.

Sam followed, having visions of tying Holly to a chair so he could stop hobbling after her on his one good leg. "What's the matter? Having trouble thinking up a fourth objection?"

He regretted the words the minute he saw the wistful expression on her face. He'd rather have her drop ten books on his toe than look like that, he realized.

"I guess Clarissa told you about me and Brad, too?"

He nodded. "Unless there's more than one 'Brad the Bad'?"

"Nope." She dropped into a big, flowery upholstered chair and took a hefty swig of her wine. She sighed. "Just the one."

He settled opposite her on the sofa. "Why does Clarissa call him 'Brad the Bad', anyway?"

"You really can't guess?" Holly eyed him curiously. "Then I'm not volunteering. Let's just say Clarissa never liked Brad much, and leave it at that, shall we?"

"Sure." Sam wasn't in any hurry to repeat what Clarissa had told him, anyway—that Holly took in wrong men like other people took in stray dogs, and had about as much success domesticating them. Despite her crack about nepotism, he just wasn't feeling that mean. Besides, it wasn't any of his business.

"On a completely different subject," he said instead, "how much are you asking for rent? I'm assuming you're still in the market for a roommate, unless you found somebody since this morning?"

Holly choked on a mouthful of wine, bringing on an impressive coughing attack. Once her breathing had returned to normal, she asked, "You're still interested?"

Sam grinned. "I don't scare easily."

"Hmmm?"

"Nothing. How much?"

She told him the rent. "But don't feel put on the spot just because Clarissa asked you to meet me. I know she must have put you up to this, but it's really not necessary." Holly narrowed her eyes and gave him a speculative look. "Besides, I'm not so sure you're the right roommate for me. I can't go around dropping things on you every day, you know."

"I didn't make the offer because of my cousin," Sam assured her. Gingerly, he propped his injured right foot on the coffee table. "And I promise I'll behave. From now on, I'll ask first before I kiss you."

She scrunched her nose at him. "And I'll say no every time, guaranteed," she promised.

He laughed. If her participation in their last kiss had been so reluctant, he couldn't wait to find out what Holly was like when she felt enthusiastic.

"You know," she mused, "maybe I could do without a roommate altogether. Brad and I will probably be back together again by Christmas anyway. I've got enough saved to tide me over between now and then."

Speculatively, she glanced around the living room. Her gaze settled on the fireplace, the centerpiece of a cozy inglenook formed by the built-in benches and pair of tall bookshelves that flanked it on both sides. It was a typical Craftsman construction, spoiled only by the hunk of nailed-on plywood that sealed the fireplace shut.

"The money you've saved—it's your renovation money, isn't it?" Sam asked.

She looked at him, surprise evident in her expression. "How did you know?"

"A wild guess." He readjusted the angle of his foot on the coffee table, grimacing at the pain the movement brought him. He didn't want to be a baby, but his toe hurt like hell. It would be a bitch driving back home.

"If I move in for the next couple of months, say, until the new year, it'll be good for both of us," he said. "You'll be able to put your renovation money to its intended use—restoring your house. And I'll already be here, so working on your renovation will be a snap. As a bonus, I won't have my mother hovering over me while I'm in town, trying to make me eat my vegetables as if I were still six years old."

She smiled. "With my mom, it's milk. 'Does a body good!' I think I'll need to be completely gray-haired before she believes I'm a grown-up."

They laughed. Sam leaned forward. "Do we have a deal?"

Holly still looked hesitant. "What about my design plan? We didn't exactly agree on renovation ideas, you know."

"Tell you what. All I ask is you let me make my case for an alternate design. If you don't like it, okay. We'll go with your idea instead. The decision's all yours to make."

"Very gracious of you . . . considering it's *my* house under discussion here." Holly smiled. "Just kidding. That sounds like a workable compromise to me. When do you want to start?"

"Let's hammer out the details tomorrow over breakfast."

At her nod, he had another suggestion. "Shall we seal the deal properly?"

"Properly?"

"With a kiss." He felt his grin widen. "Shall we seal the deal with a kiss?"

She stared at him for a second. Then, laughing, Holly put out her hand. "Are you a slow learner, or what?"

"Can't blame a guy for trying." He accepted the handshake she offered, then reached for his boot. "Now that that's done, I need to ask you a favor."

"Umm, sure. What is it?"

"Would you drive me to the doctor? I think my toe is broken."

Three

"Oh, my God!" Holly bent over and peered at Sam's foot more closely. Now that he mentioned it, his toe *did* look a little . . . unusual.

"Umm, you know the cartoon where the coyote has an anvil dropped on his foot and it blows up like a big furry balloon?" she asked, poking tentatively at his stockinged toe.

"Ouch! Yeah?"

"That was actually pretty good, compared with this."

"You're making jokes now?"

Holly glanced at him. His eyebrows drew together, making him look surprisingly fierce. Clearly, he was not amused.

"You are! You're making jokes at an injured man's expense," Sam said. "I can't believe it."

Okay, so her jokes never did go over very well. That didn't mean she couldn't try to cheer him up, she reasoned.

"I'm sorry. I really am." She actually did feel fairly awful about smashing his foot with the design book. It had seemed like a good strategy at the time. She could hardly just let him maul her right in her own kitchen, could she? Great kisser or not, she barely knew him.

"Wait here," she told him, heading to the kitchen to get the phone. "I'll be right back."

"I'm a cripple, where am I going to go?" Sam grumbled as she passed him.

Men acted like such babies when they were hurt. Holly felt bad about it, but it had been an accident, after all. She hadn't meant to *really* hurt him.

"I do *not* have furry coyote toes, either," he called from the living room.

Hiding a grin, she dialed Brad's pager number. There were some advantages to having a boyfriend who was a doctor, even if the two of them were temporarily separated. She was sure he'd agree to come over and have a look at Sam's injured toe. Brad liked to feel he was rescuing people. It was one of the things that made him a good doctor.

Plus, a house call would save her and Sam a drive to the emergency room and probably a three-hour wait for a doctor there. And if Brad just *happened* to get a look at her hunky new roommate when he dropped by, well . . . what was wrong with that?

When Holly returned to the living room with a bottle of pain reliever, the rest of the wine, and Sam's wineglass, he eyed her warily.

"Here." She tapped some of the medicine in her palm and handed it to him. "This ought to help a little."

He squinted at the label, then up at her. "How do I know you're not trying to poison me?"

"Fine." She dropped the medicine back in the vial and snapped the lid on. It wasn't until Holly glanced up again that she realized Sam had been joking. He was smiling at her, giving her the same charm-oozing smile she'd accused him of using on the waitress. Suddenly the room felt too warm, their position too intimate, his appeal too dangerously real.

Too bad that smile worked so well on her, too.

The phone buzzed in her hand. Grateful for the opportunity to think about something else besides Sam, Holly answered it.

"Holly! I told you not to page me unless it was an emergency," Brad squawked in her ear. She'd forgotten how loudly he spoke on the phone, how overwhelming his presence could be, even from a distance.

"It is an emergency." She covered the phone with her hand and mouthed, "It's Brad" to Sam. He looked interested, if a little confused.

"The Bad Boy himself?"

Holly frowned and waved her hand at him to be quiet.

"Can you come over here, please?" she asked Brad. "I think my new roommate has a broken toe. I was hoping you'd take a look at it."

"I'm a G.P., not a podiatrist. Can't you just take her to the emergency room? It's getting late, and I've got appointments in the morning."

She couldn't believe he was arguing with her over this. "He's really in a lot of pain," Holly said, doing her best to ignore the way Sam was scowling at her and waving his hands. She might have known not to make the awful admission he was in pain, especially to another man.

The phone line was silent. "Brad? Just come on over, okay? For Pete's sake, I'm sure Sam will pay you, if that's what's worrying you."

She could practically hear Brad's interest sharpen. "Sam?"

"My roommate. I told you someone was moving in, remember? Don't tell me you forgot . . ."

He hadn't forgotten. He hadn't believed her in the first place. Holly could hear it in his voice as Brad went through some lame explanation about how rushed he'd been the last time they talked. She smiled, feeling less and less *un*spontaneous by the second.

"Elevate the foot," Brad said. "I'll be there shortly."

The line went dead. Holly blinked, then replaced the phone in its stand. She turned to Sam. "He's on his way."

"It's broken, all right." Brad pinched Sam's bare big toe between his fingertips and waggled it a little.

Sam turned gray, but remained silent. Good thing, too. He appeared to be biting back several choice words. Holly doubted whatever came out of his mouth would be polite.

"Try to stay off of it as much as you can," Brad said. "Call my office if the swelling doesn't go down or if it feels more uncomfortable, rather than less."

He straightened, pulling his car keys from his pants pocket. As he turned to leave, Holly grabbed his arm to stop him.

"Let you know if it gets uncomfortable? That's it?" she exclaimed. "You're just going to pack up and leave now? What about medicine, what about a cast?"

She looked from Sam to Brad and back again. She'd arranged poor Sam on the sofa as comfortably as she could, with his bare foot propped on both pink-fringed throw pillows. It might have been a mistake to use two pillows—she'd somehow elevated his toe to roughly nose-height. Holly made a mental note to try a single bed pillow instead and turned to face down Brad.

Horribly enough, he looked about to laugh. "I can't put a cast on a toe, Holly. A broken foot, sure, but not a broken big toe."

"Must be tough to maneuver around all those other toes, eh Doc?" Sam quipped from the sofa.

Holly didn't find Sam's pain funny in the least. "I want you to do something right now, Brad. There must be something you can do."

Sighing, Brad took off his glasses, holding them in one hand while he rubbed the bridge of his nose.

"Brad!"

"I've done all I can." He handed one of his business cards to Sam, shaking his head sympathetically. "What did you do to him, anyway, Holly?"

"Me?"

Sam looked at her with renewed curiosity.

"Yes, you." To Sam, Brad added, "Watch out. This woman's a walking recruiter for personal injury lawyers. One time she knocked a ladder out from under me when I was changing a light bulb, up near this ridiculously high ceiling. I took the whole light fixture down with me."

They all glanced upward. "I just bumped into the ladder," Holly protested.

"Another time she threw a cast iron skillet at me." Brad

spread his thumb and forefinger a couple of inches apart. "Missed me by that much."

"I did not! The handle was hot, and I let go of it too quickly, that's all." As an aside to Sam, she explained, "I was concentrating on a new recipe. I told him to stay out of the kitchen." She glowered at Brad.

"Naturally, it's not limited to other people. Did Holly tell you about the time she bashed herself with a garlic press? Gave herself a really bad bruise on the collarbone," he went on blithely. "I wouldn't have thought kitchen utensils were so dangerous."

To his credit, at least Sam didn't laugh. Most people laughed at the garlic press story.

"Then there was the time—"

"That's enough for now," Holly interrupted, steering Brad toward the front door. "Thanks for stopping by. Let Thomas know I'll be calling him tomorrow to get a second opinion on Sam's toe, would you?"

Thomas White was Brad's partner, the doctor he shared office space with. Brad would have preferred his own office, Holly knew, but he couldn't afford to go it alone yet.

"Thomas is an obstetrician," Brad told her. "Toes are hardly his specialty. Take my word for it: all that's required is rest. Sam will be fine."

Sam waved from the sofa. "Thanks, Doc. And thanks for the warning, too," he added with a grin, nodding toward Holly.

She scowled. So much for making Brad jealous with her new roommate. Instead, Brad and Sam seemed intent on doing some sort of male-bonding thing, although she couldn't imagine why.

They had nothing in common, aside from gender. Brad was a successful doctor, respected by his peers. Sam was . . . not. Brad was organized, neat, ambitious, and blessed with model-quality good looks. Sam was . . , actually kind of scruffy-macho-looking, and if he were any more relaxed, he'd be asleep.

And now he was her roommate. Holly hoped she'd done the right thing. Closing the front door behind Brad, she went to check on Sam in the living room.

"You and Brad don't go together very well," he remarked.

The pain reliever she'd given him must have taken effect, because he seemed in much better spirits than he had earlier.

"What makes you say that?" Holly fluffed up the throw pillows in the brown armchair Brad had been sitting in, then bent to brush a piece of lint from the edge of the sofa.

"For one thing, you didn't give me your business card ten minutes after we met," Sam replied, dropping Brad's beige engraved card on the coffee table.

She scooped it up and put it beside Sam's wineglass, where he'd be sure to remember it later. "I didn't do your bookkeeping, either," she pointed out in Brad's defense. "If I had, you can be sure I'd have given you my card, too."

"Okay, then, for another thing, you wouldn't have embarrassed a friend for the sake of a funny story."

"I wasn't embarrassed," Holly lied. So what if she was a little sensitive to Brad's teasing? It would have been much more embarrassing to admit her embarrassment. Besides, when she and Brad went to parties together, everyone else seemed to find his jokes funny.

"Anyway, how do you know I wouldn't?" she protested. "You don't know—maybe I go around lampooning my friends all the time."

Sam grunted noncommittally. "I doubt it."

Holly raised her eyebrows.

"I can't explain it," he said with a shrug. "But I still think it's true. The two of you don't mesh."

She didn't know how true that could be when he couldn't even explain it properly. She shrugged right back at him. "You're wrong. Brad and I are perfectly well-suited for one another."

"Well-suited?" He made a face.

She'd definitely have to think up another phrase to describe her relationship with Brad.

"Yes. Brad is exactly the kind of man a girl dreams of. Even my mother loves him." It was true. Her mom had all but hired the Goodyear blimp to broadcast the news when her daughter had begun dating Brad the Doctor.

Sam looked up at her. For once his expression was serious. "Do *you* love him?"

Despite everything, Holly hadn't expected *that*. "Of course. Why wouldn't I? Brad and I had planned a nice life together."

What a strange thing for him to ask. She leaned closer to Sam, intent on picking up the wine bottle so it wouldn't leave a ring on the coffee table. The next thing she knew, he'd caught hold of her arm and was gently pulling her down.

"Sounds real cozy," Sam said. "Like a stockbroker's convention."

Holly had to brace one hand on the sofa back to keep from toppling onto his lap. Their faces were only inches apart.

"And anyway, you can't 'plan' love," he added quietly. "Brad doesn't deserve your loyalty."

"It's not just—"

Sam pressed a fingertip to her lips to quiet her. She was too surprised by the tenderness of the gesture to move away.

"I had to know," he said. "I had to ask, because even though we just met this morning, I'm already crazy about you. I had to know if there's a chance for us to—"

Crazy about her? How could that be? Stunned, she tried to pull away. His hand on her arm held her still for the rest of his words.

"—if there's a chance for us to be together. I know this sounds crazy. I always thought love at first sight was just another name for lust, but now . . . well, now I think maybe it's more than that."

"Sam—" Her voice failed her. Holly took in a huge breath and tried again. "I don't—"

"I do want you." His voice was quiet. Serious. "I'd be lying if I said I don't. But that's not all there is to this."

His gaze shifted from her eyes to her face. He moved his hand higher, stroking his thumb across her cheek in a tiny caress. The way he looked at her was somehow curious, appreciative, and unmistakably honest, all at the same time.

This couldn't be happening. Holly pushed away from the sofa, away from him.

"You've had too much wine." She grabbed the wine bottle

and nearly clobbered his injured foot with it in her rush to get away from him. "Maybe too much pain reliever, too. I'm sure you won't remember any of this in the morning."

Sam didn't move. "Yes, I will. I didn't have that much wine. And even if I didn't remember it, *you* would. You'd remember, and wonder, and pretty soon we'd be right back here talking about it again. So we might as well deal with it right now, don't you think?"

Holly thought she might be hyperventilating. "This is insane," she managed to say. Then she made good her escape to the kitchen, leaving Sam stranded atop his pillows and, she hoped, unable to follow her.

She didn't know what to do. He'd seemed perfectly sane earlier. Holly set down the wine bottle, saw that her hand was shaking, and hugged both arms around herself to keep that unsteady feeling from spreading to the rest of her.

It didn't work.

Clarissa wouldn't have pushed so hard for this roommate arrangement if her cousin really was unbalanced, would she? No, of course not. Clarissa had known Sam since childhood. Surely he couldn't have hidden some kind of crazed love-at-first-sight tendencies for that long.

Maybe this was just Clarissa's twisted idea of a practical joke. It was possible. Holly had been the unwitting victim of a number of her best friend's schemes. Usually they were funny only to Clarissa. Sidling to the doorway, she peered around the corner at the back of Sam's head, fully expecting him to be convulsed with laughter that the joke had gone over so easily.

He wasn't laughing.

Okay, so that wasn't it. Turning, Holly finished the last dregs of red wine straight from the bottle and thought about it some more. Maybe Sam was one of those people who fell in love easily. Maybe he'd just broken up with another woman and he was on the rebound, wanting to salve his ego with the nearest skirt-wearing remedy. Maybe this was simply another attempt to get her into bed, since the kiss hadn't worked earlier.

More likely, she was blowing the whole thing way out of proportion, she chided herself. Straightening her shoulders, she headed back to the living room and sat in the chair across from Sam. She folded her hands in her lap, then gave him her most level-headed look.

"I don't believe in love at first sight," she said.

"Me, neither," Sam replied, just as evenly. "At least, I didn't when I woke up this morning."

"It doesn't make any sense," she went on.

He nodded. "I know."

Holly flung both arms wide. "See? You're proving my point!" She'd finally met somebody who was even worse at arguing than she was. "It's impossible. We barely know each other. You can't love somebody you don't really know."

Sam grinned. He did that a lot, she'd noticed. Unlike Brad. Brad had really missed his calling as one of those guards at Buckingham Palace who were never allowed to smile.

There she went again, comparing the two of them. That had to stop. It wasn't fair to anyone.

"We should get to know each other better, then," Sam said.

For some reason, those words made her feel even more panicked than before. Determined not to show it, Holly said, "Well, we're going to be roommates. I guess we'll have plenty of time to get acquainted."

"I'm looking forward to it." He glanced pointedly at the empty spot beside him on the sofa. "Why don't we start right now?"

He should have looked ridiculous, a big, brawny man with his foot propped at nose-height on those pink-fringed pillows. He should have looked crazy, going on about love at first sight like he had. The trouble was, he didn't.

This spontaneity business wasn't all it was cracked up to be, Holly realized. Agreeing to let Sam move in was the most spontaneous act she could remember making, and already it was throwing her nice, steady life out of whack.

But Brad leaving her was what had really messed everything up. If seeing her with a roommate like Sam could bring Brad back to his senses—and there was still a good chance it could—it would be worth it. She and Brad made sense together. Holly had to do all she could to rebuild their relationship, to make her life the way it used to be . . . ideally, before the official eggnog-and-jingle-bells season set in.

Sam watched her, still waiting.

Holly sighed, but didn't move any closer to him. "I have to be honest, Sam. What I said before is true. I'm trying to work things out with Brad. Even though we're . . . apart . . . right now, I haven't given up on him yet. I can't."

He was silent, thinking. Then, "I hope Brad knows how lucky he is. I wouldn't have let you go in the first place."

"Thanks."

It was sweet of him to say that. But Holly had no intention of letting Brad let her go, either. Her plan was almost ready to go into motion.

"I'm pretty sure I'll be able to change Brad's mind," she said. Then she stood, turning to Sam with both hands on her hips. In her most businesslike tone, she added, "As for you, you're not looking so good—"

"Thanks."

She grinned. "That's not what I mean." Obviously, he was pretty easy on the eyes. "But I do think you should get some rest. Are you going to be all right driving home?"

Sam flexed his injured foot. "If I said I wasn't, then what?"

Then I'd say you should stay with me tonight. The thought came out of nowhere. Holly blinked. Obviously the events of the past week had affected her more than she'd thought. She was lonely without Brad, that was all—lonely and vulnerable and not at all looking forward to crawling into that big empty bed all by herself again tonight.

"Then I'd drive you home myself," she said, forcing a certainty into her voice that she didn't really feel. "I could pick you up again in the morning, or . . . or whenever you decide to move in . . ."

"Is tomorrow too soon for you?" Sam's gaze caught hers and held, clear and honest and much too perceptive for her peace of mind.

"Not at all." If she was going to be spontaneous, she was going to do it all the way. "The sooner the better."

He seemed to approve. If he'd been calling her bluff, he was pleased with the results.

After some discussion about the state of his Wile E. Coyote foot, they compromised on the following weekend for a move-in date. They ironed out the details, and Sam pronounced himself fit to drive. He lifted his foot from the pillow pile to the floor, then held up his hand to her.

"Can I trust you to help me up, or is that just asking for trouble?"

"Very funny." Holly caught hold of his hand. He squeezed back, and without thinking she glanced down at their coupled hands. His was bigger, stronger, browner—so different from hers. It was . . . it was stupid to stand there staring at his hands. She dug her heels in the rug and pulled.

She realized her mistake in the same instant the rug slid across the glossy hardwood floor. By then it was too late to correct it. She fell forward on top of him, landing with enough momentum to roll them both hard against the sofa back.

"Oooff!"

She lifted her face from his shirtfront, shook her hair out of her eyes, and found herself plastered against him from chest to knees. She was all of four inches from Sam's face.

"I think you have an unconscious desire to be close to me," he said, unsuccessfully trying to hide a smile.

"You did that on purpose, didn't you?" she shot back.

She tried to wriggle backwards so she could stand. It didn't work, partly because Sam's strong arm around her waist kept her there, and partly because she was afraid to wriggle too hard and accidentally hurt him again.

"I didn't do anything."

His chest rumbled against hers as he spoke. They were much too close. Holly wriggled a little more.

Sam's eyelids lowered slightly. She would have sworn he was looking at her lips. At the thought, her stomach did a flip. She wriggled in earnest.

"Mmmm. That feels good."

She stopped cold. He was right. It did feel good. *Really* good. She was still thinking about that fact when Sam's hands slipped from her waist and starting moving toward her hips in long, slow arcs. Holly sucked in her breath, her attention temporarily caught by the feel of Sam's hands on her body. His fingers, warm and sure, traced a path over her lower back and downward.

Reality came crashing back.

"Another inch further south," she said, "and our roommate arrangement is history."

His hands lifted. "I thought you were enjoying it."

She was. Holly would have died before admitting it. She pushed up on her elbows and Sam let her go. After a bit of maneuvering, she wound up on her knees on the sofa, leaning in any direction but his. It wasn't a very dignified position, but she did her best to sound dignified anyway.

"I think you'd better go," she said.

Miraculously, he managed to get to his feet on his own power. She guessed keeping the renovation job and retaining their roommate arrangement was a powerful incentive.

"Hey, you're the one who jumped on top of me," Sam observed with an overly innocent lift of his eyebrows. He was obviously enjoying himself.

"I'll make sure it doesn't happen again."

Her knees felt wobbly as she stood. That unsteady sensation only got worse when Sam put his hands on her shoulders.

"There's something between us, Holly. I know you can feel it, too," he said. "You can't ignore it forever."

Oh, yes, she could. She could ignore it, and she would. All she felt for Sam was the same garden-variety lust any woman would feel if she were plastered up against more than six feet of hard-muscled male. Nothing more. She wasn't going to wreck her future to satisfy it.

"I don't know what you're talking about," she lied, staring out the darkened window behind Sam so she wouldn't have to meet his eyes.

"Mmm-hmm." He squeezed her shoulders, then let his hands fall to his sides again. "Okay, if that's the way you want it."

She nodded. "It is."

It was. It was exactly the way she wanted it, Holly reminded herself as she handed Sam his boot at the door. It was the only way it could be, she told herself as she watched him get in his truck and drive away. It was the smartest decision she could have made, she congratulated herself afterward, when she got in bed and turned out the light.

It was the loneliest night she'd ever spent, she thought to herself an hour later, when she still couldn't sleep. So she got up again, took out her day planner, and set about remedying the problem.

Four

The following weekend, Holly drove with Clarissa to their favorite mall at the edge of Phoenix, a forty-five minute drive from Saguaro Vista. It was the preparatory phase of her plan: materials gathering. Unfortunately, circumstances demanded that this phase fall on the busiest shopping weekend of the year, when holiday shoppers came out in force after Thanksgiving.

"We must have been insane to come here today." Clarissa waved her arm at the throng of mall shoppers who streamed past them on both sides. "This is like feeding time at the zoo."

"I know." Holly clutched the shoulder strap of her purse tighter against her shoulder. They dodged two teenagers running past them, maneuvered around a pair of women pushing tandem strollers, then edged past a clump of men hypnotized by the big-screen showing of a football game at the electronics store.

"Have you ever noticed those stores never show anything but sports on those big-screen TV sets?" Holly asked, panting a little. Following Clarissa through the mall was a triathlon-worthy event.

"That's because purchasing power comes with a Y-chromosome, Holly Berry, didn't you know?" Clarissa replied with evident sarcasm as they veered into the potpourried atmosphere of the lingerie store next door. "Besides, it makes the balls look bigger."

She grabbed something from the nearest rack and held it out for Holly's inspection. "Hey, what do you think of this?"

Holly shook her head. "That's not clothing. It's a shiny, hot pink hair elastic. That wouldn't cover more than ten percent of me."

"That's the idea." Clarissa threw back her head and batted her eyelashes, holding the lingerie on top of her T-shirt and jeans. "Brad will love it," she promised.

"Absolutely not." Holly snatched the hanger. The pink spandex quivered as she shoved it among its pseudo-satin companions. Why did those things need a hanger anyway? Any one of them could just as easily have been packaged in a number ten envelope.

"Brad has subtler tastes. He's a classy guy. He doesn't like this kind of stuff."

Clarissa rolled her eyes as she sifted through a bin of thong panties. "All men like this kind of stuff. How 'bout some of these? They're fifty percent off."

"There's a reason for that, I'm sure," Holly said, eyeing the panties skeptically. She picked up a white pair with pale pink flowers, the most subdued-looking one in the bin.

"At least it's cotton." She looked at the price again. It really was a great deal, a third the price of her ordinary underwear. Maybe it would be a good compromise, plain in the front but sexy in the back. She could just ease her way into the new, more seductive her—a woman Brad wouldn't dream of letting go.

She picked up a few more pairs in her size, holding them bundled against her chest while she went in search of Clarissa. She found her beside a display of garter belts.

"You need one of these, too," Clarissa advised, selecting a red satin one printed with tiny green Christmas trees. She waggled it toward her. "Look! It's seasonally appropriate."

She opened one of the drawers below the display and rummaged through it, presumably for a pair of matching candy cane patterned stockings.

"Come on, this really isn't me," Holly protested, examining

the bright rows of garter belts above Clarissa's head. They looked like instruments of torture. "I don't even know how to wear one of these."

"It's very simple." Clarissa held up a pair of black seamed stockings—blissfully *sans* candy canes—then glanced at her thoughtfully. "What size, I wonder? How much do you weigh, anyway?"

"I'm going to tell you?" Holly shook her head vehemently as she reached for the garter belt and stockings. "I'm sure these will be fine."

She probably wouldn't be able to get up the nerve to wear them anyway. Not that it would matter. Her other ideas to win back Brad would be successful long before more drastic measures became necessary. Holly viewed a seduction attempt strictly as a last resort, but she wanted to be prepared, just in case. They moved on to the bras.

"Oooh—this one!" Grinning, holding the bra by its satin shoulder straps, Clarissa turned around. It was red, really red, look-at-me red. Appliquéd to the cups was a pair of what seemed to be black velvet hands, hands squeezing the . . .

"Oh, no. No." Holly shook her head.

"It's cute. You want to try it on?"

"No." Holly backed up.

Clarissa followed her with the bra. "Don't be a baby. It's about time you shed that Goody Two Shoes image and started enjoying yourself a little."

Raising her eyebrows, Holly stopped. "Goody Two Shoes?"

"You know what I mean." Clarissa pushed the bra forward. "Come on, it won't bite you."

Okay, maybe Holly was a little conservative, but she was no Goody Two Shoes. She touched her fingertip to one of the appliquéd black hands. The velvet nap wiggled slightly beneath her finger. She squealed.

"This is too much."

"Trust me."

Clarissa pushed the bra into her arms. Holly couldn't give it back without dropping the garter belt, stockings, and thong panties she was already carrying. She squished it all into a tight, inconspicuous lingerie wad and followed Clarissa toward the rear of the store.

She was browsing in a corner nook labeled Couples Cove. The aroma of potpourri and scented candles was stronger here, and the lighting was dimmer.

"Just for inspiration, we'll get you a copy of the Kama Sutra." Clarissa selected an ornate-looking book. "And some of these." She grabbed a fistful of brightly wrapped condoms. "And a couple of these." She added two bottles, balancing them atop the book.

Holly picked up one. "Aphrodisia Massage Oil," she read aloud. She peered at the other bottle. "Lover's Potion?"

"It's edible," Clarissa told her, looking helpful.

Holly dropped both bottles back in Clarissa's arms. "You've *got* to be kidding."

Clarissa's sigh was all the answer she needed.

"Have you and David actually used this stuff?" Holly whispered. She gazed at her best friend with new eyes. Clarissa had always been more adventurous than she was, but this? And what in the world did that Lover's Potion taste like, anyway?

"The point is," Clarissa replied evasively, "that these things work."

Feeling doubtful, Holly raised her eyebrows.

"Okay, I can see I'm going to have to speak your language." Clarissa sighed. "It's been scientifically proven that these things work. Take the bra, for instance—"

As if on cue, one of the black velvet fingers popped out of the lingerie wad. Holly crammed it back in.

"—scientists have proven men respond best to red and black lingerie."

Holly made a face. "Why can't men be attracted to a pretty floral print? Or, even better, why don't they think a comfy pair of sweatpants and a T-shirt is the sexiest get-up around?"

Clarissa ignored her. "Men also find the scent of vanilla arousing," she explained, nodding toward the Aphrodisia Massage Oil.

She caught hold of Holly's sleeve and steered her to the

cash register. Just before they reached it, she added, "Oh, and one more thing. Be sure to leave the lights on."

"All the lights?" Holly asked, aghast.

Appear in front of Brad, illuminated by more than a hundred watts of cellulite-revealing lamplight? Or, God forbid, in daylight? He'd see every ripple, then demand she go running with him. The last thing she'd be feeling under those circumstances was sexy.

"At least one," Clarissa specified.

She put everything she'd selected on the counter, then reached for Holly's lingerie wad and added that, too. Despite the garter belt's "seasonally appropriate" Christmas tree print, the whole mess made a pretty risqué-looking pile. Especially when combined with the book, condoms, and exotic oils.

"It's on me." Clarissa handed her credit card to the clerk, a goggle-eyed teenaged boy. "Consider it an early Christmas present."

"I can't let you—"

Wearing a no-nonsense look, Clarissa held up her hand. "I want to. Look, I know how much your plan means to you. If this'll make you feel better, then I'm glad to help. What are friends for?"

Holly disagreed. She snatched Clarissa's credit card from the clerk's hand, then offered her own instead. The shoppers in line behind them sighed.

"I'm paying," she said firmly. If she paid for it, then she wouldn't feel too bad about shoving the lingerie in a drawer until she found the necessary nerve to wear it. But if Clarissa paid for everything, Holly knew she'd feel twice as obligated to actually make use of it.

Judging by the persistence with which her friend slapped another credit card down on the counter, Clarissa knew it, too.

"Humor me. You can pay at the next store. I might even let you pick out your own clothes," she promised with a grin.

The clerk scooped up Clarissa's credit card and scanned it before they could change their minds again. Case closed.

* * *

Five and a half hours later, they headed for the mall parking lot, wearing matching red felt Santa hats and carrying enough sexy clothing to outfit a troupe of Playboy bunnies in their off-hours. Holly stopped beside her car and dropped her shopping bags on the asphalt. She dug in her purse for her car keys.

"Mission accomplished!" Clarissa beamed. "I'll bet you thought it couldn't be done."

"Not for a second." Holly lifted the trunk lid. They loaded the shopping bags inside. Shopping exhausted her, but at least now she could consider part of her plan completed. All she needed now was an opportunity to put everything into action.

She added her Santa hat to the pile and slammed the trunk shut with a feeling of accomplishment. Now that she'd taken steps toward getting her life back to normal again, the future looked a little brighter.

"I've been meaning to ask you," Clarissa said halfway through the drive home. "How did it go with Sam last weekend? Did he like your house?"

The questions were put much too casually for typical Clarissa-speak. Holly glanced at her, then back at the road.

"Fine."

"Good. Sam's a nice guy."

"Except for his broken toe."

"What?"

Holly explained the book-dropping incident. She left out the kiss that had prompted it, though. Somehow, she didn't want to share that part. Although, speaking of kisses, this might be a good time to try hanging some mistletoe around the house . . . .

"At least Brad the Bad was decent enough to pay a house call," Clarissa muttered, scanning the desert landscape through the passenger-side car window. "I hope Sam will be okay."

"He's practically as good as new already."

When Holly had phoned him earlier, Sam had confirmed that he and his Looney Tunes foot felt well enough to move in this afternoon, as planned. She'd promised to leave him a house key in one of the porch flowerpots. He might even be there when she got back home.

She tried to imagine what it would be like to live with a man like Sam, a man so impulsive he'd give a woman a scorching kiss the day they met—a man who'd talk about love at first sight with someone he barely knew.

Holly turned down Clarissa's street. "Did you put Sam up to something last weekend?"

If she had, it would go a long way toward explaining Sam's behavior. Maybe the two of them had cooked up some sort of a joke after all, and she'd fallen for it, hook, line, and sinker.

"Well . . . yes," Clarissa admitted. "I guess you could say that."

Holly's heart sank a little.

"It was my idea he meet you at the Grill. And I did encourage Sam to move into your place."

"That's it?"

"I wanted to help. God knows why you're so hung up on Brad, but I hate seeing you unhappy." *So there*, her expression seemed to say. "You promised Brad a roommate, and I helped deliver one."

Holly pulled into Clarissa's driveway. "Then you didn't . . . no, never mind." She shook her head. "Thanks for wanting to help."

Clarissa wasn't having it. "Then I didn't . . . what?"

When Holly only drummed her fingers on the steering wheel and didn't answer, she pushed a little harder.

"What do you think I did? Sam's a big boy. I can't make him do anything he doesn't want to."

Holly drew in a deep breath. "Sam told me he was crazy about me. He said meeting me made him believe in love at first sight."

Clarissa's mouth dropped open. Good Lord. She'd rendered her speechless. Holly couldn't remember the last time that had happened, if ever.

"This is still my cousin Sam we're talking about, right?"

Holly nodded. "Does he do this sort of thing a lot?"

She was starting to feel concerned. Maybe Sam fell in and out of love with a different woman every week. Maybe he was a closet Don Juan. For all she knew, he'd used this "love at first sight" line before.

"As far as I know," Clarissa replied slowly, "Sam has never uttered the word 'love' to a woman. Except maybe in bed," she amended thoughtfully, "but I wouldn't know about that, of course." She pursed her lips and squinted at Holly. "Did you sleep with him already?"

"No!"

Clarissa looked at her closely. "Then why are you blushing, Holly Berry? Hmmm?"

It was true. Holly felt the warmth spread through her cheeks and couldn't have stopped it to save her life.

"You've thought about it, then?" Clarissa pressed. "I wouldn't blame you, actually. Sam's quite a hunk—even I can recognize that, despite knowing him since he was a toddler." A dreamy look came into her eyes. "We both used to get stuck at the kid's table together at Thanksgiving dinner every year. We must have been twelve before we got promoted to the big table. And now Sam's falling for you. Wow."

"Clarissa—"

"It's okay, I won't breathe a word to your precious Bradley," she said, drawing out the name until it sounded at least six syllables long. A broad smile crept across her face.

"You and Sam," she muttered. "Wow."

"There's no 'me and Sam,'" Holly objected. "There's not going to *be* any 'me and Sam.'"

"I can't wait to tell David."

"Oh, no. You're not telling him a thing." If Clarissa's husband even suspected something was going on, the news would be all over town before midnight. "Besides, there's nothing to tell. Nothing."

Clarissa picked up her purse and swung open the car door. She turned back to Holly, frowning in concentration.

"What's that saying?" she asked. "Oh, yeah—'the lady doth protest too much, methinks'." She winked and stepped out of the car. A wave. "I'll talk to you later!"

"Bye," replied Holly glumly. She was really in for it, now that Clarissa was on the case. Starting the car again, she pulled out of the driveway and headed for the only safe haven she knew. Home.

* * *

Her safe haven had been destroyed.

Okay, maybe destroyed was a little harsh. Rearranged, redone—no, invaded—was more apt. In front, Sam's pickup truck was parked, two tires on the street, the other two on the sidewalk. Its bed was filled with assorted lengths of lumber, some bricks, and—Holly peered closer—a pair of old muddy shoes.

In the middle of the porch swing sat a squat terra-cotta pot containing a miniature fir tree strung with tiny ornaments. Next to it was a longneck beer bottle.

Just inside the doorway, she stepped over a box packed with Christmas lights, larger ornaments, and a novelty Santa figurine. Beside the sofa lay a pair of very large tennis shoes. From the kitchen came the sound of "Rudolph the Red-Nosed Reindeer"—and a loud male voice singing accompaniment.

Sam.

Holly sniffed. He must be cooking something, probably using her prized set of Calphalon cookware. The sauté pan alone cost more than a hundred dollars. She bolted for the kitchen.

What she smelled was dinner, but he wasn't cooking it. He was . . . agitating it. Sam held two white Chinese take-out cartons in each hand, and he was swinging them by their wire handles to the beat of the song still blasting in the background. As she watched, he lifted his formerly injured toe and spun on his heel. He bopped across the kitchen floor, wiggling his backside as he went.

Holly smiled despite herself. Sam danced with the kind of abandon she hadn't witnessed since the drunken festivities at Clarissa's wedding reception.

"Hi," she called out.

He shimmied across the linoleum, unable to hear her over the music and his own singing. Holly marched over to the portable stereo taking up most of the counter space in her little kitchen and switched it off. Sam paused in mid-spin, the take-out cartons still swinging.

"Great, you're home!" He didn't look the least bit cha-grined to have been caught in mid-song. "Dinner's almost ready."

Holly slung her purse on the counter. "You made dinner?"

"Don't go getting all mushy on me," he warned upon see-ing her smile. "I just ordered in. It's nothing fancy."

From the looks of things, it was nothing neat, either. He hadn't left a stone unturned—or a cupboard door unopened. For the first time, Holly felt thankful for the meticulous order Brad had always insisted upon keeping everything in. Trying to look as un-mushy as possible, she went through the kitchen flipping the cupboards closed.

Sam lifted the cardboard containers. "I was looking for some bowls to put these in. Hungry?"

"Starving."

"Really?"

She nodded.

His smile grew wider and twice as seductive. "I've got just what you need," he teased. "Come on over and get it."

Did he really mean what she thought he meant? Sam leaned against the countertop watching her, his bare feet braced against the old linoleum floor. Holly let her eyes travel up the length of his denim-clad legs, past his haphazardly but-toned shirt, to his face. What she saw there made her tremble. He meant it all right, and every sensual spin she could put on the words. *Come on over and get it.*

Her breath left her. This was going to be harder than she'd thought.

"You probably want to bring in the things you bought first, though," he said.

Holly's mind flashed on the supplies she'd purchased and the bags of lingerie, still in the trunk.

"You did go to the mall with Clarissa like you said, right? Do you want help carrying your things in?"

And let him see the stuff she'd bought? The "holiday ap-propriate" garter belt and stockings set? The massage oils? The red and black velvet groping-hands bra? No way.

She shook her head. "I . . . no, thanks. I can manage."

"Sure?"

Holly nodded.

"Okay, then." Sam indicated the food cartons. "I'll get this ready while you do. Just leave everything to me."

He couldn't know how tempting those words were . . . could he? Half on auto-pilot, Holly headed for the car to bring in the clothes she'd bought.

Just as she added the last shopping bag to the mountain of others on her bed, Sam called her for dinner. Walking back through the house, she felt his presence everywhere—saw it in the toothbrush beside hers on the bathroom vanity, in the stack of unfamiliar books on the coffee table, in the basketball game that flickered on the television.

It gave her a strange feeling. Until now, a roommate had been just an idea, a faceless entity to make good her boast to Brad and help pay the mortgage. She hadn't counted on feeling Sam's presence so strongly.

Beneath the archway to the kitchen, she stopped and stared.

Sam spotted her. "Come on, it's getting cold."

The lights were dimmed. Just beyond him, the banquette table glowed with light from the number of red and green votive candles he'd set on it, along with the bowls of food. There were two place settings, side-by-side on one long edge of the table, a teapot and cups, and a little cellophane-wrapped pile of fortune cookies for a centerpiece. Holly blinked. It was all still there.

"I thought we needed a better beginning than we had at our last dinner," Sam said when she reached the table. "Thanks for sharing your house with me."

"You're welcome."

Holly gazed across the table again, wondering at a man who'd actually eat by candlelight without being cajoled into it. The food smelled wonderful and the table looked beautiful. It looked . . . romantic. She raced for the light switch.

Sam's hand landed on top of hers before she could switch on the lights.

"Wait." He slid his fingers beneath her palm and gently lifted her hand away. "Don't do that."

She glanced up at him. He laced his fingers with hers and

came closer, *closer*, until she was backed up against the wall behind her. His other hand came to rest on the wall beside her shoulder. He pressed forward, and Holly felt his hips touch hers, then withdraw. Her breasts grazed his shirtfront. When her nipples tightened beneath the layers of blouse and bra, her breath caught and held. What was he doing to her?

"I dare you," Sam said in a low voice. "I dare you to leave everything just the way it is. I dare you to leave it and see what happens."

He pressed their interlaced hands hard against the wall. "I dare you to feel, to feel us together. Feel me."

He was hard and hot and breathless, and she was melting against him. His hips rocked, once, sending the heat deeper through her, leaving her pulsing with sensation.

Feel, feel us together, feel me.

"I can't," Holly gasped, ducking beneath his arm.

She took refuge on the other side of the banquette, the candlelight blurring from her sudden, inexplicable tears. Her whole body trembled with emotion. Whatever it was that Sam brought out in her, whatever he wanted from her, it scared her half to death. She couldn't look at him.

He switched on the lights, and Holly's breath returned with the brightness. Sam slid onto the other banquette booth. For a long time, he didn't say anything. The only sounds were the clink of the teapot against the cups and the faint swirl of the tea as he filled each one. Steam rose, fragrant and warm. Holly slipped her fingers around the heated cup and risked a glance at him.

"There's a sensuous woman inside you," he said quietly. "I think she's worth waiting for."

She shivered. No one had ever described her that way. She'd never thought of herself that way.

"Well, somebody ought to let her out," she joked, hoping to turn their conversation to safer ground. "It must be stifling in there."

Sam didn't smile. "You're the only one who can let her out."

He wasn't looking at her, and for that she was grateful. He

picked up a plate and gestured toward the serving bowls with a spoon. "Want to try some?"

She could have cried with relief at his change of topic. Holly peered in the bowl. "What's in it?"

"I'm not sure. It's better not to look too closely at Chinese food." He grinned. "But it tastes great. You game?"

"Is there MSG in it? That's bad for you, you know. Some people have allergic reactions to MSG."

Sam paused, the spoon held a few inches above the bowl. "Do you?"

"I don't know. I don't want to find out, though."

"This allergic reaction—it's not fatal is it?"

"I don't think so, but—"

"Then the Kung Pao Chicken is worth it."

With certainty, Sam scooped some on the plate. He added a generous portion of beef with broccoli, then filled the remaining third of the plate with rice. He transferred a set of napkin-wrapped utensils from his side of the table to hers, then set the plate in front of her.

Holly stared at it doubtfully. "Is this brown rice? Brown rice is healthier."

He shrugged. "I doubt it." He ladled rice on his own plate and topped it with heaping spoonfuls of both entrees. "Go on. Live dangerously."

It *did* smell good. She had to admit that much. Holly unfolded her napkin.

"It was nice of you to get dinner," she said, poking tentatively at an unfamiliar, but very precisely cut, vegetable.

Sam nodded, already chewing happily. Holly lifted a strand of something green and stringy between her fork tines and examined it. It looked like seaweed. She frowned.

"What's the matter?" Sam asked.

She twirled the seaweed around the fork and scooped up some rice to help it go down easier. "I'm just not used to eating things I can't identify," she confessed.

"Then don't look," he suggested. "Just close your eyes and take a bite."

She was being a baby. Next thing she knew, he'd be suggesting she hold her nose, or take twenty-nine bites—one for each year of her life—like the lunch ladies used to do back in elementary school.

She ate the bite on her fork, then speared a piece of chicken and ate that, too. She was the new, spontaneous Holly, a lingerie-buying adventuress who lived to try new things.

"Like it?"

She was surprised to realize she did. "Mmm-hmm, it's pretty good."

It probably had a million calories, one plateful equivalent to twenty-five Big Macs or something, like that report on the movie theater popcorn. Heart attack on a plate. She ate some more. It was addictive, seasoned with flavors she didn't recognize and filled with weird vegetables, but she liked it.

Her eyes started to water. All of a sudden, her mouth was on fire. Her lips, her tongue, even her gums, burned. Her nose started to run. She sniffed, swabbing at her watery eyes with her napkin.

"Sam," she choked out, hardly able to speak. "Sam!"

This was it. A MSG reaction. She was going to die from Chinese food. Holly waved her arm frantically.

He was beside her in an instant. "Here. Drink this."

Holly gulped from the cup he held to her lips. When that was gone, she gasped and pointed to his cup, and drank all of his tea, too. By the time she'd finished the third cup Sam poured for her, she was starting to believe she wasn't going to die after all.

"My mouth is numb." Setting the cup back in the saucer, she gave Sam an accusing glare.

He retreated to his side of the banquette. "Sorry. It didn't even occur to me you might never have tried Chinese food. I guess it *is* a little spicy, if you're not used to it."

"A little spicy? That stuff could be used to keep peace between nations." She picked up her plate and pantomimed hurling it at an invisible enemy. "Watch out, or it's the Kung Pao Chicken for you!"

Laughing, Sam refilled both their tea cups. Holly pushed her plate away. Far away.

"Maybe you ought to tell me what other things you haven't tried," he said, "so we can avoid disaster in the future." He gazed thoughtfully at her. "How about Indian food? Ever tried curry? Chicken Vindaloo?"

She shook her head. "All these new things you've got planned for me to try—are they all food-related?" she asked, curious to know what else he'd suggest.

Sam smiled. Wickedly. "Not all of them. Ever try skinny-dipping? It's a lot of fun, especially if you can find a heated pool."

There's a sensuous woman inside you, Holly.

It was dizzying to keep up with him. One minute she and Sam were laughing. The next he was gazing at her as if he wanted to devour her. No man had ever looked at her that way, not even Brad—*especially* not Brad. He was too self-disciplined for that.

"Of course, I'd never ask you to do something you didn't want to do," Sam was saying.

Holly smiled. "I get the feeling we're not just talking about Kung Pao Chicken anymore."

"I'm not. Where this takes us is up to you. But I think I can convince you to give us a try."

He unwrapped a fortune cookie and handed it to her, then selected one for himself.

"You know, some people believe fortunes like these are really suppressed wishes." He cracked his fortune cookie open. "What do you think?"

"I think whoever is paid to write these things at the fortune cookie factory would be surprised to hear that." Holly slid the thin paper fortune from her cookie.

"What does it say?"

"Your happiness is intertwined with your outlook on life."

"See? That's dead-on."

"No, it isn't. It could apply to about a million other people," she said pragmatically. "Yours is probably just as vague."

Sam shook his head. "I don't think so. I think it's right on target." He held up his fortune so Holly could read it.

"Your present plans are going to succeed," she read.

Suddenly, inexplicably, her heartbeat quickened. With a deep breath, she glanced up from the paper fortune. Sam's eyes met hers and held.

"So," she asked, trying to sound lighthearted, "what are these big 'plans' of yours?"

"To make you fall in love with me." Sam brushed his fingertip across the tip of her nose, then smiled. "I think it's happening already."

Five

Sam couldn't keep his romantic Chinese food dinner with Holly out of his mind. He tried, but it was no use. He liked her, plain and simple. And since he wouldn't be in town long enough to take things slow, there was only one thing to do.

Accelerate the process.

It was almost ten-thirty, on a November day sunny and warm enough to heat the black asphalt shingles that topped the house he and his crew were re-roofing. With a longing glance at the swimming pool glittering in the house's yard below, Sam swiped his sweaty forehead with his forearm and turned his attention to his four-man crew.

"There's fifty bucks in it for each of you," he said, taking out his wallet, just to ensure their attention, "if we can get this job finished and cleaned up by eleven o'clock."

There was nothing like cold cash to motivate a person.

Before the hour was up, Sam was home in the shower. A half hour later, he drove up to the business complex where Holly's office was. His hair hadn't even dried all the way before he approached the receptionist's desk.

She kept her head bowed as she penned a note in her spiral-bound message pad.

"Can I help you?" she asked, tearing the message from its

perforated pad. She glanced up to put it in one of the boxes atop her desk and saw him. She smiled widely.

Sam smiled back. "I hope so. I'm looking for Holly Aldridge. Is she back there?" He nodded toward the rows of precisely arranged cubicles behind the receptionist's desk.

Her smile faded. So did much of her friendly attitude when she answered. "Ms. Aldridge is away from the office for the day. Perhaps another of our associates can help you?"

It was a rote reply. Sam tried again. "Can you tell me where she's gone?"

Holly hadn't been home, or he'd have seen her after his shower. And she hadn't mentioned anything about taking the day off, either. He wouldn't have thought anything short of a national disaster could pull Holly away from her desk. Even then she'd probably grab a briefcase of work to take with her.

The receptionist frowned. "I'm afraid I can't tell you Ms. Aldridge's plans, sir. Would you like to speak with someone else?"

Sir? Brrr, it was getting chilly.

"Sam, is that you?" Clarissa popped her head over one of the fabric-covered cubicle partitions. When she saw it was him, she came around the corner.

"I'll handle this one," she told the receptionist.

After a quick hello hug, she took Sam's arm and herded him to her desk. Pushing aside some papers, her coffee cup, and a stack of CD jewel cases, she settled her hip on her desktop.

"I thought I was hearing things," she said with a grin. "Turns out it really *was* you. You curious to know how the other half lives, or what?"

"What other half?"

"The responsible half. The grown-up half. The happily married and settled-down half."

"Oh. That half." Sam crossed his arms over his chest and leaned back, mimicking his cousin's relaxed posture. He added to it an affronted look. "I'm plenty responsible and grown up," he informed her. "I've got a good job—"

"Which you treat like a lark," Clarissa interrupted with a toss of her hair.

"Like hell, I do."

"It's true. Look at that ethics charge that old sour-butt Malcolm Jeffries brought up against you over changing your student's grade."

He gave her a sharp look.

Clarissa promptly waved it away. "Your folks told me. They worry about you." Driving her point home with a jab at his midsection, she persisted. "Did you take care of that little problem yet? Huh?"

Sam felt a headache coming on. "The hearing's not until after Christmas, and it'll never fly, anyway. This thing will blow over the same way all of Malcolm's stupid charges have."

"You're probably right. Still—"

"Still, all of that is beside the point." Unwilling to devote any more thought to Malcolm Jeffries' petty machinations than he had to, Sam moved back to their original conversation. "I have a good job, which is more than can be said for most of the yucks in this town."

"You have a job that allows you to feel like a student for the rest of your life. Admit it, Sam."

He didn't want to be drawn into that old argument again. Sam was the last person anybody in his family had expected to become a college professor. He knew that. Hell, he was the last person anybody had expected to go to college, period. The people close to him didn't understand his reasons for it, and he wasn't holding his breath until they did.

"Don't you have work to do?" he asked Clarissa.

She grinned. "It's more fun to badger you."

"I was afraid of that." Sam sighed and decided to get it over with. Clarissa wouldn't let up until she found out what she wanted to know.

"As for the rest of your accusations"—he shot her a knowing grin—"I'll get married and settled down just as soon as Holly comes to her senses and says yes. Anything else?"

Clarissa shrieked. Several of her coworkers popped their heads over the cubicle partitions. Red-faced, she waved them back down again. She leaned forward and grabbed Sam's shoulder.

"It's true then! Oh, Sam, that's so romantic. Love at first

sight. I'm really happy for you." She gave a wistful sigh. "I can hardly believe it, but I'm really happy for you."

"Believe it. If you keep grinning like that, though, your boss is going to wonder what you're up to in here."

Try as he might, Sam couldn't maintain the disgruntled expression he wanted on his face. The truth was, he felt like shouting from the rooftops how he felt about Holly.

To him, she was the perfect combination: a woman who inspired love, respect, and mind-bending lust in approximately equal amounts. He grinned. The only thing stopping him from taking out a billboard to propose to Holly was the fact that she'd probably laugh in his face.

He wasn't Doctor Brad the Bad, after all.

Clarissa examined him closely. "Ohmigod! You really do mean it, don't you?"

He meant it like he meant to go on breathing, like he meant to wake up tomorrow morning. Like he meant to make Holly feel exactly the same way.

"When have you known me to be hesitant about something?"

Clarissa's eyes widened.

"Point taken." She hopped down from her desktop. "In that case, you'd better hurry."

"Why?"

"Because Holly's with Brad right now." She scanned the yellow sticky notes on her computer monitor. "That's the reason she took a personal day today. She's at the golf course, trying to talk him into giving it another go. It's part of her plan."

"Her plan?"

"Holly would kill me if I told you any more. Just trust me, okay?" After peering at a yellow sticky note, Clarissa tossed it aside and squinted at a pink one. "She left me the golf course's number in case some work-related emergency came up. Brad's tee-off time is noon. Ah-hah! Here's the number." She dialed the phone. "If you hurry, you can still catch up with them."

"And I want to do that because . . . ?"

His cousin offered a self-satisfied little smile, then thrust the receiver in his hand. "Because you and Holly belong together, that's why. Why do you think I pestered you into moving in with her? Sheesh!"

"You set us up?"

His cousin, a born matchmaker, nodded. Smugly.

"You've got to stop her, Sam. If I know Holly, she just might be able to wrangle Brad the Bad into a new commitment. One turn around the fairway, alone, might be all it takes."

At that, Sam hung up the phone. He'd make all the necessary arrangements with the golf course when he got there. After all, there was only one course in all of Saguaro Vista. Right now there was no time to waste.

Her new golf clubs hadn't seemed nearly so heavy in the sporting goods store, Holly thought as she struggled to push through the clubhouse door at the Saguaro Vista golf course without dumping the whole set on the terrace. Slung over her back by the golf bag strap, they were awkward to carry. Held in front of her, they blocked her vision.

She tried tucking the bag partway beneath her elbow like a gigantic clutch purse and nearly poked her eye out with a putter. Maybe hiring a caddie to help her would have been a good idea after all.

Then she saw Brad, standing just a few feet away. He gazed across the fairway as though searching for someone, one hand shading his eyes against, Holly supposed, the blinding glare of the green. Despite the hundred and twenty dollars he'd paid for them, apparently Brad's designer sunglasses were no match for the immaculately kept, unnaturally green grass surrounding him.

Holly tried not to feel vindicated by that, but it was hard. She'd lobbied to spend that hundred and twenty dollars of joint checking account money on something worthwhile, like new shoes. Brad had vetoed that idea in favor of the fancy sunglasses, although to his credit, he'd bought Holly a pair, too. Never mind that she'd never held onto a pair of sunglasses longer than three months without laying them down someplace and forgetting them. Sometimes Brad just didn't made sense.

Today Holly was banking on Brad making sense. She needed him to listen to reason. It was the first phase of her plan. They still hadn't discussed the issues behind their separation, and Holly was through waiting for Brad to initiate that conversation. She wanted to get to the bottom of whatever the problem was and solve it.

She felt sure that, whatever Brad came up with, she could find a way to work around it. Just to be doubly certain, she'd even prepared a list of possible rebuttals. She'd stashed it inside her golf bag for quick reference, in case she got flustered and forgot one of the points she wanted to make.

Holly felt you could never be too prepared.

Brad headed to the first hole. With a mighty effort, she hefted her clubs again and hurried after him, dodging several groups of retirees discussing the weather. Apparently, they didn't miss Minnesota winters at *all* since coming to Arizona. Also, in their opinion, chipotle-glazed grilled turkey made an excellent Thanksgiving Day meal.

She set one espadrille-clad foot onto the fairway just as Brad disappeared behind a hill. Keeping her gaze fastened on the spot she'd last seen him, Holly quickened her pace. It wasn't easy to hurry wearing a dress and cute new sandals and carrying a big leathery-smelling golf bag, but she was encouraged by the thought that she looked nice.

A few minutes later, she plunked her golf bag on the green beside Brad's.

Being apart from her hadn't affected his sense of style any—not if his neatly pressed khaki shorts and polo shirt were anything to go by. Unlike some men, Brad took pride in dressing well and looking good, from his expensive haircut to his discreetly manicured fingernails. He looked as perfect as ever— almost, Holly thought suddenly, a little *too* polished. All at once, one of the qualities that had first attracted her to him seemed . . . well, a little shallow.

Determinedly, she pushed away that disloyal thought. Where had that come from, anyway? She'd probably been influenced by living with Sam. She'd lay bets Sam had spent more time arranging that Chinese takeout dinner for her than getting himself ready for it. Afterward, he'd gotten pretty grimy retrieving her Christmas decorations from the back of the closet, too. The man just didn't care about tidiness. Obviously, his attitude was rubbing off on her now, too.

She rose on tiptoes. "Hi, Brad!"

He was surprised as all get out to see her there. She could tell by the way he leaned forward, raising his sunglasses to get a better look.

"Holly! What in the world are *you* doing here?"

"Thomas asked me to fill in for him. An, umm, emergency came up at the office."

Holly was the emergency. She'd cornered Brad's partner early that morning to ask if he'd let her take his place in his regular Wednesday golf game with Brad. Asking nicely, cajoling, and pleading had no effect on him, but Holly had finally gotten him to agree by promising to sell Thomas her fancy new golf clubs if things didn't go her way. Since she felt fairly confident Brad would respond to a reasonable conversation, it was a bet she'd been willing to make.

Brad frowned. "But you hate golf. You always refused to go with me." He shot a suspicious glance at her golf clubs. "You told me the grass they use on the fairway makes you sneeze."

"Guilty. I know I said all those things. But, Brad . . . I'm turning over a new leaf." Holly moved closer to him, watching as his gaze dipped automatically to the heart-shaped neckline of her dress. "When you left, I realized I was partly to blame for the problems between us, too. I spent so much time working, I guess I neglected you."

A measure of skepticism returned to his expression—not that she could blame him. That speech was a little over the top. Holly figured it was necessary to concede something, sort of a good faith gesture to open their negotiations.

"I want to share your interests, Brad. Like golf. So, here I am!" She nodded at her new golf bag.

"Whose is that, anyway?"

"It's mine. I bought it last weekend."

She'd chosen well, too, judging by his expression. It had been the priciest bag in the store, highly recommended by the salesperson. She'd wanted to impress her sincerity upon Brad, and it looked as if it had worked. He was all but drooling on the expensive leather.

"Why? Just in case a golf emergency arose?"

Whoops, he had her there. She blustered through it. "Yes. And since you're here, and I'm here, and Thomas isn't here, we might as well get started. Otherwise, you'll miss your tee time."

The first two holes went pretty quickly. Holly's shots were a little wide, but she thought she was doing well for a beginner. Brad wasn't quite as encouraging, but by the time they reached the third hole, he'd stopped telling her she was throwing off his entire game. She took that as a hopeful sign.

"It sure is nice and peaceful out here," she observed as Brad lined up his next swing. "I don't even see anybody else playing nearby, do you?"

He grunted.

She went on. "I was just thinking . . . this would be a perfect place for a private conversation. Take us, for instance: we have lots to talk about."

He groaned. "You set me up, didn't you?"

Trying to look innocent, Holly took her time selecting a driver from her golf bag. "What's wrong with wanting to talk to you? I deserve an explanation for your leaving, Brad. Something more than a line about how you 'need your space.'"

She pulled out a club. A wood, or maybe it was an iron. She could never remember all the different names. She tried a practice swing with it, to give Brad time to respond.

"I knew it. This *is* a trap." He gave her a dark look, hefted his bag over his shoulder, and set out after his ball.

Holly stopped practicing her swing and took up the stance the guy at the pro shop had showed her. Aiming carefully, she whacked the ball before Brad could leave her behind.

It was a beautiful shot. It sailed cleanly into the air, higher than any shot she'd made so far, straight toward the next hole. Unfortunately, Brad's body was directly in the line of fire.

"Brad, look out!"

Holly was too far away to actually see the ball hit him, but she could tell when it happened, because he staggered backward a bit. Clutching his shoulder, he swiveled to face her. She could practically feel the force of his glare as he stared up the fairway.

Amazingly, though, when Holly finally reached him, Brad was smiling. As she dropped her golf bag on the grass and leaned on her club to rest up for the next shot, he tapped his pencil on the scorecard in a cheerful manner that was exactly the opposite of what she expected.

"That's a penalty stroke for you. You're twelve over par."

Apparently a bruised shoulder was okay, as long as it helped him win the game. She hadn't realized Brad was so competitive.

"I'm sorry. That one just got away from me," Holly apologized, pantomiming the shot with her driver.

Brad glanced at her, then looked more closely. "No wonder that shot went wild, Holly. You're using a nine iron."

She raised the driver and looked at its thick, sharply angled head. "I know. I like this one. It's got a little heft to it."

It seemed logical that a bigger club might give her a bit of an advantage, since her opponent was bigger, stronger, and more experienced at the game. A look at Brad's face told her she'd reasoned wrong. Holly shrugged.

"You'll just have to teach me how to play, then." She plucked her errant ball from his hand and put it back in play. "Next time, I'll be better."

Brad shook his head. "There's not going to be a next time. Golfing with you isn't an experience I want to repeat. And you can't use a tee here."

He frowned as she scooped up the tee she'd been about to plant on the green.

"I forgot," she muttered, tightening her grip on her golf club instead. Returning to the subject at hand, she added, "We need some shared interests, Brad. How are we supposed to have a relationship, if we never spend any time together? A good relationship doesn't just happen, you know. Both people have to work at it."

His lips tightened. "You know I hate talking about this relationship stuff."

He was gazing straight at her, but Holly couldn't gauge a

thing from his expression because of those stupid sunglasses. She stared back at him expectantly.

He sighed. "I don't want a relationship that needs working at. If it needs so damn much work, maybe it's just wrong."

This wasn't what she'd expected. "That's not true."

Brad gave a mean little laugh. "Oh, yeah. I forgot. I'm talking to the expert, aren't I? Far be it for me to second-guess Holly Aldridge, the relationship expert."

The sarcasm in his tone hurt. "That's not fair, and you know it."

She could hardly believe what she was hearing. Didn't he care about salvaging things between them? If he didn't, even the neat, thorough list she'd prepared would be no help.

Brad put his arms around her shoulders and shook his head. When he spoke, his voice was gentle. "I'm sorry. But you keep pushing me to it. I told you this isn't a good time for me. I'm still adjusting to having my space."

He kneaded the tense muscles in her shoulders, then dropped his hands. He peered into her face. "Better now?"

Holly nodded, feeling disgruntled. "I guess so."

"Good. Let's get on with the game, then."

He rubbed his hands together and devoted his attention to choosing a driver for his next shot. Beside him, Holly did her best to regroup. She should have anticipated Brad's reluctance to discuss their relationship, but she hadn't.

She waited until they'd reached the back nine—and Brad was ahead of her by twenty-four strokes—before trying again.

"I thought things were going really well between us," she ventured as they walked together toward the tenth hole. As proof, she offered, "In the whole year we lived together, we never had a single disagreement. Plus, we had such a nice routine going, just like an old married couple."

Liking the sound of that, she smiled. It might have been an old-fashioned viewpoint, but growing old together with somebody you loved sounded like a pretty good future to her.

"Yeah," Brad muttered. "Just like an old married couple."

"You don't sound happy about that." She raised her eyebrows. "I thought—"

He stopped her with an irritated look. "Let's talk about this some other time. I can't concentrate with you yammering at me."

Okay. A logical appeal wasn't working. She'd have to move on to the next phase of her plan, an emotional appeal. Maybe Brad would respond better to a non-conversational approach. And if that failed, there was always the third and final phase of her plan: seduction. Though Holly didn't think she'd have to resort to such drastic measures.

Beside her, Brad frowned at the flag fluttering over the next hole. Straightening his legs, he took his next shot. He appeared to be doing an excellent job of pretending she wasn't there. She might have been invisible for all the attention he was paying to her. The realization didn't do her feminine ego any favors.

In the distance, the buzzing sound of an engine drifted over the hills between them and the clubhouse. It sounded like somebody mowing the grass, although that couldn't be, not while there were players on the course. Curious, Holly shaded her eyes with her hand and looked for the source of the sound.

A couple of minutes later she saw it: an aqua-colored golf cart, zooming straight down the path toward them. A lone man hunched over the steering wheel, driving at a speed that made the cart waver from side to side. The vibrant-colored, canopied top shimmied and snapped in the breeze as the cart came closer.

Brad squinted at it. "I didn't know those things could go that fast," he remarked, frowning. "Must be some hot-rod kid—"

His words faded when the cart squealed to a stop a few feet from them. The driver got out.

"Sam! What are you doing here?"

Feeling ridiculously glad for the interruption in her game, Holly waved for him to come nearer. She couldn't help it. It was wonderful to see a friendly face looking back at her for a change. Obligingly, Sam strode across the green, with more casual ease than should have been strictly possible for a man his size. Brad, only as tall as Holly, was dwarfed beside him.

Sam shook his hand. "Hi, Doc. How's the game?"

"Fine, thanks." Surreptitiously, Brad slid the scorecard in his shorts pocket with his free hand. "Holly's having a little trouble, though."

Sam turned to her. "Oh, I don't know about that. I saw that drive you made back there. You looked good."

The appreciative way his gaze roved over her new dress made Holly wonder if it was really her golf form he was talking about. At the moment, though, she didn't care. She felt like soaking up his praise like a flower basking in sunshine.

"Thanks." She couldn't resist an I-told-you-so look at Brad before turning back to Sam. "Would you like to join us? There's always room for one more. . . ."

Brad snickered and elbowed Sam in the ribs, man-to-man style. "She's still got a lot to learn about the game," he said. Turning to Holly, he explained, "You can't add players midway through the course. Your friend here . . ."

"Sam," the friend in question supplied helpfully.

"That's right. I remember. Your friend Sam, here, will just have to wait for another time to play with you, Holly."

Sam waggled his eyebrows at her, turning Brad's comment into the most ribald of double-entendres. He heaved a mock sigh. "Okay. I guess I'll play with you later, Holly."

They both laughed. It was hard to remain serious with Sam around, Holly was discovering.

Brad wasn't laughing—he was staring impatiently at the next hole. He cleared his throat. "Well, Sam, we've got a game to finish here, so if there's nothing else . . ."

"Actually, there is. I came out to get you, Holly. There's an emergency situation you've got to take care of."

She sighed. She might have known the instant she actually took a personal day, her first all year, a crisis would come up. She turned to grab her golf bag, but Sam had already thrown it over his back and was carrying it to the cart.

"I'm sorry, Brad. I've got to go."

He only shrugged. He'd experienced enough work-related emergencies himself to know that she had no choice but to leave. It was a familiar pattern between them. Even when they'd been living together, they'd seldom had the same days free from work.

"Let's get together in a few days," she suggested. "Is Francie's okay with you?"

Waiting for his answer, she crossed her fingers. Brad

couldn't refuse dinner with her at the restaurant where they'd had their first date, could he? It was the linchpin of the second phase of her plan.

At least in this instance, he didn't disappoint. "Call my office. We'll arrange a time."

"Okay." With one last backward glance—and a sigh for the failed first phase of her plan—Holly headed for the golf cart where Sam waited for her.

Sam drove back to the clubhouse at a reasonable speed, now that he'd found Holly and gotten her safely ensconced on the golf cart seat beside him. As they reached the edge of the fairway, he glanced at her.

"You look great," he said, admiring her short, flowery dress again. It ended a few inches above her knees and was held up by thin straps at the shoulders, the kind of thing that made him think of hot summer days at the beach. He liked it. He liked the looks of Holly wearing it.

It was a funny choice to wear golfing, though. Even given the sunny Arizona weather. He'd bet she'd meant to improve more than her golf scores with it.

"New dress?"

"Mmm–hmm," she murmured absently, digging around in her golf bag. She pulled out her fat day planner and rifled through it, flipping past what looked like a Christmas greeting card list. "When my office called, did they tell you what the emergency was?"

He stopped the cart at the clubhouse. "Well, I didn't actually say it was an emergency at your office, now did I?"

Sam felt her suspicious stare on his back while he returned the golf cart keys to the attendant.

"What do you mean?" she asked when they were alone again, walking across the parking lot toward his truck.

"Don't get mad."

Holly stopped and stuck both hands on her hips.

"You look mad."

"*You* look like you've got some explaining to do."

"Okay." Sam swung her golf bag into the bed of his pickup,

raising a cloud of dust as he did. He pulled out his keys. "Clarissa told me where you were when I ran into her at your office earlier today."

"What were you doing at my office?"

Why was she looking at him like that? "I was going to take you out to lunch, but you weren't there. So I took a chance you'd say yes and came out here to get you."

"Why do I get the feeling I've just been bamboozled out of my golf game?"

"Maybe because you were." Sam smiled, went around to the passenger-side truck door, and opened it for her. "Come on. I'll take you anyplace you want to go."

Holly crossed her arms over her chest. "I've got my car. I can drive myself."

"All right."

She didn't move.

Stepping back to make room for her to get in the truck, Sam raised his eyebrows. "Would you rather go back to your golf game instead?"

She glanced back toward the fairway. "No . . . it wasn't exactly going the way I'd planned," she said cryptically.

Did that have something to do with the "plan" Clarissa had mentioned? Sam made a mental note to get more information about it from his cousin, the matchmaker.

Holly looked indecisive, as though torn between going with him and bolting for the security of her car. "Will you bring me back for my car later?"

Sam nodded, waiting.

Grumbling something about "masculine ego," Holly uncrossed her arms and came to meet him beside the open passenger-side door.

"Does this mean you're not mad at me?"

"It means my feet are freezing," she grumbled, waggling one sandal-clad foot in demonstration.

He grinned and gave her a hand up into the truck cab. She hovered above the bench seat, swiping away the dust, papers, and CDs so she could sit down. Her voice, complaining about the messy state of his truck, came through the open window as he got in the other side.

"So what's the big emergency?" she asked once he was settled.

"Persistent, aren't you?"

She just looked at him.

"There's no emergency," he confessed, pulling the truck slowly into traffic. He shot a glance at her. "I just wanted to spend some time with you. How else am I going to convince you this love at first sight thing is real?"

Her eyes widened.

"Put your seat belt on," he added.

He felt her gaze on him the whole time she was pulling the belt across her body and buckling it. Everything in her body language screamed wariness. Sam felt like smacking himself on the forehead. Idiot. Holly probably thought he was a love-crazed lunatic. He couldn't exactly blame her for it, either. He felt like one.

"You know, you can't just go around kidnapping people from golf courses. Does this ploy actually work for you?"

"Not all the time." Sam wasn't sure, having never tried it before.

She gave a little harrumph sound. "I'll just bet. Where are we going?"

She gripped her day planner tight in both hands, probably ready to whack him with it if he got out of line. It looked heavy enough to give him a real shiner if her aim was good. Clearly Holly was a woman unused to spontaneous fun.

"We can go right back to the golf course, if you want. Or I'll take you to get your car and you can go home, to the office, wherever. It's up to you."

She loosened her death grip on her day planner. Sam relaxed, too, feeling he was making some progress.

"I almost forgot. There's something for you in the cooler." He nodded at the Styrofoam cooler near her feet.

"No, thanks. I had a lot of iced tea back at the—"

"It's not a drink."

"What is it?"

He'd never met a woman harder to give a gift to. "It's nothing sinister, if that's what you're wondering. Just open it, okay?"

It was worth every bit of trouble just to see the look on Holly's face when she opened the cooler and pulled out the miniature container of potted poinsettias from inside.

"If you're trying to soften me up with flowers, Sam McKenzie, I'm afraid you're succeeding." She smiled. "I love these! They're so Christmassy."

"It's a little early, I know. But they'll last through the holidays, I think." He grinned back at her. "The florist kept aiming me toward other kinds of flowers, but you look like a poinsettia girl to me."

"I can't imagine *why* you'd think that."

Her teasing tone didn't fool him. Holly *loved* Christmas, and everything that went with it. He'd learned that much about her after helping decorate her house—her *whole* house—for the holidays. Not that he'd minded. There hadn't been anything tough about stringing fake garland and spraying artificial snow on the windows next to someone like Holly.

Sam glanced at her again. She was still smiling, looking flushed and surprised. A sudden image occurred to him of Holly as a little girl, her red hair in two pigtails instead of the businesslike layered haircut she had now, a sprinkling of freckles over her nose. If they had a little girl someday, she'd probably have freckles, too.

Whoa. Sam slapped the brakes on that idea, shaking his head to clear it.

Returning to the matter at hand, he said, "Now that you've been kidnapped from the golf course and duly softened up, what do you want to do? Go to the zoo, to the mountains? I hear there's a winter carnival down at the fairgrounds. We could even"—he paused for dramatic effect—"go bowling."

"Bowling?"

They both laughed.

"Fun is all in how you look at it," he protested. "With the right attitude, anything can be fun. I'm going to see that you have a whole day of nothing but fun."

At the stoplight, Holly bit her lower lip. "I really ought to go back in to work . . ."

Her objection sounded halfhearted at best.

"Come on," he said. "It'll be fun. And you look as if you

could use some cheering up. Weren't things going very well with Brad back there?"

"What makes you say that?"

"Just a feeling." And the way she'd looked so miserable standing next to the guy. "What do you say?"

She took a deep breath. "First there's something I've got to know."

That sounded ominous. "What is it?"

Holly lifted her flowers. "Did you really mean to put these on ice?"

Sam laughed. "Yeah. I was afraid they'd get wilted."

"Good. In that case, maybe you're not as crazy as you seem after all. Let's go."

Six

They went to the winter carnival. Standing beside Sam as she had her hand ink-stamped by the attendant, Holly could see why he'd suggested it. Given all the rides, the flashing lights, and the junk food, it was the perfect place for a boy in a grown man's body like Sam McKenzie.

He took her hand and they walked beneath the fairground's holiday-light-bedecked archway, their shoulders nearly touching. It felt surprisingly natural to be so close to him. As long as she was being spontaneous again, Holly decided, she might as well throw herself into the experience. She gave his hand a squeeze.

He smiled down at her. "Better than golfing?"

A nod. "What should we do first?"

"Eat," he said decisively.

"Eat? It's not even dinner time."

"You do everything by the clock?"

"No, but . . . quit shaking your head at me. What's wrong with having a regular schedule?"

"Nothing." Sam gave her a goofy, smiling look she couldn't quite decipher. "There's nothing wrong with it. But I don't think my stomach's on your schedule yet. Come on."

He made a beeline for the hot dog vendor's umbrella-topped wagon, where the hot dogs spun endlessly on a revolving rotisserie. Every time he opened the rotisserie door, the scent of roasted meat wafted in the air. Holly's stomach growled.

Sam pulled some money from his wallet. "It's on me. What would you like?"

She hesitated, watching in appalled fascination as the vendor plopped a hot dog on a split bun and began piling on ketchup, mustard, relish—every condiment in the array before him. She wouldn't have thought so much could fit on a single hot dog.

"I'm not sure. Why don't you go ahead and order while I decide?"

Five seconds later, Sam, not nearly as indecisive as she was, had ordered two hot dogs with everything and a root beer.

The vendor started on his order, then paused, spoon in midair. "Chili?"

"On both, thanks." Sam glanced at Holly. "Anything look good to you?"

She examined the hot dogs again. "Well . . . yes, but—"

Waving, she caught the vendor's attention. "Excuse me, but can you tell me what those are made of, please?"

He stared at her as though she'd just started speaking Japanese.

"I mean, are they all-beef hot dogs? Or turkey? Or . . . what?"

Holly let her voice trail off. Now Sam was looking at her funny, too.

"They're just hot dogs, lady," the vendor said. "You want one or not?"

"Ummm . . . ." She couldn't decide. She was starving, but did she really want to eat something she couldn't identify—or worse, something that was almost pure saturated fat? It wouldn't be smart. If she got fat, she wouldn't stand a chance of winning Brad back with her plan. Brad disliked women who let themselves go.

"Is this another MSG reaction thing?" Sam asked. "Or is it something else? We can go to another vendor if you want."

"Is this kind of stuff all you ever eat?" Holly asked him,

wondering how he'd managed to get so big on what seemed to be an exclusively take-out diet of pizza, Chinese food, Christmas cookies, coffee . . . and hot dogs.

He shrugged. "Never thought about it much."

She'd have to show Sam how to cook himself a decent meal. At the rate he was going, he'd keel over from a cholesterol overdose by the time he was thirty-five. He needed somebody to watch out for him. He needed taking care of.

Whoa. Maybe he did, but she wouldn't be the one who did it. Had she time-warped into the fifties or something? Holly Aldridge had bigger goals than taking care of a husband.

Double whoa. Husband? She didn't know where *that* had come from. Determinedly, Holly steered her attention back to the hot dogs and tried to think spontaneously.

"Well, lady?" The hot dog vendor stared impatiently at her. Behind her, the line of people waiting was growing.

"Would you rather go someplace else?" Sam asked.

"No. Never mind what's in it. I'll take one . . . with everything, please. And a root beer, too."

Being spontaneous was starting to feel awfully good.

So was indulging her appetite, Holly decided as she licked the last of the chili from her fingertips twenty minutes later. She sipped the foamy remnants of her root beer through her straw and glanced at Sam.

He was watching her. "Good?"

"Mmm-hmm. I can't remember the last time I ate a hot dog. Brad prefers sushi."

Sam made a face.

She couldn't help but grin. As a prelude to changing the subject, she patted the picnic bench the two of them sat on. "This is nice. You really know how to treat a girl, Sam."

He gave her a wary look.

Laughing, she waved her arm at their surroundings, a prime spot near the Christmas-crafts exhibition hall. Here, multicolored holiday lights twinkled. The air was scented with the fragrance of the fir trees stacked for sale nearby. And Christmas carols burst from the speakers at the nearest booth.

Despite the lack of snow, reindeer, and naturally occurring Scotch pines, Holly found the whole effect very Christmassy.

"No, really! I mean it," she said. "It's cheerful here. And peaceful. Plus, it's nice not to have to worry about impressing anybody for a change."

"Thanks. I think."

Sam ducked his head and finished the last bite of his hot dog. When he looked up again, one corner of his lips was decorated with a little smear of chili.

"Umm, you've got a little bit of chili." Holly tapped her fingertip at the corner of her lips. "Right here."

"Here?" He probed one corner with the tip of his tongue.

"Other side."

He tried again.

"No, lower. Here, wait a minute." Grabbing a clean napkin from the pile on Sam's lap, she moved closer to him and wiped away the spot. Beneath her fingertip, the corner of his mouth raised in a smile.

"There. I got it." She dabbed the other side for good measure. "I guess nobody could eat with as much gusto as you do and not make a mess occasionally."

"Thanks."

Holly lowered her hand and made herself stop looking at Sam's lips. Her gaze settled somewhere between his shoulder and jaw.

"You need a shave," she informed him, trying to keep up her end of the conversation. The air practically vibrated between them. She needed to get back on safer ground, but before she could slide away, Sam wrapped his arms around her waist.

"I know." The tone of his voice made it plain he couldn't care less about razor stubble.

He was looking at her—she felt it. Holly risked a glance back at him, and her stupid, traitorous gaze went straight to his mouth again. They were close enough to share the same breath. Close enough to know better.

"Unless you want to be kissed again," Sam warned, "you'd better quit looking at me like that."

"Like what?"

"Like I'm an especially tasty morsel of something you stopped indulging in a long, long time ago."

Holly took a deep breath. "Maybe it's time to stop denying myself," she said slowly, assessing the dark shadow of beard stubble on his jaw. What would it feel like if she rubbed her cheek across it, just a little?

"Maybe," Sam agreed.

That brought her up short. "You sound as if you don't care one way or the other."

Didn't he want to kiss her again? Had she been so lousy at it the last time? She didn't think so, but . . . wasn't he even going to try to encourage her?

"I care." He smiled, wryly. "Do it, then."

Their eyes met. She couldn't breathe, couldn't move. Her spontaneity dissolved beneath the intensity of his expression, taking her bravado with it. This was real. No amount of rationalizing could change that.

"But do it because you want to," Sam said, his voice lowered, "and not for any other reason. Not because you're mad at your boyfriend or you want to prove something to me. Not because I kissed you first." He smiled at that. "But just because you want to."

No excuses. Holly could recognize a warning when she heard one. This one should have doused her feelings like a bucket of midwinter snow, but it didn't. Her whole body tensed with anticipation. Yes, *yes.* It had been so long.

"Yes," she whispered. "I . . . I do want to."

Sam cupped her cheek in his hand, his fingertips stroking slowly beneath her ear. "Look at me, then. Look at me and know the man you're with."

It was Sam. Scruffy, messy, love-at-first-sight Sam, and in the instant before her eyes drifted closed, he was the sexiest man she'd ever seen. She kissed him.

It was the most potent experience she could remember having. As soon as she opened her eyes again, Holly knew she'd been crazy to think one taste was enough. Being with Sam made her want to throw common sense to the wind.

She shot to the other side of the bench as if her behind was on fire. "So, what should we do next?"

She wished her voice would quit shaking.

Sam leaned his head against the bench, gazing at her with half closed eyes. "More kissing?"

"No."

"No?"

"No," she said firmly. "Besides, anybody could see us here."

"You won't kiss me because somebody might see."

It wasn't a question.

"That's right," she lied. "Wasn't once enough for you?"

"Not nearly." He ran his fingertips along the bare skin of her upper arm, raising a shivery trail of goose bumps. "Was it enough for you?"

"I have a fiancé . . . at least, I think I still do. I shouldn't even be here." She got up, then grabbed her day planner and purse. "Maybe you should just take me home."

"I'm not going to force myself on you, Holly."

"I know."

Sam reached for her hand. "Scared?"

Yes. Scared of you, scared of me. Scared of losing my best chance at happiness. She couldn't say it out loud.

"Should I be?" she asked instead. It sounded ridiculous even to herself. She tried again. "I'm sorry, Sam. The kiss was a mistake. Things didn't work out for me with Brad today, and I guess I was feeling vulnerable. I won't let it happen again. It wouldn't be fair to anyone."

Sam crumpled his paper cup and threw it into the trash can.

"Okay," he said. "I understand."

Holly wasn't sure what to expect, but it wasn't what she heard next.

"Want to hit some rides before we go?"

Saturday night. Date night, at least for the happily coupled half of the planet's population. Standing alone in the vestibule of Francie's restaurant, Holly felt decidedly in the uncoupled half. Flipping open her cell phone, she turned her back on the lovebird couples waiting for tables.

Please be home. Come on.

Clarissa answered on the third ring.

"Hi, it's me," Holly said, trying to sound upbeat. "You busy?"

"What's wrong?"

"Nothing. I . . ." Clarissa always knew when something was wrong, even when Holly tried to hide it. Her throat tightened, making it hard to speak. She blinked, staring hard at the maître d' stand. Focusing on it helped distract her long enough to finish talking. "You want to catch a movie or something?"

Silence. Holly could picture the scene, though: Clarissa sitting cross-legged on her black kitchen countertop, cordless receiver cradled to her ear, probably painting her toenails orange. Clarissa was big on beauty rituals.

"Sure," Clarissa said. "A movie movie, or a DVD rental?"

Saturday night. Date night. The movie theater would be packed with hand-holding, smiling couples. The kind of couple Holly wasn't part of anymore.

"DVD."

"Gotcha. I'll meet you at your place in half an hour."

"Unless . . . unless you've got other plans. With David, I mean. I don't want to interrupt anything."

"Don't be silly, Holly Berry. Get yourself home. And be careful, too."

"Yes, Mom." Holly smiled for the first time in what felt like hours. "See you soon."

When Holly pulled into her driveway, Sam's truck was nowhere in sight. He was probably on a date, too. So much for love at first sight.

He'd left the porch light on for her, though, and the holiday lights they'd strung along the eaves flashed merrily, too. Bathed in their multicolored glow, she trudged up the sidewalk to the front porch. She kicked off her high heels and sat on the swing beside Sam's mini Christmas tree.

The decorated plant had taken up permanent residence there, where it got plenty of sunshine during the day. Sam had insisted six inches of Christmas tree was all he needed, but his macho attitude hadn't fooled Holly one bit. His enthusiasm for hanging ornaments, cutting paper snowflakes, and blitzing the windows with spray-on snow hadn't been lost on her. He loved the holidays as much as she did. Maybe even more.

Holly sighed. They'd spent hours hanging wreaths, making red and green construction paper chains, and eating gingerbread men together. Now, cradling the little tree's terra-cotta pot with one hand to keep it steady, she dug her stockinged toes against the porch floorboards and set the swing in motion. Things with Sam might be coming up all fruitcake and mulled cider, but as far as the rest of her life was concerned . . . *that* was another story.

Things weren't turning out the way she wanted them. The worst part was, Holly couldn't figure out why. Everything ought to be peachy. You study hard, you get straight A's. You work hard, you get promoted. You find the right man, you get loved. Except she'd found the right man, and Brad didn't love her. He was messing up the rest of the equation. Where was the happily-ever-after ending?

Not that she was naïve enough to believe all relationships ended happily. Her divorced parents were proof of that. But their marriage had begun in the heat of passion. It would have been impossible to sustain that, wouldn't it? In contrast, with Brad, Holly had found a man with a background, interests, and professional goals that were all similar to hers. It should have at least increased her odds of success.

Instead it only left her feeling lonely.

Headlights swept the porch as Clarissa's sports car pulled into the driveway and roared to a stop. Clarissa got out and tromped up the walk carrying an overflowing department store shopping bag.

"Hey, what are you doing out here?" she asked.

Holly stopped the swing. Clarissa picked up the mini Christmas tree and settled herself in its place, balancing the pot on her bare knees. She plunked her shopping bag between them. They started swinging again.

"I'm just thinking about stuff," Holly said. "I haven't made it inside yet."

She hadn't wanted to go in alone. Weeknights were easier. She could stay at work late and tell herself she was being pro-ductive. There were no such excuses on the weekend. The empty house waited for her, a big old reminder of how empty her life was becoming, too.

Clarissa tapped the shopping bag. "I've got all the essentials in here. *A Charlie Brown Christmas* and some spritz cookies if you're feeling happy, *It's a Wonderful Life* and a jumbo box of tissues if you're not, and two pints of peppermint stick ice cream in either case." She smiled sympathetically. "Plus a good ear for listening. What'll it be?"

Holly burst into tears.

Clarissa stopped the swing. "I knew I should have brought a George Clooney movie, too. George is good for all occasions." She rummaged in the shopping bag, then pressed a wad of tissues in Holly's hand.

"Do you want to tell me what happened? Or should I just go wring Brad's neck right now? You did go to dinner with him tonight at Francie's like you planned, right?"

Holly nodded, sniffling.

"He stood you up. Damn him!"

"No . . . no, he didn't stand me up. He was there." Holly blew her nose and tried to get herself under control. Her nose was so plugged up she sounded like a muppet when she talked.

"He was there, but he was a half hour late," she continued. "Gina, his secretary, called the restaurant to let me know. Otherwise I probably would have left."

Yeah, right. She would have stayed out of pure stubbornness, if nothing else. Determination had served her well over the past few years. Holly couldn't admit that to Clarissa, though. She still had *some* pride left.

"How did his secretary know about your romantic dinner together?"

"I made the plans through her. You know how busy Brad is."

Clarissa shook her head. "I still think you should have left. It would have served him right."

"I'm not trying to teach him a lesson. I'm trying to put our relationship back on track again." Holly sighed. It was starting to look as if she was the only one interested in keeping things going between them.

Clarissa pulled two diet colas from the depths of her bag and cracked open a can for each of them. "Negates the calories to come later from the ice cream." She winked. "So Brad the Bad strolls in late. Then what?"

"Well, he joined me at the table. Our special table—*The Table*—where we sat on our first date."

Their first date, Holly's first blind date. Her mother had fixed her up with Brad after meeting him the day she'd closed the sale of his parents' new two-million-dollar Arizona "vacation cabin."

"Uh-huh. Good move, the special table," Clarissa said. "Part of the emotional appeal phase of your plan?"

"Yes." Holly was a little surprised Clarissa remembered the plan so well. "But Brad didn't like it. He spent the first ten minutes badgering the waiter into seating us farther from the kitchen." Holly sighed, remembering. "The poor waiter didn't know what to do. I'd slipped him five bucks to seat us there."

Clarissa tilted her head, staring up at the twinkling holiday lights. "Men can be so clueless about sentimental things. David still thinks I picked red roses for our wedding because they matched the bridesmaid's dresses best. Duh! They were the first kind of flowers he ever gave me."

Holly's mind flashed on the poinsettias Sam had given her the day of the winter carnival. Good thing she wasn't marrying Sam. Poinsettias would make a pretty goofy wedding bouquet.

"I know," she agreed. "I don't think they can help it."

She swigged some diet cola, then remembered the peppermint stick ice cream in Clarissa's bag. "Do you want to put the ice cream in the freezer?"

Clarissa carried her shopping bag inside. Holly followed, swinging her sleek new black shoes by their ankle straps. She didn't know why she'd bothered getting dressed up. Brad hadn't looked at her twice during the whole meal. If not for his perfunctory, "You look nice tonight, Holly," she'd have thought he hadn't noticed her efforts at all.

"The ice cream is safely stowed for later," Clarissa said when she came back into the living room. She flopped down next to Holly on the sofa and sat hugging her knees to her chest. "So tell me the rest. What happened after Brad finished browbeating the waiter?"

"Well, we ordered dinner." Holly paused, squinting to remember the awful truth. "You know, I always thought it was so charming of Brad to order for me when we went out someplace. But tonight . . . I don't know, it seemed a little . . . ."

She stopped and shook her head. "I'm probably just mad because things didn't work out. But I didn't like it. And it wasn't just that, either. I can't really put my finger on it. It was as if Brad wasn't really *there*, you know what I mean?"

Clarissa nodded, setting her soda can on the glass coffee table top. Holly automatically reached for a coaster, then stopped. That was Brad's rule, not hers. Whose house was it, anyway?

"I know what you mean," Clarissa said. "David is like that if I try to talk to him while he's watching ESPN. Zombie man. Not all there."

"Exactly. Brad kept looking around, as if he was looking for someone." *Or looking for an escape route.* "I had it all planned out," Holly went on. "I brought a portable CD player so I could play our favorite song. I brought pictures of the ski trip we took last December, so we could reminisce about the good times. I even alluded to the first time we, ahh . . ."

"Did the deed?" Clarissa suggested with a wicked lift of her eyebrows.

"Noodled. Brad called it noodling."

"What?"

"It's true," Holly admitted, feeling herself flush. "Whenever Brad was, ummm, in the mood, he'd kind of nudge me and say, 'Want some noodling, little girl?'"

"Gross!"

"I guess it does sound a little strange. I got used to it."

Clarissa gave her a sympathetic look. Holly shrugged.

"Anyway, nothing worked tonight. Brad didn't want to reminisce. He said playing our song would disturb the other diners, and he flipped through the vacation pictures as if they'd catch fire if he held onto them longer than two seconds apiece." Tears of frustration welled in her eyes. "What am I doing wrong, Clarissa? I'm really trying here, but I must be doing something wrong, because it's not working!"

"It's not you, hon." Soothingly, Clarissa patted Holly's arm. "It's Brad the Bad. Honest. It's got to be." She paused. "Have you ever considered he's just not the right man for you?"

"No. Uh-uh." Feeling a need to keep busy, Holly reached for the shopping bag and dug around in it. She pulled out the DVDs and plopped them on the coffee table.

"I can't give up now. Not after everything I've already invested in this relationship. What if I'm almost there? What if I just need a little more time before Brad realizes we belong together? We were really great together once."

"'Once'? What about right now? What about cutting your losses and moving on?" Clarissa insisted. "You deserve better than this."

"I can't just give up. Not yet, at least."

Clarissa threw both hands in the air. "But it's not all up to you. Maybe you've done all you can already."

Holly thought about the lingerie squashed in her bottom bureau drawer, still in its potpourri-scented bag. "Not quite everything. There's still phase three of the plan."

Groaning, Clarissa dragged the shopping bag across the polished oak floorboards.

"You mean the seduction routine," she said, her voice muffled as she searched for something in the bag. "I didn't think it would come to that."

That was heartening. It must mean Clarissa thought Holly would have convinced Brad to come back long before this.

"I didn't, either. It's my last resort."

"Oh, boy. I need more fortification for this."

Clarissa ripped open the spritz cookie box. They both grabbed a few of the delicate, sugary treats.

"I think it'll work, though," Holly said around a mouthful. "The seduction thing."

Her friend gave a skeptical snort.

"Well, aren't people always saying men think with their . . ." Holly gestured vaguely, then swallowed hard. "You know."

Raised eyebrows from Clarissa. "Their . . . ?"

"You know." Holly offered a vague hip swivel in demonstration, got even more embarrassed, and shut up.

"You can't even say it, can you?"

"I just don't want to."

Clamping her lips together, Holly grabbed the *Charlie Brown Christmas* DVD. She devoted all her attention to opening the case, popping the disc in the player, and searching for the remote.

"You can't say it," Clarissa goaded. "Admit it."

"No."

Holly found the remote behind her discoing Santa figurine. She retreated to the couch again, where Clarissa waited to jump on her like a little yappy dog.

"Geez, are *you* ever repressed," she said. "I had no idea. Come on, say it. I won't tell anybody." She was smiling now, holding back a laugh. She poked Holly's shoulder. "It's okay, you know. You're a grown woman. You're supposed to know about this stuff. Didn't your mother ever talk to you about sex?"

She bit into a cookie, scattering crumbs while she waited for Holly to speak. Before Holly could get a word out, though, Clarissa held up both hands.

"No, wait." She shuddered in mock horror. "I don't think I want to know what your mother, aka the ice queen, told you about making whoopie."

"Ha, ha. My point was," Holly said laboriously, "that I think sex appeal would work on most men. Brad included."

Clarissa—her friend, her best friend since ninth grade—snorted. Holly threw a Rudolph the Red-Nosed Reindeer pillow at her.

Clarissa ducked. "What about Sam?"

"He's a perfect example of my theory," Holly declared, feeling smug. "Sam practically sweats sex appeal—"

"Ewww."

"Okay, bad word choice." She thought about it some more. "What I mean is, he's totally centered in the here and now. The man lives like there's no tomorrow. He eats what he wants, wears what he wants . . . . Sam takes what he wants."

Shivering, Holly remembered the heat of his body pressed against hers. Remembered what he'd said as he'd all but dared her to savor the experience. *Feel. Feel us together. Feel me.*

"Sam's definitely a man who thinks with his you-know-what," she concluded. "And I'll bet he's pretty typical." *Liar,* a part of her whispered. *He's anything but typical.*

Clarissa shook her head. "Sam is in love with you."

"Sam only thinks he's in love with me. That's infatuation. There's a big difference. That kind of love can't last."

Looking sober, Clarissa pushed away the spritz cookies and wiped her fingers on a napkin. "It might, Holly. And if it did, it would be the greatest kind of love there is."

"That kind of love only happens in the movies." Holly aimed the remote at the DVD player. The opening credits rolled. "Only in the movies."

Seven

The next morning dawned bright and sunny and much too early for someone who'd slept as poorly as Holly had. She rolled over in bed, whacked the snooze button on her clock radio, and dragged a too-cheerful Christmas-print pillow over her face. Why in the world had she set the alarm for seven-thirty on a Sunday morning?

Because she'd invited her mother, along with Clarissa and her husband David, over for brunch, that's why.

Groaning, Holly pulled her matching comforter over her head, too. After her disastrous evening with Brad, hosting a brunch party fell someplace below having a bikini wax on her list of Things to Look Forward To.

Snap out of it. It'll probably be fun, she told herself as she crawled out from beneath her comforter cave. She pulled on a pair of old shorts beneath the soft cotton T-shirt she slept in—no sense ruining her nice clothes by cooking brunch in them—and headed for the kitchen to get started.

Forty-five minutes before everyone was due to arrive, Sam ambled barefoot into the kitchen wearing nothing but a pair of plaid boxer shorts and a groggy smile.

"'Morning. You look busy," he remarked as he poured himself a cup of black coffee.

"You look as though you just got up." Holly eyed his rum-

pled hair and unshaven jaw. The rest of him she tried to ignore, but it wasn't easy. The man sure looked good wearing
mostly skin and a smile. "It's after ten already."

"I know. I was out kinda late last night." He blew on his
coffee, then sipped. "Ahh . . . that hits the spot."

Holly didn't doubt it. It had been after one o'clock when
she'd finally heard Sam come home. Not that she'd been listening specifically for him, or anything. It was probably just a
coincidence that she'd still been awake finishing the last of the
peppermint stick ice cream when his key had turned in the
lock.

"Did you have a good time?" *Wherever you were?*

"Yeah." He squinted into the distance and didn't say anything else.

Poor Sam was a slow starter in the morning. Probably the
caffeine hadn't reached his brain yet.

He blinked, downed the rest of his coffee, then examined
the kitchen. "Quite a production. Are you expecting company,
or are you just especially hungry today?"

"Did I forget to tell you?" Holly maneuvered around him,
then picked up the basket of strawberries she'd bought to go
with the French toast she was making. "I invited Clarissa and
David—and my mother—over for brunch this morning."

"I'm not invited?"

"Sure you are, if you really want to join us." Holly made a
face. "I just thought I'd spare you the ordeal of meeting my
mother."

Sam remained silent. Holly sliced away the green top of a
fat strawberry with surgical precision, not looking at him. He
wasn't buying it, she could tell.

"My mother can be pretty hard to take sometimes," she
added by way of explanation. *You big chicken,* her conscience
jabbed, but it was already too late. "Clarissa and David are
used to her by now, but . . ."

"But I'm not."

"Right." Holly stemmed the strawberries faster, weak with
cowardly relief when Sam left her to pour another cup of coffee.

He came back and put his hand around hers, taking the par-ing knife from her grip. "You're going to slice more than the strawberries if you keep that up," he said, gently bumping her aside with his hip so he could reach the green plastic berry basket. "I'll finish this. It looks as if you've got a lot to do."

It was worse than she'd thought. Sam was going to be nice about being excluded from the brunch party, despite the lame excuse she'd given him. Nobody's mother was so difficult to deal with as to be unmeetable. Well, Holly's probably came close. Still, it would have been easier if Sam had gotten mad instead.

Holly took a clear glass pitcher from the cupboard and poured in the orange juice she'd defrosted. "This Sunday brunch is kind of a regular thing. My mother's been out of town the last couple of weeks, so we haven't been able to get together for a while."

Holly had hoped to avoid a meeting between her mother and Sam even longer. Forever would have been nice. If her mother met Sam, her new roommate, then Holly would have to explain what had happened between her and Brad. Her mother would be so disappointed.

"Business travel or pleasure?" Sam handed her the bowl of sliced strawberries. "Tell me this workaholic thing doesn't run in the family. Or do all of you work a billion hours a week?"

He popped a hulled strawberry in her mouth. Surprised, Holly chewed. When she finished, she said, "I don't work a billion hours a week."

Brad had never pestered her about how much she worked—he was exactly the same way. Maybe that was why they were so well-suited for each other. Of course, that might turn into a problem when they had a family together someday, but . . . but she'd deal with that when it happened.

Sam raised his eyebrows, still waiting for her answer.

"It was business," Holly admitted. "A broker's conference. My mother's a real-estate broker. A good one, too—she's a million-dollar producer."

He nodded, looking suitably impressed. "What does your dad do?"

"He's a plumber—at least he was the last time I talked to

him. He's lived in Montana ever since the divorce. I haven't seen him for a while."

Holly sprinkled sugar on the strawberries and shoved the bowl into the refrigerator. She shut the door, turned around, and ran smack into Sam's chest.

He handed her the juice pitcher. "I finished the orange juice."

"See, you *can* cook!"

"Only under pressure."

Holly put both hands around the cold glass pitcher, but he didn't release it. She had to look up at him.

"The divorce must have been hard. How old were you?"

"When they got divorced? About ten, I guess." Exactly ten. They'd announced it the morning after her birthday slumber party. "Can I have the juice, please?"

Sam handed it over. "Don't want to talk about it?"

"No. Yes. No." She swung the refrigerator door closed with her hip and hurried past him. "I've just got a lot to do, that's all. I still need to get dressed, and I haven't even started the French toast yet."

"Can I help?"

His offer barely registered. "You know, I don't have any hidden traumas over my parents' divorce, if that's what you're thinking." She just wanted to make that clear. "Lots of people get divorced."

She grabbed a sauté pan from the cupboard and plopped in slices of Canadian bacon to warm them. Waggling the empty package at Sam, she added, "In fact, *most* people get divorced. Did you ever think of that?"

He took away the bacon wrapper and tossed it into the trash. Holly couldn't believe she'd actually waved it at him like a shrewish wife on a TV sitcom. She was losing it.

Sam rubbed her shoulders as if she were a boxer going into the ring. "Tell me what to do and I'll help you," he said patiently.

She didn't deserve such kind treatment. Not when she was purposely trying to hide him from her mother. Okay, not *hide him*, exactly—it wasn't as if Sam embarrassed her. Holly only wanted to . . . delay all the explanations for a while.

"It would probably be safe to let me get the stuff out for your French toast," he offered, still rubbing her shoulders.

His hands felt really good. Holly hadn't realized she was so tense. It wasn't even noon yet. It ought to be illegal to feel tense before noon.

"It's nice of you to offer, Sam, but you don't have to help. Really. I can do it."

"I know that. I want to. Where's the bread? In the cupboard?"

He headed for the row of cupboards above the sink. Missing the touch of his hands, Holly glanced at the clock again. She felt like a sprinter at the starting line of a race. Everyone would be here soon. Any minute, in fact. She couldn't resist any longer. If Sam was going to insist on helping her she'd just have to let him, however rotten a person it made her seem.

"It's right there in the—"

"In the. . . ?"

"In the grocery store!" Holly grabbed him. "Oh, no—I forgot to buy the bread! How am I going to make French toast without bread?"

The doorbell chimed. Great—somebody was early. Holly would lay odds it was her mother. She stared toward the living room, frozen. So did Sam.

"Do you want me to get that while you go change?"

Considering the idea, Holly examined his naked chest, dark cotton boxer shorts, and bare feet. A burble of hysterical laughter stuck in her throat. "My mother would have a heart attack if you answered my front door looking like that."

Ding . . . DING!

"Okay," Sam said. "I've got a plan. I'll get dressed, go buy a loaf of bread, and sneak it back in. Nobody will ever know."

Feeling desperate, Holly nodded.

"Cover me." Grinning, Sam ducked so he wouldn't be seen from the windows overlooking the front porch, and headed toward his bedroom.

Once he'd vanished down the hallway, Holly decided it was safe to open the door. "Mom!"

"Hi, sweetie." Linda Aldridge dropped her cigarette and crushed it beneath the two-inch curved heel of her navy spectator pumps. Smiling, she enveloped her daughter in a Giorgio-scented, bracelet-clinking hug. "I hope I'm not too early."

"Maybe just a few minutes," Holly replied, smiling apologetically. Somehow she never felt quite ready for her mother. Out of the corner of her eye, she saw Sam's head peek around the hallway corner. Frantically, Holly waved him back.

Her mother glanced at Holly's shorts and T-shirt. "It must be so liberating not to feel as if you have to get all fixed up for company. You girls all look so wonderfully casual these days."

Loosely translated, *whatever possessed you to put on that pile of rags?*

Holly glanced down, too. "I haven't had a chance to change yet. I'll just be a minute. Why don't you help yourself to a cup of coffee while you wait?"

"Nonsense. I'll help with brunch."

Her mother headed for the kitchen, leaving Holly staring at her impeccably dressed back. There was a series of thumps: her briefcase, cigarette case, and cell phone hitting the countertop.

"You're lucky I got here before the rest of your guests," she called. "It looks as though you still have a lot to do."

Holly hurried to the hallway. "The coast's clear," she whispered to Sam, grabbing a handful of his sleeve to urge him into the living room. They got partway to the front door before the click-click of her mother's heels on the kitchen linoleum stopped them. Holly shoved Sam back into the hallway just as her mother appeared beneath the kitchen archway.

"Didn't you hear me? I was wondering what you want me to do with this?" She held out a sauté pan filled with shrunken, black, inedible-looking disks. They were still sizzling.

Holly leaned against the hallway arch, blocking it with her body. "Err . . . throw it out, I guess. It used to be the Canadian bacon."

Sam whispered, "I'll get bacon, too."

"Shhh," she hissed under her breath. She smiled at her mother, spreading her arms wider in case Sam was peeking around the corner again. "I think I've got more someplace. I'll, umm . . . be right there to help, okay?"

Wrinkling her nose, Linda returned to the kitchen.

Holly ducked into the hall and grabbed Sam's sleeve. "Hurry. Now's your chance."

He leaned against the wall for a minute, arms crossed, seeming almost as if he was enjoying himself.

"You look wonderfully casual to me, too," he mimicked, grinning down at her shorts and T-shirt.

Holly remembered she wasn't even wearing a bra, never mind nice clothes. She clapped her hands over her chest.

Sam pulled her to him and gave her a fast kiss. "Back in a minute," he said, and was gone before she could say a word.

Fifteen minutes later, Sam hadn't returned, and Holly was on the verge of strangling her mother with a length of sparkly garland. So far, her mother had offered advice on how to best scramble eggs, brew coffee, wrap gifts, and choose a car insurance company. She was in the middle of writing the name of a good hairdresser on the back of one of her business cards when the doorbell rang.

"Sorry, got to get that." With relief, Holly bolted to the doorway to let Clarissa and David in.

It was Sam.

"What are you doing ringing the doorbell?" Frantically, Holly looked toward the kitchen.

Her mother, thankfully oblivious to them, was humming and rearranging the place settings on the banquette table. Holly went outside and closed the door behind her. She stood nose-to-chest with Sam on the porch's candy-cane-print doormat.

"Would you believe I'm the grocery delivery boy? You can just tip me whatever you think my services are worth." Sam winked, lifting the brown paper sack in his arms.

Holly didn't feel much like kidding around. "What if my mother had answered the door and seen all those groceries?"

"What if she had?"

"She'd have known I can't even manage brunch for four people, that's what." She grabbed for the sack.

Sam held onto it. "So? She's your mom, not an entertainment critic. She's not going to care if you forgot the bread."

"You don't know my mother." Holly sucked in a deep, calming breath. "Thanks for getting this."

"You're welcome. Need anything else?"

"Yes. Just once I need to have my mother *not* criticize everything I do. Kidding," she added upon seeing the look on Sam's face. "She's not that bad. What I really need is to get this stuff inside without being seen."

Pausing, Holly thought about it for a second. "I'll go inside and get my mom away from the kitchen somehow. Just give me a minute or two, then bring everything inside, okay?"

Sam squinted at her, probably wishing he'd had more coffee before being forced to deal with her family. "Are you sure this is necessary?"

She nodded. "Thanks, Sam. You don't know what this means to me." With another deep breath for courage, she headed back inside.

Sam had a pretty good idea what it meant to Holly, despite wishing he didn't. After hearing her conversation with her mother, he was starting to understand why she was so persnickety about everything. She was trying to make everything she did mistake-proof. Trying to get the jump on her mother's constant criticism.

Shouldering the grocery sack, Sam counted to one hundred, then cautiously opened the front door. All clear. He started toward the kitchen. Halfway there, the doorbell chimed loudly enough to make his left eardrum go numb.

He was standing beneath the old-fashioned doorbell chimes mounted near the ceiling. Sam whipped open the door.

Clarissa and David looked at him, then at the sack he was holding. "Is that a door prize?" Clarissa asked with a teasing grin, "or did Holly finally kick you out for leaving your socks in the refrigerator one too many times?"

David chuckled. He and Clarissa were a perfect match. He actually seemed to think his wife's jokes were funny.

"It was just that one time," Sam said. "I set them down while I was getting a beer."

"Mmm-hmm."

He couldn't believe Holly had actually told someone about the sock incident.

"Get used to it, Sam," David put in. "I don't have any secrets left."

"Holly really told you about that?"

"Holly tells me *all* about you." Clarissa sauntered inside, sniffing. "Is Holly's mom here already? I thought I smelled that ritzy perfume of hers when we were coming up the walk."

"She's here, all right." Sam carried the groceries to the kitchen. Clarissa and David followed. "She's making Holly crazy."

"That's what mothers are for," came the sound of an evenly modulated voice behind him. A voice belonging to Holly's mother, Sam assumed.

They all turned to face Linda Aldridge. Standing on the other side of the built-in bar, she looked like an older, brittler version of Holly, with auburn helmet hair, a lot of careful makeup, and a slick business suit. She said hello to Clarissa and David, then smiled and came around the bar to meet Sam.

"Isn't it a mother's job to watch out for her child?" She offered him a bejeweled handshake—and a quick once-over. "I don't think we've met. I'm Linda Aldridge, Holly's mother. And you're. . . ?"

Sam glanced behind her, where Holly stood watching.

"I'm Sam McKenzie. Clarissa's cousin." He juggled the grocery sack to accept her handshake. "I hope you don't mind me crashing the party. I offered to . . . ah, cook."

Holly's eyes widened. She shook her head.

"My, isn't that enlightened? It's nice to meet you, Stan."

"Sam."

"Of course. Silly me." Linda put both hands together and tilted her head. "Why don't we all go in the other room and give Sam here room to work?" she suggested.

"He's not the caterer, Mom."

"Oh."

Sam bit back a grin. Now he understood why Holly was concerned about being dressed up enough for her mother's visit.

Holly hesitated. "Are you sure you don't want some help, Sam?" *Please let me help,* her expression said.

He shook his head. The least he could do was let Holly off

the hook in case the French toast tasted like soggy cardboard and wrecked her brunch party. "Leave it all up to me."

The women, except for Holly, beamed at him.

"I think it will be nice to be catered to by a man, for a change," Linda said, smiling. Clarissa agreed. Holly groaned.

"You ladies go on," David put in with a subtle lift of his chest. "We men will take care of you."

Sam didn't want to raise expectations too high, so he only smiled encouragingly. Once the women had disappeared into the living room, he turned to David. And gave him a shove.

"Are you nuts? 'We *men* will take care of you'?" He smacked his hand on his forehead, then winced. "I've got the hangover of the week—thanks to you, by the way—and you're going on as if we're culinary geniuses, here. Have you ever made French toast before?"

David shrugged. "How hard can it be? I've watched Clarissa do it."

Scowling, Sam upended the grocery sack. Two loaves of Wonder bread and a pound of bacon fell on the countertop. The selection at the mini-market on the corner wasn't the greatest, but it was at least close by.

"As for the hangover," David continued, "I'm not the one who poured all those beers down your throat last night." He gave Sam a sympathetic look. "Did you talk to Holly when you got home, like you said you were going to?"

"No. The timing wasn't right."

It never would be right, as long as Holly was hung up on making things work with Brad. After she'd left for her romantic dinner with him at Francie's, Sam had rambled around for a while in the empty house, trying not to wonder what they were doing together. It had taken him about five minutes to realize he needed a stronger dose of distraction. Somehow he'd wound up in a bar downtown until after midnight, spilling his guts to David.

"The timing wasn't right?" David shook his head. "You've got to go after what you want, Sam. Grab Holly and make her forget about Brad. Make her yours, man. Tame her!"

Sam rolled his eyes. "She's a woman, not a wild horse. Does Clarissa know about these caveman episodes of yours?"

"Are you kidding? She'd probably kick my ass if she heard me say that." David laughed and took a carton of eggs from the refrigerator. "The point is, Holly and Brad together were about as hot as day-old bread. He treated her more like a roommate than you do, if you catch my drift. Like a business partner. That guy's cold. I don't know why she can't see it."

Sam unwrapped the polka-dotted Wonder bread package and stacked the slices on a plate. He didn't want to think about Brad the Bad anymore. "Let's just get on with this."

"Besides," David persisted, "they're split. It's just taking Holly a while to catch up. She'll give up sooner or later."

Sam hoped he wouldn't be a gray-haired, arthritic old man by the time that happened. From the living room came the sound of Holly's mother, asking how things were coming in the kitchen.

"Just fine, Mrs. Aldridge," David called. "We'd better get busy." He lifted his baseball cap, then rammed it in an *I mean business* fashion on his curly black hair.

"You know, the hat makes all the difference. Now you really *do* look like a culinary genius."

David cheerfully raised his middle finger in reply. "Stand back," he said, grinning as he cracked eggs in a bowl, "and watch a *real* master at work."

"It's too bad Brad can't be here," Holly's mother said.

They all took their places at the banquette table—Clarissa and David on one side, Holly and her mother on the other, Sam perched at the end—then dug into the plates of French toast, strawberries, and bacon.

"He's working," Holly said quickly, crossing her fingers beneath the napkin on her lap. "Maybe he'll be here next time."

Sam shot her a dark look, one she understood better than she wanted to. No matter which way she turned, it seemed she hurt somebody.

"Well," her mother continued, "I wanted to invite you both to my company's annual holiday party. It's at the Cheshire Hotel downtown, two weeks from Saturday night." After chewing a bite of French toast with strawberries, she rested her fork atop her plate. "I've never had anything quite like this, boys."

Holly doubted her mother meant it kindly, but David smiled at her anyway.

"Glad you like it," he said. "Sam deserves most of the credit, though."

As a show of loyalty, Holly helped herself to another piece. It tasted a little eggy, but she wanted Sam to know she appreciated his trying to help her.

"I'd love to come to your Christmas party, Mom," she said, "but I'm not sure Brad will be able to make it."

Linda pursed her lips. "I hope he will." She leaned forward and, as an aside to Sam, added, "Brad is Holly's fiancé. A doctor. He always makes *such* a good impression at these events. We're all very proud of him."

Holly sunk a little lower in her seat. Dating Brad was the first thing she'd ever done that her mother actually approved of. How was she going to break it to her if things didn't work out according to her plan?

"Yes, Brad and I have met," Sam said. "Briefly. He's a busy guy. If Brad can't make it, Holly, I'd be glad to escort you."

Sam gazed straight at her, his eyes so blue and honest she could read his feelings in them. *Be with me.*

"It's a formal business function, dear," her mother put in, frowning. "Don't you think Sam might be a little uncomfortable? I hope this doesn't sound too harsh, but these are professional people who—"

"I don't think Sam would be uncomfortable anyplace," Holly interrupted, smiling as she gazed back at him. "No matter who was there. And come to think of it, I'm just about positive Brad won't be able to make it."

Complete silence descended. All four of them stared at her. Holly's knees starting shaking, and her throat closed up with panic. How was she going to follow up on that?

Beneath the table, Sam squeezed her knee. His show of encouragement brought a fresh sting of tears to her eyes. She had to blink them back before she could go on.

"I'd love it if you escorted me, Sam," Holly blurted.

Her mother's mouth dropped open. "What will Brad say?"

"He'll probably say he's got to work late," Holly answered truthfully, "like he usually does." She hoped she wasn't making a stupid, life-changing mistake. Taking a deep breath, she clarified. "I'd really like to go to your party, Mom. But it will have to be with Sam."

Thirty seconds later, her mother's voice broke the silence. "If . . . if you insist," she said, sounding bewildered.

Across the table, Clarissa applauded.

Despite her impending date with Sam, Holly wasn't ready to give up on her plan yet. How else was she going to get her life back to normal? How else was she going to feel like *herself* again? She'd even started skipping workouts once a week and leaving work at five o'clock most of the time, all so she could spend more time with Sam. It wasn't like her at all. She needed to re-focus on her goals.

So Holly spent the next week thinking up ways to put the final seduction phase of her plan into play. Friday night, Brad dropped the solution in her hands by asking her to stop by his office the next morning to evaluate a new accounting software package he was considering for his office.

His request couldn't have been more convenient. Even better, the place was usually deserted on the weekend.

Late Saturday morning, all systems were go.

Just before noon, Holly drove to the parking lot outside the medical complex that housed Brad's office. She couldn't pull into either of the spaces right next to Brad's shiny BMW, since he'd parked on the line between them, so she parked nearby and turned off the ignition. Her old convertible's engine clattered loudly enough to wake the dead as it gradually wound to a stop.

Wincing at the sound, Holly checked her makeup in the rear view mirror. Tasteful, yet flamboyant enough so Brad would know she wasn't the same old unspontaneous Holly, she decided. Good. She slid her briefcase across the seat. The implements of her mission—the bottles of Lover's Potion and Aphrodisia Massage Oil—clinked together inside. She checked to make sure her garter belt fasteners were still holding, gave her hair one last pat, then got out of the car.

Brad wouldn't know what hit him. The thought made Holly smile as she opened the front door with the key he'd given her long ago, then locked it again behind her. It was now or never.

Dressed only in a belted trench coat with her new lingerie beneath—Clarissa's idea—Holly navigated the wide austere corridors that led to Brad's office. The hallways were chilly. Then again, it was probably perfectly comfortable for people who were dressed. A nervous shiver passed through her. Steeling her resolve, she pressed on, the whisper of her stockinged legs sounding unnaturally loud in the deserted building.

Holly breathed a sigh of relief when her key still turned in Brad's office door. Opening it quietly, she tiptoed into the darkened recesses of the suite, where Brad kept his private office. The red spike-heeled shoes Clarissa had talked her into buying didn't make a whisper of sound on the carpeted floor, but Holly could have sworn her heart was thumping loudly enough to announce her arrival a mile away. And if the hammering of her heart didn't do it, then the aggressively musky perfume she'd dabbed on would give her presence away for sure.

Neither did. Rounding the corner, she heard the low-pitched hum of Brad's computer and the tap-tap-tapping of his fingers as he typed. She gripped her briefcase handle tighter, took a deep breath, and approached his open office door.

Her thong panties chose that moment to shoot the rest of the way up her behind.

Holly flung herself against the wall. A long, agonizing minute passed before she was sure Brad hadn't seen her. Lowering her briefcase gingerly to the floor, she flipped up the back of her tan trench coat and tried to extricate herself from her thong-panty prison.

It was a tricky maneuver, at least when performed on three-inch spike heels. Wavering a little, Holly tugged at the strip of flowered fabric. It stayed in a comfortable position for all of thirty seconds. She might as well have put on the rubber band from the Sunday newspaper, called it underwear, and saved herself a few bucks, for all the luck she had getting the thing to stay where it belonged.

She sagged against the wall to catch her breath. The way things were going, she was tempted to just back up, really slowly, and leave.

No. She wasn't giving up yet. Spreading her knees further apart, balancing precariously on her shoes, Holly tightened her grip on the thong. Nervous perspiration trickled between her breasts, dampening the red and black velvet groping-hands bra. Great, that would make a really sexy impression. Stifling a groan, she gave it another try.

Still holding the panty away from her behind, Holly snapped her knees together again, performed the greatest butt squeeze of her life, and released the thong. The thought crossed her mind that this was probably a pretty good workout: Thongs of Steel. Tight Thongs in Thirty Days. Thong Aerobics.

Oh, boy. Getting hysterical wasn't helping. But she thought the butt squeeze might. Reaching back, Holly gave it one last try, squeezing for all she was worth this time. As long as she stayed clenched, the thong stayed put. Success!

Smiling triumphantly, Holly grabbed her briefcase and glanced up. Brad leaned against the door frame, his arms crossed over his chest, watching her.

"I thought I heard something out here," he said mildly. "I was afraid the cleaning lady was having a heart attack, judging by all the thumping on the wall and the heavy breathing."

He raised his eyebrow—just one, a trick that always irritated her a little because it made him look so superior. Also because she couldn't do it.

"You're late," he said. "I thought you'd changed your mind."

"Are you kidding?" Holly laughed, stepping closer to him. *You can do this. Confidence is sexy,* she told herself. "I'd love to have a look at your, ahh . . . hardware, Brad."

He frowned. "It's software. Didn't I tell you that?"

Geez, he used to understand innuendo.

"That's not what I meant." She clarified her intentions with a caressing hand on his starched shirtfront. The sharp scent of Brad's aftershave hit her with the force of a dozen memories, helping to shore up her courage. Lowering her voice seductively, she said, "I've got more than accounting software on my mind."

Brad lifted her hand from his shirt, then straightened his glasses. He peered closely at her. "You should get that hoarseness checked out," he said, stepping backward. "It might be bronchitis."

For a second, Holly wished she did have some virulent, highly contagious illness. Something Brad could catch from her that would make him feel miserable, but wouldn't be life-threatening.

In her normal voice, she said, "I feel fine. I just think we've been apart long enough, don't you?"

Think sexy, Holly commanded herself. *It's your last chance—be bold.* She advanced toward him. Brad backed up, all the way into his office. Slamming the door shut with her foot—hey, this was fun!—Holly tossed her briefcase on the leather sofa that lined one wall and reached for her coat sash.

"You didn't really invite me here to look at software, did you, Brad?" she whispered.

"Holly! What's gotten into you?" Trapped between her and the rosewood executive desk at his back, Brad gaped at her. "This isn't like you at all."

"It's the new me," she murmured, actually starting to enjoy herself. It was like playing a role in a movie. It was like riding a roller-coaster, drunk, at midnight. Not that she'd ever really done something like that, but Holly was starting to believe the new, *spontaneous* her just might try it.

Smiling, she finished undoing her coat sash and raised her fingers to the lapels. "Come home, Brad. We can be so perfect together. I know we can."

Inch by inch, she slowly opened her coat. His eyes widened. It was just the reaction she'd hoped for. Encouraged, Holly raised her knee to the desk, high enough for Brad to see her garter and the top of her stocking.

The pressure of balancing on one foot snapped the spike heel clean off her shoe. She went down like an anchor tossed overboard.

"Holly! Are you all right?" Brad crouched in front of her

and caught hold of her arms. Briefly his gaze dipped to the groping-hands bra, then upward again.

"I'm fine," she said, feeling ridiculous. "Help me up?"

He helped her to her feet, then hot-footed it behind his desk, putting some distance between them. While his back was turned, Holly seated herself on the sofa and belted her coat closed again. Somehow, it didn't feel right anymore.

Brad sat, looking awkward and embarrassed for them both. He stared at his desk blotter, patting the nape of his neck—a sure sign he was mulling something over. She crossed her legs, waiting.

"I'm not sure what to make of this," he finally said. "Have you been reading one of those women's magazines or something?"

As a matter of fact, she had. She'd gone to the library and searched the periodicals index for appropriate articles, articles which might spark some ideas for her plan. Holly wasn't going to admit that to Brad, though.

He straightened in his chair and glanced at her. "This isn't about . . . sex." He cleared his throat, looking vaguely prudish—something she hadn't noticed in Brad before. "It's about making a decision that will affect my life for years to come. I won't rush into a greater commitment without considering all the factors. It's part of the 'space' thing I've been talking about lately."

Holly leaned back. Okay, so seduction hadn't worked. She was willing to speak practically with him.

"Exactly how long do you think this . . . consideration is going to take?"

She slipped off her shoes and set them on her briefcase. The motion made the Lover's Potion and Aphrodisia Massage Oil clink together inside. Maybe she could still return the un-opened bottles for a full refund. She wasn't likely to find a use for them now.

Brad patted his neck again, then smoothed his open palms over his desk blotter. "I don't know, but I'm very close to making a decision."

Hallelujah. Brad was "very close" to deciding their fate.

"I'm not sure how much longer I can wait," Holly said.

It was the end of the line. The end of the plan. She'd tried everything she could think of, short of handcuffing them together. Even then, Brad would probably resist making a commitment. It had to be up to him now.

"I understand." His forehead wrinkled with concern. "After all, you've probably got that biological ticking clock thing going on. I've been thinking about it. You're not getting any younger, you know."

Holly couldn't believe what she was hearing. "And you're not getting any smarter."

She rose from the sofa with as much dignity as she could muster. Gathering her shoes and briefcase, she headed for the office door. There, she stopped.

"I need to know what your decision is—about us—by the end of the week."

Brad blinked up at her. After a minute, he asked, "Does this mean you won't evaluate my new accounting software for me?"

Had he always been this self-centered?

"I don't know," Holly said, throwing his words back at him, "but I'm very close to making a decision. Bye, Brad."

Eight

"I've gotta be crazy," Sam said to David mid-morning on Sunday. "Of all the women in this town—"

"And we both know there are so many in Saguaro Vista—"

"Of all the women in this town," Sam continued, scowling at Clarissa's husband, "I've got to pick one that's obsessed with another man."

They were sitting on Holly's kitchen floor, trying to pry up the remaining few feet of old yellow linoleum so they could lay a new wood floor. It was the last big renovation project to be tackled, but given their progress so far, Sam almost wished they'd chosen something easier, like rewiring the whole house.

The linoleum seemed to have been welded on somehow. Either that, or the original concrete slab was really an eight-inch-thick slab of linoleum. With a heavy metal spatula, Sam pried at the one corner he'd managed to loosen. As usual, it barely moved.

"She'll come around," David said. "Holly's a smart girl."

He rammed his spatula beneath the section of linoleum he was working on and pulled. About an inch of flooring came up. David swore.

"Louder. Maybe you can cuss it out of there," Sam told him, grinning.

Of all the men who worked for his dad's construction company, David was the only one who'd agreed to help Sam with Holly's renovation project. As soon as the other workers had heard the job was renovating Holly Aldridge's house, they'd all found other things to do with their nights and weekends than earn a few extra holiday-shopping bucks. Sam didn't understand it.

"I know Holly's smart," Sam said, returning to their earlier conversation. "What I didn't bargain on is how determined she is, too. She doesn't know the meaning of surrender."

David stopped prying at the linoleum long enough to point the spatula toward Sam. "And *you* do?"

Sam laughed. David had him there. "I'll surrender just as soon as Holly does. Until then, I'm going to do my damnedest to convince her we belong together."

The slam of the front door put an end to their conversation. A few seconds later, Holly stomped past the archway to the living room. There was a thud as something hit the floor, then the sound of Holly muttering to herself.

"I don't know, Holly. What's gotten into you, Holly? Might be bronchitis, Holly."

Her voice sounded low-pitched: a pissed-off imitation of a man's voice. Brad's voice, if Sam guessed correctly.

Still muttering, she came into the kitchen, clutching a pair of red high-heeled shoes to her chest. She was dressed in a raincoat. She dropped the shoes on the counter and frowned at them. A small red thing rolled off the countertop and landed on the other side, almost in Sam's lap. It was one of her heels.

He held it up. "I can fix this for you, if you want."

Holly screamed.

She lurched over the counter, staring at him. "Why didn't you say you were down there? You just about gave me a heart attack."

"I didn't mean to scare you," Sam said, looking back at her. She'd done something to her hair. There was a pouffy spot on top big enough to stash a pack of gum in, and it was all curly on the ends. It looked good, in a wild kind of way.

Holly examined the ripped up floor, then the two of them sitting amid their spatulas, the heat gun, assorted tools, and Sam's open red tool box. Her gaze rested for a second on the jumbo bag of red and green Christmas tortilla chips he and David had shared for breakfast, then moved up to Sam again.

"Are you sure you two are doing this right?" she asked doubtfully. "You've been at this for days. The floor looks worse than ever."

"It's supposed to look this way, at least until the new floor is all the way in," David interrupted, saving Sam from answering. "How ya' doing, Holly?"

"Fine, thanks." From the sound of it, she'd rather chew nails than talk civilly to anyone.

"Oookay. . . . Sorry I asked." David grinned and went back to work again.

Holly took a deep breath, visibly trying to calm herself. She gave David a wavery, apologetic smile. "I'm sorry, David. You guys want some help? I can change and be back in a couple of minutes."

She touched her fingers to her coat lapels, started pulling them apart, then stopped. Her face reddened. Surprisingly, so did her chest. Sam hadn't realized a woman could blush all the way down to . . . down to where her shirt should be, if she was wearing one. Holly wasn't wearing a shirt. Probably, she wasn't wearing much of anything else, either.

Holly shoved the raincoat closed again, holding it tight against her throat. "I'll be right back."

Hastily, she turned toward the archway.

All at once, Sam understood. "How's Brad these days?"

She stopped, holding onto the archway edges with both hands. Her fingers tightened.

"None of your business." She raised her head and, with sudden decisiveness, marched all the way back to the middle of the kitchen where he and David sat. "How did you know?"

"It didn't take a genius to figure out all those lingerie bags in the trash. But your raincoat was the dead giveaway."

Sam examined her broken heel, still in his hand. "What I can't figure out is how this happened." He grinned. "You want to tell us about it?"

David looked interested. Holly looked mad.

"No." She turned, scooped up her shoes from the counter, and headed for the living room.

Sam waved the heel of her shoe. "You want me to fix this, or what?"

He couldn't stop smiling. If Brad could turn down Holly—and he must have—when she was wearing nothing but a raincoat and some sexy lingerie. . . . Well, Sam's chance of a future with her looked a whole lot brighter, all of a sudden.

Holly belted her raincoat tighter, then came back and snatched the heel from him. "No. I'll fix it myself."

She examined the little nails embedded in the broken heel, then flipped over the shoe and centered the heel in place. Biting her lip thoughtfully, she glanced around the kitchen, studiously ignoring him. An instant later, her eyes lit up. Picking up her other shoe, Holly held it like a hammer, high above her head. She took a deep breath and slammed it down hard on the broken heel.

The heel flew like a red leather bullet, straight at Sam's head.

"Ow!"

Distantly, he heard the heel clatter to the floor. Holly gasped and skidded across the linoleum to where he clutched his head with one hand. It still stung where the heel had smacked into it.

"Oh, Sam—I'm so sorry! Are you okay?" Gently, she lifted his hand away, then peered at his scalp. "I don't think you're bleeding."

Beside him, David picked up the broken heel and held it out to Holly. "Here you—"

"Oh, no you don't!" Sam grabbed it, glaring at them both. "You want to arm her again? I thought you were my friend."

He shook off Holly's hand and got up. Taking the heel from David, Sam picked up the broken shoe from the counter.

"*I'll* fix this." He gave them both a look that dared them to disagree. He shouldn't have been surprised when Holly did. She grabbed for the broken shoe.

Sam held it just out of reach. She gave a little jump. He lifted it higher.

"I can fix it. I've gotten along just fine until now without your stupid he-man fix-it routine, you know. I'm not helpless."

He-man? "You're a menace," he shot back.

"Give me my shoe, please." The words emerged through clenched teeth, just before Holly jumped again.

She missed, probably because Sam stood six inches taller than she did. It wasn't difficult to keep the shoe away from her.

He had a devious thought.

"Show me what's under your coat," he offered, "and I'll give you your shoe back."

"What? No."

"Come on," Sam coaxed, dangling her shoe, the bait, just out of reach. He grinned.

She kicked him in the shin.

"Ow!" He dropped her shoe.

Holly picked it up with a smug little smile and flounced off, muttering something about getting into some normal clothes so she could help.

He stopped her. "Oh, no. You're not helping."

"Why not?"

"We've already covered this ground, haven't we?"

She glared at him.

"You're not going to kick me again, are you?"

Holly shook her head. "Come on, Sam. I'm having kind of a hard day. Why don't you quit trying to change the subject and just tell me why you don't want me to help?"

"Because you're dangerous, that's why."

Looking offended, she crossed her arms over her chest. "Only when provoked. I asked you nicely to give me my shoe, and you didn't." She nodded at the broken heel. "Hitting you with that was an accident, and you know it."

"So was breaking my toe with that damned ten-pound book," Sam pointed out, waggling his bare foot in demonstration, and remembrance. "Now you want me to let you wreak havoc on the floor? With tools?" He shook his head. "I'd have to be crazy."

David grinned at that. "What was that you were saying earlier about being crazy?"

Sam cut him off with a look. He didn't need to be reminded that he'd called himself crazy, and crazy about Holly, just fifteen minutes ago. David shrugged and dug into the bag of tortilla chips at his feet, removing himself from the argument.

"It's my floor," Holly insisted. "I want to help. All you have to do is show me how." She studied the shards of yellow linoleum scattered at their feet. "It doesn't look too difficult to me."

She gave him a shrewd look. "Maybe you don't want me to find out how easy this is. It would hurt your handyman's ego." Her gaze darted over to David. "Is that why he won't let me help?"

David looked about to choke on a green tortilla chip with the effort of holding back a laugh.

"Well, I dunno." He gazed speculatively at Sam. "Are you worried about your masculine ego, Sam?"

If that chip didn't get him, Sam promised himself *he* would.

He frowned at Holly. "You really believe that?"

"No, but I really do want to help. I've been working all week and I haven't had a chance to do anything. Come on, Sam. I'm a quick study, you'll see."

She smiled encouragingly.

Sam decided to surrender to the inevitable before she dug any deeper. "Fine. Have it your way."

Her smile deepened. Sam's didn't. He felt like a sap. Holly headed for the bedroom to change clothes. Too bad he couldn't persuade her to keep on the raincoat and lingerie.

"Be sure to put on something old," he warned. "Whatever you wear is going to get wrecked."

She waved a hand over her head. "Okay. I'll be right back!"

Sam turned to David.

"We're in for it now," he grumbled.

He was more right than he'd expected, but not in the way he'd thought. A few minutes later when Holly emerged from the bedroom, Sam stopped in mid-scrape to stare. Holly's wild new hairstyle was small change compared with how she looked geared up for renovating.

"These are the oldest, grungiest things I could find." She waved her hand at her faded University of Arizona T-shirt and old denim cut-off shorts. "Okay?"

"Uh, okay." Sam tried to quit staring, but it was impossible. In those shorts, Holly looked completely different. It was a glimpse of the kind of woman she must have been before Brad and his tight-assed ways got a hold of her, before she'd plotted out her plan for life and set the map in stone. He wondered if it was too late to smash the map and start over.

But that would have to come later. For now he'd have to settle for teaching Holly how to tear up an old linoleum floor. Kneeling next to her, Sam showed her how to look at the edges of the floor for places that had lifted over the years, then pry them up further with a heavy metal spatula. He showed her how to pour in a little adhesive solvent to loosen the glue, and how to scrape up the stubborn pieces that sometimes remained, so the subfloor would be level.

When Sam turned to check on her progress a few minutes later, Holly was working diligently. Beside her sat the evidence of her labor: a tidy stack of linoleum pieces, a dustpan filled with debris, and the tortilla chip bag, now filled with linoleum shards. For a radius of two feet around her, the floor was swept conspicuously clean.

Holly crouched on her hands and knees, mopping it with a sponge.

"We're not going to eat from this floor." Sam tried, and failed, to keep his grin hidden. "Work first. Clean later."

She didn't stop. "A neat workspace will make the job go quicker."

She sounded breathless from her enthusiastic mopping. She whipped out an old towel and dried the floor, her backside swinging enticingly in rhythm with each stroke of the towel.

Her denim cut-offs revealed more than they hid, especially in the places where she'd dried her damp hands on them. Beneath the soft, thin fabric of her old T-shirt, her breasts kept time too, swaying gently as she worked. Sam's gut tightened. He really was crazy.

Clapping his hands to dislodge the worst of the dirt, he looked at David and Holly in turn. "What do you say we break for lunch?"

When they didn't answer, he raised his eyebrows. "Lunch?"

David glanced at the tortilla chip bag. "I'm still pretty full from the Christmas chips."

Scowling, Sam got to his feet. "Then you can stay here and finish up while Holly and I go to lunch." He turned to her. "You'll want to change first, right?"

She looked exasperated. "I just did, remember? What's wrong with what I've got on?"

"Nothing." Nothing except that it made Sam want to take all of it off. Nothing except that it showed him a side to Holly he'd never seen before, and he liked it. Too much.

"Nothing. I just thought you'd want to wear something more ... ahhh ...." He searched his brain for a reason that would appeal to her. "Something more appropriate."

Something *un*sexy.

"You sound just like Brad," Holly accused, scrambling to stand on the slippery linoleum. She pointed her finger in Sam's face. "Well, I'm through with men telling me what to do and what to wear and whom to see. Do you hear me?"

He backed up, pushed more by the impact of her unexpected temper than the pink fingernail she was poking at him. He'd obviously touched a nerve by telling her to look appropriate.

It wasn't a mistake he wanted to repeat in the future.

"I'll do what I want, when I want to do it." Holly's voice rose. "If I want to dance naked on *my* floor, in *my* kitchen, in *my* house, then I'll do it! And you can't stop me!"

"Why would he want to?" David put in, grinning.

Holly threw her wet sponge at him. It landed with a wet splat on his nose, then plopped to the floor.

She was spoiling for a fight. She looked at Sam as though she were mentally rolling up her sleeves, a prize-fighter ready for the next match.

He held up both hands in surrender. "Okay! Wear what you want."

"I will." Holly flounced away.

So much for his brilliant plan to get her into some different clothes. Maybe next time he ought to try reverse psychology. For now he'd have to admit defeat. Maybe if they went someplace dark. . . .

Hell, he was a grown man, wasn't he? It would take more than the sight of Holly in a pair of short shorts, looking fresh from a roll in the hay, to take Sam McKenzie down.

In the foyer, she paused, keys in hand. "You fellas coming, or not?"

Sam nodded.

"We'll take my car," she announced when he and David got to the front door.

She seemed about six inches taller, flush with the thrill of running the show. Proud of herself. Despite everything, Sam felt glad for her. Maybe that roadmap of hers was splintering a little already.

Holly could have kicked herself for saying they'd take her car. She'd been so pleased with the way she'd asserted herself with Sam, she'd forgotten there were three of them going to lunch—one more than would fit comfortably in her two-seater convertible.

To their credit, neither Sam nor David said a thing about her mistake as they piled into Sam's old pickup truck instead. Sam got behind the wheel. Holly slid across the wide bench seat to take her place in the middle, leaving David smashed up against the passenger-side door. To give him more room, she scooted a little closer to Sam.

The truck was just like Sam, big and messy, but in perfect running order. When he turned the ignition key, the engine purred to life quietly as a luxury sportscar's. The stereo system he turned on sounded even better than the expensive one Brad had so rudely repossessed after their split.

Sam raised his eyebrows, seeking her approval of the radio station he'd tuned. Holly nodded, surprised he'd bother to check with her at all.

She probably shouldn't have been. From the day she'd met him, Sam had wanted to please her. To pleasure her. In that, too, he was exactly *un*like Brad. She shivered and turned her attention to the things jumbled inside the truck, a much safer subject than Sam's feelings for her.

Her inspection ended abruptly with the warm, unexpected feeling of Sam's hand on her bare thigh. Her gaze shot downward as he slid his hand along the inside of her thigh. He moved toward her knee until his tanned arm lay against her, then he gripped . . . the gearshift. It was right between her legs.

Their eyes met.

"Excuse me," Sam said. "I hope this won't be too uncomfortable for you."

The sparkle in his eyes told her he wasn't *too* sorry about their driving arrangement. Trying to retain the upper hand, Holly shrugged.

"As long as you're not uncomfortable," she said solicitously. "I guess I can stand it as long as you can."

He stroked her thigh with his thumb. "I'll remember that," he promised with a wink, then he set the truck into motion.

Sam could make a grocery list read like erotic innuendo, Holly thought. She didn't know how he managed it. *Maybe you want it to sound that way*, a part of her nudged. *Maybe you're the one who wants him.*

She shoved the thought aside and tried to focus on her neighbors' holiday decorations as they drove into town. She tried not to think about the hungry way Sam had looked at her this morning, when he'd realized how little she had on beneath her trench coat. She tried not to remember the feel of his body against hers, to relive the kisses they'd shared, to re-experience the heat and intensity of his mouth on hers.

Who was she kidding?

Holly sighed. Being around Sam made her priorities go so far underground she couldn't remember what she wanted anymore. She remembered feeling certain Brad was the right man for her, that marrying him was the only sensible thing to do. She'd thought he was the ideal man to share her future with.

All of a sudden, that future looked awfully bleak.

She didn't want to fail. That's what would happen if her plan didn't bring her and Brad back together again. She'd fail.

She'd probably ensured failure by giving Brad a deadline to decide about their future together. Holly hadn't been able to think of another alternative. She didn't want to end up like her mother had after the divorce—alone. Alone and . . . yes, a little bitter, too. Holly supposed that a great, passionate love gone wrong could do that to anybody.

Even Sam? She glanced at him. As usual, he wore low-slung jeans and an attitude so relaxed that being with him was like the best vacation she'd ever had.

As though he sensed her gaze on him, he gave her a smile, then looked back at the road. No, Holly decided, probably not Sam. Love wouldn't dare go wrong on Sam.

They had lunch at the Downtown Grill, and afterward they brought David back to pick up his car at Holly's house. Still sitting in the driveway in Sam's truck, they watched him make a U-turn in the street, then drive away.

"So, should we go in and finish up the floor?" Sam asked.

He looked as if he'd rather dye his hair green than go back inside and scrape more linoleum.

"No. I've got other plans for you."

"Really?" He nudged closer and wrapped his arm around her shoulders. "Tell me all about it."

"Well." Holly smiled up at him, feeling better now that she'd been fortified with a double cheeseburger and fries— and a hefty helping of Christmas cookies from the City Bakery. "First we'll go to the formal wear shop downtown . . ."

"Yeah . . . ?"

"Then we'll pick up your tuxedo. Did you forget my mother's Christmas party at the Cheshire is next weekend?"

Sam groaned and started the engine. "I thought you were kidding about wearing a tuxedo."

"Nope. I already ordered one for you. Just in case you, um, *forgot.*" Her smile broadened.

"You don't leave much to chance, do you?"

"Not usually. Let's go."

At the formal wear shop, Holly picked up the dress she'd ordered for the party. Sam reluctantly accepted a black tuxedo and the full dress regalia that went along with it.

"Can I try on the dress, please?" Holly asked the sales-person. "Just to make sure it fits before I take it home?"

"Certainly." The clerk nodded toward a curtained area at

the rear of the small shop. "The fitting rooms are right through there."

Murmuring her thanks, Holly headed to the changing rooms. She chose one of the three mirrored alcoves and pulled the curtain closed behind her. After hanging her dress on the hook provided, she shucked her shorts and T-shirt at warp speed.

Brad had always hated shopping with her. Holly supposed most men were the same way, including Sam. She wanted to hurry so he wouldn't have long to wait.

Someone entered the cubicle next to hers and dragged the curtain shut with the metallic scrape of the hanging rings against the chrome rod. Whoever it was, she was tall. Holly glimpsed a headful of shaggy blond hair over the partition before she bent down again.

She shrugged and stepped into her new dress. One zip, thirty seconds of fiddling with the shoulder straps, then . . . voilà. She looked in the mirror.

It was a great dress, the sexiest one she'd ever owned. White, mid-thigh length, and close-fitting, it needed only a matching sheer chiffon scarf to accessorize it. Holly arranged the scarf over her throat, leaving the ends to trail down the dress's low-cut back. Uncertainly, she scrutinized the effect.

"You look great in white," Sam said. "It sets off all that red hair of yours."

He winked down at her from the neighboring dressing room. At that moment, Holly decided the expensive designer dress was worth every single cent it had cost her.

"You're not supposed to be back here," she whispered. "What are you doing?"

"Trying on my stuff," he answered reasonably. He propped his arms on the partition, making it wobble. "There are only these three little rooms, you know. Was I supposed to change out there in front of the three-way mirror like one of those Chippendales guys?"

Holly pictured him doing an exotic dancer's bump and grind routine, slowly stripping off his clothes in front of the big mirror. The idea had merit.

"Of course not." The way he was looking at her, she couldn't resist preening a little in her new dress. Pivoting, she glanced over her shoulder at him. "Do you really like it?"

"Come next door and I'll show you how much."

"I'm serious."

"So am I." Sam grinned. He disappeared from sight behind the partition. There was a rustle of fabric, then the sound of a zipper. He reappeared. "Pants fit."

He must have been talking to her in his underwear. "Good."

He struggled into his white dress shirt. "I meant what I said. You look great. The only way you could possibly look better is if you were wearing that white dress at our wedding."

He ducked behind the partition again, swore, and re-emerged a minute later with his bow tie draped loosely around his open shirt collar. He waggled one end of it.

"Can you help me with this thing? I think it's possessed."

Holly gaped at him. Sam took one look at what had to be her stupefied expression and said, "Never mind. I guess the saleslady can tie it for me. I just won't take off the monkey suit until after the party."

"Did you just say, 'our wedding'?"

His expression turned serious. "Yeah. What did you think I had in mind? Seducing you and skipping town the next day?"

He waited for her answer, but somehow Holly's brain had turned to Jell-O. That was exactly what she'd thought, she realized. She'd thought that if she let herself fall for Sam it would only mean heartache when he left.

She nodded slowly. "Umm, yes."

This was getting way too serious. She turned to the mirror again. She fiddled with her dress strap, trying to disguise her confusion.

"Aren't all men commitment-phobic, anyway?" she asked lightly. "What makes you so different?"

The curtain slid away. Suddenly, Sam was there. He closed the curtain behind him, secluding them both in the tiny cubicle.

He looked good in a tuxedo, even with it only half on. No, make that *especially* with it only half on. Holly experienced a brief, ridiculous impulse to duck beneath his outstretched arms and run as far away as she could. It didn't happen, because she couldn't move.

"I'm different," he said, "because I'm the man who loves you."

"You shouldn't be in here," Holly babbled. "You shouldn't say things like that, and not so loudly, either. Somebody might hear you."

"I don't care who hears me." He pulled her against his chest, wrapping his arms around her. "I'll take out a billboard if it means you'll listen. I'll put an ad in the paper." He grinned. "I'll wear one of those signs you strap on and walk around with. I'm in love with you."

"You only think that," Holly said with certainty.

She stared at the walls, at the curtain, at her feet—anyplace but at him. Why had they started talking about this in the first place? Hadn't she had enough cold reality for one day?

He splayed his fingers along her shoulder blades, lightly teasing her bare skin. Halfheartedly, she tried to shrug away his touch.

"It's only that love at first sight thing," she said.

"Not anymore."

Sam drew her closer, his fingertips pressing harder. When his mouth lowered to hers, Holly stopped thinking altogether. His kiss was slow and deliberate, filled with passion and sweetened by longing. It hinted at promise and possessiveness alike. When it was over, she felt limp in Sam's arms.

"Is that proof enough for you?" he asked.

Rational thought returned.

"No. It only proves there's a . . . a sexual attraction between us." She put a good eight inches between them by retreating to the tiny triangular bench in the changing room corner. She felt damp and disheveled, and fiercely aroused. "Nothing more. You've got that love at first sight thing in your head and you're too stubborn to give it up."

"I'm not the only stubborn one," Sam pointed out. "Are you saying all this to convince me? Or to convince yourself?"

With a sigh, Holly pressed her thighs together to stop the

ache he'd aroused—just a natural reaction, she assured herself.

She glanced up at him. Sam leaned a shoulder against the partition and stuffed both hands in his pockets. He didn't say anything else.

"You have a life in another city. A life I know almost nothing about, aside from the bare facts," she said. "And I—"

"What do you want to know?"

"Oh, Sam, that's not the point. Don't you see?" She wanted to cry, caught between hope and fear and a bunch of feelings she'd never experienced before. At least there was logical thought to cling to. "You have your life and I have mine, and they're happening in different places. When the new year gets here, you'll be gone."

Sam shook his head, but she couldn't stop until he understood.

"You drop the idea of marriage on me as if it's as easy a decision to make as picking what brand of toothpaste to buy. I'll bet you haven't thought, really *thought*, about any of this."

"I spend most of my time thinking of you."

But that wasn't the same as planning a future together. Holly shook her head. He didn't understand, and she didn't know how else to explain it.

But she couldn't resist when Sam dropped to his knees in front of her. He wrapped his arms around her, resting his head on her thighs. His hair felt silky against her bare skin. He breathed deeply, then hugged her tighter.

"It'll work out." Sam's voice sounded muffled. "We can make all those details work."

Her throat tightened. She wanted to believe it, wanted to believe *him*. She wanted to be as sure as Sam was. But she couldn't be.

"How? What about my job—and yours? Where would we live? Oh, Sam—how can it work out?"

He remained silent. Tentatively, she raised a hand to his head and buried her fingers in his hair, stroking. It felt good. *He* felt good—and so did Holly, when she was with him. But was it enough?

"Ms. Aldridge, are you all right?" The voice came from

outside the dressing room, but it was grew louder every instant. "Mr. McKenzie? Where are you?"

The salesperson pulled open the curtain. It took just one look at Sam's head buried in Holly's lap to get them both kicked out of the formal wear shop. For life.

Nine

The Cheshire Hotel was the finest in all of Saguaro Vista. It catered as much to the local golfing crowd that spilled over from the city course as it did to the temporarily resident senior citizens who liked to spend their winters someplace warmer than North Dakota.

Tonight, in honor of the holidays, the Cheshire's elegant lobby had been decorated in shades of ivory and gold. An enormous Christmas tree filled one corner, and orchestral Christmas carols drifted through the cinnamon-spiced space.

"Thanks for bringing me tonight," Holly told Sam as they stepped inside together. "Big formal parties aren't really my thing. I'd hate to face this alone."

He smiled at her. "You're not alone anymore."

His words sounded *so* wonderful. Holly couldn't help but savor them. Even when she'd planned her life with Brad, she hadn't thought of them as being truly *together*, two halves of one whole. Their lives had already been more separate than that. If Brad's decision was to move their relationship forward, she realized, she'd have to find a way to deal with that.

But that was for later. For now, she and Sam had a party to get to. Leading the way, Holly headed for the ballroom where her mother's gala was in progress.

"If word's gotten around about what happened in the formal wear shop," she said as they passed through the lobby, "I'll probably *never* be alone. The owner is one of the biggest gossips in Saguaro Vista. People probably think I'm the town hussy by now."

For some reason, though, the idea of being on the receiving end of the townspeople's censure didn't bother her as much as it used to. Despite all appearances to the contrary, Holly knew she'd done nothing wrong. That seemed more important.

"You'll see." She grinned up at Sam. "They'll be lining up to date me."

He tightened his arm around her waist. "Not if I have anything to say about it, they won't."

At the party, Holly's mother was the first to greet them. She floated over, doubtless fueled by several glasses of Christmas wassail punch, and linked arms with her daughter.

"I'm so glad you both could come," she said.

Amazingly, her smile seemed genuine. Even Holly, who'd expected disapproval instead, was convinced. It was a relief to know her mother wouldn't disown her for appearing in public without Brad.

"Thanks, Mom." Holly nudged Sam. "Doesn't my date look handsome?"

Linda examined him from the top of his head to the soles of his dress shoes. "Yes, he does. You clean up nicely, Steve."

"Sam."

"Oh, of course. I'm sorry." She turned to Holly with a frown. "But *you're* another story. You didn't try that hairdresser I told you about, did you?" Licking a fingertip, she swept her daughter's hair away from her face. "No, I can see you didn't. Your hair still has that *rumpled* look."

"I like it this way, Mom," Holly said, but she gritted her teeth and dutifully endured her mother's fussing.

Wearing a satisfied smile, Linda stepped back to survey her handiwork. "There. That's better."

Holly stifled an urge to rearrange her hair into the style she'd arrived with. Hey, it was the holiday season: the season of goodwill. She could afford to let this one go.

"Now," her mother announced, "I have to speak with Mayor Anderson about his new house. If you'll both excuse me?"

They said their good-byes, and Linda disappeared into the crowd of brightly dressed women and tuxedo-clad men.

Holly watched her go with a clear sense of relief. After having all but refused to go to the party unless Sam escorted her, she'd been worried about how her mother would react. It looked as though the only problem her mother had with Sam, though, was remembering his name.

"You know," Sam said, "your mother has an overdeveloped mothering instinct. But I think she means well."

Surprised, Holly looked up at him. "You do?"

"Sure. If she didn't care, she wouldn't spend all that energy trying to tell you what was best for you."

Grinning, he accepted two cranberry margaritas from a passing waiter. He handed one to Holly, then raised his glass. "To true love."

"To relentless men," she said, raising hers also.

"Touché."

They both drank. Sam set his glass on a damask-skirted table, then looked around. "Now that we've greeted, made an appearance, and toasted each other, can we slip out of this shindig?"

"You don't like parties either?"

Tugging at his bow tie, he made a face. "Not this kind. I've had enough of these press-the-flesh, networking things to last a lifetime. But I'll stay if you want to."

Holly thought about it. "Now that my mother has already talked to us and restyled my hair, I don't think she'll miss us if we make an early getaway. There are just a few people I want to say hello to."

Her "few people" took nearly an hour to say hello to, especially since she had to introduce Sam to each one. Surprisingly, no one asked her about Brad, and for that Holly was grateful. She didn't want to make any explanations, at least until everything was settled between them.

Outside the hotel, the Christmas ambiance continued. Lush evergreen wreaths decorated the stucco exterior walls, along with red velvet bows and trailing lengths of ribbon. A row of paper luminarias, filled with clean sand and lighted candles, lined each side of the saltillo-tile path around the landscaped grounds. There wasn't any snow, and the jingle bells were strictly of the recorded variety, but Holly loved it.

Sam caught hold of her hand and squeezed gently. After that, she loved it that much more.

"Why do you have to go to so many parties if you don't like them?" she asked him, reaching up to brush her fingertips along the canopy of feathery mesquite trees. Within their branches, tiny Christmas lights twinkled.

"Goes with the job." He shrugged. "I guess there's a certain amount of glad-handing that goes with any kind of work."

"But construction?"

"No, my other job. My far-away life in Tucson. Remember? The road to tenure is paved with hard work, publication, and about a million faculty parties."

At that, Sam looked so aggrieved that Holly had to laugh.

"See? That's exactly what I was talking about earlier. I've spent so much time seeing you rip my house apart—"

"Hey! I think the remodeling is going well."

"—that I forget about your alter ego. What's it like to be a college professor?"

They passed an open archway. The sounds of conversation and holiday music drifted outside.

"It's probably not the way you imagine it," Sam replied. "Less ivy-covered halls of academia and more *Animal House*. I teach night classes—Composition, Literature, and some remedial English—mostly to returning students."

"Dropouts?"

His expression was indecipherable. "Sometimes. Or sometimes my students are just people who've had life interfere once too often with their plans. They're the ones old enough"—he frowned—"no, *determined enough*—to really value what they're learning."

Stopping abruptly, Sam pulled her close. "And that's probably more than you ever wanted to know about any of it."

With no warning at all, he danced her the rest of the way down the luminaria-lit path.

142 *Lisa Plumley*

By the time they stopped, Holly was breathless. So was Sam, but he didn't seem to mind. She decided she should have been taking spontaneity lessons from him all along. He made it all seem so effortless.

Wondering why they'd stopped dancing, she looked around. They'd arrived at a landscaped border of fuchsia bougainvilleas. In the darkness beyond it, the hotel pool shimmered turquoise, surrounded by a deserted deck and more candle-filled luminarias.

"Mmmm. The water looks good." Sam gave her a reckless wink. "Let's take a swim."

"It's December!"

"It's December in Arizona," he reminded her. "We live in the desert, remember?"

"It's still too cold for swimming."

He shrugged. "The water's probably heated."

"The hotel pool is for hotel guests only. They're very strict about that here," Holly argued. "They have security, you know. Besides, we'd have to go home first and get swimsuits."

"Who said anything about swimsuits?"

She put both hands on her hips. "My dress is new, and your tux is a rental. You'll forfeit your deposit if you take a dip."

Sam grabbed his tie and yanked it free. "Who said anything about wearing clothes?"

Five minutes later, Sam was as naked as the day he was born, chest-deep in the warm water of the hotel pool. Feeling carefree, he ducked his head underwater and came up shaking drops of it from his hair.

"Come on in. The water's fine," he called to Holly.

She shook her head and held her ground at the edge of the pool. He couldn't read her expression, but the moonlight caught every sexy curve beneath her white dress, teasing him with her nearness. So close and yet so far.

"Don't make me come over there and get you," he warned with a grin.

She didn't budge. Sam swam closer.

"You wouldn't dare," Holly said when he was halfway there.

"I wouldn't?"

He stood, making rivulets of water run from his body into the pool. Holly developed a sudden, apparently overwhelming interest in the lush bougainvilleas that secluded the pool area from the rest of the hotel. She crossed her arms over her chest, staring fixedly into the distance. On a lounge chair just behind her, his dress shoes, tuxedo and shirt lay where he'd dropped them—now folded neatly, thanks to Holly.

"Nobody's around." Sam started toward her through the shallow end, goose bumps prickling his skin. It was a lot warmer in the water than out of it. "Come on. It's fun."

"I never said I'd go skinny-dipping with you," Holly reminded him, pushing her bare toes against the pool deck. She'd taken off her shoes while his back was turned, and stowed her strappy sandals on the lounge chair beside his clothes.

She chewed her lip, looking vaguely guilty. "I'm not . . . Well, you might as well know the truth. I'm not really the spontaneous type. It was all an act."

"You're kidding."

"It's true. I can't help it."

Sam came closer. She backed up.

"I even planned the whole spontaneity thing," she confessed.

"If you're trying to scare me off, it won't work. I'm already hooked." He smiled. "I'm at your mercy."

Her eyebrows lifted. Holly did look at him then, but only at his face. She studiously avoided the bare-naked rest of him. "You're at my mercy?"

"Absolutely."

He reached the steps, almost close enough to grab her. Almost close enough to drip pool water on her bare feet. Sam was laying himself bare for her, naked in every way. The idea of that was enough to send a sane man screaming to the hills, but he wanted Holly to know the man who loved her. If that made him crazy, then Sam didn't care.

"Okay, then." She narrowed her eyes at him in a contemplative, amused look. "If you're really at my mercy, prove it."

"What do you want me to do?"

"Stand back. I'm afraid you're going to toss me in the water."

He laughed, moving closer. "Very perceptive. The idea had crossed my mind."

"Well?"

"Anything but that." He scooped her in his arms and carried her toward the pool.

"Let me go!"

"If you don't quit kicking and wriggling, I just might drop you." Sam stopped at the pool's edge. He grinned at the woman in his arms. "Well?"

"Okay, okay," Holly relented. "Just let me down first."

"No way. You'll chicken out."

"I won't. I promise. Look! I'll prove it." Giving him an unreadable glance, she unwound her scarf from her throat. The sheer fabric fluttered as she tossed it to the lounge chair. "See? I'm all ready to go."

He decided to risk trusting her. "That makes two of us."

Taut with anticipation, Sam lowered her to the steps. At the first lap of water over her toes Holly shivered, but she was as good as her word. Biting her lip, she held his biceps for balance and waded farther. Her white dress dampened by inches, clinging to her thighs and hips, highlighting each subtle curve and intriguing hollow. Too quickly, pool water enveloped her from the waist down.

Surprise lit her features. "It *is* warm!"

To his astonishment, she dived underwater, dress and all.

In the pool lights he glimpsed her movements, fluid and graceful as she swam. Her red hair was a dark cloud around her face; her dress a whispery white trail. Moments later, she'd made it to the opposite end of the pool.

Naturally enough, Sam realized, she was making him chase her for every inch of progress.

He did, swimming after her with powerful strokes. Catching Holly with both hands around her waist, he drew them both to the surface. She laughed, her skin sparkling with dampness. Her dress molded wetly to her body—to his hands—as though it had been designed exactly for this. Her face shone with elation, framed by her chlorine-scented, slicked-back hair.

"I didn't think you'd do it," Sam said, panting a little.

"I'm braver than you think," she informed him, wriggling slightly as she clutched his bare shoulders. "I've been doing all sorts of risky things lately."

"Oh, yeah?"

A grin. "Yeah."

"Risk this." Digging one hand in her hair, Sam tipped her head back and kissed her, hard.

She welcomed him with a ferocity that matched his own. Damn, but he wanted her. He dragged Holly closer, loving the feel of her tight against him, the feel of her breasts pressed against his bare chest.

They drifted in the water, mouths still exploring, and all he wanted was to never stop touching her. With a groan he kissed her neck—small, deliberate bites, then tongue-sweet kisses along the base of her throat. Holly moaned, the low, husky sounds she made as potent as wine. They sent desire shivering through him. She felt it, too, felt and breathed desire with every sigh, savored it with every bite of her fingernails against his back.

"Oh, Sam . . ."

It was too much and not enough, all at once. He cupped her breasts, making the water eddy between them, and through her soaked dress her nipples rose to meet his thumbs. He stroked slowly, slower, making the good feelings last. Holly made him feel something beyond simple desire, beyond anything he'd experienced before. He wanted to strip away her dress, wanted to take her there in the water, on a lounge chair, on the pool deck. He wanted somebody to shut off the lights that were blinding him.

Sam squinted past Holly. At the pool's edge, an industrial-strength flashlight was trained directly on them. Beyond the brightness, he saw the silhouetted figure of a uniformed, pot-bellied man.

"Break it up, folks," the man drawled. "Or get a room, at least." He chuckled. "This here's a private pool, and it's closed for the night."

The hotel security guard—Sam realized that had to be who it was, judging by the uniform—motioned with his flashlight.

"I'd hate to have to arrest you both for indecent exposure, too, along with the trespassing charge," he said without a trace of regret. "So you'd best put your clothes on, sonny."

"I can't believe he actually had us arrested."

Shaking her head, Holly gripped the cold bars of the holding cell issued to her and Sam at the county jail. She peered down the dank corridor leading to the front of the jail. No action there. Except for the snoring of the drunk who'd been asleep in the adjacent cell when they arrived, everything was quiet.

Behind her, one of the gray metal cots squeaked as Sam sat on it. He rested his forearms on his thighs and loosely clasped his hands together, looking almost as relaxed as he had in the middle of the pool at the Cheshire Hotel. He was dressed now, except for his tuxedo jacket and tie. They lay where he'd tossed them at the foot of the cot's mattress.

"I feel like a criminal," Holly complained, brushing vainly at her wrinkled, still-damp dress. Its matching scarf hung limply around her neck. She ran her tongue over her teeth, wishing fervently for a toothbrush.

She headed for the cot—barefoot, because they'd kept her high-heels for some inexplicable reason—and stopped in front of Sam. There was no way she'd actually sit on the mattress. Who knew what kind of people had used that thing?

"But then I guess I have a criminal record now, don't I?" Holly went on. "I've been arrested and booked into jail."

Booked into jail. "Booked into" sounded wrong, as if she'd made reservations at an exclusive resort. Sure, *Casa de la Criminal*.

None of this seemed to be making a dent with Sam. Holly waved her arm wildly at him.

"Into jail!" she wailed, feeling slightly hysterical. "Do you know I've never even been *inside* a place like this before, much less been thrown into one?" She paced across the gritty concrete floor. "Here I am, in jail," she muttered, halfway to herself. "The slammer, the joint, the hoosegow. Dear Lord, what am I *doing* here?"

Sam gazed calmly back at her. "It's only a trespassing charge. The hotel decided to get tough with us, thanks to the vandalism problems they've had lately."

She frowned, remembering the lecture they'd endured in the office of the hotel manager while waiting for the Saguaro Vista police to arrive. As if *she,* a perfectly upstanding citizen, were likely to vandalize lounge chairs, dump paint in the water, or paint graffiti on the pool deck. The very idea rankled.

"So it's a night in jail, no sleep, and a fine," Sam continued. "It's no big deal."

Holly gaped at him. "What are you, a career criminal?"

"I've had my share of scrapes with the law."

"What?"

This was what she got for being spontaneous. She'd become involved with a wanted man. A felon. An ex-con, maybe. It sounded like a bad late-night "B" movie. *Babes Behind Bars, Part Two: Sam Returns.* Holly grabbed the cell bars again and gazed toward the door leading to freedom. She might have known changing her life would lead to disaster.

"It wasn't anything serious," Sam said. "Some stupid high-school pranks, a couple of drunk-and-disorderly charges. I've changed my ways since then."

He tried a grin. Holly wasn't having it. Sure he was charming—the dangerous ones always were, weren't they?

"I'll just bet you've changed your ways! Changed them right into jail again, you mean. Why didn't you tell me you'd been arrested before?"

"It never came up." He shrugged. "This will blow over in no time, you'll see. Don't worry. Everything will be fine."

"Fine? No, it won't be fine."

She felt like shrieking at him, but she didn't. She was afraid they'd put her and Sam in separate cells if they argued too loudly. The only thing worse than being locked up in a jail cell would be being locked up in a jail cell without Sam.

She was still mad, though. Mad and scared. Holly jabbed her forefinger at his chest.

"This is what comes of being irresponsible," she told him. "This is what comes of crazy stunts like skinny-dipping in a private pool at midnight. *This"*—she paused for emphasis— "is what happens when you don't plan ahead."

Her point made, Holly stomped to the other end of their cell. She crossed her arms over her chest, not looking at him. Wait until the people at her office heard about this. She'd probably be fired on the spot. After all her hard work, too.

It just wasn't fair. Why, oh why, had she let Sam talk her into going swimming with him?

"You can't plan your whole life." He crossed the cell, then stopped behind her. His hands lowered to her shoulders, warm against her bare skin. "You can't plan who you fall in love with." He kissed her shoulder. "Life happens to you. You have to take the good with the bad."

Holly whirled to face him. "Oh, no, I don't. I'm not standing by waiting for life to take its chances with me. Only a fool does that. Everything I've gotten, I've gotten because I worked my tail off for it. I've done a damned good job of it, too!"

Her eyes filled with tears. Why did that always have to happen when she got mad? Angrily, she blinked them away.

"So don't you tell me to just take what life hands me," she cried. "Because I won't do it."

"So now I'm a fool, then?" Sam stepped back. "Now I'm the stupid one, because I'm not a neurotic, compulsive Felix Unger wannabe with a retirement plan and a set of matching towels?"

She gasped. "I should never have told you about that!"

"About which, the retirement plan or the towels?"

"Neither!"

"You tell 'em, sister!" the drunk from the next cell shouted. He'd awakened during their argument and now had his grizzled old face pushed halfway through the bars to watch the final round. He waved his fist in encouragement, then winked at Holly.

"Give 'em what for, honey," he slurred.

Sam's eyes narrowed. His face darkened. Holly had never

seen him mad before—it was an education. Their whole relationship was an education in mistakes *not* to repeat again.

Sam nodded toward the drunk. "Friend of yours?"

Holly glared at him.

"No, wait. You wouldn't have anything to do with someone who wasn't *perfect,* would you?" Sam asked. "You can't be bothered with somebody who's made a few mistakes."

"Somebody such as . . . an ex-felon like yourself?" she inquired with a lift of her eyebrows. "I know better now."

Hurting too much to look at him any longer, she turned away. Sam didn't try to stop her. Stony silence descended upon their cell, only to be broken by the scrape of a key in the door at the end of the corridor. They both looked expectantly toward it.

Brad walked in, followed by the key-wielding guard.

"Somebody page me?" he asked with a grin.

Holly could have cried with relief. Reaching their cell, Brad put his fingers through the bars to clasp her hand. He looked like freshly shaved and showered heaven, right down to the pressed crease in his casual cotton pants. Brad wouldn't have let her down. He'd never have gotten her locked into jail.

"Oh, Brad! Thank God you're here." She tossed back a meaningful glance at Sam's stony face. "It's been awful."

"What the hell is he doing here?" Sam asked.

"He's here to get me out of this godforsaken place. I paged him. Because I *knew* he'd come."

The guard unlocked their cell and swung the barred door open.

Brad rushed in and grabbed her hands. "Are you all right?"

"I'll be fine," Holly answered. "Once I'm out of this place."
And once I get over Sam.

"I already called David and Clarissa to bail us out," Sam gritted out through clenched teeth. "They'll be here any minute."

Holly linked arms with her rescuer, then glanced at Sam. "How was I supposed to know you had a plan to get us out of here? It's not as if you've ever planned anything before."

His eyes turned gray with pain. "You're right. If I had, I'd have planned not to fall in love with you."

He held her gaze, daring her to look away first. Daring her to say he didn't really love her.

Holly couldn't do it.

"Goodbye, Sam," she whispered, her throat thick with unshed tears. "I'm sorry things had to end this way."

Ten

Watching Holly walk away on another man's arm was one of the hardest things Sam had ever had to do. He could only stand, frozen, as she and Brad stepped out of the jail cell and walked together down the corridor. The guard slammed the door shut, locking him in again.

Without a backward glance, Holly was gone.

She'd made her choice. Brad.

He should have known better. He should have known a woman like Holly wouldn't really change. She'd told him all along, hadn't she? *I'm trying to work things out with Brad. I haven't given up on him yet.*

Of course, not ten minutes later she'd been kissing Sam, responding to him as though they were the hottest of lovers, reunited. But what did that prove? Not a damn thing. Only that they were two healthy, sexually-aware adults who knew a great kiss when they felt one.

Sam lay on his back on the narrow cot, one arm thrown over his eyes. He closed them, trying to blot out Holly's image. He shouldn't still want a woman who'd just dumped him. He still wanted Holly. He was an idiot.

The door at the end of the corridor opened again. Sam sat up. Clarissa hurried inside, followed closely by David. She reached his cell and wrapped her fingers around the bars.

"Geez, Sam. It's been years since I've seen you like this."

Weakly, Sam grinned. He gathered up his jacket and stuffed his black tie in the pocket. "I'll bet I wasn't wearing a tuxedo last time."

"You look very nice." His cousin wasn't smiling. "Unlock this," she snapped to the guard.

Her tone suggested horrible consequences if the portly guard didn't snap to it. He must have recognized the threat, because he did. Then he backed out of Clarissa's way.

"Uh, you're free to go, mister," he mumbled.

Sam headed down the corridor with Clarissa and David, then picked up his personal things in the jail's office. Outside, the bone-jarring Sunday morning sunlight did nothing to warm him.

The instant the doors of the county jail closed behind them, Clarissa grabbed his arm.

"What was Holly doing with Brad?" she asked, frowning. "We ran into them in the parking lot, but he was hustling her into that gaudy red car of his. We didn't have a chance to talk. What's going on, Sam?"

"Simple. She picked him." Sam shielded his eyes against the sunlight and scanned the parking lot. "Where did you park?"

"Over there." David pointed to their blue Wagoneer, parked at the edge of the lot in the meager shade of a Paloverde tree.

Sam slung his tuxedo jacket over his shoulder and headed in that direction. "Would you mind driving me back to the Cheshire Hotel? I had to leave my truck in the parking lot and ride over here with Saguaro Vista's finest."

"Sure." David unlocked the driver's-side door, then reached in and unlocked the back door directly behind it.

Sam opened the door and threw in his jacket. He was about to follow it onto the back seat when Clarissa grabbed him again. Somehow, she'd wedged her body into the space between the back seat, Sam, and the opened door. She scowled at him like a bulldog having a bad day.

"'She picked him.' Is that all you're going to say?"

Sam thought about it. "Yeah."

"Come on, honey." David glanced over his shoulder at his

wife. "Get in. You can badger Sam about his love life on the way to the hotel."

"Hmmph."

Clarissa got in and proceeded to do just that. While David steered the Wagoneer through town, passing gaily-decorated Christmas displays and lots selling discounted fir trees, she tossed questions at Sam.

"Why was Holly leaving with Brad? Why didn't she just wait for us?" She jabbed her husband. "And how can the two of you act like nothing just happened?" Clarissa paused, fixing them both with a stern look. "Is this a guy thing?"

Sam sighed. "Which question do you want answered first?"

She swiveled in the front seat, straining her shoulder safety belt to the limit so she could glare at him. "I'm serious. This is a serious thing."

"It's an over-with thing."

Morosely, Sam gazed out his window. The glittery holiday displays only made him feel worse. Christmas was supposed to be a time to spend with the people you loved. Unfortunately, the woman *he* most wanted to be with had chosen another man to make merry with.

He turned back to Clarissa. "Holly didn't wait for you because she didn't know you were coming to bail us out. I didn't tell her. I thought she knew I'd get us out of jail, for Chrissakes! I'm not a total screw-up."

He fisted his hand against his knee. He wasn't a screw-up at all, not anymore. A long time ago Sam had woken up to the fact that he'd been wasting his life away. Wasting his potential in a haze of parties, women, and the search for a good time. So he'd screwed his head on straighter and found something better.

He was far from perfect, but Sam liked to think he helped most of his students. Once in a while he even came across someone like himself, someone drifting along. Sometimes he gave them a nudge toward bigger goals for themselves, and saw them realize they could do more than they'd thought. Someone like Jiggly Jillian Hall.

"You're not a screw-up at all," Clarissa protested. "You're a respected college professor."

"Yeah," David chimed in, "your wild days are behind you, buddy . . . with the obvious exception of today." He grinned into the rearview mirror. "You want to tell us what you were doing naked, with Holly, in the middle of the pool at that ritzy hotel?"

"No," Sam said flatly. The memory of being with Holly, so close together, hurt too much to think about. He wouldn't do it.

"I really thought Holly would buckle long before this." Clarissa shook her head. "With Brad out of the picture, and you right there in her house, I thought you were a shoo-in. You seemed like just what Holly needed."

"Honey," David said as he turned into the hotel's curved drive, "why do I smell a matchmaking rat in all this? Hmmm?"

Clarissa lifted her chin and gave him a sly smile. "It didn't hurt us any to get thrown together by somebody who cared." She winked at Sam.

He smiled. He was the one who had introduced the two of them: his friend from college, David, and his loudmouthed cousin, Clarissa. A perfect match. Maybe some kind of matchmaking genes ran in the family.

After giving David directions to the correct area of the parking lot, Sam grabbed his tuxedo jacket. He was seriously considering burning the damn thing. It had brought him nothing but trouble. Since he'd put it on, he and Holly had been kicked out of the formal wear shop *and* arrested. For someone like Holly, that was probably too much social censure to swallow all at once.

"It doesn't matter," he told Clarissa. "Holly got Brad. I hope she's happy with him."

"No, you don't. You hope they're miserable together and she comes back to you. Admit it."

So what if he did? It wasn't going to happen.

"They belong together. They're perfectly well-suited for one another."

"Oh, geez. Now Holly's got you believing that junk, too? David, she's brainwashed him. We've got to do something."

Her husband and Sam only stared blandly at the parking lot.

Clarissa smacked the back of the seat with her hand, looking exasperated. "Hello? Sam? You don't fall in love with somebody just because you share shoe sizes and an interest in Keogh accounts."

David pulled up to the left of Sam's truck. His Wagoneer swayed, then stopped.

Sam opened his door. "You're preaching to the converted," he told Clarissa. "Thanks for the ride."

"Wait a minute!"

His cousin jumped out of the Wagoneer right behind him. She followed Sam to his truck and leaned against the driver's-side door, arms crossed.

"You're not going anywhere until I get some answers."

"Oh, yeah?" Sam caught hold of her upper arms, lifted her a few inches above the blacktop, and set her down out of his way. He unlocked his truck door.

"That's not fair! I'm only here because I care about you, and you know it."

He cracked open his door, then faced her. "I'm tired," he said gently. "I'm dead tired and a little pissed-off and a lot sick of talking about this. It feels as if my heart got stuck in a vise and twisted like hell. So cut me a little slack, okay? We can talk about this when I get back."

Clarissa came closer and wrapped her arms around his middle. Contritely, she laid her head against his chest. "I'm sorry. I'm so sorry things worked out like this, and—"

Her head rose sharply and she released him. "And did you just say we'll talk about it when you get back? Back from where? Where are you going?"

"I've got to get away."

Sam climbed in his truck. Inside, it still smelled like Holly's flowery perfume. Her lipstick tube was still tucked in the passenger-side visor where she'd left it before the party. He gripped the steering wheel tighter. There was no way in hell he was going back to her house and watch her rebuild things with Brad.

Goodbye, Sam. I'm sorry things had to end this way.

He was sorry, too. Sorry things had ever begun, only to turn sour at the end. He shoved his keys into the ignition and started his truck. The sooner he left, the better.

"Sam, where are you going?"

"Back to Tucson. I've got to be there anyway—my ethics hearing is scheduled later this week. Remember Malcolm's charges about changing Jilly's grade?"

Clarissa nodded. "Malcolm's a worm. You can tell him that for me when you see him." She grinned, looking cheered by the thought.

"After that, I don't know." Sam shrugged. "Maybe I'll try to pick up some tutoring work. Take my mind off things."

"I don't think you should go," Clarissa said unhappily.

"I can't stay here." He pulled the truck door closed and rolled down the window instead. He drummed his fingers on the edge of it, needing to be gone. Needing to forget.

She sighed. "I know. What should I tell Holly?"

His heart twisted again. "Tell her . . . tell her if she decides to take a chance, I'll be waiting. Tell her love at first sight is real." He paused. "Tell her I still believe that fortune cookie was right."

"Huh?" Clarissa looked puzzled.

"She'll know what it means." Sam put his truck in gear.

"Wait. You want me to tell her about a fortune cookie?"

He gazed sadly at her. Why was he still hoping?

"On second thought, just tell her I said good-bye."

He pulled out of the parking lot and onto the highway. Pretty soon, Sam was making good time toward Tucson—the direction exactly opposite of the one he really wanted to go.

Just after sunset, Holly arrived home in Brad's BMW. As she and Brad pulled in her driveway, she peered at the darkened windows of her house and knew things really were finished between her and Sam. He wasn't there.

Her heart sank. Part of her had been hoping, admittedly without reason, that Sam would be waiting for her. Beside her, Brad cut the BMW's engine and stretched his arm across the back of her seat, looking satisfied with himself.

"I'm certainly glad I didn't hire an outside consultant to evaluate that accounting software for me. It would have cost me a bundle."

It was as close as Brad would come to a thank you. Somehow, he'd persuaded her to look over his new software package for him after all. She'd spent the whole afternoon in his office setting up portions of it for him.

"I'm glad I could help," she said.

She shifted uncomfortably on the car's leather seat, feeling awkward and overdressed in the conservative beige dress and matching jacket Brad had bought for her earlier. The clothes had been waiting in the car when they'd left the jail. He'd insisted on taking her to his new, luxurious condominium to shower and change before heading to his office.

Brad's condominium had all the warmth of a modern-art museum—all slick surfaces and cold, hard edges. Even the landscaping outside was cold, a mixture of granite boulders accented with knifelike desert agave. Holly hadn't wanted to admit how well its austerity suited him.

"Do you want to come inside?" She nodded toward her dark, empty-looking house. "The renovation is practically finished. It looks nice. I'd like you to see it."

Brad shook his head. "No, thanks. I've had enough reminders of your friend Sam's handiwork for one day."

She looked away, remembering all the times she'd mentioned Sam's name. So many things reminded her of him. She hadn't realized how much those references might hurt Brad.

"I'm sorry, Brad. I'm sure I'll stop doing that soon."

"I hope so. The guy was ruining your reputation. Getting you thrown out of stores—getting you arrested!" He pursed his lips. "I'm afraid your exploits didn't do my reputation any favors, either. Everyone in town still links the two of us."

Brad reached into the back seat and retrieved her white party dress, newly cleaned and wrapped in a drycleaner's bag. Still holding it, he opened his car door and got out.

Holly watched him walk around the front of the car. He paused, wiped a spot from the hood with his sleeve, then proceeded to her side and opened her door.

"I *will* walk you up to your door, though," he offered with a smile. "It's the least I can do as a gentleman."

She let him help her out of the car and walk her to the front porch. Brad arranged her dress across the porch swing.

"I do understand about Sam." He faced her again. "In fact, I admire your quick thinking. Letting him move in was a good way to get your renovation done cheaply."

"It wasn't like that. Sam was . . . a friend." A friend and more, someone who'd always thought of her happiness. How could Brad make their relationship sound so mercenary?

He waved away her explanation. "Whatever. It doesn't really matter, now that your little plan finally worked."

"My . . . plan?"

He spread his arms, an odd sort of smirk on his handsome face. She couldn't read his expression very well, because he still had his sunglasses on, even though it was getting dark.

"You got me," he announced.

"What?"

"You got me. You got what you wanted with your plan. *The Plan*. It was all there in your day planner."

"You read my day planner?" Holly grabbed the porch wall and leaned against it, needing its support.

Brad frowned. "Only by accident. I saw my name on some of the pages. Naturally I was curious." In an apparent, and misguided, attempt to lighten the mood, he added, "Once I got going, though, it was quite a read."

"You had no right. That was private."

Holly had thought being unceremoniously dumped on the night of the romantic dinner that wasn't was bad. She'd thought being ridiculed, then ignored, on the golf course was bad. She'd thought being turned down while dressed in her most seductive clothes was bad. This was worse.

"Are you actually making fun of me because of something you read while you were snooping?" she asked, her voice shaking.

A horrible thought occurred to her. How long ago had Brad read about her plan? Had he known, almost from the start, what she was doing? The idea was humiliating.

"It was really very flattering," he insisted. "What man could resist being the subject of such—"

"When did you read it?" she interrupted. She pushed away from the porch wall to confront him. "When?"

"I don't see what you're getting so upset about. It was just a stupid little thing—"

She snatched Brad's damned black sunglasses from his face so she could look him in the eye, then straightened to her full height. Wearing her heels, she had a good two inches on him. For once, it felt good.

"When?"

He blinked nervously, his face pale and somehow diminished without the glasses he always wore. "This morning. While you were in the shower."

She fought the urge to whip off her spike-heeled shoe and hurl it at him. *"Why?"*

"I wanted your mother's phone number at her real estate office." He glared at her as though she were being completely unreasonable. "I called to find out how much we might get for your house. To find out if Linda would list it for sale."

Wearing an aggrieved expression, Brad snatched his sunglasses. Holly felt too stunned to care. Dumbstruck, she sank on the porch swing. Her dress, still in its drycleaner's bag, crinkled beneath her. She didn't have the energy to care.

"You know I always hated this old house, Holly. We should start fresh. Start over in a new place, like my condo. Now that we're together again—"

"No."

"Huh?"

"No." Oh, Lord. She'd been such a fool. How could she have been so blind?

She'd been so afraid of failing. So afraid of winding up alone. So certain the problems in their relationship could be—should be—fixed, if only she tried hard enough.

Holly shook her head. "No, Brad. We're not together. I'm not sure we ever were." She gazed steadily at him, her certainty building with every passing moment. "I tried everything to make things work between us. Everything. Do you know what I just realized?"

Cautiously, Brad shook his head. He was probably still reeling from the realization that he wasn't taller than Holly after all.

"It's not my fault."

It was true. Her plan should have worked. Probably *would* have worked—on anyone who really cared for her. Anyone except Brad the Bad. Holly wasn't the failure in their relationship. Brad was. Realizing the truth of that was like a shot of pure sunshine to her battered spirit.

It wasn't her plan that had won him back. Her plan was only one big, ego-stroking joke to him. Brad's need to save his own reputation had made him come back, not to mention his need for a part-time accountant.

Holly narrowed her eyes at him. She'd gotten what she wanted, all right—only to find out it wasn't worth having.

"I think you should leave, Brad."

"Be serious." He gave her his most charming smile. "Don't make more of this than it really is. You said it yourself. We belong together."

Holly stood, then gathered up her dress. "Not anymore. Frankly, I'd rather be alone."

He stared at her. "You *will* be alone," he said meanly. "Even your handyman's gone, thanks to the kiss-off you gave him at the jail this morning. And you won't get a second chance with me. Not this time."

He waited, probably expecting her to change her mind. To beg him for that second chance he'd preemptively refused. To revert to the old, desperate, do-the-right-thing Holly he remembered.

When she didn't, he looked astonished. Then angry. Red-faced, Brad clomped awkwardly down the steps. Standing beside the lighted Santa-with-reindeer display Holly and Sam had erected on the lawn, Brad turned.

"How does it feel to be unwanted?" he asked snidely.

Holly didn't want to hurt him. She really didn't. So she only gazed at him for a long, thoughtful moment.

"Maybe you should ask yourself that question," she said quietly. Then she turned, unlocked the door, and slipped inside. Alone.

* * *

"You're crazy," Clarissa said a few days later. Hands full of Christmas CDs, she plopped down on the floral-upholstered armchair beside Holly's newly repaired fireplace. "You've got a man who loves you—Sam, in case you're wondering—and you're letting him get away."

"It's too late to stop him." Holly poked glumly at the fire. "He's already gone."

She'd never been able to use the fireplace before. She'd never even seen it when it wasn't boarded up. But somehow, whenever she laid a fire log, struck one of the special, extra-long matches, and hunkered down beside the resulting blaze, it made her feel closer to Sam.

It was absurd, but Holly experienced the same kind of cozy feeling whenever she used the new porcelain sink he'd installed in the kitchen. She felt it when she hung pictures on the freshly painted walls, and when she encountered the new hardwood kitchen floor on her bare feet instead of the old yellow linoleum.

She missed him.

"He's only gone because he thinks you chose Brad," Clarissa insisted for what had to be the hundredth time. "Call him. I gave you the number."

Holly shook her head. "I can't. What if Sam doesn't want me anymore? What if he hates me? I couldn't stand it if I called him and he hated me."

She replaced the wrought iron fireplace poker in its holder, then curled up on the sofa. In its corner were the pink-fringed throw pillows she'd used to prop up Sam's injured foot. Reminders of him were everywhere. Holly picked up a pillow and hugged it in her lap.

"I still have my memories. At least this way I can still dream of what might have happened." She shuddered. "I can't call Sam. I was so mean to him at the end! How could he ever forgive me?"

"You're right. He never will," Clarissa deadpanned. "He's probably sticking pins in a Holly Aldridge voodoo doll right now. He's probably telling total strangers how lucky he was to get away from you."

Holly covered her face with the pillow. Clarissa was right. She felt horrible.

"You know, I even ordered a pizza from Angelo's last night. And Kung Pao chicken the night before," she confessed forlornly, her voice muffled by the pillow. She looked up. "My throat burned like crazy, but it wasn't the same without Sam."

She'd taken to sleeping in Sam's bed in the guest bedroom, too. Worse, she hadn't even changed the sheets first. She imagined they smelled vaguely, but wonderfully, like Sam. She was turning into a real basket case.

"I was *kidding!*" Clarissa shrieked. "Geez. Get it through your head, Holly Berry. Sam. Loves. You. He's not going to stop. You should have seen his face when he left."

Holly dared to lower the pillow. "Really?"

Her friend threw her hands in the air. *"Yes.* What do you think I've been trying to pound into that thick head of yours for the past three days?"

"I still can't call him. I just can't take a chance like that."

"Do it."

Holly shook her head. "I can't."

"You can. Do it."

Trying to ignore Clarissa, Holly pulled a fresh tissue from the supply she had taken to keeping in her pocket. She blew her nose.

"You know, I haven't even been in to work since last Friday," she admitted.

"I know. I work there too, remember?" Clarissa gave her a sympathetic look. "Anyway, you've probably accrued about a thousand sick days. You deserve it." She got up and sat beside Holly on the couch, then gave her a hug. "That only proves my point, hon. For you, missing work is like breaking the law."

Holly sniffled. Clarissa had a point. This was serious.

"This is a chance you can't afford *not* to take," Clarissa said. "Isn't true love worth it?"

Holly took a deep, quivery breath. Then she voiced her greatest fear. "What if Sam doesn't want me anymore?"

Clarissa looked solemnly at her. She gave her a squeeze. "There's only one way to find out."

"You sure about this?" Sam's landlord pushed the lease agreement across the kitchen table for Sam to sign.

"Yeah." He scanned the document, then scrawled his name at the bottom and handed it over. It was a done deal.

Beside him sat Jiggly Jillian Hall. Her two toddlers—a boy and a girl, both with identical curly, pale blond hair—played noisily in his apartment living room. He could hear their toys banging, and the sound of their babyish laughter.

Jillie gave him a worried look. "I hope they won't break anything."

"Nah." Sam grinned at his landlord. "The furniture comes with the place, and I'm sure it's been through worse. It would take a jackhammer to make a dent in any of it."

"Hey, you're making me look bad," his landlord protested. "There's nothing wrong with that stuff." He peered semi-suspiciously at Sam. "You sure about this deal? Maybe you're having second thoughts about losing a nice, cheap apartment like this."

"I already told you. I'm not." Sam got up and shook hands with his landlord. "Thanks for everything. Just don't go raising the rent on Jillie, here. She's got a lease, remember?"

"Yeah, okay."

His landlord picked up the lease, took a copy for himself, then headed for the front door. He was still muttering something about, "never had no kids here before," when he left. Sam didn't think it would be a problem. The day he'd first moved in, the landlord had gone on at length about "never had no college students here before."

Besides, Sam had already overheard him telling Jillie what nice little rugrats she had. Despite his bluster, the guy was a softie at heart.

Picking up his last moving box, Sam went in the living room to say goodbye to the kids. Jillie followed him.

"It's a great place," he told her. "I hope you'll be happy

here. With two bedrooms it was always too big for me, anyway."

She smiled. "Oh, we will be, professor! This is the best Christmas present anybody ever had. The kids never had their own room before. They'll be just tickled."

Jillie looked pretty happy herself. Sam grinned back at her. The movement felt strange. He hadn't been feeling much like smiling lately. Losing Holly made everything look gray.

He wished Jillie good luck. After they said their goodbyes, he hefted his box again and carried it outside to his truck. Sam shoved it in place atop the rest and tied the whole mess down. He'd be on his way in no time.

Honk! Honk! At the sound, Sam turned, shading his eyes to peer down the street. A little white convertible, horn blaring with as much enthusiasm as its tiny size could muster, zoomed straight toward him. Holly was at the wheel.

Holly was going to run him down, judging by the speed she was traveling. Maybe three days with Brad had sent her over the edge. Sam figured a guy like Brad could do that to a person.

She wrenched the car to a gravel-crunching stop a few feet away and leaped out without opening the door. Sam rubbed his eyes. He had to be hallucinating. Either that, or dreaming. Holly had way too much decorum to jump out of a car, especially when she had on that sexy white dress of hers, which she did.

"Sam!"

"Holly?"

"I can't believe I found you."

She threw herself in his arms and clamped herself to him so tightly it would take a crowbar to pry her away. She was real, all right. Sam would have recognized the feel of Holly in his arms no matter how it happened.

"I drove straight here," she said, the words rushing out, "but I went to the University first and you weren't there. So then I went looking for your apartment, but I got lost. I was driving around in circles, then I saw your truck. And here I am!" Holly paused for breath then plunged ahead. He couldn't get a word in edgewise. "Sam, Brad and I are through. For good this time. I was a complete idiot. Can you forgive me? Please forgive me! I'm so sorry for everything."

At that moment, she noticed his truck bed, piled high with moving boxes and the rest of his things.

She stared. "Where are you going?"

"I—"

"Is it because of me?" she babbled before he could answer. "Were you trying to get away before I got here? You *were*, weren't you? I'll *kill* Clarissa if she's the one who called to warn you."

She sagged in his arms, close to tears, looking desolate. And gorgeous. And like everything he'd ever wanted.

Sam pulled Holly close and kissed her. When he raised his head again, she looked slightly dazed. Sam took advantage of the opportunity to explain.

"Clarissa didn't call me. I—"

Holly gasped. "Oh, no. You lost your ethics hearing, didn't you? I can't believe it! Those—"

She squinted, probably trying to think up something really vile to call the university faculty.

Sam grinned down at her. "No. I didn't lose. In fact, Malcolm's ridiculous charge got thrown out. Laughed out, actually."

In fact, Malcolm's complaint hadn't even reached the stage of a formal ethics hearing. But because of Sam's moves from Tucson to his parent's house, then to Holly's, the corresponding notices hadn't reached him. He hadn't found out about it until he arrived.

"I quit. I took another job, one where I wouldn't have to deal with somebody like Malcolm Jeffries. Life's too short to spend your days working with a jerk like him."

Her eyes widened. "Oh."

"What, no lecture about job responsibilities? No warnings about the dangers of unemployment? No speeches about the necessity of planning ahead?" Sam pressed his hand to her forehead. "Are you sure you're feeling all right?"

They both laughed.

"I'm feeling fine," Holly said, obviously recovering from her surprise. She nearly purred with the certainty of her statement. "And you don't need a plan, because *I've* already got one for both of us."

"You do?" He kissed her shoulder, then her neck.

"Yes."

She pressed a slip of paper in his hand, folding his fingers tightly around it. "You were right all along. I *was* falling in love with you. I was just too stubborn and too dumb to admit it."

Sam unfolded the paper. In his hand was the fortune-cookie fortune from their Kung Pao chicken dinner. *Your present plans are going to succeed.*

"I love you, Sam," Holly whispered. "And I never want to lose you again."

He held her close, his lips against her hair. "You never will." Sam considered turning a few happy cartwheels on the lawn, then dismissed the idea. He'd have to let Holly go in order to do that. "Damn, I missed you. There's no way I'll lose you again."

"Well," she said, sounding businesslike despite the fact that her face was squashed against his chest, "I want to make sure of that."

Stepping back, she sucked in a deep breath. "Marry me. I've already got the dress. See?" She held out both hands and turned in a circle. "You said it was perfect for a wedding."

"Wow." Shaking his head, Sam admired the woman he loved. "When you make a decision, you really take it all the way."

"Are you kidding me? I don't do *anything* halfway." She smiled. "Is that a yes?"

Sam picked her up. He twirled her around in a circle, and now he was smiling, too. "Yes. Yes, yes, yes, yes, yes!"

Eleven

It was going to be a perfectly romantic Christmas. The tree was lit, the holiday music was cheerful, the eggnog was cold. Even the weather had cooperated, in the form of a rare desert cold front that made snuggling up together in front of a toasty fire an absolute necessity.

Things started going uphill from the moment Holly's husband Sam came home, carrying her holiday favorite—poinsettias. Juggling the flowers, he shucked off his shoes, stripped off his jacket, and came toward her in the soft glow of the Christmas lights.

"Power go out?" he asked.

"Nooo." Smiling, Holly patted the sofa cushion.

Sam placed the flowers on the coffee table. "I'm kidding. I recognize a romantic Christmas Eve when I see one."

Gently, he pushed his wife backward against the cushions. His fingers delved in her hair, stroking. His mouth found hers, and their bodies settled familiarly—exquisitely—together.

"Where's the pizza from Angelo's?" He grinned. "You can't perform a cheap pizza-and-wine seduction routine without it. Not even at Christmas. I'm not easy, you know."

Holly rubbed her cheek against his, then nuzzled his neck. She loved him more every day. "The pizza is in the kitchen, as usual. But I've got other plans for you. And they're happening right here."

"I love them already," Sam said, bringing her close for another kiss. "As it happens, I've got a few plans of my own."

Holly noticed the sprig of mistletoe in his hand. She smiled and dropped the matching sprig she'd been hiding. As far as romantic Christmases went, this one was starting out . . . perfectly. She had a feeling it would end that way, too—happily ever after.

"Ho, ho, ho," she murmured, and kissed him back.

CHRISTMAS
HONEYMOON

One

It wasn't every day a girl checked into the honeymoon suite of a posh hotel.

Especially alone.

Sucking in a deep breath, Stacey Ames paused beneath the neon-studded entrance of the Atmosphere Hotel. Like everything else on the Las Vegas Strip, the hotel's massive porte-cochere popped with thousands of flashing lights. Never mind that it was only four o'clock on an ordinary Friday afternoon in December. The illusion of glamour, she supposed, had to be maintained constantly.

Maybe all that va-va-voom lighting would perk up her sun-starved complexion and wilted hairstyle. Something sure had to. After more than five hours spent driving from her cousin Janie's wedding to the hotel, Stacey felt about as glamorous as a wrung-out washcloth.

Behind her, tires squealed on the pavement. She glanced backward long enough to glimpse her red rented Honda Accord skidding around the corner toward the hotel's hundred-acre parking lot. The poor car all but spun on two wheels, thanks to the valet's energetic driving.

She'd have to check her rental car agreement's insurance provisions, just in case Mario Andretti, Jr. got too carried away. Making a mental note to do that when she got safely to the honeymoon suite, Stacey picked up her two hastily packed suitcases. She shrugged her purse higher on her shoulder and girded her courage.

Time to get on with the charade.

It'll be fun, she told herself as she pushed through the hotel's heavy glass doors. A three-day weekend of sun, fun, and fulfilling family obligations. Every girl's dream getaway.

Good thing they had free cocktails at these places.

The instant she stepped into the hotel's futuristic-themed lobby, a cacophony of jangling slot machines blasted her. So did the sound of murmured voices and a Muzak version of "Santa Baby." She hoped a similarly orchestrated "One Hundred Greatest Romantic Hits For Lovers" wasn't featured in the honeymoon suite. That just might be the thing to make her end this sham, promise or no.

When she'd awakened in Phoenix this morning, she hadn't planned on being drafted into emergency faux-bride duty. Her wardrobe showed it, too. Dressed in her usual jeans, sweater, and a jacket, Stacey felt downright dowdy next to the vacationers in the check-in line. But, cheered by thoughts of getting to her room and soaking in a hot bubble bath until she turned pruney, she managed to tough it out.

When her turn came, Stacey approached the hotel desk.

The immaculately coiffured clerk glanced up. "May I help you?"

"I have a reservation. Under the name of, ummm, Parker. Richard and Janie Parker."

The woman frowned in concentration as she typed the names. Then she beamed up at Stacey. "Oh! The honeymoon suite. How exciting for you. Congratulations!"

"Thanks." *Please just give me the key. Don't ask any questions,* Stacey prayed. *Please, please, please.*

How like Janie it was to ask her, possibly the world's worst liar, to take her place at the hotel.

It would be a miracle if she weren't found out before sunset. The people at the hotel would tell Aunt Geraldine her niece had tried to pawn off her wedding gift on somebody else, and she would get mad at Janie. Janie, when she got back from the

Bahamas with Richard, would get mad at Stacey for bungling the whole thing. Before long, none of the family would be speaking to each other.

For the sake of the promise she'd made to her cousin, Stacey had to get through the weekend with her real identity undiscovered. She'd just have to find a way to pull it off.

"Married." The desk clerk sighed. Her eyes went dreamy, just like Janie's did when she spotted a shoe sale. "You must be thrilled," she chirped, going back to the terminal in front of her. "I got married last June."

Pushing buttons, she described her bridesmaid's dresses, the flowers, and the wedding toast the best man had made.

Stacey nodded and smiled, doing her best to gush right along with her—without revealing her own *non*-bride status. It was just her luck to be checked in by the hotel's talkiest, cheeriest employee. A woman like this was meant to work at Disneyland greeting little kids, not at one of Las Vegas's trendiest new resort hotels.

Still chattering, the woman rifled through a pile of room keycards. She selected one and started handing it to Stacey. With her hand midway there, she stopped.

"Oh, but you'll need two keys, won't you? Silly me." She grabbed another card. "But where's the happy groom?"

She frowned toward the hotel's entrance, then at the conspicuously empty area surrounding the reservation desk.

"Oh, ahhh . . ." *Think, dummy.* Nothing came to mind. Why hadn't she planned for this question? Stacey gestured vaguely toward the bank of glass doors leading outside. "He's, ahhh—"

"Getting the rest of your luggage?" The clerk waved her hand, smiling conspiratorially. "I always pack too much, too. Mark—that's my husband—well, he says you shouldn't bring more than you can carry yourself, but that's ridiculous, don't you think so? How would I ever bring what I needed then?"

"Right," Stacey agreed. Giving the woman what felt like a completely inane grin, she nodded at the keycards. "I'd better just go on up without him, I guess."

"Oh!" The woman tittered. "Sorry. Here you go!" She held out the keycards, then paused. "Shall I keep one here for your husband to pick up?"

Since Stacey's "husband" was strictly imaginary and about as likely to turn up as Rudolph the Red-Nosed Reindeer . . . .

"I'll take both." Stacey grabbed them. "I'm trying to get a head start on my husband, since I'm planning a . . . surprise."

"Ahhh. Say no more." With a wide, woman-to-woman grin, the clerk relinquished the keys. "Good luck with that. Oh, and don't forget to visit our special holiday buffet. All the food is red and green! And the Holiday Extravaganza show is a must-see, too! The showgirls dress up in Santa suits, and—don't tell your hubby I told you this—the hunky holiday elves are a real showstopper!"

The idea was mind-boggling. "Wow. And they say Christmas doesn't come to Las Vegas."

"Oh, it definitely does. Enjoy!"

Making her getaway, Stacey scurried across the crowded lobby. She passed a glittering display of Christmas ornaments, each at least six feet in diameter. Everything really *was* bigger and fancier here, she guessed. A Muzak rendition of "White Christmas" serenaded her in the elevator. And on the fourteenth floor, one of those "hunky holiday elves" got on and rode with her all the way to the top.

Yep, Christmas had come to Las Vegas, all right. So had Stacey Ames, fresh from Phoenix and sans fake husband. Now all she had to do was keep her head low and keep her real, non-bridal identity a secret until check-out time.

Piece of fruitcake, she assured herself. How tough could it possibly be?

"Quit worrying," Dylan Davis said, speaking into his cell phone with one hand and steering his Jeep through the bumper-to-bumper Las Vegas traffic with the other. "I said I'll handle it."

On the other end of the line, his friend Richard sighed. "When I asked you to do this, I didn't know things had gone sour between you and Stacey. Janie told me all about it. You—"

"Everything will be fine," Dylan interrupted. Ducking his head, he frowned through the windshield at the highway exit sign overhead. "The Atmosphere, you said?"

"Yeah. Janie's aunt booked us into the honeymoon suite for the weekend as a wedding surprise."

"Nice surprise." At least it would have been, if the newly-weds hadn't already paid for a trip to the Bahamas themselves.

But their loss was his gain. Thanks to the generosity of Janie's Aunt Geraldine—and her yen for surprises—Dylan was about to have a second chance with Stacey. He'd blown it the last time. He didn't mean to make the same mistake twice. If he had to swing from a trapeze like one of those Cirque du Soleil performers, he'd do it. Whatever it took to win Stacey back.

Feeling more determined than ever, Dylan steered the Jeep toward the next exit. At the rate cars crawled off the highway toward the Las Vegas Strip, he'd be lucky to get there in time to spring his *own* surprise much before sunset.

"Get on that plane with Janie and get going, you worry-wart," he told Richard. "I'll handle everything here."

"That's what I'm afraid of."

A muffled thump sounded on Richard's end of the phone line, then bumping. A second later, Dylan heard something scrape across the receiver, then, "Okay, okay."

If he knew Janie, she was giving her new husband an ear-ful. Patiently, Dylan nestled the phone between his ear and shoulder and eased his Jeep down the off-ramp. Cars whizzed past in the right-hand lane, streaming toward the turn that led to the surface streets.

The phone crackled. "Listen," Richard said loudly, as though he'd returned his full attention to their phone conversation. "I gotta go. But watch yourself out there. If you screw up and break Stacey's heart again, you'll never sing bass in this town again."

Dylan grinned. "Janie's parting shot, I presume?"

"Mine, too. You know how—"

"Quit worrying." He frowned at the brake lights shining between him and the stoplight at the bottom of the ramp. "Stacey's a big girl. She can take care of herself."

"Like hell she can," Richard returned. "Especially when it comes to you."

"What am I, the Terminator of romance?"

"According to Stacey? Yeah."

"She'll change her mind." *God, he hoped she changed her mind.*

He said his good-byes to Richard and Janie, then plopped his cell phone on the Jeep's passenger seat. Its occupant, Ginger, sprawled across the upholstery with about as much canine grace as usual. He gave her a pat.

"You know, for a girl dog, you don't have much feminine mystique."

He scratched between her furry, perked-up ears. She sneezed, quivering with the joy of being the center of attention. She rolled over so he could rub her belly. Dylan rubbed absent-mindedly, his thoughts returning to Stacey.

Now *there* was a female with feminine mystique to spare. He hardly ever knew what the hell she was thinking. He had to be insane to jump back into the three-ring circus that was dating Stacey Ames.

On the other hand, he'd be even crazier not to.

Dylan turned onto the next street, his gaze darting toward the space-age 'atinum spire of the Atmosphere Hotel rising above the Las Vegas skyline. Stacey didn't know what she was in for. But he was going to love showing her.

In the honeymoon suite's pink marble bathroom, Stacey slipped deeper into the hot, peppermint-scented bathwater she'd drawn. Her muscles relaxed for the first time since she'd stepped into the church for Janie's wedding this morning.

What an adventure *that* had turned out to be. First, Janie had burst into tears at her bachelorette party the night before, thanks to Stacey's brilliant idea to have a male stripper dressed as a police officer come to the door and pretend to arrest the bride. Then, at the wedding, Janie had had the train of her wedding gown ripped off, thanks to Stacey accidentally stepping on it while spotting a cute usher.

By the time Aunt Geraldine had presented the bride and groom with their surprise wedding gift—*after* they'd scrimped and saved for a nonrefundable trip to the Bahamas—Janie had

had all she could take. She'd run from the room wailing, leaving Stacey to explain away her cousin's trauma as a case of newlywed nerves.

And to step in and solve the problem.

Now here she was, chest-deep in a bubble bath foamy enough to get lost in, in a hotel suite bigger than the whole closet-sized apartment she lived in back in Phoenix. *You know,* she thought, sculpting herself a new pair of forty-four double-Ds with the suds, *this might actually be fun.* A little relaxation, a little shopping, a little honeymooner champagne . . . yessir, she could get to like spending a weekend in Vegas.

Stacey raised her foot from the water and examined it. Yep, just about wrinkly enough. After a few more minutes' soaking, maybe she'd get dressed and head down to the casino to try her hand at a slot machine or two.

The phone jangled. Luckily, hotel patrons in Las Vegas apparently felt it imperative to remain connected at all times. Beside the neatly lined-up toiletry bottles on the pink marble vanity stood a cordless receiver. Dripping, Stacey rose from the tub and leaned halfway out to answer it.

"Oh, Mrs. Parker!" the woman from the front desk yelped. "I hope everything's all right with your room. Is everything satisfactory? Do you need anything?"

"Everything's fine," Stacey replied, feeling extra naked. *As soon as I hang up, I'm throwing the phone out the window.* "Thank you for calling. If that's all, I'll just—"

A giggle came from the receiver. "I just wanted to give you a little advance warning, because of your, you know, surprise. We girls have to stick together, I always say."

Listening with half an ear, Stacey murmured, "Uh-huh."

Water puddled on the plush rug beneath her left foot. Frowning at it, she balanced on the foot that was still in the bathwater so she could shake herself dry on the left side, at least.

"He's on his way up," the clerk said urgently. She lowered her voice to a girlish whisper. "I just gave him his keycard a few seconds ago." She paused. "Whoops! There he goes into the elevator."

"What?" Stacey lowered her leg back to the rug, still

poised between the tub and vanity but too confused to move. Goose bumps spread along her arms and sped toward her toes. "You gave who a keycard?"

"Why, your *husband*, of course."

"My husband."

Silence. Then, tentatively, "Yes, your husband. Is there . . . a problem?"

Her husband? But Richard and Janie were already at the airport, waiting for their honeymoon flight. Who in the world . . . ?

"Mrs. Parker?"

This had to be some kind of mistake. Had to be.

"Uh, I'm here." Her mind wasn't, though. It was someplace else entirely. Like Panicville. "Thanks for calling. I guess I ought to get ready!"

With a ridiculous, panic-induced titter, Stacey disconnected the line. Clothes. She needed clothes. She slammed the phone in its stand and twisted to pull her other foot from the bathwater.

Knock—knock—knock.

Her heart revved into overdrive. So did her foot. It splashed from the water, sending an arc of complimentary Happy Holidays brand peppermint-scented foam across the bathroom— and sending Stacey flat on the floor. She landed on her backside in a puddle, staring in the direction of the knock on the door.

Knock—knock—knock.

Ouch. Rubbing her aching, soggy butt, she glared toward the sound. Maybe if she ignored it, whoever it was would just go away. He'd obviously made a mistake. He needed the *other* honeymoon suite, the one with an actual bride in it.

Just in case, she pushed herself up and hobbled across the bathroom. Shivering, she yanked the white monogrammed hotel robe from its hook and slipped her arms inside the sleeves. The thick terrycloth stuck to her wet skin, but at least it was warm.

Knock—knock—knock.

Okay, this was ridiculous, Stacey decided, tying the robe closed at her waist. She was hardly going to skulk around in her honeymoon suite, dripping, while some poor libidinous bridegroom knocked around outside. For all she knew, that wasn't even his knuckles he was rapping against the door.

Now there's the kind of guy you want to invite in, Janie would have said with a wink. Unfortunately, Janie and her ribald sense of humor weren't there. Stacey was. With a quick swipe at the foggy bathroom mirror and a last pat at her scraggly brown ponytail, she headed toward the door.

Something scraped against it. The knob clicked.

The keycard. The woman at the desk said she'd given one to Stacey's "husband."

Panicked, Stacey scanned the room for a weapon. Her suitcase? Too bulky. Her purse? She carried hot pepper spray in a holster inside, but there wasn't time to grab it. *Think, think.*

Her gaze settled on her blow-dryer's cord, dangling from the bathroom vanity to the floor. She followed it upward from the plug to the two-thousand watt, gun-shaped business end.

The door swung inward.

If personal care appliances were all she had to defend herself with, that's what she'd use. Adrenaline pumping, Stacey lunged for the blow-dryer. The plug slapped her bare leg. The dryer's weight filled her hand.

"Mrs. Parker?" asked a rich-timbered masculine voice.

A *familiar* masculine voice.

The broad, jacket-clad shoulder that edged into view around the door nudged her suspicions. The rest of the hard-muscled body that followed confirmed them.

Dylan Davis. Here. Dear Lord, she had to be imagining him. Maybe hallucinating. Stress could do that to a person, couldn't it?

But he sure *looked* real. Tall, dark-haired and grinning, he filled her doorway. His arms were laden with an overcoat-wrapped bundle of what she assumed constituted luggage for a Peter Pan type like him, and above it his eyes sparkled with good humor. The bastard.

"Aren't you missing a husband?" he asked.

He added another smile to the mix. This was the part, Stacey supposed, where she was supposed to fall at his feet in gratitude. *Fat chance.*

"I spent the whole wedding trying to avoid you." She aimed the blow-dryer nozzle at him.

His gaze went to it, and his eyebrows raised. His stupid smile widened, too. Damn him.

"What are you going to do? Style me to death?"

Stacey stretched her arm back, letting the blow-dryer cord spin through her fingers until she held a good hank of it. She twirled it in the air, working up momentum. Then she walloped him with it.

It was the least Dylan Davis deserved.

The hair dryer whacked him right in the temple.

"Ouch!"

The dryer rebounded off his forehead, bashed off the wall, and came at him again. Dylan ducked, his head stinging, and tried to keep from dropping the trench coat-wrapped bundle in his arms. Easing it into the crook of his arm, he grabbed the hair dryer with his other hand.

"Same old Stacey." At the sight of her, he was completely unable to keep a goofy-feeling grin from his face. "I knew I should have taken out accident insurance before I came here."

She crossed her arms over her chest, hair dryer swinging beneath her elbow, and glared at him. "That *wasn't* an accident."

"Uh-huh."

God, she looked great. Between the half-tied bathrobe she had on, the bunched-up, shiny brown ponytail she'd stuck her hair in, and the fire in her eyes, she'd never looked sexier. But maybe that was just his skewed perspective talking. Because actually, Stacey looked miffed. Adorably miffed.

Adorably miffed? part of his brain jeered. *Hell-o. You're way far gone over this one.* He had to get a hold of himself.

Okay, maybe *miffed* was understating it. *Mad as hell* was more like it.

On the other hand, he'd pretty much expected that. Now he just had to change her mind—about him, about them—and he didn't plan to leave until he'd done it.

Dylan let go of the hair dryer. "You always say that. Right after you stomp, drop, smash or hurl something at somebody."

"I did that on purpose, you creep."

Okay. Clearly, Stacey needed time to adjust to the surprise of seeing him. Giving her exactly that, Dylan devoted himself to studying the suite.

The room stretched outward, luxurious and spacious and awash in mid-century modern design details. A carpeted sitting area with a pair of angular loveseats. A sleek media center. Chairs arranged around a table featuring a triangular plate of cellophane-wrapped Christmas cookies.

A bank of windows let in the desert sunshine, and the suite's vaunted view of The Strip, belying the fact that it was only a week until Christmas. In an adjacent room, a big double bed covered with a cushy black silk comforter awaited.

He liked it. All of it.

"Nice place," Dylan said, looking back at her.

"You're not staying."

"Who's asking?"

"Not me."

Beneath his trench coat, Ginger wiggled. Stacey's gaze went straight to the lump of coat covering the dog. Her eyebrows lifted.

"But you were *thinking* about it," he said to distract her. "Admit it. You want me as much as I want you."

She swung the hair dryer back and forth in front of her like a lion tamer tossing a whip from hand to hand. Her eyes told him Stacey would have found the analogy wholly appropriate. Something inside him ached at the thought.

"I want you to leave," she said.

Dylan kicked the door closed with his foot.

Her eyes widened. She stepped backward, and a flush rose beneath the gaping neckline of her robe, tinting the cleavage he remembered so well a nice shade of pink. The heck with looking at the room. He liked watching her more.

She advanced toward him. "Get out of here."

Dylan wasn't sure if she realized exactly how menacingly she'd started whirling the hair dryer again. Probably not.

"Don't you understand? Take a walk," she went on.

Ginger's tail popped from beneath his trench coat. It started wagging.

"Scram. I don't wa—" Stacey snapped her mouth shut, staring at the fluffy, golden-colored tail beating against his hip. "*What* have you got under there?"

He lowered Ginger to the carpet and pulled off his coat. Free at last, the dog sneezed and trotted over to have a good sniff of their new companion. Her tail wagged so fast it made her whole hind end shake.

"You had to say the 'W' word, didn't you?" Dylan asked.

"'W' word?" Stacey's eyebrows dipped. Absently, she crouched beside his dog and patted her head.

With a blissful closing of her doggie eyes, Ginger rolled on her back. All four furry legs lolled in the air.

"Yeah, don't say it a—"

"What do you . . . ?" Her eyes brightened. "Oh, *walk*!"

Yip!

Ginger tried to scramble onto four paws. She thunked her muzzle on the carpet, looked vaguely confused, then made it upright. From tail to whiskers, her whole body quivered with undisguised canine glee. Walk—walk—walk.

Dylan shook his head. "Sorry, girl," he told her. "Not right now." Crossing his arms, he looked at Stacey. "I had enough trouble just smuggling her in here. What'd you have to go and do that for?"

"Sorry. I didn't know." She bent to the dog, crooning as she smoothed her hand over Ginger's fur and scratched beneath her muzzle. "Sorry to get you all worked up for nothing," she told the dog.

She glanced up at Dylan, her eyes clear, golden brown . . . and suspicious. "Whose is she?"

"What do you mean, 'whose is she?' She's mine." He crouched near the bathroom door and whistled. "Come here, Ginger."

The damned traitorous dog rolled her eyes and licked Stacey's hand. Not so much as a tail thump indicated she'd heard him.

"Ginger. Come."

She sprawled heavily atop Stacey's feet, nearly toppling her over. Stacey grinned for the first time, presumably at his failure to make even a dog listen to him, and went on petting her.

Dylan snapped his fingers. "Come."

The dog yawned, stretching her muzzle wide. She plunked her head on the carpet and closed her eyes.

"Smart dog," Stacey observed. "More women ought to try resisting you like that."

"Ha, ha."

She grinned. With a final crooning pat, she left Ginger in a contented heap and crossed the room toward him. Dylan watched her, mentally gauging his chances of being treated as kindly as the dog.

Judging by his reception so far, they were pretty bleak.

"Seriously," Stacey said. "Who'd you borrow her from?"

"What do you mean, who'd I borrow her from? She's mine."

"Yours." She snorted and glanced back at Ginger. "Right."

"I'm hurt." Dylan did his best to look it. "Why can't I have a dog?"

She tightened the belt on her robe and scrutinized him through narrowed eyes. The hair dryer still poked from beneath her elbow, but Stacey hardly needed it. Her icy composure was all the defense required. Dylan practically felt himself shrink a couple of inches just standing there.

"You're not the dog-owning type," she said simply.

As though that actually explained anything, she rocked back on her heels and waited for him to answer. *Bet you can't*, her expression said.

Bet I can, he thought.

Dylan stepped nearer, close enough to sense the candy-cane-scented dampness on her skin. Close enough to touch her. God, how he wanted to touch her.

"I've changed," he said.

Her head came up, sending her ponytail swinging. "I don't believe you."

"I can convince you." He pried the hair dryer from beneath her elbow and shoved it safely on the foyer table where he could keep an eye on it. "Let me convince you, Stacey. I'm not leaving until the weekend's over. I promised Richard and Janie. So you might as well give me another try."

Two

Give him another try.

It really *was* Dylan. No one else would have had the guts to make a statement like that, especially after all that had happened between them. Besides, it was just like him to barge into *her* honeymoon charade and try to take over.

Stacey glanced past his lean, jeans-clad hip at the blow-dryer, wishing she still had the semblance of protection it offered. She needed protection—against the hurt of getting involved again, against the loss of identity doing so had led to before. *Against him.*

Dylan Davis. A guy who could break your heart with one hand and still make you want him with the other.

"No way." She shook her head, squinting up at him. "Huh-huh."

Holding her head high, she stepped briskly past him to open the suite's door. The faint spicy musk of the soap he used wafted to her as she passed. The memories it engendered made her stupid heart beat faster . . . even though experience had told her exactly how hopeless such a reaction really was. But she just couldn't help it.

And that was all the more reason for Dylan to leave.

"I want you to go." Stacey opened the door and nodded toward the opening. Her knees wobbled, but her robe hid the telltale motion from him. Thank God. "I don't know how you knew I was here, and I don't care. I just want you gone."

"Why?"

With apparent casualness, Dylan stepped closer and propped one big hand on the wall beside her head. His shirttail, typically untucked, brushed across the front of her robe. She had to crane her neck upward to see him clearly. Even then, the masculine breadth of his shoulders and chest filled her vision.

Her gaze caught and held on his haphazardly buttoned shirt placket. One of the buttons had slipped partway from its buttonhole. She automatically began to stick it back where it belonged, to make him look more like the successful software engineer he was and less like a person who got dressed in the dark.

To take care of him, like the idiot she'd be if she let him back into her life again.

She shoved her hands in her robe pockets instead. He'd probably left it that way on purpose, knowing it would drive her nuts.

"'Why?'" she repeated, squinting up at him. "'Why?' Maybe because you're smothering me, that's why."

She meant it as a joke. The strangled laugh that came with it wrecked the punch line. Scowling, she pushed herself against the wall, wishing she could disappear into the stylish wallpaper.

What was Dylan doing looming over her, anyway? He couldn't have proved her point better if he'd tried. Men never could leave well enough alone. They had to be in charge of everything. All the time.

After Charlie, she just wanted to be on her own for a while. Was that so wrong?

No, it wasn't. And she'd be damned if she'd let Dylan Davis back her into a wall like this. Literally.

"You ought to stick with zippers," she muttered, poking at his shirt placket as an excuse to move forward again. *Coward*, she told herself. "You look as if you got dressed wearing mittens."

Dylan made a face. He tucked his chin to his chest to try to see what she was pointing at.

Too quickly, he stopped. "You look as if *you're* trying to scare me away," he said, tilting his head sideways to study her.

She felt like a bug under a microscope. Pinned.

"I can't help it if you dress like an eight-year-old." Hating the way her voice quavered when he came closer, Stacey gestured vaguely at his close-cropped, dark-haired head. "Look. Your hair's all sticking up on one side, too."

The pathetic thing was, on him it looked pretty cute. But there was no way she'd admit it.

"I left the top down on the Jeep. I wasted no time getting here." Dylan scooped his hand under her chin and tilted her face upward. "Finding you."

His hand felt warm and solid and two hundred percent as good as she remembered. Stacey wavered, her knees wobbling harder—and so far, he'd only touched her chin. She had to get him out of there.

She jerked her chin from his palm. "Look, you dumped me, okay? I'm over it. We didn't click—"

"Oh, we clicked, all right—"

"And anyway, I've only been divorced from Charlie for a couple of—"

"Charlie was a jerk."

"—months." This wasn't working. He wasn't even listening to her. Just like her ex-husband. *Retreat*, she decided. Tossing her head, Stacey tried to step backwards.

The wall stopped her. Damn. She'd forgotten all about it.

Dylan cupped her cheek in his palm and lowered his gaze to her lips. "Scared?"

Oh, boy. She remembered that expression of his—remembered it too well. He planned to kiss her. Unfortunately, part of her craved exactly that.

"No. Smart," she shot back. "You've got a wandering eye, Dylan. Sooner or later, your hands and heart would have followed. I don't need the heartache. It's just as well we ended it when we did."

Actually, *he'd* ended it. But the illusion of a friendly, adult agreement strongly appealed to her pride. No point in whining.

Dylan's expression sobered. His gaze slid upward from her lips to her eyes. While she should have been glad at that small sign of progress, Stacey couldn't manage it.

"I'm not your worthless ex-husband. Give me a chance to prove it."

"No."

"Come on," he coaxed. "It's almost Christmastime. Consider it an early Christmas present?"

Oh, boy. Now he looked extra irresistible, like a kid on Christmas morning: all big, dreamy eyes and contagious eagerness.

"No." She ducked beneath his upraised arm, diving for the open doorway. Anything to put a little distance between them. Something big and lumpy on the floor blocked her path. A towel, she supposed. Giving it a hearty kick and a stomp, Stacey headed into the hallway.

Behind her, Dylan yelped and grabbed his foot.

Geez, the woman was as dangerous as he remembered.

Clutching his toe, Dylan hopped to the doorway of the honeymoon suite. In the hallway, gilded by the light of a sconce behind her, Stacey glared at him with her arms folded across the front of her robe. Beside him, Ginger poked her muzzle between his knee and the doorjamb and stared out, too.

Then she trotted onto the red and beige harlequin-patterned carpet to join Stacey.

Rejected by his woman. Betrayed by his dog. It didn't get much lower than this.

From down the hall came a faint ding. Dylan turned his head toward the sound, then realized it was the elevator stopping on their floor. Great. He looked at Ginger, busily scratching her ear, then toward the bank of elevators. If anybody spotted him with a dog in the hotel, they'd throw him out for sure.

He'd never get close to Stacey that way.

"Ginger. Come!"

Her tail thumped. Her paws didn't. The mechanical swish of the elevator doors opening echoed down the hallway. Two elderly women carrying Fashion Show Mall shopping bags and a man in a bellman's uniform got off. They clustered briefly in front of the mirrors opposite the elevators.

"Ginger, come on." Dylan squatted in the doorway and snapped his fingers. The dog didn't move. Hell. Standing, he reached for her collar.

With a toothy doggie grin, Ginger wagged her tail and shuffled closer to Stacey, just out of his reach. The movement earned her a pat on the head and a crooned, "Good dog."

Down the hall, the two women pushed the elevator buttons again and got on the next car that stopped. But the bellman started down the hall toward the honeymoon suite.

Stacey turned her head, saw the bellman approach—and smiled. "You're out of here," she said to Dylan.

She was going to squeal on him. And since Ginger was stuck to her side like Velcro, there wasn't a damned thing he could do to get the dog out of sight before the bellman got there.

Unless it involved getting Stacey inside the room first.

"That's what you think." Leaning forward, Dylan grabbed Stacey's elbow and hauled her up against him.

She whacked into his chest with a surprised whoosh of breath. He held both her arms, keeping her close, then glanced down. Predictably, Ginger trotted into the room. Success!

"Hey!" Stacey looked down at the dog wagging beside her, then up at Dylan. Her eyes widened.

Looking fiercely determined, she sucked in a big breath and got ready—ready to yell for the bellman, Dylan felt sure.

"Oh, no you don't." He pinned her arms to the wall and kicked the door closed. Before she could do so much as squeak, he brought his mouth down hard on hers.

At least it started out hard. The second their lips met, though, the kiss took on a softness all its own. His fingers tightened on the silkiness of her wrists, and his wits went walking. To heck with shutting her up. This was what he really needed. Moaning, Dylan pressed against her, demanded more . . . and got it.

Stacey's bare foot slammed into his shin. Pain shimmied toward his ankle.

"Youch!" he bellowed, releasing her with a glare.

"Oww!" she echoed, glaring back at him. She raised her foot, wiggled her big toe, and scowled at his shins. "What are those made of, solid steel?"

"I'm supposed to apologize because you hurt yourself *kicking* me?" The ache in his shin flared along with the words. He wanted to rub it away, but he'd be damned if he'd show any weakness in front of her. "You've got to be kidding me."

"That wasn't just kicking. It was self-defense."

"Yeah, just like the blow-dryer attack was on purpose." Dylan shook his head. *"That* was kicking."

Her robe billowing behind her, she flounced toward the door. She swung it open and stuck out her head. "Excuse me! Bellma—"

Dylan yanked her inside. "Look. Do you want to get us both kicked out of this place?"

"No. Just you."

Stacey shook her arm from his grasp. The movement made her robe twist crookedly around her middle. Jerking it straight again, she tied the belt tight enough to make him wince.

"I'm serious, Dylan. Nothing you can say will make me give you another chance. Your timing stinks, and I've got a honeymoon charade to worry about. You're not invited. Get it?"

"Are you sure?"

"Aaarrgh!" Stomping past him to the bathroom, she picked up the phone from the vanity. "Either quit manhandling me and get out of here," she said, waggling the receiver toward him, "or I'm calling security."

Dylan folded his arms and leaned against the doorjamb. *Nice tub,* he noticed, peering inside the pink marble room. *Big enough for two.* "Do you really want to do that?"

She blew out an exasperated breath. "What is it with you? Learn to take no for an answer." Ducking her head, Stacey punched zero on the phone and raised it to her ear.

Damn. He was blowing it again.

He lurched forward to pluck the receiver from her hand

and felt himself skidding across the marble instead. Sudsy water squeaked beneath his shoes. Arms pinwheeling, he tried to keep his balance. Stacey's surprised face flashed in front of him. A second later, he landed in a heap at her feet.

This was some kind of stellar impression he was making.

"Be—because," he stammered, trying to look comfortable on the floor with water seeping into his jeans, "if you really want to carry off this honeymoon pretense for Janie, I can help you."

She clicked off the phone. "How?"

Ice cold. Because he'd hurt her, Dylan knew, and regretted every moment since they'd split. He'd played his cards wrong, ducked out of the game just as it heated up—and all because of Janie's cockamamie theory that Stacey wanted to keep things light after her divorce. No serious relationships.

Naturally, what had he done? Fallen in love with her. Their timing couldn't have been worse. Dylan had figured he'd get over her if they spent some time apart. Instead, the distance had only made him realize he'd been an idiot to let her go.

He looked up at her. "I'll be your husband."

"My husband?" She couldn't have heard him right. Stacey stared down at Dylan, tapping the phone against her shoulder. "What do you mean?"

It was *so* hard not to crouch down beside him and make sure he was okay. If anyone knew exactly how hard that marble floor was, it was Stacey. Her backside was intimately acquainted with it. Dylan's descent had *looked* funny, but it must have hurt.

He shifted his weight and got to his feet, wincing at the effort. She doubted he realized it, though. Dylan was a classic tough guy. Too brawny to show any weakness to a mere woman.

The big baby.

"I mean, *you're* supposed to be Janie. In the honeymoon suite, right?" He leaned on one foot as though favoring an injury and propped his hand on the vanity. Deftly, he slipped the phone from her grasp and replaced it in its stand.

Stacey frowned. "Are you . . . ?"

Okay? she'd been about to ask.

No. He was the one who'd barged in, totally uninvited, and started bossing her around. She refused to feel sorry for him.

"—serious?" she finished instead. "I suppose *you* want to be Richard?"

"Yeah. I talked to Richard and Janie before they left. I volunteered to help."

I'll bet. Breaking her heart once hadn't been enough for him, apparently. What kind of weird ego trip was that?

He wasn't getting a second crack at her. First she was getting him out of this room, then she was getting on with the honeymoon charade. By herself. Period.

Stuffing her hands in her pockets to keep from reaching out to steady Dylan, Stacey skirted past him. "I don't need help. I was handling things just fine until you got here."

She reached the suite's sitting area, chose one of the austere white-upholstered chairs, and flopped on it. Ginger followed her. Naturally, so did Dylan.

He settled opposite her and rested his forearms loosely on his thighs. The motion made her gaze wander over those hard-muscled legs, those lightly tanned arms . . . . *Whoa.* Forcing her gaze upward, Stacey met his eyes.

He grinned. The rat. He must have caught her gawking at him.

"Tell me that kiss didn't affect you," he said.

"It didn't affect me," she lied. Truth was, it was the greatest kiss she'd had all week. All month.

It was the greatest kiss, the *only* kiss, she'd had since their breakup, but Stacey was hardly going to admit that to him. The last thing she needed was to encourage a guy like Dylan, a guy who was even bossier than Charlie had been—and who was twice as hard to resist.

She was only just beginning to crawl out from under the dark, stifling blanket of her ex-marriage. Being married had sent her identity so far underground, just getting her own credit card had been an ordeal. She still didn't own a car. After four years of gradually sliding deeper and deeper into Charlie's life, her own interests seemed alien to her. So did making her own choices.

She didn't need Dylan around mucking things up.

"It didn't affect me." This time, she dared to meet his eyes. They sparkled back at her, green and intelligent and filled with a good humor she longed to possess. "So you might as well leave. Satisfied?"

"Not yet."

He leaned forward, making his meaning plain. *Not satisfied . . . but he meant to be.* And the thing was, she'd bet he'd satisfy *her*, too. It had been a struggle not to sleep with him before, when they were dating. She'd wanted to. But just when Stacey had decided to make her big move, Dylan had called it quits.

Now, alone together in a hotel room with no divorcée date protocol to put the brakes on things, who knew what could happen?

Why couldn't she just be immune to him? It would make everything so much easier. But her stupid thumping pulse rate made a lie of her wish.

"I promised Richard and Janie I'd stay the whole weekend," he said. "So you might as well accept my help. I'm not leaving."

That's what you think. Stacey opened her mouth to tell him so, but a strange scraping at the door made her pause. What if someone was listening? She could hardly be caught arguing with her "husband" on her honeymoon.

She peered around the gaily decorated cookies on the table. A long white envelope slid beneath the honeymoon suite door and dropped on the carpet.

Probably a room service menu or something, she decided. It gave her an idea.

"Why don't we go out to dinner and talk things over?" *That way, I can get you out of my room and out of my life.* "That way, we can, ahh—"

"Don't you want to see what that is?" Dylan interrupted, nodding toward the envelope at the door.

She waved it away. "Later. So, what do you say? We could, ummm, discuss strategy."

He stared at the envelope. "It looks like a note. Are you sure?"

Geez, he was like a dog with a bone. Why did he always assume she didn't know what she wanted?

"Positive." Stacey fought an urge to glare at him. "Because if we're really going to do this, what we need is a strategy. A honeymoon pretense strategy."

Dylan raised his eyebrows. Stacey raised hers, too, trying to seem as though she actually meant to leave the hotel room with him.

"It might be important," he said.

"Aaarrgh!" He hadn't come to help. He'd come to drive her crazy. She stood, slapping her hands onto her thighs. Ginger bounded over, tail wagging.

"If you're so curious, *you* go look," Stacey said, glancing curiously at the dog.

At her feet, Ginger flopped both paws playfully onto the carpet and buried her muzzle between them. She peeked up at Stacey, her tail sweeping with impressive speed from her upraised waggling rump.

She looked from Ginger to Dylan. "What's with her?"

"She thinks you want to play." Silently, he mimicked her thigh slap. "I think she likes you more than me," he added forlornly.

"Oh, I don't know about that. You——" *No.* She wasn't going to be nice to him. She had to stay on course. "Umm, what about dinner?"

As an answer, he went to the door and scooped up the envelope. It didn't do much to tell her his plans, but it did give her an excellent opportunity to watch him unobserved. So she crouched down to pet Ginger and did.

He caught her at it just as she reached hip level. "See anything you like?"

What wasn't to like? Rather than let him see the truth in her eyes—she did have some pride left—Stacey shrugged and flopped back into her chair. "Nothing I haven't seen before."

"Ouch!" Dylan shuddered, grinning as he handed the envelope in her direction. "You really know how to hurt a guy."

"Comes from dating guys who stand you up and leave you with four pounds of steak from the romantic dinner that wasn't." She turned the envelope. *Mr. and Mrs. Richard Parker*, it read in flowery script on the front. "My next-door-neighbor's dog was overjoyed, though."

Frowning, Stacey slit the envelope. Out fell a glossy brochure, two pairs of tickets, something that looked like a detailed itinerary, and a note written on a piece of embossed stationery.

"Oh, no." She turned over the brochure. The words *Romantic Escapades* leaped from the page in inch-high letters, above a picture of a carefree couple strolling hand in hand along the beach. Dropping it like the time bomb it was, Stacey picked up the letter instead.

Surprise! it began. *Dear Janie and Richard . . .*

"Oh, no. It's another honeymoon surprise."

Dylan leaned over her shoulder. His arm came partway around her to rest on her chair's arm for balance. Even worse, his lips brushed past her ear. At the feel of their soft heat, a shiver raced through her.

Oh, boy.

"Aunt Geraldine's got some bag of tricks." He read along with her. "Show tickets, golf passes, his-and-hers massages . . . and what's this?" He picked up a foil-inlaid invitation card. "Free psychic readings for couples. Wow."

"Aunt Geraldine's into that stuff," Stacey muttered.

What was she going to do now? The "couples weekend" her aunt had arranged for Janie and Richard could only work with—let's face it—a couple.

"I wonder what she'll say about us," Dylan mused.

"Who?"

"The psychic." He bent his head lower, ostensibly to examine the card. His jaw smoothed warmly past her cheek. "I'll bet she says we belong together."

"We're already together. We're the honeymoon couple." Whoops. Had she already accepted his plan? Having him so near only scrambled her thoughts. "I mean—"

"I know what you mean." He leaned to the side and grinned at her. "After this, you've got no choice but to draft somebody to be the happy groom."

Stacey tapped the brochure against her lips and gave him a suspicious look. "Did you arrange this?"

"Me?"

"I wouldn't put it past you. You probably rented Ginger, too, just to make a good impression."

"Rented?"

"Well, why not?" She gestured toward the dog, improvising madly. "Why bring her, when you know they don't allow dogs in the hotel?"

Hey, that wasn't bad. She was holding her own with Dylan. Maybe she *could* handle a whole weekend alone with him. Stacey crossed her arms and legs, wishing she had on something more substantial than bathrobe and bare skin.

"Hmmm?" she prompted.

He slipped to the front of the chair and bent to gently cup her shoulders in his hands. Shaking his head as though she couldn't be farther off-base if she tried, Dylan said, "Let's be realistic, okay? I don't think—"

"Hmmm?" She cocked her head, considering tapping her foot for good measure. *Patronize me, will ya?* Charlie had tried that tactic, too. Every time she was right about something.

Dylan made a face. "How about that dinner?"

"Delaying won't work," Stacey warned. His gaze dipped to the neckline of her robe, and she added, "Neither will that."

He grinned. "Can't fault a guy for trying."

What was he hiding? "Well?"

"Ginger goes just about everyplace with me," he finally said, lowering his hands from her shoulders and looking embarrassed. "If I leave her home, she goes into some kind of doggie tantrum."

"Hmmm. Must be spoiled."

She might have said "worthless" or "stupid," given the aggrieved look he gave her. Stacey bit her lower lip and glanced at Ginger. "Sorry."

Dylan gazed at the dog fondly. "She's not spoiled, but I think she had a rough upbringing." As though sensing his attention, Ginger got up and trotted to him. She nudged his hand with her nose, and he patted her between the ears. "She's a stray. Turned up in the office parking lot a month or so ago, skinny as a stick, matted with dirt. No collar."

He puckered his lips at the dog, blowing her a kiss as he petted her. It was an unconscious motion, Stacey felt sure. Something inside her softened because of it.

Dylan straightened, blinking like somebody walking into the summer sunlight. "Nobody claimed her, so I kept her."

"You rescued her, you big softie." Stacey couldn't keep a silly grin from her face. "I didn't know you had it in you."

"I'll rescue you, too, if you'll let me. You need help with this honeymoon thing, especially now with Aunt Geraldine's latest surprise."

Stacey bit her lip. If she didn't pull off the honeymoon charade well enough to convince Aunt Geraldine that Janie and Richard had used and enjoyed her wedding gift surprise, it would cause no end of family feuds. She did need help.

But why, of all the men in the universe, did it have to come in the form of Dylan Davis?

"I don't know. Maybe I can just hide out here in the honeymoon suite until the weekend's over. I'll mail Aunt Geraldine a few hotel postcards from Janie and Richard, and that'll be that."

Dylan's gaze dropped to the pile of tickets, brochure, and itinerary in her lap. "Your aunt knows most of these people, remember? She'll know it if nobody collects on the rest of her 'surprise'."

He was right. *They're mostly old friends and they'll treat you right*, Aunt Geraldine had said in her note. *Just because they gave me a discount, doesn't mean you two newlyweds will have less fun.* Even the psychic was a personal friend.

Stacey sighed. "You're right."

"I know." He braced his hands on the chair's arms and gave her a serious look. "So, do we have a deal?"

Three

He was in.

Well, mostly in, Dylan amended to himself as he strolled beside Stacey an hour later into the neighboring hotel where their dinner-show reservations had been made. Mostly in, because she'd only agreed to let him stay for one night. On the honeymoon suite sofa. Wearing pajamas, if possible. And only on the condition he didn't make any moves on her when they got back to their room.

He'd agreed. At this point, those were all the concessions Stacey was likely to make. He'd work on the rest later.

After all, she hadn't said anything about not making any moves *before* then.

Grinning, Dylan put his hand to the small of her back and guided her through the hotel's enormous casino. Like every other resort hotel in Las Vegas—heck, like every supermarket and fast food joint—the Renaissance had its share of slot machines. Then some. Beneath gothic-style arches and rows of flashing lights, gamblers stood cheek by jowl, scooping up the coins jangling into the slot machines' bins.

"That's how Aunt Geraldine won her fortune." Stacey pointed to one of them. "She used to take the tour buses up here with my Uncle Bert almost every month . . . before he passed away last year, I mean," she added, looking wistful. "They had so much fun together."

Dylan slid his arm to her waist and hugged her closer. Amazingly enough, she let him.

"They got married here, did you know?" she asked. "In one of those wedding chapels down on the Strip."

"Maybe that's why she wanted Janie and Richard to have a honeymoon in Vegas."

She smiled up at him, leaving him with the distinct impression that, finally, he'd said something right. Dylan wanted to rack his brain to repeat the accomplishment. The trouble was, he was as clueless about what made that the *right* thing to say as he was about what made his usual comments the *wrong* thing to say. He settled for the guy-tested method of keeping quiet and nodding thoughtfully.

"I think you're right," she said. "Sweet, isn't it?"

They neared the mammoth slot machine she spoke of, one big enough to merit its own pedestal and spot lighting at the end of the row. Her fingertips grazed its metallic face.

"This isn't the machine she won on, of course." Stacey paused beside the slot machine to gaze upward at the Renaissance's brightly colored medieval banners and beyond them to the suits of armor posed nearby. "This hotel wasn't built then."

She stopped, frowning slightly. "You know, that's odd. I would have expected Aunt Geraldine to arrange the honeymoon surprises at some of the older hotels, the ones she was familiar with. Not one that's as nearly new as this one."

Ding—ding—ding. The warning bells in his head were totally appropriate, Dylan knew. But that didn't mean he had to like the little buggers. If Stacey guessed the truth already . . .

Tightening his hold on her waist, he swept her against him fast enough to make her dressy black dress flare up behind her. He had to make her quit questioning the honeymoon surprises, and he had to do it now.

"Let's try it." He whirled her in his arms so they stood side by side, facing the slot machine. He scrounged in his pockets for change, turning out his wallet, his hotel key card, and two gold-wrapped condoms.

Stacey raised her eyebrows at the condoms. "Try what?"

"Well, I've never gotten lucky atop a giant slot machine," he deadpanned, pretending to consider the idea, "but I'm game if you are."

"Sorry. I'm afraid of heights."

"Afraid of heights?" Dylan pocketed everything again. *At least she'd quit wondering about the rationale behind Aunt Geraldine's honeymoon surprises.* "We need a smaller model, then. How about we climb up on that row over there?"

He nodded toward the row he spoke of, where a gray-haired lady wearing a purple silk jogging outfit busily fed quarters into two machines at once.

"Let's not." Stacey scanned the glittering row of machines and the woman in front of them. "She looks like my grandmother."

"Always a mood breaker." Scooping his arm around her waist again, Dylan approached the monster slot machine. "Come on. It'll be fun. Maybe we'll win."

"I really think we ought to keep a low profile. And what about our dinner reservations? We'll be late for the show."

"Quit worrying. Here. You go first." He handed her a twenty and nodded toward the bill-feeder on the face of the slot machine. "You just slide it in, like the change machines at the Laundromat."

"Laundromat? You mean you're actually that domesticated? I thought you still took your laundry home to mom."

"Ha, ha."

"First a dog rescue and now this. Wow." Stacey made a deliberately sappy face at him, but made no move to take the money. "I swear, you might turn out okay yet."

"Enough with the dog. I'm already okay. If you'd quit looking out for Generic Faithless Male Scum, you might see that."

She cast her gaze downward. "I—"

"Never mind. Let's gamble." He slid the money into the tray himself and rubbed his palms together as the machine racked up their twenty-dollar credit. "This one looks lucky to me."

"It looks like a good way for us to get into trouble to me."

Nervously, Stacey glanced around them. "Let's just get on with the honeymoon surprises, okay? Dinner-show first."

"Come on, try it. Pull the handle."

She stepped backward. "Nobody ever wins on these big machines." She glanced toward the stairs that led to the dinner-show theater. "They're just for show."

"Tell it to that guy." Dylan pointed at the poster-sized photo of the previous twenty-five-thousand dollar winner displayed beside the slot machine. "He looks pretty happy with this loser slot machine of yours."

Nibbling her lower lip, Stacey looked at the picture.

"Aunt Geraldine would be proud." Dylan gave her a little push forward. "Come on, you pull the handle first."

"We should try to be inconspicuous."

"Then you shouldn't have worn that sexy dress."

She rolled her eyes. "If I try it, will you try to keep a low profile for the rest of the night?"

"Do you really think that's the best way to carry off this honeymoon imposter thing?"

She nodded. She also stroked the slot machine handle. Something about the way she wrapped her hand around it made his brains go south.

"Okay." He held up two fingers. "Low profile. Scout's honor."

"Good." Stacey wrapped her other hand around the handle, raised on her sandaled tiptoes, and squeezed her eyes shut. Poised there, she started moving her lips.

Dylan leaned closer to listen. He heard only the Muzak "Jingle Bell Rock" chorus and the din of the casino surrounding them. She wasn't even whispering, just moving her lips as though carrying on a conversation with the gold ball at the top of the slot machine handle.

He peered curiously at her face. "What are you—"

She yanked the handle down and the whir of the machine cut off his question. They both stepped backward, watching the mechanism spin. Two cherries snapped into place on the winning line. Two more cherries. He heard Stacey suck in her breath.

A lemon.

"Maybe next time you ought to kiss it first, instead of chanting at it," Dylan said. "Or else talk loud enough for the machine to hear."

She looked sideways at him. "I was wishing for good luck."

"Then next time it's bound to work."

Grinning with enthusiasm, she grabbed the handle again. She raised on tiptoes, closed her eyes . . . then cracked one open to look at him. "Do you want to do it this time?"

"Nah." It was too much fun watching her, anyway. "Go ahead. We've still got fifteen dollars left."

"Okay."

She closed her eyes, got herself settled, and started moving her lips. Dylan leaned closer, wishing he'd learned to read lips.

She pulled the lever. It spun madly. Three utterly mismatched fruits clicked in place along the line.

"Rats." Stacey flopped flat-footed again and looked up at him. "I thought we had it that time. Why don't you try?"

Dylan stepped forward. He positioned himself like one of those guys with a mallet at the test-your-strength machine at the county fair and yanked the handle.

"Yup, that ought to do it." He hooked his thumbs in his belt loops, then stepped back so there'd be plenty of room for their winnings to spill out.

This time, the items that came up weren't fruit. They weren't even all on the fruit level of the food pyramid. He and Stacey frowned at the display, then at the five dollar credit remaining.

"Let's do it together," they said in unison.

She grinned at him as they reached for the handle, and Dylan felt a great surge of solidarity. So what if they were a couple of gambling fiends who couldn't make it to dinner on time? At least they were together.

They pulled. Stepped back. The slot machine spun.

A silver dollar plunked in the coin tray.

"Whoopee!" Stacey threw herself against his chest, jumping up and down with glee. "We won, we won, we won!"

Dylan held her about as well as he could while dancing a jig. This winning was heady stuff. So was the feel of Stacey tight against him, trembling with excitement. He wanted more.

The purple jogging suit lady leaned over to congratulate them. "You kids won because you worked together." She winked. "That's the secret."

"Do you think so?" Stacey asked her.

Grinning, she clutched Dylan's arm with both hands and leaned into it, apparently unaware of her position. One flex of his biceps, and he'd know if her silky dress fabric was really as thin as it looked. He'd also know whether or not she had anything on underneath it—not to mention what temperature the room was.

Grow up, he told himself. Enough with regressing back to ninth grade. Tamping down the urge to flex, Dylan nodded in what he hoped was a thoughtful and mature manner and tried to get in on the conversation again.

"Everybody says there aren't any real tricks to winning at gambling," Stacey was saying.

"Not just gambling, honey," the purple jogging suit lady said. "Life, too." She propped her plastic casino cup of coins against her ample hip and looked them up and down. "But you two look like a good pair."

Great opening. "We're newlyweds," Dylan volunteered. "Just got married this morning, in fact."

"Oh! Congratulations!" Mrs. Purple Suit's expression turned dreamy, like women's always did when confronted with babies or puppies or anything else that was really, really tiny.

If women liked small things so much, then why were guys so worried about the size of their—

"That's wonderful!" she gushed. "Just wonderful!"

"Thanks." He tried to ignore the dagger-laced look Stacey threw him. What was the matter with her, anyway? This was the perfect opportunity to cement their honeymoon façade. "We're on our honeymoon, in fact," he went on, hugging Stacey tighter.

Her elbow jabbed his rib.

"Huh—" came his breath. "Huh, huh, huh," Dylan said,

trying to turn it into a laugh. "Yep, just me and the missus, on our honeymoon over at the Atmosphere."

Me and the missus? He'd morphed into Ward Cleaver all of a sudden.

Mrs. Purple Suit didn't appear to notice. Her gaze turned to Stacey, and her smile broadened. "Don't you want to show me your ring, honey? I couldn't wait to show off mine."

Stacey stiffened beside him. A ring! What ring? They hadn't thought of that. As unobtrusively as he could, Dylan tucked her left hand in his rear jeans pocket.

"Awww, we don't want to brag, do we honey?" he said through another Cleaver-bright grin. He felt like the bumbling husband character in a TV sitcom.

"I don't know if I'd call it bragging."

Stacey tried to wriggle her hand out of his pocket. Keeping his smile intact, Dylan clamped his hand on her wrist.

She leaned toward the purple jogging suit lady and whispered, "He's a little self-conscious about . . . its size."

"I am not!"

They both smiled sympathetically at him.

"Really!"

Mrs. Purple Jogging Suit patted him on the shoulder. "It's all right. Everybody's got to start somewhere."

"That's what I told him." Stacey smiled serenely as she wormed her fingers around in his back pocket. "It's not the size that counts, I said, it's—"

It's ticklish. "It's really not that big a deal," Dylan interrupted.

"Oh, I understand," the woman said. "Lots of men are that way. You know, some women think the small ones are endearing."

"Do you really think so?" Stacey asked innocently.

Her fingers wriggled amongst the stuff in his pocket. Another second, and she'd get her hand loose enough to flash her nonexistent wedding ring. Dylan tried to hold her wrist tighter.

She goosed him.

"Yeow!" Both women looked at him, eyebrows raised. Stacey had the gall to smirk, too. "Oww, oww, oww," he went on, letting go of her wrist to glare at his watch as though *that* had somehow caused all the ruckus.

"Look at the time." He shook his head with what he hoped looked less like an overwhelming urge to pinch his "wife" and more like husbandly concern. "We'll be late if we don't get going, Snookums."

Stacey batted her eyelashes at him. He hadn't even known women could actually *do* that outside of cartoons.

"In a minute, Pudding," she cooed. Regally, she extended her hand, knuckles facing. Dylan closed his eyes.

Inconspicuous, she'd said. *Let's keep a low profile,* she'd said. And here she was, flashing her embarrassingly bare knuckles at a total stranger.

"Awww," the purple jogging suit lady said. "That *is* sweet. Congratulations again."

Dylan opened his eyes.

The purple jogging suit lady turned to leave, shaking her cup of quarters. "Good luck, you two. I'd better get back to it before my luck turns cold."

"Nice meeting you," Stacey called, waving.

Dylan only stared at the diamond and gold wedding band flashing on her finger beneath the casino's brilliant lights.

"Where did you get *that*?" he asked, glancing up to make sure Mrs. Jogging Suit had reached her slot machines again. She had. He grabbed Stacey's hand to make her quit waving, then scowled down at the ring on her finger. "Well?"

"You didn't think I'd try to pull off this honeymoon ruse totally unprepared, did you?" she asked, batting her eyelashes some more.

He squinted at the ring, then at her. "You didn't even think to bring along a pretend husband for this honeymoon ruse," he pointed out. "How well-prepared could you have been?"

Stacey puckered her lips, appeared to think about it, then pulled her hand out of reach.

"It was from Charlie," she admitted. "I used to be married, remember?" Turning, she scooped up their silver dollar winnings. "Come on. We're already late for dinner." She tossed the coin to him.

Dylan caught it and followed her toward the dinner theater

entrance. "Why do you still wear your wedding ring? You've been divorced for months."

Did she still care about her ex-husband? Was that why she didn't want to get involved with him again? Hell. Why couldn't anything be easy with her?

Stacey stopped at the edge of the stairway leading to the theater just as he caught up with her. She gazed thoughtfully at him, and a strange expression crossed her face. Then she shrugged.

"Why shouldn't I wear it? I like it."

"It's puny."

She smiled at him—one of those irritating, superior smiles only a beautiful woman wearing heels and a skimpy cocktail dress could give. *Mister, you're putty in my hands*, it seemed to say.

"Does it bother you? Because I could take it off if you're . . . jealous, or anything."

Was that hopefulness in her expression?

Nah. Just pleasure at teasing him, Dylan figured. He wrapped his arm around her waist and gave her an enigmatic smile of his own.

"No more than pretending to be my wife bothers you." He guided her downstairs to the dinner theater. "And you seem to be handling *that* pretty well. So, are you hungry? Let's eat."

Dylan's hand slid onto her knee for the fourth time just as the Renaissance's special medieval dinner was served.

Stacey held her breath and looked down. His tanned, muscular arm stretched right across her lap with two hundred proof masculine assurance, and his hand cupped her knee as though it belonged there. Slowly, his fingers spread wider, then started inching up the inside of her thigh.

She waited for him to goose her the way he had the first two times. He didn't. Instead, his palm skimmed higher on her leg, then stopped just below the hem of her dress. Beneath it her skin prickled—not because the huge, arena-style theater was cold, or because the rustic wooden benches they sat on were too rough, or because of any other harmless thing she could name. Just because it was Dylan touching her. Dammit.

Their waiter approached, dressed in a laced-front medieval tunic, some sort of buccaneer sash, and brown leggings. Apparently somebody had decided a true "Middle Ages" look required lots of spandex. Stopping in front of the long wooden table she and Dylan sat at side by side with the rest of the show-goers, the waiter brandished a pitcher of something.

He smiled. "Shickenzoop?"

They both stared up at him. "Pardon me?" Stacey asked.

He twitched the pitcher. "Shickenzoop."

As though that explained anything, he mimicked pouring it into the teacup-sized pewter bowls in front of them.

She looked into her empty bowl. It, along with a matching pewter plate, a mug of water, and a heavy cloth napkin, had been at their table when they arrived. Dylan looked into his bowl, then at her.

"Shi—cken—zoop," repeated the waiter, scanning the long row of pewter bowls lining the rest of their table. He sighed, looking as though he might pour the contents of his pitcher on their heads if they didn't catch on pretty soon.

"Shi—cken—zoop," Stacey repeated, speaking slowly enough that he'd be sure to hear her plainly.

Dylan's lips nuzzled her ear. "Gib—ber—rish?" he whispered. His tentative tone matched hers perfectly.

"Cut it out," she whispered back, but she couldn't help smiling.

The waiter looked into his pitcher and nodded. "Shickenzoop." *That's what I said.*

"Sure. Why not?" Dylan pushed his bowl forward with his free hand. She felt his shrug all along her thigh as his arm moved with his shoulder. "We'd love some."

The waiter poured milky broth into their bowls, then moved on down the row. "Shickenzoop," he said loudly, like a peanut vendor at a ballgame. He stopped in front of the next couple at their table. "Schickenzoop?"

Interrupted in the middle of the tankard of ale they were sharing, they both looked at him with puzzled frowns. "What?"

"Just take it," Dylan said. "It's easier that way."

He turned his smile on Stacey and caught her in the middle of trying to twist her wedding ring from her finger. She started scratching furiously in the hope of faking a massive itch beneath the gold band.

He raised an eyebrow. "Allergic to rings? Or allergic to marriage? Or is it just that ring in particular that's giving you trouble?"

Actually, it was the fact that she couldn't wrest the darn thing from her finger that was giving her trouble. She'd gained a few pounds since her wedding to Charlie four years ago, but Stacey would rather die than admit her ring was too tight to take off.

She plunked her hands in her lap. "Acupressure," she mumbled, staring into her bowl of Shickenzoop. "Massaging your ring finger relieves stress."

"I know a lot of single guys who'd agree with you. They like to keep that area nice and limber. And unencumbered."

"You among them?" She picked up her bowl and sniffed, trying to seem as though his answer didn't matter one way or the other. *It didn't*, Stacey told herself. It was simply idle curiosity among friends that made her ask. Nothing more. What did it matter to her if he wanted to remain a bachelor the rest of his life?

"Are you kidding?" Dylan stroked his thumb over her bare thigh and gave her an exaggeratedly goofy grin. It was, she was beginning to realize, his "newlywed husband in love" look. "They could slap a pair of handcuffs on us and I wouldn't mind." He waggled his eyebrows suggestively. "There's nobody I'd rather be hog-tied to than you, babe."

"Hog-tied, huh? I'm flattered." She sipped from her cup, and Dylan did the same. The broth inside tasted salty, slightly meaty . . . she thought she even detected a noodle. Lowering her cup again, Stacey peered inside. So did Dylan.

"Shickenzoop," he said, "is . . ."

". . . chicken soup!" she finished, laughing. "No wonder the waiter looked at us so strangely."

The rest of the meal arrived in less cryptic form—savory roasted game hens, chunks of potatoes, broccoli spears, and individual loaves of crusty bread. The waiter served every-thing with an elegant dip of his medieval spandex-clad knee, then retreated as the lights lowered, signaling the beginning of the Renaissance's featured show.

"Excuse me!" Stacey called after him.

He turned. The linen cloth he carried over his bent arm whipped along with him, passing mere inches from another diner's eyebrows. She ducked, then glared toward the source of the trouble.

"Sorry!" Stacey called with a wave.

The waiter stopped in front of their table. Assuming his presence meant he was listening, she asked, "May I have some silverware, please? There doesn't seem to be any at my—"

"We don't use utensils in the Middle Ages." He glanced meaningfully at the other diners' place settings. They were all, Stacey saw, devoid of utensils. "Perhaps your . . ." His gaze shifted to Dylan, and he arched his eyebrows.

"Husband," Dylan supplied helpfully, wrapping his arm around Stacey's shoulders. "We're newlyweds."

"Husband can help you." With that suggestion, the waiter glided away from them—to retrieve his Shickenzoop pitcher, no doubt.

Biting her lip, Stacey examined her plate. Around her, the other diners had begun biting into tiny roast drumsticks and breaking off chunks of bread. Spotlights played over the arena and the packed-earth floor in its center. The show was about to begin.

"I guess we'd better make like newlyweds." Dylan scooted closer. He raised his hand, and something warm and spicy-smelling nudged her lips. A piece of roast chicken, she guessed.

"I—" As soon as her mouth opened he slipped the first bite between her lips, leaving her no choice but to chew. She did, and was surprised to find it tasted delicious. "Mmmm. It's good, but I—"

But I can't get a word in edgewise, between bites. Next came a piece of warm bread with butter. It melted in her mouth, rich and yeasty and exactly as chewy as good bread should be.

"Mmmm."

Dylan watched with a smile as she chewed and swallowed, then he used his thumb to brush away a crumb from the corner of her lips.

"Really, I can do it my—" she started to say, but he only shook his head and fed her a bite of herb-scented roast potato.

"We're newlyweds, remember?" he said. "We've got to make this look good. Besides, don't you find this romantic?"

Actually, considering the way he did it . . . she did. His attention was all for her, his actions focused on selecting just the right morsel to satisfy her, his gaze centered on her lips as he gave her one taste, then another. To be the focus of so much attention was more than Stacey had expected—more than she'd experienced in a long time, too. Maybe ever. At the end, she and Charlie had rarely shared meals together at all, much less tried anything like this. With a sexy half smile, Dylan broke off a thin spear of broccoli and brought it to her lips.

Yuck. Broccoli was way too ordinary for a setting like this. Raising her head, Stacey made a face and pressed her lips together.

"What, you don't like anything that's good for you?" Dylan followed her movements with the broccoli. Slowly, he drew it across her lower lip.

The sensuous glide of it nearly made her open her mouth without thinking. Good grief! Leave it to a guy like Dylan to figure out how to make vegetables sexy.

"And I had you pegged as a good-girl type," he teased, tracing the edge of her mouth again. "Still no? Then maybe you're in the mood for something a little more dangerous."

His gaze met hers. It felt as though he was seeing her, really *seeing* her, for the first time. The sense of discovery she saw in his eyes made her mouth go dry and her pulse beat faster. Around them, the lights dimmed all the way and festive Christmas-style show music began playing, but those things might have been a hundred miles away for all the notice Dylan paid them. He must have dropped the broccoli on her plate because she didn't feel it against her lips anymore, but Stacey didn't want to look away to find out.

"On the other hand, you and I have different ideas about what's dangerous, don't we?" he murmured, lifting his goblet of water from their tabletop. Ice cubes clinked together softly as he raised it between them, then swirled it. "To you, this is just water. Plain and cold and that's all. But to a man who hasn't drunk for hours, a thirsty man, it's everything he needs." His gaze joined with hers, then lowered again. "And to me, it's opportunity."

"Opportunity?"

"Mmmm-hmmm." Dylan stroked his fingertips against the goblet, leaving slippery trails of condensation on the glass.

He raised it higher, gazing into the water as though considering whatever opportunity he'd meant, then brought the goblet nearer to her. Stacey sensed its chill just above the bare skin at the neckline of her dress.

"Opportunity for sensation," he explained, raising it to her lips. "Maybe for you, that's a little dangerous." Slowly, he tipped it forward, allowing her to drink.

She did, knowing he watched her and feeling acutely aware of her reliance on him. Dylan knew her thirst, controlled the glass . . . and her satisfaction. The water slid down her throat. Shivering at the icy wetness of it, Stacey leaned forward for another sip.

He tilted it away. "More?" He watched her over the goblet's rim. She nodded, but still Dylan held it away. "Tell me what you want."

His low, rough voice sent a shiver through her.

"You have to tell me what you want, because it's all up to you. Everything." He leaned closer, and his body heat mingled with hers and the iciness of the water between them. "I have what you need. You only have to ask."

Stacey couldn't speak, couldn't move. This was more than thirst they spoke of, more than anything they'd shared so far. He was asking for her trust, offering her the freedom to choose what she wanted . . . and she didn't, she realized as she stared into the goblet, really know what that was.

"What you need depends on how you feel," Dylan went on, raising the goblet to her cheek in a sort of caress.

Cold bloomed where it touched her. Stacey gasped at the delicious sensation it aroused, automatically arching her neck to expose more of her overheated skin to the glass's icy touch.

He pressed it gently closer, lowered it to her throat, and goose bumps prickled along her arms in the wake of his movements.

"See? This feels twice as cold because you're so hot." He watched her, moving the goblet to her lips again. "More?"

More what? her poor muddled mind asked. The thread of their conversation was lost to her, swept away beneath the giddiness she felt at his words—her, hot?—and the incredulity of her response to him. *He's dangerous*, her heart whispered. But the rest of her couldn't have cared less for the warning.

"More," she answered.

Dylan's eyes gleamed, green and wicked in the arena's dim light. He raised the goblet to her lips. Stacey brought her hand to his wrist to steady it, but rather than let her drink, he tipped the glass away again.

"I'll do it. Much as I'd enjoy seeing you in a wet T-shirt"—his gaze roved over her body, then lifted—"or wet dress contest, that's not what I have in mind." A smile crooked his lips as he raised the glass. "For now, at least. Trust me."

Trust me. Easy for him to say. He wasn't the one risking a lapful of ice cubes. Nevertheless, Stacey let him tip the glass to her lips. She sipped the icy water, wildly conscious of him watching her, and dared to raise her gaze to his.

Dylan stared at something over her shoulder. Bam! The seductive mood he'd woven went straight down the tubes, right along with her thirst for his attention. *Dummy.* She should have known better than to think he'd have eyes for her alone.

Stacey quit drinking and slid sideways on their bench just in time to avoid the unbalanced goblet's descent. Dylan wasn't so lucky.

"Youch!" He jumped partway up, sending the goblet tumbling the rest of the way to the floor. Water and ice cubes dripped from his pants.

Twisting to look over her shoulder, Stacey spotted the hotel employee he'd been staring at, a flower girl selling roses to the diners, and shook her head. She *really* should have known better.

"Maybe that'll cool off your libido a little bit." She smoothed her dress and gathered her purse so she could leave. "Suddenly, I'm not hungry anymore."

A few yards away, two knights on horseback galloped into the arena to prepare for the first joust. The crowd cheered.

Dylan shook his hands dry and gave her a dumbfounded look. "What?"

"Your libido," Stacey said louder, trying to make herself heard over the thundering hoofbeats of the jousters. "Cool off your libido."

The music swelled along with the crowd's enthusiasm and drowned out her words.

"What?"

"Oh, for Pete's sake." She looked at him, dripping and shivering, and decided he'd had enough punishment already. "Never mind. I'm leaving."

Four

Outside in the neon-spangled December night, Stacey hailed one of the taxis parked beneath the Renaissance's porte-cochere. She hurried toward it with her heart still thumping from her race through the casino. Near as she could tell, Dylan hadn't followed her from the arena.

He was probably busy getting the flower girl's phone number, she thought sourly as she slipped in the back seat of the taxi. Going to dinner with him had been a bad idea. She should have listened to herself and refused to go along. Next time, at least, she'd know better than to give Dylan the benefit of the doubt.

Leaning forward, Stacey told the Santa-hat-wearing driver her destination. Serenaded by the Christmas music on his radio, she settled on the upholstered seat as he maneuvered into the heavy Las Vegas traffic. Judging by the number of cars and pedestrians on the infamous "Strip," it could take days to reach her hotel again.

Shaking her head, Stacey scrounged in her purse for a compact and lipstick to put herself together with. She might feel as if she had "gullible" tattooed on her forehead, but that didn't mean she had to look the part. If and when Dylan caught up with her, she wanted to look as polished as possible.

Maybe then he wouldn't guess how close she'd come to making a complete fool of herself over him. Again.

She cracked open the compact she'd found and swiveled up her lipstick with a shaky hand, then peered in the mirror to put it on. *Idiot*, her expression said. *Dylan wants something, all right, or he wouldn't be here—but it's not you.*

Let me convince you, Stacey. Give me another try, he'd said, but what did that mean, anyway? Did he want to start dating again? Did he only want to keep his word to Janie and Richard, and help her pull off the honeymoon suite charade?

Maybe, she thought dismally as the taxi inched forward in traffic, Dylan had realized he'd spoiled his studly dating record by dumping her before sleeping with her, and now he just wanted to seduce her. Then dump her. Again.

Lipstick accomplished, Stacey stared out the taxi window at the flashy casinos they passed. Spotting the cheerful sixty-foot Christmas tree in front of one hotel only made her feel more morose. This was some Christmas season so far, wasn't it?

It wasn't that she honestly believed Dylan was as bad as she made him out to be. It wasn't even that she was worried about her honeymoon imposter status being found out. At least not *much*. No, what really bothered her was her own indecision. If she couldn't even trust her own judgment anymore, what did she have left?

The last time she'd been involved with Dylan, Stacey had been freshly divorced and about as eager to start dating again as a fish was to rumba on the beach. She'd only agreed to go out with him as a favor to Janie and Richard, who'd gone to college with Dylan and thought he'd be the perfect dating re-entry partner: good-looking, successful, and not the least bit interested in a serious relationship. Tailor-made for a skittish divorcée.

Or so she'd thought.

Until she'd started falling for him.

Dumb, dumb, dumb. The very instant she'd started having couple-type thoughts about Dylan, he'd sensed it and scrammed. Did men have early commitment warning systems, or what? It wasn't as though she'd wanted to nail him down and marry him on the spot. She needed to get used to running her own life again before getting involved with another man. She needed . . .

She needed to find out if that flash of black and red had really been Dylan running alongside the taxi, or if she'd only imagined it.

Craning her neck, Stacey stared out the taxi's side window toward the sidewalk bordering The Strip. Pedestrians in red and green Christmas sweaters surged along the narrow space, toting shopping bags, cameras, and even cocktails. Multicolored lights brightened their faces, but none of those faces, it seemed, belonged to Dylan.

Whew. She *had* imagined that glimpse of him. Maybe a guilty conscience could do that to a person. Although why she should feel guilty, Stacey didn't know. After all, *he* was the one she'd caught ogling another woman in the middle of their "honeymoon" date.

Except she did feel guilty. Guilty for dumping ice water in his lap, and foolish for running out on him the way she had. If she was going to pull off the honeymoon charade, she'd have to think first before acting.

The driver stopped at a corner to let a stream of tourists pass on their way to the holiday show at the Bellagio's fountains. Stacey settled back again, trying to put the evening's dinner debacle out of her mind. She put her things back in her purse, gazed out the windshield at the red traffic light overhead—and something slammed against the passenger-side window.

Dylan. His face, penitent and pleading, pushed close to the glass. He rapped on it, motioning for her to let him in, saying something she couldn't hear clearly.

Not that she wanted to hear it. Whatever interest she had in listening to him or relieving her former guilt attack evaporated once she saw the huge bouquet of red roses he cradled against his chest. So, he thought he'd buy her off with flowers, did he? He had another thing coming.

Stacey surged across the back seat and slammed her palm

on the knob that locked the taxi door. At almost the same instant, the traffic light changed. The taxi drove forward.

Dylan jogged beside it, dodging pedestrians and a bicyclist.

"Roll down the window!" He mimicked cranking the handle down. She didn't and he jogged faster, trailing fallen rose petals along the side of the street. Noticing that fact, he held the bouquet closer.

"For you!" he called, catching up with the taxi as it idled in traffic again.

Stacey glanced at what had to be at least three dozen long-stemmed flowers bundled against his chest. He must have hit on every flower girl at the Renaissance to accumulate that many. The cad.

She leaned closer to the driver. "I'll pay you fifty bucks if you can get me to the Atmosphere in the next five minutes."

He grinned at her in the rearview mirror. "Yes, ma'am."

He accelerated. Stacey fell back against the seat. Dylan's voice, "Staaaceey. . . !" faded like a bad Brando impression. She caught one final glimpse of him waving the roses overhead before the taxi changed lanes and left him behind.

They changed lanes again, shot across The Strip, ran a yellow light, and screeched to a stop in the next clump of traffic. Jittery and soon to be fifty dollars poorer, Stacey swiveled in the back seat. She looked out the rear windshield.

No sign of Dylan. Whew! She'd lost him.

So how come she didn't feel relieved?

Stuck on Las Vegas Boulevard, Dylan revved his Jeep in front of the Atmosphere, swearing under his breath at the two police cars and the taxi that blocked the curved drive to the casino's entrance. Must be a fender-bender. Great.

Shoving his fingers through his hair, fighting for patience, he stared up at the palm trees bordering the drive. Someone had strung Christmas lights on their jagged trunks and along their fronds. The multicolored, twinkling lights lent the tropical trees an old-fashioned air of holiday joviality, much like the vendor hawking eggnog lattes on the corner did.

Not that Dylan was feeling especially ho-ho-ho at the moment. Not since Stacey had run out on him. Damn. He shouldn't have pushed her so hard during dinner. He should have known she'd be looking for an excuse to bolt.

Like an idiot, he'd come on too strong. Now it would be twice as hard to get through the weekend with her. He'd probably lost every inch of ground he'd gained, and all because of his stupid roving eyeballs. And the roses, of course.

Reminded of them, Dylan glanced at the bouquet on the passenger seat. A little wilted from being waved about, but still pretty nice. He'd had to buy out both flower girls at the Renaissance to get them, and had almost missed catching up to Stacey because of it.

"What do you mean you won't take a check?" a woman said near the taxi-police car clump. "You just got done telling me you wouldn't take a credit card, which I don't have anyway, so that's kind of beside the point, but how am I supposed to pay you? What else is there?"

Stacey. He'd have recognized her voice even at normal decibel levels. As it was, she was nearly wailing. Dylan whipped out his Jeep keys, grabbed the bouquet, and hefted himself upright using the Jeep's roll bar. Yep. There she was, standing in the middle of the parked cars beside the squat taxi driver and two uniformed policemen.

"Cash, lady!" yelled the taxi driver, rubbing his thumb and fingers together in a show-me-the-money gesture that spoke every language. "Ya heard of it?"

"Of course I've heard of cash! But haven't *you* heard of the computer age? These days, even fast food joints take credit cards."

"Maybe, lady. But Mickey D's *doesn't* take checks, and neither do I."

Grinning, Dylan tossed his keys to a valet and headed toward them. He couldn't have come up with a better way to pull a knight in shining armor routine if he'd planned it himself. This taxi driver was heaven sent—even if he *had* nearly run over Dylan earlier.

"Sir, you'll have to move your vehicle," one of the officers told the taxi driver. "You're blocking the—"

"I ain't moving until I get paid," the driver interrupted, looking belligerent. He glared at Stacey. "She even promised me extra to ditch some loser with a bunch of flowers."

Hunching her shoulders, she scooted closer to one of the police officers. "I told you. I don't have any cash! I must have lost it someplace, or—"

She spotted Dylan. The rest of whatever she was saying came out in a garbled series of mismatched syllables. "Or, or," she tried to rally, "or I could go to an ATM. Please? I swear you can trust me." Smiling wanly, Stacey blinked up at the officer nearest her. "Really, I'm very trustworthy. Ask anyone."

"Ask me." The driver snorted. "The guy she tried to stiff on the fare."

The officer shook his head. "I'm sorry, miss—"

"Sugarlumps!" yelled Dylan, smiling broadly. He reached them in two quick steps, then thrust the bouquet in Stacey's arms.

"Hey, that's him!" the driver cried. "The loser with the flowers!"

"He's not a loser," Stacey said. "He's, he's . . ."

Dylan could almost see the wheels turning in her mind. Suddenly her eyes brightened. She gave him a smile even more syrupy than the one he'd tried out on her at the Renaissance show.

Of course, *his* smile had been sappy and genuine. Stacey's probably wasn't, especially in this instance. But if Dylan had his way, she'd look at him like that and mean it by the time the weekend was up. It was something to look forward to.

"He's my husband." Her voice emanated false cheer as her gaze met Dylan's. "Isn't that right, honey?" she added through her smile, turning to face him so the others couldn't read her desperate please-stick-to-our-story expression.

She clamped both hands on his shoulders. *Help me!* she mouthed.

"Trust me," Dylan said.

He covered his whispered words with a loud smacking kiss on her lips. She nodded, looking scared but willing to bluster her way through whatever they had to do.

"It's going to cost you, though," he warned.

Grinning at the thought of the friendly repayment he'd exact, Dylan hauled her up against his side. He put on his best sitcom husband face. "I'll take care of this, Sweetcakes."

He offered his hand to the closest policemen. "Richard Parker!" he boomed, shaking hands with each of them in turn. "What seems to be the trouble, officers? Don't tell me it's my little lady, Janie, here."

Stacey raised the flowers. "Richard's going to kill you," she muttered from behind them. "You're making him sound like Fred Flintstone."

"I guess that makes me Barney Rubble, then. You know, Fred's buddy," he whispered. "I'm kinda tall for the part, though. Don't you think so?"

Her smiling, up-and-down perusal made him feel tall enough to touch the top of the Atmosphere. This hero business had potential.

"It seems your wife can't pay the taxi driver," one of the officers said. "And he won't move his taxi out of the drive until she does."

The driver waved a strip of paper at Dylan. "She's paying this ticket, too! You're lucky I don't charge you for lost wages. What kind of bubble brain tries to pay for a taxi with a check?"

"Bubble brain?" Dylan repeated.

The driver looked uncertain.

"This is my wife you're talking about, pal." Dylan stepped closer, then reached in his pocket.

Both officers straightened, instantly alert.

"Sorry, lady." The driver darted a glance at Stacey.

Dylan bared his teeth at him. "I don't think she heard you."

"I'm sorry about that, ma'am!" He shoved the ticket in his pants pocket, then wiped his palms on the wide bottom of his sweatshirt. "I'll, uh, take care of the ticket myself."

"Good idea." Pulling out his wallet, Dylan withdrew two ten dollar bills and gave them to the driver. "That ought to about cover it from the Renaissance to here, right?"

"Uh, yeah," mumbled the driver, counting the money. He pocketed it, started to walk back to his taxi, then stopped and looked over his shoulder. "What about the extra fifty bucks?"

Dylan's hand stilled midway through folding his wallet. "Extra fifty bucks?"

Beside him, Stacey seemed to shrink a couple inches. "I, umm, promised him a little extra money."

"Fifty bucks?"

She bit her lower lip, twisting her purse strap tight enough to cut off circulation to her wrist. She nodded.

"Big tip."

"It wasn't . . . exactly . . . a tip."

"Nah, it wasn't a tip," agreed the driver. "Well?"

Sighing, Dylan opened his wallet again. "What's it for?" he asked Stacey as he counted out fifty dollars.

"Ummm . . ." She shifted her weight from foot to foot, looking like a kid caught red-handed with her hand in the cookie jar. "I paid him extra to get rid of you back there. When you were chasing the taxi."

Dylan raised his eyebrows and handed over the money. No, *he* was paying extra to get rid of *himself*.

"Next time, just make sure you can fork over the dough before making a promise like that. Okay, Lovey?"

Stacey mumbled her assent—and something that sounded like "Tigerlips," if he wasn't mistaken—then buried her face in the roses.

With everything apparently in the clear, the police helped escort the driver and his taxi onto the street again, leaving Dylan and Stacey alone.

"Now that that's taken care of," he said, grinning, "it's payback time."

Stacey ducked into the crowd and bolted down The Strip.

"You're fast," Dylan told her an hour later, inside the conservatory at the Bellagio. He braced his hand on one of the low marble walls and gazed at the winter wonderland all around them, trying not to show he was winded.

He'd chased her down The Strip, past several casinos, into an array of shops, and finally to the Bellagio. An Olympic runner would be breathing hard after all that. "I almost caught up to you when you stopped to check out that shoe sale."

Stacey grinned, but she was panting, too. "I had a pretty big head start on you by then." She strolled beside him along the conservatory's pathway, still holding her bedraggled bouquet of roses. "I figured I could always use a new pair of shoes. It was worth the risk. Besides, you *didn't* catch me."

Her eyes were shining, her face rosy with the aftereffects of their chase. Damp tendrils of chestnut-colored hair clung to the back of her neck. Still smiling, she turned her face to the conservatory's display of thousands of poinsettias.

All around them, Christmas cheer abounded. Above the poinsettias, enormous ornaments, each one bigger than a Humvee, hung suspended from the ceiling on invisible wires, gleaming in shades of metallic red and green and gold. Lights twinkled everywhere. Magnificent fir trees sheltered an indoor ice pond, and around them stood caribou-shaped topiaries and a 25-foot-long topiary train—complete with a smoking stack. Apparently, in Las Vegas, no holiday spectacle was too over-the-top.

Stacey gazed at the lights and ornaments and flowers, her face aglow with wonder. "It's beautiful, isn't it?"

"Beautiful," Dylan agreed. But the view was ordinary compared with the way she looked to him now, relaxed beside him. She might have been a different woman than the one who'd greeted him warily at the door to the honeymoon suite earlier. No less beautiful but twice as appealing . . . because now she was beginning to feel comfortable with him. "So are you."

Stacey laughed. She raised her hand to wipe away a streak of smudged mascara.

"Come on, Dylan. There's nobody around to hear us." She nodded her head to indicate the sparsely populated conservatory. She hunched her shoulders, fiddling with a rose petal. "You don't have to be Mr. Honeymoon when it's just us."

"I'm not. I—"

"It's okay. After all, you did your best to act like a honeymooner back at the Renaissance, and I kind of put the kibosh on that, didn't I?" With a short laugh, Stacey twisted a rose petal from its place and smoothed it between her fingers. She stared up at the conservatory's fully decorated Christmas tree.

"I'm sorry about that, Dylan. I shouldn't have run out on you the way I did."

He couldn't believe she was taking the blame for . . . for what? Dylan still wasn't sure exactly what had gotten her all riled up during dinner, and at this rate he wasn't likely to find out.

"I think you skipped a step." He put his hand to her shoulder and smiled at her. She didn't glance sideways to see it, though, so his good faith gesture was wasted. "I never—"

I never figured out what all the trouble was, he started to say, but before he could get the words out, Stacey twisted off another rose petal and interrupted.

"Please. I don't want to keep fighting with you." She looked into his face at last. "I can't stand it." More rose petals followed the first, twisted, scrubbed between her fingertips, then dropped on the growing pile beside her. "You were doing your best to pull off the honeymoon charade, and I . . . I overreacted. I'm sorry. Let's just leave it at that, okay?"

Her gaze, brown-eyed and imploring, met his. Stacey might not want him there at all, but if they were going to be forced into cooperating on the honeymoon charade, Dylan realized, it was obviously important to her that they do it peacefully.

"It means a lot to you that people get along, doesn't it?"

He placed his hand over hers to keep her from shredding the other two and a half dozen red roses he'd given her. She looked at his hand, startled, then at the pile of petals she'd made. Her cheeks pinked.

"That's why you're doing this," he went on. "The honeymoon charade, I mean. To keep the peace."

"Yeah. I'm a real peacenik." Stacey offered him a rueful smile. "That's why I bashed you with a blow dryer and almost got you run over tonight. If I were you, I'd get the heck out of Dodge before the real shooting starts. You might get *really* hurt."

He was already hurt. Hurting without her. Only it had taken him too long to get it through his bone-headed brain. "I'm not going anyplace."

"Oh, that's right. I forgot. You gave your word to Richard

and Janie, didn't you?" She frowned sympathetically. "You're honor-bound for the whole weekend."

That wasn't what he'd meant about staying, but he couldn't pass up an opportunity to solidify his alibi.

"You've got it. The whole weekend. Especially now, with all those honeymoon surprises still to get through," Dylan said, trying to fake a little resistance to having to go through with the charade for two more days. "We've got a full lineup tomorrow."

"Let's keep a low profile this time, okay?"

He raised two fingers. "Scout's honor, remember? I'll try to impersonate Richard a little more, umm, quietly, if you'll agree not to get Janie arrested."

He stuck out his hand for a deal-making handshake.

Stacey blushed at his mention of her run-in with the police but slipped her hand in his anyway. "It's a deal. I never did thank you for rescuing me from the taxi driver, you know."

She squeezed his hand gently. Dylan used it to pull her closer. She had no choice but to come, since her other hand was filled with the tissue-wrapped flowers.

"You can thank me now. You still owe me, remember?"

He raised his hand to her cheek. Beneath his fingertips her skin felt softer than the roses. The feel of it lured him closer.

"Thank you," she said hastily, ducking her head. She tried to turn her face away, but Dylan tipped her chin up with his knuckles and gently shook his head.

"That's not what I meant," he said, cradling her cheek in his hand. He stroked her again, and the roses Stacey held between them started to tremble, filling the air with their perfume. "My payback demand is a thank-you kiss."

"A thank-you kiss?" She squinted at the few people standing near them. "But there's hardly anybody here to impress. You know, with our just-married honeymoon bliss. We should wait until—"

"The charade isn't why I asked. Kiss me."

The faint rustling of the roses underscored his words. Was she afraid or excited? Her trembling could mean either one, and he didn't want to scare her. He *did* want to kiss her . . .

THE BENEFITS
OF BOOK CLUB
MEMBERSHIP

- You'll get your books hot off the press, usually before they appear in bookstores.
- You'll ALWAYS save up to 30% off the cover price.
- You'll get our FREE monthly newsletter filled with author interviews, book previews, special offers and MORE!
- There's no obligation —you can cancel at any time and you have no minimum number of books to buy.
- And—if you decide you don't like the books you receive, you can return them. (You always have ten days to decide.)

PLACE
STAMP
HERE

kiss her long and hard and make the past melt away so they could start again.

"Kiss me," Dylan said, "and I'll call it even."

That reasoning she could accept, he saw. The roses stilled, and the hunted expression left her face. Stacey raised slightly, her hand still linked with his, and quickly pressed her lips to his. She started to lean back . . . and Dylan stopped her with a hand to the back of her neck. His fingers kneaded in her hair, and its softness sifted through his fingers like silk.

"You're welcome," he said. *More*, he thought.

Her eyes closed briefly, then opened again to focus on his mouth. "I . . . you're welcome, too."

The roses dropped to the floor. Heat passed between them, and Dylan hardly dared move for fear of scaring her away. An instant later Stacey's mouth found his again, and it was as though nothing had ever come between them. She was Stacey, his Stacey, warm and tempting as he remembered. She brought both hands to his shoulders and kissed him harder. He was lost, falling for her all over again, and he wanted to tell her, tell her how he felt and how much he'd missed her, except just as he thought it he literally *was* falling. Backward.

She'd unbalanced him by leaning forward. Dylan tightened his hold on her and tried to keep them upright without breaking their kiss. Hell, he'd be nuts to end a kiss like this one. He slipped his arm around her middle and held her close.

"Mmm-mmm," Stacey moaned, deepening the kiss. "Mmm-mmm . . ."

Briefly, Dylan wondered if she'd mistaken his maneuverings for increasing passion. He leaned forward, preventing them from toppling over. But then her kiss made him wild, made him forget where they were and who was around . . . and what was happening.

Teetering, he grabbed for leverage and caught an armful of woman instead. They both toppled backward into the bed of poinsettias.

Their mouths popped apart. Stacey sprawled atop his chest, looking disheveled, disoriented—and sexy as hell. Also confused. But she wasn't jumping up off him right away, so Dylan decided to savor the experience.

He smiled, wanting to feel nothing except the curving softness of her body pressed against him. Something sharp poking
into the back of his shirt changed his mind and sent his attention to less good-feeling parts of his anatomy. It felt like
dozens of tiny needles stabbing him in the back, like cactus
spines or midget shish kebab skewers or maybe even swizzle
sticks, which somehow seemed more suited to the glitz of Las
Vegas than anything else.

It felt like rose thorns working their way into his shoulder
blades.

Because it was.

"*Youch!*" Rearing upright, Dylan rooted in the poinsettias
for the limp flowers Stacey had dropped behind him. He held
them out to her. "Let's try that again. Without your instruments of destruction behind me this time."

But it was too late. She was already getting to her feet,
yanking down her dress as though it was supposed to come to
her *ankles* instead of just above her knees, filled with apologies and the same damned misplaced modesty she'd given him
before.

Hell.

"Sorry." She took the flowers from his hand. They dropped
in her grasp, several blossoms bending over the tissue paper
with broken stems and crushed petals. "I didn't mean to attack
you like that." Stacey tried to prop up one of the roses, then
plucked a poinsettia petal from her hair. "One minute I was
thanking you, and the next . . ."

She pressed her lips together and shook her head. Guiltily,
she looked around the conservatory, as though expecting the
kissing police to come skulking by at any second.

"For Pete's sake," she blurted. "I had us both sprawled all
over the Christmas display! I just don't know what happened."

He did. They'd connected, *really connected*, for a minute.
And it scared her.

"Let's try it again," Dylan offered. "Maybe we'll be able to
figure it out."

As an attempt to lighten the mood between them . . . it didn't.
Probably because yearning still sounded in the sandpapery rasp
of his voice, still showed in the shadows he felt in his eyes. He

wanted her too much. No amount of kidding around would change that.

She shook her head. "We'd better just go."

As though punctuating her words, snowflakes began drifting from the ceiling. Airy and magical, they floated over the conservatory's fir trees like figments of his imagination.

Stacey cracked a rueful smile. "Look out. Apparently, I'm even capable of changing the weather now."

"It's okay." Dylan stepped out of the poinsettia bed, then did his best to fluff up the crushed flowers. "I'm pretty sure that's part of the attraction. It *is* supposed to be a winter wonderland, right?"

So long as Stacey was beside him, it felt as if it was, too. But apparently she didn't feel the same way, because she fiddled with her purse and then the strap on her sandals and then the straps on her dress, as if any one of those things might have flopped down from the sheer force of their kiss.

Actually, as kisses went, that one might have been scorching enough to accomplish it.

But that was beside the point. He and Stacey might be on slightly more civil terms with each other now, Dylan realized, but as far as she was concerned he was still a danger to be reckoned with. The wary glance she sent his way told him that much. It looked as if he was back to square one.

The trouble with that was, their kiss had done nothing to satisfy his yearnings for Stacey. If anything, it had only brought back everything they'd ever shared and made him want that closeness more.

He put his hand to her waist to guide her toward the exit, wondering how he'd ever been dumb enough to let her go in the first place. They were right for each other. Dylan was sure of it. All that remained was convincing Stacey of that fact before the honeymoon suite charade, and especially his part in it, was discovered.

Five

Stacey sensed the morning sunlight on her face, screwed her eyes more tightly shut, and rolled over in bed. Something big, warm and solid blocked her path. Feeling muzzy-headed, she opened her eyes . . . and looked into Dylan's face, only inches from hers on the neighboring pillow.

"Aaack! What are *you* doing here?" she shrieked, scooting madly backward. Her backside met empty air at the edge of the bed. With two feet of empty silk sheet between her and Dylan, she was able to relax long enough to stare back at him. "Well?"

He smiled. Actually *smiled*, first thing in the morning. The only time her ex-husband had ever smiled first thing in the morning was when they'd . . . no, never mind. The morning quickies Charlie had insisted on every Sunday definitely did *not* bear remembering.

"You're supposed to be sleeping on the loveseat, remember?" She clutched the comforter to her chin. "We agreed!"

What had she put on to sleep in last night? She couldn't remember. Was it her faded oversize Arizona Wildcats T-shirt or her more respectable, if boring and scratchy, flannel pajamas?

More importantly, what was Dylan wearing underneath the covers?

"I did sleep on the loveseat." Casually, he angled one elbow on the pillow and propped his head in his hand.

The sunlight shining through the honeymoon suite windows captured the good-natured gleam in his eyes and burnished his dark tousled hair with lighter-colored highlights. Why, Stacey thought grumpily, couldn't Dylan have awakened looking like an ogre and smelling just as bad? And what *was* he wearing, anyway? He'd only pulled up the sheet waist-high, but she couldn't catch a glimpse of anything beneath it.

She bet he slept in the nude.

"But I've been up for a while," he went on, oblivious to her wonderings. "I had to smuggle Ginger out for a walk."

He tossed a smiling glance at the dog sprawled, snoring faintly, near the honeymoon suite door.

"I can see it wore her out."

"No more than last night did." When they'd returned to their room, they'd found Ginger surrounded by colorful pieces of shredded Las Vegas attractions brochures, chewing up the M-Z section of the Yellow Pages. Obviously, they'd tasted better than the ordinary dog food and water Dylan had left for her.

"Anyway, I stopped and ordered breakfast from room service while I was downstairs. I thought it would look more honeymoon-ish if both sides of the bed looked slept in when the food arrived."

"Oh." So much for her plans to go out for breakfast at one of the restaurants nearby. How typically Dylan, to decide *for* her what she wanted to eat.

She'd just have to try and put a good face on it, for the sake of the honeymoon ruse, Stacey decided. But first she needed to get out of bed. And to do that, she had to be dressed.

Trying to seem casual about it, she stuck her hand under the comforter and touched her shirt. At the feel of the thin washed cotton in her hand, she remembered that she'd compromised last night and worn her Wildcats T-shirt *plus* her flannel pajama bottoms.

Too bad the latter were lumped someplace at the foot of the bed, discarded in the middle of the night when it had gotten too hot to sleep with them on. She was sleeping in a T-shirt and panties. Nothing special . . . except she'd never actually worn such a getup in the company of Dylan.

And she didn't intend to now.

"Breakfast, huh?" Trying not to jiggle the mattress, Stacey fished around with her foot, hoping to hook her pajama bottoms. "Sounds good."

"Mmmm-hmmm." He didn't sound like he was contemplating scrambled eggs. "I figured you'd rather sleep in than wrestle with the room service menu. I don't know what you usually have for breakfast." Dylan gave her an innuendo-laden grin. "But I think you'll enjoy what I ordered. It's special."

Thump—thump. Her heart turned over at the purr in his voice. The sleepy, let's-stay-in-bed look in his eyes didn't help her composure much, either. She had to get out of that bed before her body got the better of her brain and convinced her to attack Dylan again, the way she had at the conservatory last night. Biting her lip, Stacey dug her toes in a promising lump then realized it was part of the sheet. Rats.

"This is nice, isn't it?" Dylan grabbed hold of the headboard for an anchor and yawned as he stretched. His toes popped out from beneath the sheet at the end of the bed. The muscles in his arms flexed, then relaxed again. He resumed his propped-on-the-pillows stance and smiled at her. "Being together like this, I mean."

Stacey's gaze dipped from his dark-stubbled jaw to the broad expanse of his shoulders and muscular chest. Geez, he looked amazing. She made herself return his smile. "Yeah, uh, nice."

Find those pajama bottoms! her brain yelled. She wiggled and scooted sideways, still searching with her toes. How could being in bed with a man discombobulate her so much? It wasn't as though she hadn't spent four years sleeping next to a male person every night. Well, almost every night. Except for when Charlie had been working overtime, or out of town, or . . . .

Face it. He hadn't been Dylan. And it wasn't just sculpted chest muscles or gorgeous green eyes or cute rumpled hair she was talking about, either. Charlie would never have put himself out to help her with something like the honeymoon ruse. Period. Dylan would—was—and if his help with the police and the taxi driver yesterday was any indication, she knew he'd stick by her to the end, too. Even if she made him mad.

Maybe, just maybe, she could trust him a little.

A very teeny-tiny little.

But it was a start. Heartened at the thought, Stacey let herself relax a bit, still probing the bottom of the mattress with her foot in the hopes of finding the rest of her clothes. "So, what's on the agenda for tod—aaaay!"

She'd scooted too far backwards. The mattress dipped with her weight and she went with it, straight off the edge.

Clutching fistfuls of comforter, Stacey landed on the floor with half the covers twisted around her. A pillow bounced on her head, then dropped on the carpet. She frowned at it. *Cool move, Stacey. Way to look sophisticated.*

Way to hide her T-shirt and panties getup. Aaack! She flung part of the comforter over her exposed legs just as Dylan leaned over the edge of the bed. His arm swept sideways. His hand, filled with something he'd picked up from the mattress, appeared over the side of the bed. He grinned and held whatever it was aloft.

Her pajama bottoms.

"Looking for these?"

"Give those back!" Holding the comforter plastered against her hips for a shield, Stacey grabbed for the pajamas.

Dylan raised them higher. "Say please."

"What? No!" She snatched, missed, and scowled. Ginger, apparently awakened by all the excitement, bounded over with her tail wagging. She barked at Dylan.

"Shhhh!" they said.

Ignoring them both, the dog put her paws on the mattress. Her tail swished, narrowly missing Stacey's nose. She hauled her from the mattress, letting the dog plunk down beside her.

"Figures," Dylan said. "As usual, she's on *your* side."

"She's on the *right* side," Stacey told him, leaning over to pet her. Ginger licked her chin, nicely showing some doggie allegiance. "Now give me those pajamas."

"Make me." He had the audacity to laugh.

She grabbed the pillow from the floor. His grin faded.

"Oh, no, you don't." Backing up on his knees, he held up

his arms to ward off the pillow. Speaking from between his elbows, he said, "I have to warn you, you don't know who you're messing with here."

"Oh, yeah? Who?"

"Pillow fight champion of Camp Wigwam, that's who." He inched his fingers toward one of the remaining pillows. "Two years running."

"Oooh, I'm scared." Stacey grinned, releasing her blanket long enough to yank down her big T-shirt. Grabbing her pillow, she twirled it by its corner and tried to look menacing. "I've got you beat by a year. *Three* year champ, Camp Weehawken."

"Camp Weehawken's a bunch of girls." He draped her coveted pajama bottoms over the headboard like a pirate flying his flag on a stolen ship.

Or a matador inciting the bull to charge. Except Stacey felt more mulish than bullish.

"I'm going to get those anyway." She raised an eyebrow with mock regret. "So you might as well surrender."

"Never. Besides, I've got more ammunition than you do." Turning partway, Dylan picked up his pillow and passed it from hand to hand, treating her to a pirate's roguish grin and a revealing view of his sleeping attire, too. He was wearing, she saw, a pair of green striped boxer shorts. And nothing else.

The broad planes of his chest narrowed into a tight stomach that had to cost him a thousand crunches a day. Between passes of the pillow, Stacey glimpsed narrow hips and the finely muscled strength of his thighs as her gaze skimmed lower, followed the crisp green-and-white stripes of his boxers.

Mercy, but the man kept some kind of body hidden beneath those sloppy T-shirts and baggy jeans of his! She'd never have guessed, never have thought to . . .

To wallop him with a pillow. *Stay focused*, she ordered herself. His attempts at distraction wouldn't work on the likes of *her*.

"But I've got better aim." She squinted up at him with her best Dirty Harry impression to hide the fact that he *had* distracted her, at least for a nanosecond. "Hand over my pajamas."

Her cover-up came too late. He'd already caught her all but counting the pinstripes on his underwear.

"Do you like what you see?" Dylan asked, as smoothly as though she'd never spoken between ogling him and making her demand. How come he always seemed to guess what she was thinking? Stacey sure as heck never noticed him ogling *her*. Suddenly, the notion made her feel sort of miffed.

Oh, no, it didn't. That was ridiculous. What did she care what Dylan thought of her? She had no intention of cozying up to him again and risk having the honeymoon suite charade exposed because her attention was someplace else.

"I see my clothes draped over the headboard like panty raid souvenirs." She twirled her pillow overhead. "Hand them over."

"Come and get 'em."

"Bully."

"Chicken."

She hurled her pillow. It flew at Dylan's face with a satisfying *thwap!* and slid into his lap. Too late, Stacey realized she'd let go of it. Rats! Now she was defenseless. She'd only meant to whack him once, just to show she meant business.

"Looks like you'll be the one surrendering," he informed her, grinning at the pillow, then at her. He lowered his pillowcase-covered ammunition—and lowered his voice. "I promise to be lenient in my terms. Amnesty's granted for a kiss."

The seductive tone of his words raised goose bumps along her arms, but Stacey wasn't ready to surrender.

"You wish. I'm not giving up." She cast about for another weapon. Her gaze lit on her other pillow, tilting precariously at the edge of the mattress. Biting her lip, she snaked her hand toward it.

Dylan snatched it first. "Uh, uh, uh. That's mine." He pretended to think about it. "I guess you could always take off your T-shirt and wallop me with it, for lack of a more lethal weapon." He waggled his eyebrows with overplayed lasciviousness. "On the other hand, that might be most lethal of all. What do you say?"

"I say you're out of there." Stacey grabbed the portion of silk sheet still remaining on the bed and tugged. He was kneeling on top of it. All she had to do was pull, and Dylan would come tumbling to the floor too, minus a couple degrees of smugness *and* his pillow stockpile.

She wrenched harder. Nothing budged except her. Dylan had captured the sheet's other end and started pulling.

"Hey!" She kept hanging on. Her backside bumped across the carpet. Beside her, Ginger scrambled out of the way, breathing blasts of doggie breath into her face as she went. "Hey!"

"All's fair in love and war."

Tug-of-war she *wasn't* a champion at. But where brute strength couldn't take her, Stacey figured as she pulled, cunning would. Sneaking a glance at Dylan, she saw he'd added both hands to his sheet-pulling efforts. Perfect.

She let go. Just as she'd hoped, Dylan flopped on the bed, thrown backward by the force of his own strength turned against him. With a yell of triumph, Stacey scrambled on the mattress and trampled on her hands and knees over the sheets, atop Dylan, and over to the bedpost. She yanked her pajama bottoms free.

She whirled them overhead like a cowboy's lasso. "Woohoo!" she crowed, putting her hands on her hips and settling back onto her heels. "Don't mess with the Weehawken champ."

Laughing, Dylan raised his arms and tee'd his hands together to make a time-out signal. "You win," he groaned. "I'm no match for your stealth."

He struggled up on his elbows and peered down the length of his body at her on the bed next to him. They were so close their hips nearly touched, but Stacey felt too triumphant to care. She grinned hugely, feeling carefree, with laughter still tugging at her lips. How had she forgotten how much sheer *fun* Dylan could be?

"Is that what they teach you at girl's camp?" he complained. "Fighting dirty?"

"Awww, you big baby." Pursing her lips in a pout, Stacey leaned forward. She patted his chest sympathetically with her hand that wasn't holding her pajama bottoms. "You're the one picking fights with me. Maybe next time you'll . . . ahhhh!"

Suddenly, she was airborne. Her pajama bottoms, so hard-won, went flying. The next thing she knew, she was flat on her back amid a pile of pillows with her hands anchored over her head in Dylan's fists. The heat from his body seared into her skin.

Straddling her, he leaned over and smiled. "Gotcha."

Her eyes widened. His strong thighs hemmed in her hips on both sides, his hands held her arms immobile, and his chest nearly touched hers because he leaned so close. Worse, she realized as a brush of unexpectedly cool air whisked over her belly, her T-shirt had ridden up past her thighs. It felt as if it was puddled someplace around her navel. This was a danger-ous situation. Very dangerous.

And to be immediately gotten out of.

Stacey wiggled experimentally beneath him. Dylan's gaze went straight to her breasts. She felt suddenly aware of their jiggling, happily braless state beneath her T-shirt. She froze. Unfortunately, her chest didn't. Instead of cooperating with her mind, her body went right ahead and responded to his at-tention. Her nipples puckered, pushing against her shirt in a way she would have immediately covered—if she'd had the use of her arms.

"Play with fire and you might get burned." Dylan's gaze roved lower. "Or maybe that's me getting burned. God, you're gorgeous."

Gorgeous? Wow, nobody had ever called her . . . no, she wasn't falling for this. Remembering her theory that Dylan only wanted her to sleep with him and repair his studly dating record, Stacey hardened her resolve and stared back at him. "Let go of me."

Dylan eased his hold on her hands long enough to caress her fingers and smile. He looked so boyish, so openhearted, that she wanted to throw caution to the wind and abandon her suspicions. Lulled by his smile, she sank a little deeper against the mattress. When his answer came, his voice was just an-other soothing lure, easing her against the tangled sheets and further into her tangled emotions.

"Are you sure?" He slid his fingers up, down, in between hers, gliding over each sensitive fingertip in turn.

Shivering, she tried to get a hold of herself. For Pete's sake, only their fingertips were touching. That wasn't enough to make her tremble, to make her want him, like this. Yet when Dylan looked down at her again, Stacey felt his gaze touch her like the softest of caresses. She wanted to sigh beneath it.

"Ummm . . ." Of course she was sure. Wasn't she?

Her moment's indecision cost her the choice. His hands tightened on her wrists and pushed them into the plump pillow beneath. Her breath caught.

"Yes, yes, I'm sure! I'm sure."

"Sure of what?" Dylan's head lowered, and his stubbled jaw whisked past her cheek. Stacey couldn't move, couldn't think, as his mouth found her earlobe, nibbled gently, then kissed below it. "Sure of this?" he asked, moving his lips against her neck. "You only have to tell me what you want, Stacey, and I'll give it to you. Do you want this?"

He kissed her neck, her jaw, brought his hand low to cradle her head and hold her still as he sucked the place where her neck and jaw met, doing things with his mouth and tongue and teeth she'd never dreamed could feel so good. "Do you want this? Because I swear I'll stop if you ask me to."

Please don't make me stop his body said as his hand tightened in her hair. *Love me. Let me love you.* Smiling, Dylan looked deeply into her eyes and stroked his thumb across her cheek. "You make me crazy. God, I should have never let you go."

Let her go. No, she didn't want that. Stacey knew that much, despite the warning bells in her brain telling her that was exactly what she ought to be asking for.

No, what she wanted was to arch against him, to tangle her legs with his and feel his hairy calves tickle hers, to stroke his back and feel him shudder beneath her touch. She wanted to feel him kiss her again, to let him take her mouth, her heart, her soul, and make her his.

"Please." She dared to bring her hands to his arms and grasp the finely wrought, muscular support she found there. "Please . . ."

She felt languid yet taut as a strung wire, sleepy yet more alive than she'd been in months. Looking into his eyes, Stacey dug her fingertips on his arms and levered herself closer. Her gaze drifted to his lips. *Kiss me,* she thought. *I need you to kiss me.* Dylan's weight shifted as he moved to comply, reading her desires in her eyes or her mouth or maybe her plaintive cry. *Please . . .*

His lips neared hers. A thud sounded at the door. Someone knocking. The sound roused Ginger. She barked—just once, but it was enough to make Stacey aware of her situation again. She tightened her hold on Dylan at the sound, realized he'd already released her hands and it was she—she—who'd practically attacked him yet again, and the spell was broken. Another knock came. Dylan's mouth brushed hers . . . and Stacey bolted from the bed.

"No!" Shaking, she yanked down her T-shirt and leaped onto the carpet just as Dylan's head thunked onto the mattress. There was an odd popping sound. Something powdery and sweet-smelling puffed up around his head.

"Ahhh! My eyes!" Yelling, Dylan scrambled upright, swabbing at his eyes with both fists. White powder drifted like a cloud in the air above him, then gradually sifted back down on his head like an exceptionally even-spaced, and exceptionally bad, case of dandruff.

Her aromatherapy powder. Stacey snatched the broken paper sachet from the indentation in the mattress where Dylan had landed just as another knock came at the door.

"Room service!" someone called. Ginger snuffled at the bottom edge of the door then pranced in front of it, eager for some human company that might pay attention to *her*. She cocked her head when nobody moved and gave a blowsy doggie sneeze instead. *Hey, somebody's here!*

Dylan coughed loudly to cover the sound, his gaze darting toward Ginger. "Shhh!"

"Room service!" came a suspicious-sounding voice from the hallway. "Mr. and Mrs. Parker?"

"You broke it!" Stacey waggled the smashed and empty sachet toward Dylan.

For some reason, the sight of it made her want to weep. It

was a foolish reaction, she knew, but no less true. Geez, she was a mess, her emotions too close to the surface to be trusted. Blinking hard, she waved the paper at him as though he could repair it somehow—make it whole again.

He grabbed the sachet with one hand and peered at it, temporarily abandoning his attempts to wipe his face clean. "Gingerbread Dreams?" he asked, reading it.

"It's aromatherapy, Christmas style." She crossed her arms. "It's *supposed* to be relaxing." She'd needed it last night after her encounters with Dylan, but he was the last person on earth she'd admit it to. "I use those sachets sometimes to wind down at night. I must have forgotten it was beneath the pillow."

Another knock came, along with a more urgent, "Room service!"

"Just a minute!" Dylan called toward the door of the honeymoon suite, sounding surprisingly polite for somebody who was wearing boxer shorts, an even dusting of ginger-scented powder, and nothing else.

"Wind down, huh?" he asked as he headed to the door, brushing drifts of Gingerbread Dreams from his head and shoulders as he went. He ushered Ginger into hiding in the suite's bathroom with a push to her wagging rump and closed the door. "No wonder I feel so calm right now."

He grinned and nodded toward the bed. "Better get in bed, snookums. Otherwise, you'll give the room service guy an eyeful."

Joking. He was actually joking about being the victim of yet another of her accidental disasters. Stacey couldn't believe it. Did *nothing* get Dylan rattled?

Only you, a part of her whispered. Ignoring it, she dove for cover, hefted an armload of black silk comforter, and made it into bed just as a uniformed hotel employee wheeled his room service cart into the honeymoon suite.

"Good morning, Mrs. Parker, Mr. Parker." He sniffed, wrinkling his nose at the conspicuously ginger scented air, then parked his cart and turned to address them. The poor man nearly jumped a foot at his first sight of Dylan's powder-whitened face.

"Aromatherapy accident," Dylan said solemnly. "Dangerous stuff."

"I'm sure." The hotel employee peered at the amazing whiteness of Dylan's face. He'd seen stranger things, Stacey supposed, during his tenure at the hotel. "Would you like me to send up someone from our spa to help you?"

Dylan waved his hand. "Nah. I'll just take a walk—"

"Ruff!" barked Ginger from inside the bathroom.

"—down there after breakfast if I need to," he finished, his eyes widening. His gaze met Stacey's, and she had the feeling they were thinking the same thing. *The 'W' word.* Walk—walk—walk.

Whoops.

The hotel employee's attention veered from Dylan's face to the closed bathroom door. His frown made his face look a little like an unhappy mustachioed fist. "Is that a—"

"Hack, hack!" Loudly, very loudly, Dylan started coughing. A lion with a hairball caught in its throat couldn't have been louder. Finally, the hotel employee whacked Dylan on the back, and his coughing fit subsided.

"Thank you," Dylan croaked. "Terrible, being hit with this rotten cold on our honeymoon and all."

"Yes, I'm sure." With one parting glance at the bathroom door, the man shrugged his shoulders. He clattered the silver-covered dishes on his room service cart. "I hope you're not under the weather, too, Mrs. Parker."

Stacey stared at the bathroom door, wishing it were possible to mind-meld with a dog. *Be quiet,* she tried anyway. It couldn't hurt to try.

"Mrs. Parker?"

"Honey?"

"Mrs. Parker!"

"Sugarcakes?" Dylan kicked discreetly on the bedpost, jolting Stacey back from her mind-meld attempts. She looked up to see the room service guy stroking his mustache with narrowed eyes—eyes aimed suspiciously at her.

"She's a little hazy before the caffeine kicks in," Dylan explained.

"Oh! Ha, ha," Stacey managed. She glared at Dylan for the

kick—couldn't he have found a less jarring way to get her attention?—and clutched the covers to her chest. *Hazy, huh*?

"I guess you're right, Dumpling," she purred. "A girl's gotta have *something* to get her motor running in the mornings."

Behind the room service guy's back, Dylan pantomimed a dagger to his chest. With a silent howl of pretend anguish, he staggered backward, then grinned. Stacey stifled an answering smile and turned her gaze toward their visitor.

"So sorry we kept you waiting in the hallway earlier," she said sweetly.

"Oh, that's all right." He winked at Dylan.

Dylan whipped the imaginary dagger behind his back and gave him a leering sort of man-to-man grin. Stacey could've kicked *him*, never mind the bed post.

"The honeymooners are always that way. Sometimes we just give 'em a few minutes, then leave the food at the door if they don't answer." The hotel employee picked up a delicate white china cup and saucer, then poured coffee into it from a silver pot. "Of course, with a special order like this one, we didn't want to do that." He carried the steaming coffee to Stacey. "Here you go, ma'am."

She took the saucer in her hands and inhaled the rich brewed scent appreciatively. "Thank you," she said, and realized it was really Dylan she thanked most.

Even after spending the night with his six-foot frame cramped on the loveseat, even after being walloped, evaded, out-raced, and told to leave more times than she could count, he was still dedicated to pulling off the pretend-honeymooners thing for Richard and Janie.

In his own overbearing, take-charge way, of course.

Still, Dylan *was* trying to help. Unfortunately, the fact that he was being nice about things only made it twice as hard to resist him, which made it twice as hard for Stacey to keep her mind where it belonged—on the honeymoon ruse. If she couldn't handle the honeymoon deception better than she'd handled Dylan so far, her family's peaceful coexistence was doomed.

They were almost all she had left now. Four stifling years spent married to Charlie meant she'd socialized more with his business colleagues and their wives than with her own friends. Since her divorce, Stacey had started rebuilding her old friendships, but they were still a long way from the solid, just-us-gals relationships she used to enjoy. The last thing she wanted was to wreck things with her family, too.

She wouldn't. Not if there was any way to prevent it.

Grimacing, Stacey sipped her coffee just as Dylan emerged from the bathroom and shut the door behind him, looking clean and better than he had a right to after all he'd been through since showing up yesterday. The moment the door shut, Ginger started scratching. Dylan coughed to cover the sound. Stacey, trying to be helpful, did too. The hotel employee only raised his eyebrows and went on working.

Before long, Ginger apparently got tired of the game and quieted. Stacey imagined the dog chewing up the plush pink bath mat and grinned. Maybe Dylan's dog went everyplace with him, but she'd bet Ginger got him into his share of trouble, too.

Just like her, unfortunately.

Dylan ambled to the room service cart and lifted lids from its covered dishes, releasing the delicious aromas of toast, scrambled eggs, maple syrup, coffee, and the sharp tang of citrus.

"Smells good." His gaze shifted to her, and an appetite wholly unrelated to food rose in his expression. "Hungry?"

Her pulse leaped. How in the world did he keep doing that to her, with only a glance and a handful of words?

She ought to be nice to him, Stacey knew. She ought to make their honeymoon façade look good. But the way Dylan looked at her made her heart perform a sudden, unsettling mamba in her chest, and the only thing she really wanted to do was run.

"Actually," she wound up saying, "I'd hoped to go out to eat, rather than have overpriced room service food."

Dylan appeared crestfallen.

So did the room service guy. Banging the silver dishes, he poured a cup of coffee for Dylan and sloshed it in his hand. "Everything else will be along in a minute, sir."

"Thank you." Dylan held his cup in one hand and shook

spilled coffee from the other. He sucked the outer edge of his thumb, looking over his wrist at Stacey. "This won't just be overpriced room service food," he promised. "This will be something special. You'll see."

Setting his cup on the room service cart, Dylan picked up a plate and spooned what looked like scrambled eggs on it. He added two strips of bacon, stabbed a pancake with a fork and plopped it on the plate's edge, then poured maple syrup over the whole thing.

"Sit up." He nodded toward the headboard. "You're about to be served breakfast in bed."

Before she could protest being served breakfast while she was still half-dressed, four more hotel employees came in through the opened honeymoon suite doorway. Uniformed and carrying instruments, they gathered beside the room service cart. All four of them stared at Stacey, then turned expectantly to Dylan. "Are you ready for us, sir?"

"You bet!" Looking boyish and pleased with his surprise, Dylan stuck the plate of food in Stacey's hand. "That is, breakfast in bed *with music*. I'll bet you've never tried this before."

She hadn't. Balancing her filled plate in one hand, Stacey hauled the covers higher and watched the musicians. They quickly tuned up, then launched into a twangy-sounding Christmas carol. Grinning, they drifted toward her and surrounded the bed. The music got louder. So did the sound of someone banging on the wall of the neighboring hotel room.

Dylan ducked beneath the upraised arm of the violinist, carrying a filled breakfast plate of his own. Climbing on the silk comforter, he settled against the headboard beside Stacey with perfect assurance, despite the fact that he still wasn't fully dressed.

"Do you like it?" he asked. "Are you surprised?"

"I'm surprised, all right." What she *wasn't* was hungry. Not with a T-shirt and panties wardrobe and four strange men grinning down at her as they played the southwestern version of "Merry Christmas, Baby." For Dylan's sake, and for the sake of the honeymoon charade, Stacey picked up a strip of bacon and nibbled it.

The music picked up tempo. Dylan smiled at her, bobbing

his head along with the music as he packed away forkfuls of pancakes dripping with butter and maple syrup. Trying to get into the swing of things, Stacey forked up some scrambled eggs.

They shook off her fork and landed in her lap. She tried another bite. It wiggled off the tines, too. That's when she realized the bed was vibrating. The musicians' knees bumped rhythmically against the mattress as they played their hearts out for the "honeymooners." Somebody pounded again on the other side of the neighboring hotel room wall, but everyone else seemed too engrossed in the music to notice.

This was way too much activity for a Saturday morning.

And Dylan was doing far too much to take over the honeymoon suite charade. This was *her* problem. She'd be the one to solve it. Her way.

"This isn't very inconspicuous," Stacey remarked. Doing her best not to flash the six hotel employees gathered around their bed, she eased her plate onto the bedside table then snuggled the comforter up to her chin again. "I thought we had a deal."

"What?" Dylan cupped his ear and leaned closer.

"Inconspicuous, remember?"

The musicians charged into the final chorus of the song. Their hotel room neighbor banged away at the wall, suddenly sounding strangely as though he was keeping time with the music. It was like breakfasting amidst a full-blown holiday fiesta.

Dylan frowned. "What? I can't hear you."

"Please make them leave."

"What?"

"*Make them leave!*" Stacey yelled as the music stopped.

Shocked silence filled the honeymoon suite. The musicians froze in place, their instruments lowered halfway. The guitar player shook his head. Five pairs of sad eyes—Dylan's included—stared back at her.

"Sorry," she peeped.

"My wife gets terrible migraine headaches," Dylan explained rapidly, rising from the bed with more quick thinking than Stacey would have credited him with. "I'm sorry. The music was wonderful, but I'm afraid that'll have to be all for now."

Guilt-stricken, Stacey pulled the black silk comforter over her head and listened to Dylan explain away their abbreviated morning serenade. Their neighbor had quit banging on the wall, she noticed. Dylan would be disappointed: he might not have called the hotel management to complain yet. You couldn't get much more conspicuous than having yourself reprimanded by the management for unruly behavior.

Probably that had been Dylan's plan all along. Why not? It wasn't *his* family at stake. He'd decided on a course of action for the honeymoon suite charade, and by God, he meant to follow through with it. No matter what she wanted.

Money rustled in his wallet, many pairs of feet shuffled toward the doorway . . . then, silence. Stacey poked her head out.

"What did you think you were doing?" she yelled, scrambling for her pajama bottoms. She found them and managed to pin Dylan with her most scathing look as she yanked them on beneath the covers. "All I wanted was a nice, peaceful breakfast in a little café someplace, away from all the craziness of this hotel—and especially away from this honeymoon suite. So what did you do? Invite in four people to join us!"

"Aunt Geraldine—"

"Don't even give me that." Shaking, Stacey threw back the covers and, finally dressed, leaped out of bed. She stomped over to where Dylan stood and put her hands on her hips. "This might have been another one of Aunt Geraldine's honeymoon surprises, but you took every possible advantage of it."

"I thought you were enjoying it."

She had been. A little.

But that was beside the point.

"You're just, just, just"—she cranked her arm in the air, trying to summon up an explanation—"just taking over everything! You bulldozed in here, made me take you on as a partner in this stupid charade—"

"Wait a minute. You agreed that I—"

"No, *you* agreed." Stacey shook her head. "You agreed you should be here. You agreed you weren't leaving until the weekend was over. *You* agreed I needed help."

Dylan gazed over her shoulder, probably hoping she'd wrap up her tirade soon so he could go back to his pancakes. His indifference only infuriated her more. Even now he wasn't listening to her.

Just like Charlie.

"As usual," she said as she folded her arms to hide her trembling hands, "you didn't stop to consider what I wanted."

His gaze slipped to her face. His expression sobered. "That's not true," Dylan said quietly. "All I thought of this morning was what you wanted. What you'd like."

She unfolded her arms and paced across the suite. Why couldn't he see how everything he'd done made it impossible for her to even find out what she wanted? He hadn't so much as asked what she wanted for breakfast or where she wanted to go—or what kind of musical accompaniment she'd like, Stacey fumed. Dylan was a man who intended to be in charge, and he'd put himself squarely there.

"But what about our deal, our deal to be inconspicuous?" She hated the wail in her voice but was unable to squash it in time. "You're breaking our deal right and left."

"I only thought of what would please you." Crossing the suite's plush carpet, Dylan stopped beside her and rubbed his hands gently along her shoulders. "I didn't mean to make you mad."

"That's what they always say."

He dropped his hands from her shoulders. Obviously, Dylan had no defense. "No. But I'll bet that's what your ex-husband used to say. The difference here is, I mean it."

Wavering, Stacey stared at him, trying to gauge if what he said was true. Was she overreacting because of her past with Charlie?

No. Dylan really *was* trying to take over the honeymoon charade. The breakfast had only been more proof of that. Still, she supposed it was possible he meant well.

She bit her lip, then reached out to touch his shoulder. "Oh, Dylan, I don't know. This whole thing has me going nuts. If I survive the weekend, it'll be a miracle." He couldn't help wanting to be in charge. That was just the way he was. Who was she to hold it against him? "I'm sorry. I didn't mean—"

He held up his hand. His gaze swept the room service cart and their empty bed, then came to rest on her face. "No need to explain." His mouth twisted into a half smile that somehow hurt her more than the anger she expected. "I understand. You've got me confused with someone else. We'll have to change that, won't we?"

She gazed up at him without the slightest idea how to reply. She'd been so certain of his motives. But if Dylan really didn't care what she wanted, then why did he look so disappointed?

"Enjoy your breakfast," he went on quietly. "I'll be in the shower, getting ready for the rest of this charade. We've got a golf date in a little more than an hour."

Before she could answer, he disappeared into the bathroom and closed the door behind him. Hugging herself, Stacey stared at the door as the shower spray turned on, punctuating the end of their discussion.

The end of the easy playfulness between them.

And the end of her certainty about anything.

Six

"Not quite what you expected?" Dylan smiled at Stacey, stretching his arms overhead with a golf putter in hand.

If her expression was anything to go by, she'd expected to set foot on a course very different than the one they'd arrived at twenty minutes ago in fulfillment of Aunt Geraldine's next honeymoon surprise.

Of course, he could be totally off-base.

It wouldn't be the first time he was wrong about her.

Dylan lowered his putter and leaned on it, watching the enticing sway of Stacey's hips as she traveled the length of the path leading to their tee-off point.

"No, not quite what I expected," she called, propping her putter over her shoulder. She stepped toward him looking like some department store's version of Sporty Femininity, wearing canvas sneakers, a flippy white skirt, and Dylan's favorite bit of attire, a chest-hugging pale pink sweater. "But I like it. It's cute."

So was she. She stopped next to him, beside the statue of a giant saucer and teacup emblazoned with the words Tee-Time, and looked around. The miniature golf course surrounding them was filled with meandering paths, statues, the requisite windmill, a pond with a waterfall, and huge plaster apple trees.

Shading her eyes, Stacey gazed over it all. "Finally. We can just relax and be ourselves for a few hours."

As a dig about their breakfast-in-bed plans gone awry, it was pretty mild. But the memory of her reaction to this morning's surprise added enough bite to her remark to make it sting. Dylan still wasn't sure how things had gone so wrong, so fast.

Strike one, the Renaissance dinner.

Strike two, the breakfast serenade.

Strike three . . . and he'd be out of the action for good. If he was going to convince Stacey to give him another try, he'd have to be more careful the next time he planned a romantic surprise.

Turning, Stacey flipped her putter from her shoulder. It swung through the air with a whoosh, forcing Dylan to duck or else be brained with the thing. He surfaced at eye level with her waist as she spun around.

"What are you doing?" she demanded.

Not thinking about miniature golf, that was for sure. Her snug sweater had ridden up as she moved, revealing a smooth glimpse of belly and driving all golf-related thoughts straight out of his mind. Probably part of her strategy.

"Warming up," Dylan improvised, making good on his claim by touching his toes a couple of times. He straightened to a skeptical wrinkling of her nose and added several side-to-side windmills for good measure.

Stacey raised her eyebrows. "The better to play competitive mini-golf, I suppose?"

"Yeah. Aggressive game, if you play it right." He bent his knee in a quadriceps stretch, grabbing his foot and raising it until it touched the back of his pants.

He smiled. She'd never believe his cutthroat mini-golf story, but it was too late to turn back now. He'd just have to show Stacey he was serious. About this, about the honeymoon charade . . . about having a second chance with her.

Any self-respecting guy would still be mad at her, after her blatant lack of appreciation for his first Big Romantic Gesture. Looking at her now, Dylan guessed his willingness to forgive and forget meant he valued spending time with Stacey more than he valued that particular brand of self-respect.

He grabbed his other foot and repeated the quadriceps stretch, ignoring her open skepticism. "You'll be sore tomorrow if you don't stretch out," he warned. "Don't come crying to me if you wake up and can't move."

"That's what the masseuse is for."

She twirled to pick up one of their assigned golf balls. Her skirt flared with the movement. So did Dylan's body heat level. The woman could interest him more with a glance in his direction than most women could with a bikini, a bucket of body oil, and a blatant invitation.

"I'll put myself in the masseuse's capable hands," Stacey added. *Speaking of body oil*, Dylan groused silently. She tossed her bright orange golf ball into the air and caught it again neatly in her palm. "And come out feeling better than ever," she finished, smiling at him.

He hoped not. Dylan didn't think of himself as a violent man, but the idea of the nameless honeymoon surprise masseuse touching Stacey made him feel like punching the guy in the nose. He gazed out over the golf course to cover the sudden surge of unearned possessiveness he felt and tightened his grip on his putter.

"So," Stacey said, sounding tentative. "Do we start here?"

He turned to find her frowning down at the bright indoor-outdoor carpeted green, still tossing her ball. Nah. She couldn't mean what he thought she meant.

"You've never played mini-golf before?"

"You say that as if it's un-American, or something."

She hadn't. "It *is* un-American. What kind of childhood did you have, anyway?"

"A perfectly normal one," she assured him.

"Not without mini-golf." He edged up behind her, guided Stacey's putter in her hands, and covered her fingers with his own. "First you hold the putter." He bent low enough to speak against her ear. "Just like this."

"Okay." She sounded deadly serious, as though they were discussing taxes, or maybe an impending shoe sale. "Just like this?"

"Good." Dylan eased his hands over her wrists, straightening them, then over her forearms and up to her slender biceps. "When you swing, the power comes from here. And also"— he cupped her waist and felt her body tremble in his arms— "from here."

"Ummm, shouldn't we start with the ball first?" Her voice sounded as though she'd been holding in her breath and released it all to speak. "Dylan?"

"We'll get to that." He stroked his cheek along hers under the pretense of adjusting her stance. Sweat beaded between his shoulder blades and rolled beneath his faded shirt, sweat that had nothing to do with the desert sun beating down on them both. "We've got all the time in the world."

She stilled. Her head came up. "No, we don't."

"What do you mean?"

"Look." Glancing back at him, Stacey cupped his chin in her fingers. She turned his head toward the entrance to the mini-golf course.

A tall, aggressively stylish blond woman stepped on the green. She paused with one hand to her sunglasses and surveyed the course. The desk clerk from the hotel.

Dylan frowned. "Did she give you the twenty-minute blow-by-blow account of the bouquet throwing at her wedding? Or was I just lucky?"

"Nah. I was lucky the same way. Except I was treated to a rendition of the wedding toasts. Verbatim." She looked over her shoulder at him. "What's the matter, you don't like weddings?"

"Not unless I'm a participant." He watched as she swung her purse by its shoulder strap, caught it in her hands, and started rummaging through it. "What are you doing?"

"Trying to come up with a disguise." She pulled out a crushed white hat, a tube of something, and a dark pair of tortoiseshell sunglasses, then grabbed his arm. "Come on."

He had just enough time to grab their putters and the balls before she hauled him by the forearm behind one of the fake apple trees. Dylan ducked to avoid one of the eight-inch red painted apples, then hunkered down beside Stacey. She grabbed the pretend tree trunk with one hand and peered around it.

"It's her, all right." Looking businesslike, she crouched beside Dylan and dropped her supplies on the green. She shoved the sunglasses on her head like a headband, grabbed the tube, and squeezed a blob of something baby blue in her palm. Squinting, she eyed Dylan.

"So," he said, "we're hiding back here because. . . ?"

"Because I need time to think before dealing with somebody else from the hotel, that's why." Stacey grabbed his chin, turned his head to the side and back again, then frowned fiercely. "Also because this time I'm leaving nothing up to chance." She dipped her forefinger in the baby blue goo. "Hold still."

"Whaddya mean?" Dylan slurred, finding it hard to talk with her hand clamped onto his chin like a vise. "She's just a hotel employee. What's she going to do, dial direct to Aunt Geraldine and turn us—hey!"

He caught her wrist partway to his face. The goo on her fingertip gleamed in the sunlight. So did her ex-husband's wedding ring. Unreasonably, he wanted to twist it off and drop it in the murky mini-golf pond. Instead, he nodded at the blue goo. "Where are you going with that stuff?"

Stacey cocked her head sideways as though being forced to explain things to an especially backward partner in crime. "I'm going to make sure you're *inconspicuous*."

She sounded fairly smug, he thought, for a person supposedly afraid of having her honeymoon deception found out any second.

"Not with that stuff, you're not."

"Quit being a baby. It's just zinc oxide ointment. Sunscreen. You don't stop needing sunscreen just because it's winter, you know."

"It's blue." Dylan backed up as far as he could without leaving the concealing shade of the thick plaster tree trunk. He raised an eyebrow at her. "Is this your idea of revenge for this morning? Are you sure that's not eye shadow, or rouge, or something?"

"As if I want blue cheeks." She blew a deep breath and crab-walked over to him, then locked her vise grip on his chin again. Her flowery scent, soap or shampoo or something else, washed over him, successfully scrambling his thoughts enough that Dylan quit squirming for a second.

Stacey seized the opportunity. "And anyway, you're being ridiculous." She peered speculatively at the goo on her finger. "You'd look awful with blue eye shadow. It would totally clash with your eyes."

Dylan smirked. "Ha, ha."

"Besides, that wouldn't look very inconspicuous, now would it?" Her gaze darted toward the blond hotel desk clerk, then met his. "Now hold still."

Her finger, laden with shimmery blue, came closer.

Dylan eyed the stuff warily. "I don't care if we're found out." He leaned far enough away that she couldn't touch him. "I'm not letting you smear that stuff on me."

"If you keep arguing with me, you're going to blow our hiding place. Trust me, will you?"

Trust me. It was what he was always asking her to do for him. How could he refuse?

He couldn't. Hell.

"Only if I get to smear some on you, too."

Hey, that might actually be fun. Grinning, Dylan thrust his face forward again.

"Fine." She came closer, peering at him intently.

He admired the curve of her cheek, the delicate arch of her eyebrows, the straight, even line of her nose. He tried not to indulge his suspicions that Stacey was about to give him his first beauty makeover.

"Cute freckles," he said, hoping to distract himself with a little conversation. Too late. Her finger smoothed cool goo on the bridge of his nose. He jerked backward.

She smiled. "I don't have freckles. Hold still. This will only take a minute."

She did have freckles, a pale smattering just over the bridge of her nose and the top of her cheeks. They looked cute.

"Yes, you do."

She plopped her sunglasses on her face. "Quit trying to distract me." She dabbed a couple more times, spread her goo-covered finger across both his cheeks, than examined her handiwork with a critical expression. "I guess that'll do."

Keeping her baby-blue covered palm aloft, Stacey dug into her purse, muttered something. She pulled out a mangy-looking Diamondbacks baseball cap and a pair of aviator sunglasses. Dylan leaned over, looking into the depths of her purse.

"Have you got any snacks in there? Maybe a hank of bratwurst or a spare Thanksgiving turkey? I'm getting kind of hungry, and it looks as if you've got room for—"

She smacked him in the knee with the cap. "Ha, ha. Here, put these on."

She shoved the cap and aviators toward him. Leaning closer, she turned up his shirt collar, too. He felt like The Fonz.

"I happen to travel prepared," she said staunchly. "There's no crime in that."

"These look like men's sunglasses."

"They are." Stacey shrugged. "They used to belong to Charlie. I haven't seen him lately to return them."

Dylan looked at the hat and sunglasses in his hand, having a satisfying vision of himself stomping the stuff into dust. Sighing, he put them on instead. "How come you're still carrying around your ex-husband's personal belongings?"

"Look. I only divorced Charlie. I didn't hire a hit man to rub him out, or anything. Sheesh. To hear you talk, you'd think I'm packing a Charlie Ames voodoo doll in here." Stacey fiddled one-handed with something inside her purse.

"Are you? Because I think the voodoo idea actually has some merit."

"Ha, ha."

Dylan adjusted his hat brim, then reached over to scoop a little of the blue oxide goo from her palm. Time for *his* turn at finger painting.

"You're supposed to put it on the angled, prominent parts of your face," she instructed, setting her purse down. "Like your nose and chee"—Stacey looked up at him, mid-sentence, and burst out laughing—"ch—ch—cheekbones," she choked out, trying to stifle her amusement.

He frowned. "What's so funny?"

"You." She caught his expression, looked chagrined, and tried to settle down by coming closer so Dylan could apply some goo.

Except when she got there, her gaze roamed over his hat, his sunglasses, his turned-up collar, and his undoubtedly bizarre-looking goo-smeared face. He could tell she lost the battle to quit laughing right there. Her lips quirked. A sound something like a snort came out. She pressed her mouth tightly together.

"Go ahead," she said, pushing the words between barely moving lips. Stacey removed her sunglasses and nodded toward his hand, indicating the ointment. "I'm ready. I think."

Dylan raised his goo-tipped finger and swiped a gob of baby blue onto her nose. Her gaze wandered from his face upward, then made another circuit around his head. Her body started shaking. With suppressed laughter.

He rested his forearms on his thighs. "*What?*"

A laugh burbled from between her lips. "You look like The Invisible Man. All you need is a trench coat and you're in business."

"Very funny." She was probably right, but that didn't mean he had to like it. Here he was, trying to do things her way— her supposedly *inconspicuous* way—and she couldn't quit giggling over it. "Wait until you see what you look like when I'm finished with you."

"You wouldn't dare."

"Try me."

"Shhh! I think I hear something."

Dylan heard it, too. The desk clerk's cheery, high-pitched voice, floating toward them from the Tee-Time cup.

"Come on, Mark! Let's get going! I've got to be back at work this afternoon!"

"Okay, honey!" a chipper-sounding male voice answered.

Great. There were two of them. Identically buoyant.

"Hurry up." Stacey stuck her face forward.

You asked for it. Loading up his fingertip again, Dylan smoothed out the blue goo until it covered her whole nose, plus her supposedly nonexistent freckles. Then he dunked into the ointment again and drew three thick stripes on each of her cheeks. He finished up with fat blue dots in the center of her forehead, above each eyebrow, and on her chin.

A masterpiece.

By Picasso, maybe.

"Done." He accepted the tissue she offered to wipe off his hands and scrubbed them clean of ointment. "You'd better give it a minute to dry."

"Thanks." Smiling with the pleasure of a woman in charge for the first time, Stacey fanned her fingers in front of her face. She grabbed two handfuls of her shoulder-length hair, twisted them behind her head, then squashed her white floppy hat over the whole bunched-up assembly. She eased on her sunglasses with conspicuous care. "I think we're set. Let's go."

Dylan eyed her hat. "Okay, Little Buddy."

"Huh?"

"We look like The Invisible Man meets Gilligan."

Just for a second, her face took on a wary expression. "You're kidding, right?"

"Yeah." If following her idiotic plan was his only chance of getting in Stacey's good graces, you bet he was kidding. Dylan helped her to her feet, waited as she brushed off her skirt, then gathered up their golfing gear. "Of course I'm kidding."

He still wasn't convinced this would make them look inconspicuous. However, the further he followed her loose-limbed, graceful sway toward Tee-Time, the less he cared. It was enough just to be together. Cooperating, for a change.

Halfway to the giant teacup, Stacey stopped so fast her tennis shoes squeaked. Dylan, too engrossed in admiring her to have full control over his feet, bumped into her. She teetered—half-unbalanced by the weight of her monster purse, he figured—then grabbed his arm and managed to spin around to face him.

"Hold it." She whipped her purse between them. In the spirit of cooperation, Dylan propped it up with his hands while she shuffled things around in it. "I forgot this."

She pulled out a disposable camera.

She slung it by its strap around his neck, then stepped back to examine the effect. "That's it! You look like the perfect tourist."

"Or maybe Claude Raines on vacation."

Stacey smiled. "Now you're getting into the swing of things. Let's go."

"Whew! That was close!" Stacey muttered two hours later, feeling triumphant and not a little bit vindicated from the safety of her perch in the Jeep's passenger seat.

"Nah." Dylan braked beneath the Atmosphere's porte-cochere. He turned off the ignition, leaned against the steering wheel, and gave her a heart-stopping grin. "Not close at all. Admit it. Your plan worked."

Stacey shook her head. "I must have been out in the sun too long." She pretended to fan herself with the souvenir pennant he'd bought her at the mini-golf course. "Are you actually agreeing with me that my *inconspicuous* method worked best?"

"Best?" His grin widened.

Despite his Invisible Man-as-tourist getup, she thought he looked pretty fantastic. *It figured. Not even a disguise could make Dylan Davis look goofy.*

"I didn't say your plan was the best." He tossed the keys to a valet. "I just said it worked. This time."

"This time, huh?" Stacey watched him round the front of the Jeep, then stop beside her seat. "This time and every time, you mean."

Dylan grunted noncommittally. He held up his hand, and she took it, too happy with the recent turn of events to try to force an agreement out of him. Their golf game had been a success, they'd remained relatively incognito, despite some amused glances from the other mini-golf patrons, and, most importantly, they'd actually learned to cooperate.

Surely before too long he'd come to the realization that,

when it came to the honeymoon charade at least, she was right.

And he was wrong.

As though reading her thoughts, Dylan tugged her hand. "Let's go, Sweetiepie. Your *husband* is starving."

Stacey stumbled from the high Jeep seat, flew across the pavement, and wound up squished up against his chest. His arms enfolded her. For a minute, their embrace felt so real and so right that she only stood there, enjoying it.

Then common sense returned.

"Thanks for the game." She twisted out of his arms, then stepped back. She eyed the huge glass front doors of the hotel.

Safety? Or just another accident waiting to happen?

"It was my pleasure."

He sounded as if he meant it. All the connotations his words implied sent excitement shimmying down her spine.

"Now," he went on, taking Stacey's arm and heading with her toward the hotel entrance. "Where do you want to go for lunch?"

She smiled up at him. "Hey. You *can* be taught!"

"Ouch!"

"Sorry."

But not sorry he'd listened to her this morning. All during their golf game, thoughts of their argument over the breakfast serenade had churned in her head. It was a relief to know her efforts in speaking out hadn't all been for naught.

"Actually," Stacey said as their reflections loomed larger in the doors in front of them, "do you still have that silver dollar we won last night? I thought we might take advantage of our good karma and try our luck before lunch. What do you say?"

"Good idea."

Letting go of her arm, Dylan lunged for one of the doors and yanked it open for her. Mr. Chivalry. She liked that. Yammering noise and more Muzak Christmas carols whooshed at her as Stacey stepped into the casino lobby.

"Feeling lucky, are you?" Dylan caught up with her. "That's good. So am I. Maybe we can pull off this honeymoon thing, yet." He fished around in his pockets, came up with their silver dollar winnings, and tossed the coin in the air. "So, where should we spend this baby?"

Stacey bit her lip and looked around the casino. In every direction, rows of jangling slot machines gleamed in the multicolored overhead lights, stretching far into the corners of the room. Coins clanked into some of their bins with the thrilling sound of winning, but obviously she couldn't pick those. They were already taken.

Yet suddenly, for some reason, it seemed very important that she choose well. Important to maintain the new spirit of togetherness between her and Dylan, important to validate the good luck they'd enjoyed so far . . . important just for the fun of winning.

"I don't know," she said, turning to Dylan. "You pick."

"Oh, no. I'm not picking. If I wind up choosing a bum machine, somehow you'll make it sound as if I did it on purpose, just to wreck your honeymoon charade."

Did she really seem that eager to place the responsibility for the success or failure of the honeymoon charade on his shoulders? So far, most of it had been thrust in their laps, ready-made in the form of the honeymoon surprises and their stay in the suite. It wasn't as though Dylan had anything to do with that. After all, they'd *both* volunteered to help Richard and Janie.

"No, I wouldn't," Stacey protested.

"It's your idea. You pick."

"Really. I don't mind if you pick."

"I don't want to."

She crossed her arms, feeling frustrated. "How about if I close my eyes and hold out my hand, and you steer me toward one of the slot machines? That way, technically I'm choosing, but—"

"Uh-uh." Behind his sunglasses, Dylan looked as though he was trying very hard not to laugh. "Will you just make a decision already?"

"Fine." Trying to look determined, Stacey strode to the nearest row of slot machines and examined them. Maybe one of them would seem luckier than the rest.

After a few minutes, Dylan said, "It's just a dollar. Go ahead and pick one. I thought you felt lucky."

"I do." But she wanted a lucky slot machine, too. Unfortunately, no hunches were hitting her the way they did to people in the movies. The machines all felt exactly the same.

Dylan touched her shoulder. "The luck isn't in one of these machines. It's inside *you*. Go ahead. You can't lose."

Drawing a deep breath, Stacey examined the machines again. She pointed to the one nearest her. "Okay. Eeny, meeney, miney, mo—"

"Arrgh!" Dylan slapped his forehead, knocking his Diamondbacks cap askew. "I can't believe it's this hard for you to make a decision."

Defensively, she frowned at him. He was too busy wiping off the blue zinc oxide smear on the heel of his hand to notice. "The rate of inflation will rise before you manage to spend that silver dollar," he said, talking over her rhyme. "Our winnings will be worth ninety-nine percent less by the time we get them."

". . . told me to pick the very best one," Stacey went on chanting at the glittering faces of the four machines in front of her. "And you are not it!" There. One down. She started again, more quietly this time.

"Done!" she announced a minute later. She slapped her hand on the winning slot machine and shot Dylan a triumphant look.

Finally his answering expression said. Stacey didn't care. Adopting her best gambler's voice, she held out her hand, palm facing. "Hit me."

"Like, with a ruler?" he asked, grinning. "The nuns at parochial school used to do that, but I don't think you've—"

"Give me the money, you goofball."

He pressed the silver dollar in her palm. Hefting it, Stacey hesitated before dropping it in the slot machine. It felt heavy and important, its weight a talisman of impending good fortune.

"Wait." Looking suddenly serious, Dylan wrapped his hand around hers, cradling the coin within their united grasp.

Heat crept from his fingers to hers, turning the silver warm in her palm. "First, a kiss for good luck."

He bent his head. Stacey's heart pounded. He should have looked ridiculous, still decked out as the ultimate tourist. She should have felt silly, standing in the middle of a crowded casino looking the way she did, with her hair all bunched up beneath her crumpled Gilligan hat and her blue zinc oxide nose and her movie-star-incognito sunglasses.

But all she felt was beautiful.

Because of Dylan. Because of the way he touched her and because of the caring in his voice. Tenderly, he raised one hand to the back of her neck, and all at once time stood still.

The frenzy of the casino receded, leaving her aware of nothing but the anticipation between them. Stacey leaned forward, mesmerized by the gentle feel of his touch. *Kiss me.*

She pressed her palm to his chest and discovered his heart beating as wildly as her own. Smiling, she raised her head. At the same moment Dylan's mouth met hers. His kiss felt hard and demanding, warm and giving, all at the same time. It swept her mind clean of everything but this moment. This man.

Their sunglasses clinked together and slid. His hat brim jabbed at her forehead. Stacey didn't care. She wanted more of his kiss, his teasing tongue, his smooth nipping teeth that set her lips tingling with pleasure. She returned his kiss with a passion that curled her toes—and, she hoped, his. Her fingers tightened on his shirt, seeking support in a world turned unpredictable and anchorless.

It was as though they'd never separated. Being in Dylan's arms felt familiar and bittersweet, flavored with the memories they'd shared months before. His mouth opened over hers again, his tongue stroked over hers again, and Stacey welcomed him with a fierceness that surprised her. She wanted him.

Now. Later. Both, she didn't care. She wanted Dylan and only him . . . no matter what his loving cost her.

He ended the kiss. Awareness crashed back to her. The music, the casino lights, and the murmur of voices all flooded her senses. Trembling, Stacey withdrew her hand from his chest.

Dylan caught her wrist midway. Over the rims of his sunglasses, his gaze pierced straight through her own smoky lenses. Suddenly, she felt grateful for their partially concealing protection. Otherwise he'd certainly see her emotions, too new and exposed to hide, reflected in her eyes.

Holy cow. *She wanted Dylan*. Even after all this time.

"Did you . . . ?" His voice sounded rough. "Did you just . . . ? No." He shook his head. "No. Never mind."

"What?"

The steel in his grip and the heated rasp of his voice intrigued her—made her almost unbearably curious. Had he felt the same things she had? The closeness, the familiarity, the *attraction*?

Apparently not, she decided when Dylan released her wrist. He shoved his sunglasses back where they belonged, heedless of the smear of blue that doing so added to his eyebrow, and tried a crooked smile.

"It's nothing." He opened his hand over hers and unfolded her fingers to reveal the silver dollar within. Dylan nodded to the slot machine behind her. "If that kiss didn't bring us good luck, I don't know what will."

He wasn't going to tell her. Of course, that didn't *really* matter, Stacey told herself. After the honeymoon weekend was over with, they'd go their separate ways just like they had before. Wouldn't they?

"Me neither." She attempted to push down the disappointment she felt with a smile of her own. *Two could play at this game*. She raised the coin to the slot. "Ready?"

Dylan held up both hands with fingers crossed. "Ready. If we win, I get to sleep in the bed tonight. Another night on that loveseat and my knees will be permanently crooked."

Stacey smiled. What were the chances of their winning with a single coin? That was a goodwill gesture she could afford to make.

"Okay." She pinched the coin between her fingertips. "It's a deal."

Closing her eyes, she wished for good luck and dropped in the money. Dylan reached around her and pulled the slot machine handle.

"Here goes." He wrapped his arms around her waist from behind, then propped his chin on her shoulder. Together, they watched the mechanism spin.

A bunch of cherries locked in place on the center line. Another bunch of cherries locked in place beside it. Two matches! Stacey held her breath. She felt Dylan's chest expand against her shoulder blades with an indrawn breath of his own.

The mechanism spun. A third bunch of cherries spun onto the line. Stacey blinked. They'd won?

They'd won.

Won big, judging by the high-pitched jangling of the slot machine bells. Coins clanked into the bin and just kept coming, pouring in a shower of silver. Numbly, Stacey stared at it for a second before reality kicked in.

They'd won!

She shrieked and grabbed Dylan. He looked as shocked as she did. "We won! We won!" she yelled, shaking him—probably shaking him silly, but too excited to stop. "We won!"

"I get to sleep in the bed." As he gaped at the outpouring of coins, a huge grin spread over his face. "We won!"

Money kept on clanging into the slot machine bin. Other casino patrons gathered around, pointing and talking and smiling. Somebody shoved a plastic cup in Stacey's hand, and she held it beneath the stream of money. Another cup for her and two cups for Dylan weren't enough to contain the overflow.

By the time the casino management arrived to congratulate them, the money had slowed to a steady ping-ping into the pile Dylan had started collecting in his shirt. He held his shirt hem beneath the flow of coins like a farm wife collecting eggs from the golden goose, grinning at least as happily as Stacey was.

They were celebrities in an instant. Passersby offered their congratulations, then raced to their own slot machines with renewed faith. Winning could and did happen.

"Congratulations!" boomed the uniformed casino employee who arrived, partner in tow.

He looked like a ringer for a professional basketball player, tall and lean and with hair shaved to within an eighth of an inch all over his head. His partner, a petite brunette with a digital camera hanging from a strap around her neck, stepped forward, smiling too. They both seemed thrilled that Stacey and Dylan had won in their casino.

The brunette put her hand forward and clasped both of theirs in turn, patient enough to allow Dylan to juggle his shirtful of coins before shaking his hand.

"Congratulations!" she echoed. "What are your names?"

Names, names. For a second, Stacey felt too bedazzled to say. During the handshaking, the basketball player lookalike had somehow guided her and Dylan into a standing position beside their winning slot machine. Between that and the unreality of having actually won, she could barely think straight. Beside her, Dylan seemed in a similar state, cradling his shirtful of coins with a beaming smile.

"Dylan Davis," he said.

"Stacey Ames," she said at the same time. Wow, this was sooo neat! It had to be a good omen, a positive sign for their honeymoon suite collaboration.

"Fine, fine." The brunette made a note of it, then raised her camera. She edged closer as Mr. Basketball explained how to cash in their coins with the casino.

"You're our fourth big winner of the day," he said, speaking with at least as much blatant cheeriness as the hotel desk clerk brought to her job. Maybe chipper behavior was a hiring prerequisite for the hotel.

"Stand a little closer to each other," the brunette instructed. "Okay. Now raise your cups—sir, your shirt will do nicely, thanks—and say, 'We won!'"

Obediently, Stacey and Dylan shuffled together. "We won!" they shouted in unison.

It wasn't until the brunette's camera flashed in their faces and blinded Stacey that she realized what they'd done less than a minute earlier.

They'd given out their names.

Their *real* names.

Whoops.

Seven

"I still don't see what the problem is." Dylan swiped his hotel key card through the reader at the honeymoon suite door.

Stacey stared at him. He had to be kidding. They'd given away their real identities, had pictures taken to prove it, and made possibly the most public spectacle of themselves with winning. How could he not see the problem?

"We told them our real names!" Miserably, she followed him through the unlocked suite door. "That's the problem."

Ginger danced at her feet, shimmying with joy at their return. Stacey gave her a pat, then dragged herself to the sitting area and brushed off the remnants of what looked like chewed-up hotel stationery—Ginger's latest doggie entertainment, she guessed—so she could plop on the loveseat.

Their absences weren't fair to Ginger. Maybe they ought to spend the rest of the night in the honeymoon suite, to avert another doggie meltdown.

Behind her Stacey heard Dylan crooning to Ginger, saying something about chewing up his shoes instead of the curtains. A minute later he landed on the loveseat beside her, forcing her to tug her purse out of his way and onto her lap.

She hugged it. If only money really did buy happiness, then maybe she could find some way out of this mess. Her half of their slot machine winnings had to be good for something, didn't it?

Dylan leaned over, looking exaggeratedly patient. It was the same expression he'd worn since she'd whispered her revelation about their name slipup to him at the hotel cashier's office.

"I'm telling you. You're worrying too much about this."

Grrr. If there was anything Stacey hated, it was being told her worries were insignificant. She tried buying time to respond with a little patience by taking off her sunglasses, folding them, and stowing them along with her Gilligan hat inside her purse. It didn't work.

She still wanted to scream at him.

"Oh?" Adopting an expression of polite surprise, she combed her fingers through her stringy hair. Fear of hat head had prevented her from trying to deal with it until now. A shower was definitely in order.

"Is that right?" she asked. "Exactly what makes you think I'm worrying too much?"

"All they asked for were our names. All they did was take our picture and hand us some money. As far as they're concerned, we're not even guests of this hotel. They didn't ask us where we were staying, you know."

He was right. They hadn't. "Probably because they already knew. We *are* supposed to be the honeymoon couple, you know."

"In this town, honeymoon couples are a dime a dozen," Dylan pointed out. "On The Strip alone there must be fifty wedding chapels. Maybe more. Do you think we're the only 'honeymoon' couple around?"

"But—"

"Trust me. Nothing's gone wrong. Aunt Geraldine will never catch word of this. Not unless you tell her yourself." He whipped off his aviators and ball cap and handed them both to her, then raked his fingers through his hair. It stood on end like short brown spikes. "Are you going to tell her?"

"Of course not!"

"Because the way you're going on about this, a person could get the idea you're trying to sabotage the honeymoon charade. If you are, you might as well cut to the chase. Just call her up and spill the beans right now. It would sure free up the rest of my weekend."

"How dare you!" Stacey stuffed the sunglasses and cap in her purse with enough force to make Dylan wince. Good. At least that meant he was paying attention. "Of course I'm not trying to sabotage the honeymoon charade. What a ridiculous thing to say."

Throwing her purse on the loveseat—wishing she could throw it at *him* for making such an outrageous suggestion— she stomped to the bathroom. Scowling, she picked up a comb and looked in the vanity mirror.

Her face stared back at her, flushed pink beneath a thick coating of baby blue zinc oxide war paint. Those were the only words for it. War paint. Three stripes streaked across each of her cheeks. Thumbprint-sized dots marched across her fore-head and chin. Her nose was a blue blob.

"Ahhh!"

Thumping footfalls sounded outside the bathroom. Dylan poked his head around the corner, his face filled with concern. His gaze whipped over her, just as though it *wasn't* completely obvious what was the matter.

"Are you okay?" he asked.

"Okay? Am I okay?" Stacey shook her head at her mirror image. "No, I'm not okay! On top of everything else, some-how *you*"—she poked her finger at his chest—"managed to make me look like a crazed lifeguard! Am I supposed to be *okay* with that?"

Stacey gripped the pink marble vanity and looked again at her mirror image. She'd actually appeared in public like this? Actually had her picture taken like this?

"What have you done to me?" she wailed. Her fingers tin-gled on their way to going completely numb, but that was the least of her concerns. Her greatest concern was . . . strangling Dylan.

Or at least giving him a coat of war paint to match.

He took one look at her and backed up, turning his head left and right like a fugitive searching for a hiding place.

"At least now you're not so worried about the honeymoon charade," he said. "Ha, ha."

Wisely, he retreated. She circled him through the sitting area, around the loveseat, and past the plate of Christmas cookies. Ginger yapped at her heels, wanting in on the game.

"Not now, girl," Stacey told her. "This time he's all mine."

Her gaze searched the room, landed on her purse, and an idea struck her. A devious idea. But Dylan deserved it. She picked up her purse.

"You told me to hurry up." Doubtless wondering what she was up to, he glanced at her purse. "I was just going for even coverage."

"Even coverage, huh?" Opening her purse, Stacey pulled out a tube of pomegranate-colored lipstick and a midnight blue-colored eyeliner pencil. She held up the lipstick to the sunlight streaming through the honeymoon suite window and squinted at it. Yes, it would do nicely.

He thought war paint was funny? She'd show him war paint.

"Even coverage, huh?" She felt a devilish smile lift her lips. "Funny you should mention that."

Dylan backed up, skirted the edge of the bed, and stopped on the other side. "If this is about the honeymoon charade," he said rapidly, "it's really no problem. The hotel's not going to call Aunt Geraldine."

"Oh, no?"

"No." His gaze zipped to the lipstick, then to the eyeliner pencil. He smiled too, but his grin looked a little wobblier than hers felt.

It was kind of a thrill to have the upper hand for once. Stacey did, after all, still owe him for his dirty trick at the end of their pillow fight.

"The ones we really have to worry about," Dylan said, "are the honeymoon surprise people. The ones who know Aunt Geraldine personally. If anyone's going to rat on us, it's them."

She stopped. He had a point.

But so did she. A cosmetics point. Two of them, in fact.

"You'd like that, wouldn't you?" She wielded her trusty lipstick and eyeliner. "You know, I'm starting to wonder if maybe you're just here to mess up my honeymoon charade. Is that it?"

The more she thought about it, the saner that crazy idea seemed. Why else would Dylan have tried to war paint her into public ridiculousness? Tried to take over the whole honeymoon façade? Tried to goad her into calling Aunt Geraldine and confessing everything?

But why?

"No." He backed up some more. His eyes followed the path of the cosmetics she wielded, but he kept on grinning. "Stacey, put the makeup down. Let's just talk about this like two reasonable adults."

"You're patronizing me now?"

"Don't be ridiculous."

"See! There you go again!"

"Aaack!" Dylan shoved his hands in his hair. Clearly, things weren't going the way he'd planned. He backed up into the window and stood there, silhouetted by the light.

"It wasn't enough that you broke up with me all those months ago." She advanced almost close enough to touch him—or paint him, which was what she really had in mind. "You had to come back and try to break my heart all over again, didn't you? Let me tell you something, Dylan, that's really twisted. I can't bel—"

"I broke your heart?"

She snapped her mouth closed, assaulted by the silence that fell between them. Dear God, had she really just blurted out what she thought she had?

"I broke your heart?" This time his voice was a broken whisper, slipping past her defenses right into the heart in question. What had she done?

She tried backpedaling first. "I mean, back when we were first dating, I—"

A goofy grin spread across his face, dissolving every bit of aggravation she'd felt before. Damn him. How did he keep doing that?

Dylan reached for her. His big hands closed around her hips, then traveled a sensuous trail up to her waist. The possessiveness inherent in his touch left no doubt he knew she was lying about how she felt. Stacey's breath caught, held, keeping time with the bump-skip rhythm of her heartbeat.

"That is," she choked out, desperate to retain what little rational thought she had left, "part of me thought maybe we—"

"Shhh." The tender smile on his face tantalized her almost as much as the slow squeeze and release of his hands on her waist. He drew her closer. "I really broke your heart?"

"You don't have to sound so happy about it."

"I'm not happy."

His gaze met hers. His body heat touched her, penetrated her clothes to wrap around her heart. This wasn't how it was supposed to be . . . her confessing her stupid inability to get over him, him savoring every word. But somehow, Stacey couldn't pull away.

"You *look* happy," she groused. "You're grinning like a kid at Christmas."

"I'm grinning because I *feel* like a kid at Christmas." Dylan tipped her chin up with his hand and looked into her eyes. "Which is only appropriate, right? It's almost Christmastime. And I have to say . . . I've never received a better gift."

"A better gift than my humiliation? Ha." Stacey jerked her head away. "I don't know—"

"Let me start over." He smiled, and something in his expression made her heart skip a beat. "I'm sorry. I'm so sorry to have hurt you." He caressed her chin, her neck, her shoulder . . . but he might as well have reached in and touched her heart. "I thought I was the only brokenhearted one. I was a fool to let you go, Stacey."

Him? Broken-hearted?

Because of *her*?

It was too much to take in all at once. "But what—"

"Richard and Janie told me all you wanted was a casual relationship," he explained. "When I started falling for you, I . . . I panicked, I guess. From where I stood, the whole thing looked doomed."

"Doomed?" It hadn't been doomed. She'd been falling for him, too.

But she'd never told him so. Just like she'd tried to hide her feelings from him during the whole honeymoon charade.

Amazed at her own blindness, Stacey felt like slapping her forehead. How would she ever start getting what she wanted if she never admitted what it was?

"So I bailed out." Dylan's face twisted at the memory. "In my own defense, it seemed pretty smart at the time." He smiled again, laughing at himself. "I thought I'd actually get over you. But it was the dumbest thing I ever did."

She looked up at him, wanting to ease into his arms, to enjoy the feel of him holding her . . . but afraid to do it. "Why are you telling me this? Why me, why now?"

"Sheesh. Do I have to spell it out for you?"

Grinning, Dylan slipped the eyeliner pencil from her hand and peered at the tip. Apparently satisfied it would write, he turned up her wrist and started scrawling something on the underside of her forearm.

"Hey! That tickles! Haven't you already done enough damage to me with makeup today?"

He paused and looked up at her, still holding the pencil poised above her skin. "Do you really want me to stop?"

Was he kidding? She was dying of curiosity. Stacey bit her lip. "No," she admitted.

"Good." The soft pencil moved across her skin, forming letters, then words. Between Dylan's sloppy handwriting and the fact that he was holding her arm sideways, she couldn't tell what it said. He wrote more, his smile widening, then released her wrist. She looked down.

I love you.

Holy cow.

"I lou . . . I Lou?" she read, too rattled by the words to believe what they said. A joke seemed worlds safer. "You're Lou?"

He cupped her face in his hands. For once, Dylan looked absolutely serious. Something indescribably tender filled his gaze, and in that moment Stacey believed—no matter how incredible they were—the words he spoke next.

"No, silly," he said gruffly. "*I love you.*"

The lipstick drooped in her hand. Stacey tightened her grasp so she wouldn't drop it, then uncapped the slender tube. With trembling fingers, she swiveled up a half-inch of red.

Without her being aware of having reached for him, Dylan's wrist was in her hand. She turned it, exposing the underside of his forearm and, holding her breath, drew a curvy red question mark. She looked up at him.

His eyes darkened, but a smile curved his lips. "Always the skeptic, aren't you? I'll have to cure you of that. There's no reason in the world you can't believe me."

He raised her other arm and wielded his eyeliner pencil again. Its soft point scrawled over her arm.

Yes.

Then, in capital letters going all the way from her elbow to her wrist: *I LOVE YOU STACEY.*

She grinned. Once Dylan made a commitment, it looked as if he really went all out. Pursing her lips, she grabbed Dylan's other arm and drew a red lipstick heart. His free arm tightened on her waist as she embellished the heart with an arrow piercing through the edges.

He grinned as he watched her draw. "You had to make yours fancier than mine, didn't you?"

"It's not a competition," Stacey answered, stalling for time, trying to sound about a hundred times more lighthearted than she felt as she added a couple of feathers to her arrow.

What if he was kidding? Or, given the possible fiasco they might have made out of the honeymoon charade, trying to cheer her up?

I love you. It danced inside her head like a pink jewelry box ballerina, surprising and beautiful . . . and likely to stop with no warning at all.

Why? she wrote inside the heart she'd drawn.

Dylan wrinkled his forehead and read. "Why?"

She nodded, suddenly afraid to look up at him. He'd probably be mad. Maybe she'd spoiled the whole thing. But it was better to know the truth now rather than later, wasn't it?

"Yes," she whispered. "Why?"

Eight

Dylan hesitated, then cupped her jaw and raised her face to his. "A million reasons."

His voice wrapped her in warmth and half-forgotten wishes, seductive enough to make her hurl caution to the desert sun and melt right along with it. A million reasons . . . a million reasons to love her. Wow.

Stacey's knees wobbled, an unmistakable side effect of whatever spell Dylan was weaving. Like a sorcerer's lure, it kept her plastered happily next to him as the rest of her thoughts unraveled. She and Dylan, Dylan and she—together. Right now. It was almost too much to believe, too much to hope for.

Just believe him! her body screamed, but her head had gotten used to watching over the rest of her, and it had other ideas. Stacey swiveled her lipstick higher and smoothed her palm over his biceps as though it were a bumpy sheet of paper, then wrote. *Sex?*

Dylan gave her a roguish smile. "That's one reason. Let me show you some more."

He smoothed her sweater sideways, baring her shoulder. He stroked his pencil over her skin. Slowly, its tip circled the rounded edge of her shoulder with feather-light touches, then curved toward her neck. The sensation felt surprisingly erotic. Every nerve ending along her arm and shoulder tingled. She watched him draw, his face close enough to hers that she could detect the faint beginnings of beard stubble shading his jaw. If she leaned over a couple of inches, she could kiss him.

Mmmm. Good idea.

He frowned slightly, intent on his handiwork, then raised his pencil with a grin. "There."

Already missing the teasing stroke of his pencil, Stacey tucked her chin to her chest and peered at her shoulder. He'd drawn a chain of interlocked hearts.

"Show off." Playfully, she wrinkled her nose at him. How much more of this could she take before she caved completely? As a sexual conquest, she'd be no contest—not after a little more of Dylan's body graffiti. But maybe, just maybe, it was more than that.

Oh, how she wanted to believe it was more than that! She closed her eyes and made a quick wish. *Please. If this is only a dream, just let me sleep in, for once!* When she opened them again, Dylan smiled.

"That was just warming up."

He added a wink that left her noodle-legged and leaning. All this time, she'd thought she disliked men who winked. Winkers belonged in the same class with fanny-pinchers, street corner hooters and guys who called you "Babe". Didn't they?

Unless they were Dylan.

His fingers, blunt-edged and so much stronger than hers, twisted up more eyeliner. He raised his eyebrow at her. "Hold still, now. We don't have an eraser."

"What are you going to do?"

"I'm giving you those reasons you asked for." He bared her other shoulder, stroked his fingers over her skin like an artist testing his canvas, then wrote *Sexy*.

"We already covered that."

Was she nuts, arguing with him over it? *Shut up*, she ordered herself.

"No, we haven't." He lifted his gaze from her bare shoulder to her eyes. "This is a reason. *You're* sexy."

"Oh." She felt her face heat and realized she was blushing. "Umm, you are, too."

Dylan looked pleased. She looked him over, pretending to test her judgment. Her gaze wandered a leisurely arc from his big feet to the top of his mussed-up hair, lingering over points in between . . . muscular legs, jeans, a broad chest covered by his untucked shirt, wide shoulders, arms made for holding her, and a sappy, sexy grin. Yeah. *Sexy* was the only word for Dylan Davis.

He slipped his finger inside the scooped neckline of her sweater, just barely touching her skin. He lowered the soft cotton just enough to expose an inch or two of writing space.

Dylan touched the eyeliner to a place just below her collarbone, then smoothed it slowly sideways. Stacey shivered in reaction, biting her lip. She was supposed to hold still during this? It was torture.

But torture of the very best, most teasing kind. The eyeliner pencil moved, guided by his warm fingers, creating a path of ticklish, heightened sensation. His breath followed, fanning gently across her skin. It made her yearn for his lips, his hands, to follow the same path.

Touch me, she thought, and felt only the teasing glide of the eyeliner point. *Touch me.*

Dylan stopped writing and stepped back. Grinning, he caught hold of her arms and twirled her around. The next thing she knew, she was backed up to the huge honeymoon suite window. Sun-warmed glass heated her back, her arms, her thighs. It was nothing compared with the feel of his hands holding her there. She wanted this, wanted him . . . wanted to know what else he'd written. Stacey lowered her chin, trying to read the loopy midnight blue letters he'd drawn.

"Caring," Dylan said, tracing them with his finger. He raised his hands to smooth her hair from her face, then smiled. "You care about people more than anybody I know. You take care of them. Worry about them. You love them." He delved his fingers in her hair, drawing her closer to him. "*Love me,*" he whispered. "Let me love you."

She wanted to—wanted to answer him—but the longing she glimpsed in his eyes stunned her too much to speak. By the time Stacey regained her wits, Dylan had already moved on.

He flashed her a smile. "But maybe you want the rest of those reasons first."

Withdrawing his hands from her hair, he used them instead to trace the sides of her body, gliding past her shoulders, her arms, the indrawn curve of her waist. His fingers pressed on her hips, creating a new wave of sensation as his thumbs kneaded through her clothes, speaking his desire in a way no words could.

He dropped to his knees at her feet. His jaw caressed her bare belly, unerringly finding the few inches of skin left uncovered by her hiked-up sweater. Her stomach contracted, her pulse raced, and her knees wobbled harder, sending her flat against the heated window at her back. His lips nuzzled her belly button.

Yelping, Stacey grabbed his head. "What are you doing?"

Lazily, Dylan turned his face upward, using her hips for an anchor. "Looking for more bare canvas. You do want the rest of those reasons, don't you?"

Reasons? "Yes. *Yes*." Anything. She'd have agreed to anything to keep him close. "Please, don't stop."

"Oh, I won't stop," he promised, raising her T-shirt hem. Dylan peered at the gently curved slope of her belly and pattered his fingertips delicately along the waistline of her skirt. "This looks good. How about right here?"

He raised his eyebrow at a rakish angle, looking up at her. Stacey swayed in his arms, supported only by his hands, the sunny window, and the strength of his will. She murmured something meant to be agreement. It sounded more like a moan.

"Yes?" He poised the eyeliner near her belly button.

She wanted to scream for him to put his hands on her instead, to quit torturing her with that smooth pinpoint of sensation. Curiosity made her bite her lip to hold in the demand. She nodded.

He drew. She waited, quivering, as he stroked eyeliner loops and curlicues over her tummy, forming words she couldn't read. Tantalizing sensations she couldn't escape. And yearnings only Dylan could satisfy. Impatiently, Stacey buried her fingers deeper into his hair. Her breath came faster the further he wrote. Her spine felt liquid, useless to hold her much longer. Urged by the inexorable tug of his hand on her hip, she arched her pelvis forward, silently pleading for another touch, another stroke, for just one instant of skin against skin.

"Uh, uh, uh," he cautioned, giving her another belly nip. "If you wiggle, I might have to start all over again."

Oh, God . . . anything but that. She'd never survive. Stacey stiffened, flattening her palms against the window behind her. For an instant, she wondered if anyone could see her there, silhouetted in the sunlight with Dylan's head almost in her lap. Then she remembered they were on the hotel's top floor. No one but passing bluebirds could see them.

"Mmmm," Dylan moaned against her, still writing. His breath penetrated her thin skirt, searing all the way to her panties beneath. "You smell good. Sweet, like honey and cinnamon. Sweet . . . all over."

Stacey gasped, trembling harder. More writing would be hopeless. In her condition, she could barely stand. What was he doing to her?

"Mmmm." The husky rumble of his voice vibrated all the way to her heart and set fire to her senses. Dylan plucked his fingers along her skirt hem as he finished writing. He leaned back to examine the words. "I like it."

Cool air rushed over her skin. Somehow, Stacey managed to find the ability to speak, even though her brain had probably overheated fifteen minutes ago. "What does it say?"

He touched his fingertip to one side of her belly. "Smart," he said, tracing the word he'd written there. "Smart enough to have a brilliant career, a brand new life . . . and the wisdom to give me another try." Smiling, Dylan looked up at her. "You are giving me another try, aren't you?"

"That's what this is." Her heart raced as she admitted it—to herself and to him. "Starting over."

Dear God, that *was* what it was. Starting things over between them. If it was foolish, so be it. It was too late to turn back now.

"Generous," Dylan went on, his fingertips underlining the

second word he'd written in a loopy curve above her belly button. "You're generous here, spending your weekend making sure no one in your family gets hurt. Generous to still be friends with your ex-husband, no matter what a louse he really is." He frowned, as though that particular generosity escaped him. "You spend time helping your family, time helping all those pharmacy interns you oversee at work—"

"Enough!" Stacey protested, laughing. Dylan even remembered the details of her work at the pharmacy? She couldn't believe it. "You're making me sound like Mother Teresa!"

"But miles sexier." He raised his hands to her waist, then backed her sideways toward the table and chairs that formed a sort of honeymoon suite breakfast nook near the window. "*Miles sexier.*"

"That's a relief."

Her hip touched the smooth edge of the table. Stacey stopped, smiling up at him. Miles sexier, huh? She felt it, given the appreciation in his gaze as he looked at her. Somehow it infused her arms and legs with unexpected grace, lent her hips and breasts a *femme fatale's* curvy seductiveness and her voice a siren's alluring huskiness.

"I wouldn't want to disappoint you," she said.

"You won't. There's no way you could."

He smiled and lifted her onto the table as easily as he might have lifted a coffee cup to his lips, and with the same expectation of something good to come. She whooped and grinned, grabbing his shoulders.

"I've got you." He helped her scoot in position on the table.

Sure. He had her all right—but for what? Filled with anticipation, she wrapped her arms around him and fingered the fine hairs at the nape of his neck. He smelled good, like soap and musk and creamy zinc oxide, all put together. Nose to nose with him, Stacey looked into his eyes.

What she saw there made excitement sizzle up her spine. Desire. Hunger. And the tenderness that had been her undoing since the moment he'd confessed his broken heart. All of it for her.

She held her breath, waiting for Dylan to make his move. *Kiss me, kiss me.* Any second now he'd cradle the back of her head in his big hand, pull her closer, cover her mouth with his and spin them both into warm, wet, bliss.

Instead, Dylan's hand flattened just below her ribs, easing her backward. She felt herself falling backward on the table.

"What are you doing?" Letting go of him, she balanced herself on her elbows and blinked away her visions of long, languorous kisses. Instead she gazed, half-reclining, down the length of her body at him.

Rather than answer right away, Dylan fit his palms around her knees, drew her legs apart, and settled himself between them with a satisfied smile. "That's better."

She'd say. He fit there veeery nicely.

"I'm showing you the next reason."

In demonstration, he trailed his fingertip to her belly . . . and the last word he'd written. Somehow, he'd managed to hold onto the eyeliner, probably with intentions of torturing her some more. Too bad she couldn't reciprocate. She'd dropped her lipstick shortly after Dylan had dropped to his knees.

He traced the flowing letters he'd written. Stacey squirmed beneath his touch, only half-listening as he spoke.

"Brave. You were brave enough to leave your husband and start over on your own. Brave enough to do a hell of a job of it, too, to hear Richard and Janie talk. Brave enough to stand up to me when—"

"Dylan, enough." Stacey pushed herself to a sitting position. "Enough talking, enough writing . . ." *Enough teasing*, but she couldn't say that aloud. Balancing on one elbow, she spread her hand along his chest, his shoulder, trying to pull him closer, feeling his muscles flex beneath her fingers. "Enough, enough," she whispered as his mouth neared hers. "En—"

His kiss smothered her words, merged their mouths in a union so powerful it made her dizzy. God, yes, this was what she needed. Blindly, she grabbed for him. Something clattered on the tabletop and rolled—the forgotten eyeliner, she guessed vaguely—then Dylan held her close as he kissed her, smashing her against the warmth of his chest with one strong arm.

His hand flattened and circled over her back, raising her sweater higher, pulling it tight across her breasts. Her nipples pushed against the knit cotton, friction-sensitized and tight with excitement. Her thighs strained to bring her closer, trembling to lift her higher from the table and catapult her all the way against him. She wanted to feel every hot inch of him pressing on her skin, wanted to drag him onto the table with her.

The table. They were sprawled on a table, too eager and aroused to wait, and the realization of their position excited her even more. Loving it, Stacey met him greedily, opening her mouth wider, welcoming the pressure of his lips and the gliding, forceful strokes of his tongue. She whimpered in the back of her throat, wordlessly asking for more as she held him tighter.

Taking his lips away for one aching instant, Dylan slammed his hand on the table beside her hip. "*Mmmm, yes,*" he murmured. Then he lowered his head again . . . and gave her all she wanted.

This was no warm-up kiss, no exploratory kiss or make-up kiss. Between them, there was no need, and she felt about as warmed up as was possible to be without bursting into flames. Tongue-sweet and hot with need, this was a hungry kiss. A starving, can't-get-enough kiss.

Jubilant to finally have what she needed, Stacey lost herself in him, pressing as hard as he did, giving everything. Triumph surged through her. She'd show Dylan to go on talk, talk, talking . . . she'd show him what she wanted, and it wasn't more conversation. Her fingers dug into his shoulder, seeking the hard man beneath and capturing nothing but warmth and a handful of woven shirt.

That shirt needed to be gone. Now. It buttoned right over the skin she wanted to feel next to hers, covered up all the strength that cradled her and held her still for his kiss. Arching higher, Stacey took her mouth from his, then planted both hands on Dylan's shoulders and tugged.

The damned shirt wouldn't budge.

"What's the matter with this thing?" She frowned at it as

though the sheer force of her impatience could melt the clothes standing in her way. "Take it off."

"Mmmm." Dylan looked at her through half-closed eyes. "You first."

How could he be so calm about this? Stacey felt like ripping off his shirt however she could, leaving him in tatters like the Incredible Hulk. There'd be time enough for her to get naked later. Right now, what she wanted was him.

Naked.

Shivering, she fumbled with his shirt buttons. Brute force finally got most of them through the four or five buttonholes that made up his shirt placket. She whipped her fingers beneath his shirt to tug it off . . . and the delicious texture of his skin beneath her palms stopped her instantly. Heat surged into her hands, emanating from his skin along with the scent of Safeguard and sunshine. Crisp masculine hairs tickled her fingers. She roved higher, loving the feel of him.

"God, you're killing me," he moaned. "Take it off, take it off."

"I am." Stacey spread her palms over him, letting his chest hair tickle her splayed fingers. She found the small, sharp point of his nipple and flicked it with her thumb.

Dylan shuddered and closed his eyes. "*Now*. Take it off now."

"Mmmm. Maybe I've got a mind to try some body painting of my own." She slid her hands to his back so she could press her chest against his. "I think I've got my lipstick around here somepla—"

"Later."

He thrust his hand in her hair and used it to tilt her head back. Her scalp tingled as his mouth descended on hers, taking her breath away. Needy and passionate, his kiss destroyed whatever urge to tease Stacey had left. She only wanted him.

Now.

Dylan ended the kiss. She grabbed two handfuls of his shirt and tugged. His shirt slid past toned skin and muscle, bared his stomach, his chest . . . and Stacey stopped pulling, temporarily blinding him as she abandoned his shirt to smooth her hands over him. God, he felt gorgeous.

She flexed her fingertips, sank her nails barely into his flesh and felt him shudder beneath her palms. It was heady stuff to have such power over a man like Dylan. Maybe she'd leave him like this for a while, just long enough to satisfy her urge to—

"Hey!" His hands came up, grappling for his shirt. Evidently, he had other ideas besides letting her ogle him.

Stacey tickled his underarm.

"Yeow!" Laughing, Dylan doubled over sideways, wrenched off his shirt, and came up facing her with the promise of retribution written on his face. He bunched up his shirt. Threw it over his shoulder.

And grabbed her sweater instead.

She stopped him with a kiss that started out hard and fast and only got hotter. Hooking her fingers in the waistband of his pants, Stacey hauled him between her thighs and went on kissing him.

He tasted hot and clean . . . he felt even better than that. Past reason, past anything but wanting, she took his hand and pushed it flat against her body, making his palm skim past her hip, her waist, her ribs. Guided by her hand, his fingers closed around her breast and squeezed gently. Oh, God, he touched her as though he couldn't get enough. His other hand came up to cover her other breast and she pushed herself into his palms, needing that contact more than she needed breathing.

Stacey moaned into his mouth as he caressed her, her nipples peaking hard against his hand. More, more . . . groping, fumbling, she worked one-handed at his fly, using her free hand to keep herself from falling backward. Her thumb found his pants' first riveted stud and pushed it through its buttonhole.

Breathing hard, Dylan stared at her hand, watching her unfasten the next stud, and the next. She watched too, thrilled by the erotic sight of her pink-manicured nails against his darker skin, by the contrast of her hand on his rough clothes and the smooth flare of his dark hair vanishing beneath them. His erection strained against his pants, its hard length exciting her into working faster.

He kissed the nape of her neck, nipped and sucked and

made her wild with teasing love bites that trailed up the side of her neck. He nuzzled her earlobe, sending the heated rasp of his breath against her sensitive skin. "God, you feel good," he whispered against her ear. "Mmmm . . . so soft."

Feverishly, Stacey twisted the next button on his pants. She wanted to see him, to feel him . . . she dug her other hand in his waistband for leverage and finally got two more buttons free. Almost there.

Dylan's hands slid beneath her sweater, letting in cool air then sweet, dizzying warmth as he unfastened her bra clasp and cupped her bare breasts in his hands.

Quivering, she bucked against him. "Ahhh, Dylan . . . *yes*. Please, touch me. . . ."

He caressed her, stroking his thumbs over her nipples, sending heat and pleasure shimmering through her.

"Please, please," she begged, hugging her knees to his hips to keep him close. His rough pants rubbed against her thighs, exciting her even further.

Slowly, so slowly, Dylan eased her sweater higher. Stacey bit her lip, trying to keep from screaming as he pulled it over her head and trailed the bunched-up fabric over her shoulders, her breasts. He finally dropped it on a chair. There was no way she could wait for him to take off the rest of her clothes, not at this pace. Eagerly, she slid off her bra and dropped it beside her shirt, then reached for him.

"Wait." He caught her wrists in his hands and held her arms at her sides. "I want to see you. I have to see you."

His eyes flashed, dark with need. His gaze devoured her, moving hungrily over her body.

"Beautiful," he said. "Oh, God . . . you're so beautiful."

He cradled her face in his hands, stroking his thumbs over her cheeks as he kissed her. He pulled her close enough that her breasts rubbed sensuously over his chest, driving her wild with the need to have more . . . more of this, more of him, more love.

Moaning, Stacey arched against him, pushing her knees harder into his hips. Her hands roved across the hard, muscular span of his back, searching for a way to bring him closer still. His hands, trembling and impatient, worked at her waistband. She needed him too much to wait. Raising her hips from the table, Stacey scrambled to take off her skirt. Fabric rustled as Dylan whipped it down her legs and onto the floor, leaving her dressed in only her panties.

He shoved off the rest of his clothes and pushed them aside with his foot, dragging her into his arms again. Their bare skin touched everywhere, warm and sleek with sweat. His erection pushed against her thigh, silky and hard and incredibly hot. Stacey wrapped her fingers around him, loving the feel of him pulsing with life against her palm. Groaning, Dylan dipped his head and kissed her.

"Make love to me," she whispered, feeling him throb eagerly in her hand as she spoke. "Here. Now." His fingers touched the lacy edge of her panties, then dipped lower to fondle her through their silky fabric. It clung to her body, warm and wet with her arousal. "*Please.*"

"Mmmm. Forever," he promised.

His smile for her was a hungry man's, all appetite and anticipation of the pleasure to come. Dylan eased off her panties, then slowly, *slowly*, found every private place needing his touch. Stacey writhed beneath his hand, clutching his shoulder for support against the storm of pleasure he created inside her. Tighter and tighter her need wound, spiraling almost out of control.

Dylan moaned with her, taking in every tremor and cry, every aching plea she made. His harsh, honeyed whispers swept past her ear, offering sweet suggestions of the loving, erotic things he'd make her feel. Now. Later. Forever. She whimpered, drowning in pleasure and greedy for more.

"Yes." He gave her everything her shivering, aching body needed, touching her with endless, loving strokes. "Yes, Stacey, ahhh . . . you feel so good," he moaned as she bucked against his hand. "Mmmm . . . come for me now. Let it go. Ahhh . . ."

Her orgasm exploded through her. Fierce waves of pleasure made her clutch him blindly, a creature of sensation alone. She hadn't dared open her eyes before she heard the tiny sound of tearing foil. *Yes.* That meant he'd soon be inside her. She helped with the condom, watching their hands mingle as they worked together, panting, to put it on.

Their gazes met. Stacey smiled, silly with eagerness and discovery and love. Dylan smiled, too, his a crooked grin that vanished as he pulled her closer across the table. She reached for him, kissed him.

"I need you," she whispered.

"You've got me."

He dragged her close, holding her hips in his hands, and entered her with one smooth, powerful stroke. *Bliss*. Nothing had ever felt this good. Her eyelids fluttered closed as she met him, mindlessly, thrust for thrust. Tremors shook her, made her grasp at his back, his waist. He held her bottom in his hands and raised her higher, gliding inside her, thrusting harder. His hands clenched convulsively on her buttocks, squeezing and releasing her as their loving urged him closer and closer to completion.

Dylan buried his face in her shoulder. Hoarsely, he panted against her skin, calling her name. She met every thrust of his hips, needy and breathless as another orgasm shook her. Her body squeezed around him with exquisite release, drawing him closer.

Suddenly, he stilled. He cried out, thrusting again. Again. His body rocked against her, and his arms tightened hard around her. His teeth sank into her shoulder, sending a fresh wave of pleasure spiraling through her.

"Ahhh, Stacey. Oh, God," he cried, slumping against her. Dylan's breath whooshed past her shoulder, and his hands eased. Cracking his eyes open, he gazed at her, still breathing hard. His fingers brushed her tangled hair from her face, then he lay his forehead against hers. "You're incredible." A crooked smile lit his face. "What a woman I picked to love."

She couldn't speak, too overcome with emotion and their frenzied lovemaking to form any coherent thoughts. Smiling, Stacey caressed him, then kissed his shoulder.

"Next time," he promised, "we'll take our time."

He wiggled slightly, and her smile turned wicked. "Hmmm . . . feels as if you're already ready for next time."

"Noticed that, did you?" Dylan gave her a teasing, gliding thrust, just enough to remind her of all they'd shared. "Mmmm. I'd hoped you would."

He cupped her breast in his hand. His tongue circled her nipple, sending ripples of new, raw pleasure through her.

"There are some places I haven't quite paid enough attention to," he murmured, sucking gently. "I'd better start remedying that right now."

Stacey could hardly wait.

Nine

Hooked. That's what he was, Dylan decided the next morning as he scrubbed at a swirl of pomegranate-lipstick love words on the inside of his thigh. *Hooked*. And he loved every minute of it.

Standing alone in the steamy shower, he scrubbed a little more, then realized ordinary soap and water wasn't going to remove the *Lovetiger* on his thigh—or the *King of Love* on his shoulder, or any of the other, spicier words Stacey had branded him with last night. Her lipstick, as she'd informed him too late with a saucy grin, really was new, improved, and famously indelible. He guessed he'd just have to get used to wearing her sexy opinions all over his body.

Dylan grinned and rinsed. *Tough job.*

He shut off the water and ran his fingers along the smooth pink marble walls, feeling his grin widen. Memories of his night with Stacey tumbled over themselves in his mind, better than a dream and twice as erotic. They'd made good use of that inviting pink marble shower and bathtub, he remembered as he reached for a towel to dry off with. Good, mind-blowing use.

They'd also taken advantage of the corner table, the bed, the armchair in the sitting area . . . his body still thrummed with the lightning touch of her hands and mouth and skin on his. He and Stacey had come together as though they'd been made for each other.

Which was only natural. They had. He'd never met a woman who intrigued and tempted and fascinated him more than Stacey did. Until her, he'd never known what love could be. He was lucky as hell she'd taken a second chance on him.

A second chance on them.

Lucky, lucky. Dylan had half a mind to forgo packing and head down to the casino. As good as he felt today, he was practically guaranteed to win big. But he'd promised Stacey he'd pack their things while she made use of their prepaid massages in the hotel fitness center, and he wasn't about to disappoint her by breaking his promise.

In any case, he still had some loose ends to tie up with the honeymoon surprises. Whistling "Have a Holly Jolly Christmas," he shook his head, sending water droplets pinging across the pink marble. He rubbed the towel over his water-beaded body, then stepped out of the shower. Time to get packing.

Sunday had already arrived, bringing with it the end of the honeymoon charade. And the end of their weekend together.

He shouldn't mind, Dylan told himself as he rumpled his fingers through his hair and examined his jaw in the mirror, deciding whether or not to shave. It wasn't as though they wouldn't be seeing each other back home in Phoenix. After last night, anything felt possible between him and Stacey.

He leaned toward the mirror, rubbing his hand along his jaw, and decided he ought to at least try to look civilized for her sake. Resigned but still whistling, he reached for his razor and glimpsed something shiny on the vanity. Curiously, he bypassed his razor and picked up the smooth circle of gold that had caught his eye instead. As soon as his fingers touched it, his whistled carol stuttered to a surprised stop in his throat.

It was Stacey's ex-wedding ring.

Dylan rubbed the thin gold band between his fingers, watching it glimmer beneath the bright vanity lights. He'd never seen her without it. The fact that Stacey had left it behind now could only mean one thing.

"Whoo-hoo!" he hollered, jigging naked into the honeymoon suite. "She loves me, girl!" he yelled at Ginger. With his dog frolicking at his heels, Dylan jived to the window and whooshed his arms overhead like a Super Bowl fan doing the Wave of Love. "Hey, Las Vegas! She loves me!"

Ginger hunkered down and tucked her muzzle on her paws, her hind-end wagging along with her tail.

"Stacey loves me!" he told her, grinning like an idiot.

His dog joined in the celebration with a sneeze and a rollover that left all four paws lolling in the air. Dylan gave her belly a vigorous rub, his mind and heart still reeling with the significance of Stacey's actions. She hadn't said the words last night, not that he remembered—and he would have definitely remembered—but her leaving behind her ex-wedding ring could only mean one thing. Not only did he love her . . . *Stacey loved him back.*

Too happy to hold still, Dylan got up and cha-cha'd across the suite. "She-e-e-e loves me, cha-cha-cha-cha-cha-CHA!"

The door swept cautiously open. Stacey came in with her purse slung over her shoulder, wearing boots, a sexy pair of jeans, and a vibrant orange sweater. She looked gorgeous. She looked bemused, probably at the sight of him dancing naked around the suite. She looked . . . a lot less interested than he'd hoped she'd be, seeing him dancing naked around the suite.

Dylan smiled and boogied toward the woman he loved, slipping the shiny gold harbinger of all his happiness safely on his pinky so he wouldn't dance it off.

"Good morning!" He crushed Stacey to him for a fast kiss. Grabbing her hand, he twirled her away from him and back again, then caught her waist and two-stepped them both into the sitting area. "How was your mass—"

"Dylan, stop! Stop! This is terrible."

She wrenched out of his arms and pushed herself away from him. She gazed up and down his body, squeaked out a startled sound at the sight, buried her face in her hands.

"Geez." He waggled his eyebrows at her. "You seemed to like everything okay last night."

A huge snuffle came from behind her hands. Her shoulders shuddered. He could see her trying to get a hold of herself long enough to speak.

"This can't be happening!" she wailed.

"It was only dancing." What the hell kind of massage did they give in this place anyway, to leave her in a mood like this? Dylan stepped toward her, gesturing vaguely to the bathroom. "I'll go put on a towel or something if you want me to."

Stacey sniffled and peeked through her fingers. "Oh. Oh!"

Her hands went to her sides, making desperate little fists against her jeans. Again her gaze whipped over him, and a blush rose in her cheeks. Laughter, slightly hysterical and utterly confusing, burbled from her lips.

"Oh, Dylan. I didn't mean *that.*"

He stared at her for a minute, then shook his head. "I'd better get dressed anyway."

"Really!" She trailed him to the half-packed suitcases lying open on the bed. "I just-just—"

Stacey faltered and stopped, her gaze slanting over him as he yanked a pair of jeans from his duffel bag and pulled them on.

"I just . . . do you do this often?" she asked in a small voice.

"You mean the naked boogie?"

She nodded, not looking at him. He grinned and touched her chin.

"I'm not sure. This is the first time I've tried it," Dylan leaned down to whisk his fingertip over her lips, making her draw in a quick breath in reaction. He smiled gently. "But I'm pretty sure I could only manage it when I'm in love. Deeply, crazily in love."

Her lower lip wobbled. An instant later, her face crumpled in a wail louder than the first one had been. Turning away from him, Stacey sank on the bed in a disconsolate heap, sending clothes toppling to the floor. A bottle of shampoo thumped down and rolled beneath the bed, joining whatever else lurked in the wasteland beneath a hotel bed's dust ruffle.

"Stacey?" He knelt beside her, taking her hand between both of his and squeezing. This was more than a reaction to bare naked joy dancing. "What's the matter? Did something happen during your massage? Was it something I said? Did I do something, any—"

She shook her head. A tear fell on his wrist, then another. Whatever this was, it was serious.

"Honey, whatever it is, I can help." Dylan rubbed her hand softly between his. "Just tell me what's the matter."

"You'll hate me," she choked out between shuddering breaths. She shook her head again, pressing her lips together. Still they trembled, and another tear coursed over her cheek. "It's too awful."

"There's nothing you can say that'll make me hate you. What's the matter?"

He raised his hand to brush away a tear from her cheek. She grabbed his hand, spreading his fingers and staring at the gold band on his pinky. Her gaze lifted to his.

"I was keeping it for you," Dylan told her, slipping it off. "You left it in the bathroom." He held the ring out to her.

She took it and wrapped her fist around it, then promptly started crying harder. She folded both arms around her middle, shaking her head.

"I thought I didn't need it." Stacey looked up at him through shimmering, tear-filled eyes. "I thought we—you and me—that we—"

"We can!"

"We . . . Dylan, I wrecked everything. Just now. Everything. I was at the masseuse's, having the most wonderful massage." Sniffling through her tears, she rifled through her purse and pulled out an apple, a day planner, a box of condoms. "Here," she said absently, handing them to him. "I got these while I was out."

"The economy jumbo pack," he remarked, turning over the box. He tossed it in an open suitcase. "I didn't know they made these."

"You just have to shop around."

Elbow-deep in her purse, Stacey grabbed her wallet, then dropped it on the black silk comforter. A bottle of calcium supplements, a roll of tape, and a jump rope followed. Dylan raised his eyebrows. A jump rope?

She spread her arms, scowling down at her purse. "Where are my tissues?" she demanded in a quavery voice, picking up her bag and giving it a hearty shake. Things rolled and clanked together inside. How much more could possibly be in there?

"So you're having the massage," he prompted, handing her the box of hotel tissues from the nightstand. "Then what happened?"

She blew her nose, then stared up at him mournfully. "Please don't be mad."

"I won't be mad."

"Swear it."

What had she done? "Cross my heart." He whipped his hand in an X over his chest. He sat beside her on the bed, shoving things aside with his hip to be closer, and wrapped his arms around her. "I love you. Nothing can change that."

Her face crumpled. "I wrecked the whole honeymoon charade!" She burrowed her face in her hands. "I hadn't had my coffee yet, and I was feeling sooo good after last night, and the massage was so. . . . Oh, Dylan, there's no excuse." Stacey paced toward the sitting area and back. Balling her hands into fists, she met his gaze dead-on. "The masseuse recognized me from our picture."

"Our picture?"

"Our winning picture. From yesterday. 'Say we won!', remember?" She pantomimed snapping a picture, then grimaced.

"Is that all? That's not so bad. Maybe she—"

"She caught me, Dylan. She asked me, point-blank, why I was using two names." Her gaze swerved guiltily to his. "I couldn't lie. Not like that! I spilled everything . . . the whole story." Her hands shook as she picked up the fallen clothes from the floor and stuffed them in one of the suitcases. "It's finished."

"Wait. You think I'll be mad at you because you couldn't tell a bold-faced lie?"

Hell, that was one of the reasons he loved her—because she was so kind-hearted. Because she was the kind of woman who'd go out of her way to help her family.

Her family. The family Stacey felt sure she'd let down, because she thought she'd given away the honeymoon charade.

"Don't you get it?" She didn't look at him as she shoved

things industriously back in her purse. "*The masseuse knows Aunt Geraldine*. She's a personal friend, remember? She's probably on the phone with her right now. My family will never forgive me when word of this gets out."

Wailing, Stacey threw down her purse and twisted her hands in front of her. "I'm sorry, Dylan. I wrecked this for you, too, and all you were trying to do was help Richard and Janie." She raised her chin. "I'll explain, though. You were doing things my way in the end, even though you didn't agree. I'm responsible. You won't—"

"No." He stood to pull her into his arms. She nestled against him with her head beneath his chin, softer than he'd dared hope for and all the woman he'd ever wanted. Dylan hugged her tighter. "No, you're not explaining anything," he said against the silkiness of her hair. "I love you, and I won't—"

"I love you, too."

Her whispered words arrowed into his heart, into his soul. He'd dreamed of hearing those words from her. Now the dream was real.

"At least there was one good thing in all this." Stacey shifted in his arms so she could look up at him. She gave him a quivering, hopeful smile. "At least I found you again."

"We found each other." Dylan touched her cheek. He kissed her, long and slow and sweet. "I wouldn't give up this weekend for anything."

Stacey stepped away, then breathed deeply, like a runner preparing for a long-distance race.

"Me, neither." Her smile steadied. "I'd better call Janie. And Aunt Geraldine." She raised her chin staunchly as she reached for the bedside phone. "I've got some explaining to do."

"*No!*" Dylan grabbed for her and captured nothing. She'd already slipped away from him.

She picked up the phone, then pulled her day planner from her purse. "I know I wrote the number of their hotel in the Bahamas in here someplace." She balanced the phone between her ear and shoulder as she turned pages, searching.

He slapped his hand on her day planner.

She stared up at him, her eyes wide. "Dylan?"

God, it wasn't supposed to be this way. She loved him. He loved her . . . too much to see her hurt by something that he'd set in motion. It was up to him to finish it.

"Don't call," he grated out. His gaze sought hers. Dylan drank in the sight of her, closed his eyes to concentrate on her scent and the feel of her next to him. He opened his eyes. "Don't call."

"What?" Stacey wrinkled her forehead. "I have to, I—"

"The masseuse doesn't know Aunt Geraldine. Neither did the mini-golf people or the breakfast serenaders or anyone at the Renaissance. The honeymoon surprises were a hoax." He held himself rigidly, forcing himself not to touch her. "I arranged them all."

"*You* arranged . . . ?" She shook her head and tried to pry his hand loose from her day planner. "That's sweet, but avoiding the facts won't make this go away. You know how I feel about the men in my life making decisions for me. Not again. *Never again*, after Charlie. I told you, and you listened. You wouldn't lie to me about—"

He slapped a receipt on her day planner page.

"You're just trying to make me feel better." She overrode his actions with faster talking. "You-you . . ."

Her voice faltered and stopped as Dylan added another receipt to the pile.

"Aunt Geraldine paid for the hotel, but everything else was my doing," he said harshly. "I knew you'd be here, and I took advantage of the situation to try to win you back."

Stacey's mouth dropped open. Her gaze locked on his, filled with surprise and dawning belief. She glanced at the growing pile of receipts, then lifted one in her trembling fingers.

"The Renaissance," she read. "Tickets for the dinner show." She picked up the next. "Mini-golf passes, arranged by Las Vegas Travel. Massage package, hotel extras . . ."

The receipts drifted to the floor, and pain drained the color from her face. Her eyes, when she looked at him, filled with tears. "All lies?"

Dylan's throat ached, making it hard to speak. "I already checked out by remote. As far as the hotel is concerned—and

Aunt Geraldine—Richard and Janie had a fabulous honeymoon." His hands fisted and flexed, wanting to touch her and ease her pain somehow, but it was too late. He was the one who'd caused it. "Your honeymoon charade is safe."

Stacey's tears shimmered and fell. "Damn you, Dylan."

He closed his eyes. *You did the right thing, the only thing*, he told himself.

It didn't matter. All he wanted was her.

He heard the phone being replaced quietly in its cradle, heard suitcases snapping shut. He sensed her presence, her warmth, in front of him . . . almost as though she'd reached out to touch him and withdrawn her hand at the last moment.

"Goodbye," Stacey whispered.

The next sound Dylan heard was the door closing behind her, leaving him more alone than he'd ever been.

He'd lost her.

They'd lost each other.

Ten

"I heard from Aunt Geraldine this morning."

At the sound of Janie's voice, Stacey looked up from her miserable contemplation of her first peppermint mocha of the morning, glad to have company at the Phoenix café she and her cousin both frequented. Janie chugged toward her across the holiday-decorated outdoor seating area, waving a packet of something and grinning her elfin smile.

Elfin. It was the only way to describe pert, petite Janie, with her black pixie-cut hair, tilting green eyes and penchant for gauzy, pastel-colored dresses. Reaching Stacey's table, Janie dropped her purse, an eggnog latte, and a slew of shopping bags packed with wrapped Christmas gifts, before settling in.

"You did?" Stacey asked. "You heard from Aunt Geraldine? She must have gotten your thank-you letter, then. What did she say?"

Please say she said nothing about the honeymoon charade.

She held her breath, waiting for the verdict. It had been almost a week since she'd returned home, and a day and a half since Janie had returned from her *real* honeymoon.

It had been the longest five days of her life.

"She said she was glad Richard and I had a good time." Janie winked, then opened the packet she'd brought and slipped out a stack of glossy photos. She handed the bundle to Stacey.

"Pictures. Of our Bahamas trip. I just picked them up on my way here."

"Thanks." Stacey shuffled through them, watching images of a smiling Janie and Richard slide through her fingers—on the beach, at their hotel, boating on the ocean, looking honeymoonish and carefree. Envy stabbed through her. *That could have been you and Dylan.* Better not to think about what might have been.

"That's all she said?" Stacey asked instead. "Nothing else?"

"Aunt Geraldine? There was more, but don't worry." Janie waved her fingers. "She doesn't know our secret." She sipped her eggnog latte, then stirred it with a sobered expression. "I'm sorry to put you in such a spot, Stace. I was desperate. You know that. Otherwise—"

"It's okay. Everything worked out, so, so—"

So, suddenly, she couldn't go on. To her horror, Stacey burst into tears. Shaking, she realized she couldn't quit crying, either, and bawled harder.

"Hon, hon—what's the matter?" Janie asked, wrapping an arm around her shoulders.

Stacey leaned shamelessly into her, grateful for her tear-hiding sunglasses. Everyone at the café might hear her blubbering away, but at least people driving by in their cars with their windows rolled up wouldn't *see* her doing it. At the thought of the public spectacle she was making over herself, she wailed harder. This was so unlike her.

Janie handed her a scratchy paper napkin. "Blow," she ordered. "Can you tell me what's the matter?"

She shook her head and snuffled into the napkin. "I-I—"

"Is it Dylan?"

The world got waterier. Stacey took off her sunglasses and swabbed at her eyes with another napkin, nodding.

"That rat! I knew it." Janie stabbed her coffee stirrer in her cup with a vicious frown. "I'll kill him." She brushed back Stacey's hair and set their foreheads together, looking into her eyes. "Or would you rather have him maimed?"

Janie's loyalty pushed a feeble-feeling grin onto Stacey's face. Trying to take her mind off her troubles, she fumbled to put the Bahamas pictures back in the envelope so they wouldn't get soggy. She took a deep, shuddering breath, then shook her head.

"Okay, not maimed, I guess. You big softie." Janie smiled wickedly. "Financially ruined? Publicly humiliated? He deserves it for hurting you." She squeezed her hand. "You just tell me what you want, hon, and I'll make sure you get it."

Stacey thought over the past lonely days, remembered her weekend with Dylan and everything they'd shared. It had felt so real, so right, between them.

"All I want is Dylan," she said sadly.

She blurted out the whole story, right up to Dylan's confession that he'd been the one to arrange the honeymoon surprises. Janie nodded wisely, finished her second eggnog latte, complete with red and green sprinkles, then narrowed her eyes.

"So he actually *did* quit telling you what to do." Thoughtfully, she stroked the side of her paper coffee cup. "And he actually *did* try to carry off the honeymoon charade your way. Right?"

Stacey nodded. "He only told me the truth because he thought I was going to confess everything and make all of you disown me, bec—" Realization struck her. Dylan hadn't had to tell her a thing. He'd only done it to protect her, knowing how much her family meant to her.

And sacrificed himself in the process. Because he was in love with her. *Deeply, crazily in love.*

"Holy smokes! What have I done?" Stacey bolted to her feet, scattering coffee cups and swizzle sticks. "I've got to find him!"

Janie grinned. "Sit back down. I've got a plan."

Stacey was all ears.

Hell. The last place he wanted to be, especially on Christmas Eve, was the Atmosphere Hotel. Dylan screeched his Jeep to a stop beneath the glittering porte-cochere, eyeing the hotel about as eagerly as he would a lumpy Christmas fruitcake.

Something happened with Aunt Geraldine's credit card, Richard had told him. *The hotel wants payment for the honeymoon suite stay.* The Parker's credit card, tapped to the limit after their Bahamas honeymoon, had already been refused.

Cash only had been the hotel's request. Today. Or things would get ugly.

Feeling responsible, Dylan had volunteered to drive to Vegas and straighten things out himself. Now he wished he hadn't. He was already hurting enough without this.

Memories of Stacey haunted him as he tossed his keys to a valet and headed inside. The usual Muzak Christmas carols and ritzy decorations brought less holiday cheer than he'd hoped, and walking past the noisy casino called up a hundred more details he didn't want to remember. The feel of Stacey beside him. The lure of her perfume. The cocky expression she'd worn while challenging him to their pillow fight.

The sound of her voice when she'd told him she loved him.

Hell. Feeling surly and lost, Dylan stalked to the reception desk and pulled out his wallet. "I'm here to pay for a stay in the honeymoon suite last weekend. I was told you'll only take cash."

"The honeymoon suite, sir?" The same chipper, newlywed blonde he remembered from last weekend looked up at him. Her grin widened.

He frowned. "Yes. How much to—"

"Oh! It's you!" she interrupted, looking giddy. "The person you need to see about this is right over there."

She pointed to the nearest row of slot machines.

The row of slot machines containing the one he and Stacey had won on. Great.

"Who?" he asked. "How will I know—"

"Oh, you'll recognize the person you need to see," she assured him, winking. *Winking?*

Feeling suspicious, Dylan put away his wallet. Grumbling, he stomped toward the casino. The *last* thing he wanted to do was revisit anyplace he and Stacey had been to together. Who'd set up this ridiculous system, anyway? He guessed he'd just have to watch for someone wearing a hotel uniform and hope they had more facts at their disposal than the ditzy desk clerk. Then he could pay up and get the hell away from there . . . get on with his lonely Christmas Eve.

He pushed through the crowds, nearing the familiar row of slot machines. The winning picture Stacey had told him about loomed at the head of the row—another Technicolor memory of the two of them decked out in kooky hats and blue goo, holding up their winnings. Another memento of all he'd lost.

Dylan frowned and looked away.

At the head of the row, the scent of roses reached him, nearly overpowering in their sweetness. He felt just grumpy enough to dislike the aroma. Someone's perfume? They must have ladled it on, he groused as two gamblers swerved out of his path. The place smelled like a million roses.

The crowd parted. In the open space revealed along the gleaming slot machines, he glimpsed the roses: actual roses, masses of deep, rich red ones, and the woman holding them.

Stacey.

His heart slammed to a stop, then kicked into double speed. She hadn't spotted him yet, he realized. She gazed out over the huge bouquets, half hidden by their spreading petals, nibbling on her bottom lip and rising on tiptoes to see over the crowd. Looking for someone.

Him?

Dylan walked nearer, his stride eating carpet in two-foot chunks. Stacey saw him. A tremulous smile spread over her face. He felt an answering smile light his own.

He'd been had, he realized. Lured here under false pretenses, just so Stacey could get her hands on him again.

He didn't mind one bit.

"You came!" she said when he reached her. Clutching the flowers tighter, she raised the whole quivering mass with a jerky movement of her arm. "These are for you. I know they're not very Christmassy. Ho, ho, ho, you know. Season's greetings, and all that. But they, um, had special meaning."

She thrust them in his face, thorns and all.

"Ahhh!" Dylan grabbed them. "You almost put my eye out!"

"Sorry." Stacey stared at her feet. A blush climbed her cheeks, and her voice shook when she spoke. "I guess I'm a little nervous."

"There's no need to be." Smiling, he tucked his hand in the nape of her neck and drew her to him, his heart so filled with love and gratitude he couldn't wait to touch her. He nodded at the flowers and the casino surrounding them. "I guess this means there's no payment mix-up over the honeymoon suite?"

"No. Everything's fine." Stacey gazed up at him, flushed and soft and adorably determined. "I'm sorry to bring you here like this, but I didn't know what else to do." Hesitating, she bit her lower lip. "I'm sorry, Dylan. So sorry. I didn't understand, but now I do. I should have never let you go."

"Then don't." His lips curved in a smile as he kissed her. "Let's not let each other go, ever again."

"Never," Stacey agreed, melting against him with a smile of her own, probably unaware she was standing on his foot.

Dylan ignored the pain, too happy to squabble over little things like smashed toes. They'd heal . . . and so would his heart, starting now.

"I love you." She linked her fingers with his, giving him a tinsel-bright smile. "I love you so much."

"I love you more." He grinned as he pulled her away from the slot machine and into the swelling crowd of gamblers along with him. "Much more."

"I love you times a million," she countered, hugging his arm as they walked.

The roses flopped in his other hand, bouncing in rhythm with their steps and sending a flowery scent in the air.

"I love you times infinity." Dylan paused. "Do you think the honeymoon suite is free? We might want it later."

"Might?" Raising her eyebrows, Stacey pulled something from her purse and pushed it in his hand. A hotel key card. "I already booked it."

"You're my kind of woman, Stacey Ames," he said, watching her bounce up on her toes to push the elevator button.

"Going up?"

"Not until you earn it." Dylan swept her in his arms along

with the roses. "I'm carrying you over that honeymoon suite threshold as a real bride this time."

Not much later that afternoon, he did.

And his merry Christmas bride?

She loved every single minute.

A BABY FOR CHRISTMAS

One

Saturday morning, Chloe Carmichal woke up with a naked man in her bed.

Of course, she was naked too, but that wasn't the point. The important thing was, this wasn't just any old sunstruck, Arizona spring morning, and the man asleep beside her wasn't just any old golden-haired, buffed-up guy. This was the morning after the night she'd never forget, and the fella snoring with his legs tangled around hers and his arm slung around her waist was Nick.

Her best friend in the whole world.

Maybe now he'd realize how perfect they were for each other. She'd spent three years living next door to him—three companionable, let's-be-pals, excruciatingly platonic years. Last night everything had changed.

Oh, boy, how it had changed. Feeling giddy, Chloe snuggled closer to Nick's warmth and fought the urge to wake him up just to tell him how happy she was. That wouldn't be fair, not after the late night they'd spent together. He deserved at least another ten minutes' sleep.

Maybe five.

Nick snuffled and turned over. His arm whipped from her waist and sailed toward her head like a sleepy stealth missile.

Chloe ducked just as it smacked into her pillow. Whew. She
never knew sleeping with a guy could be so dangerous.

Too excited to sleep anymore, she used his movement for
cover and slipped out of bed to go freshen up. Maybe she'd
even put together a little breakfast *à deux*. After last night,
they could both do with a recharge.

Her feet hit the floor. Behind her the covers rustled, and
Nick gave a soft muffled moan before going back to sleep.
Chloe's heart skipped a little higher. Nick was in her bed!

Nick was with her.

Oh, sure. She and Nick had never shared more than a hug
before last night. And yeah, he did just happen to be slightly
on the rebound from what'shername, the mean, commitment-
hungry brunette he'd been dating until yesterday. But, Chloe
told herself as she emerged from the bathroom and pattered
down the hall, that was all in the past. From now on, things
would be different. Way different. Last night he'd seen another
side to her, and things could never go back to the way they
were before.

Never go back. In the kitchen, the thought of losing all the
closeness she and Nick had shared over the years made her
pause. Could their friendship survive becoming lovers? What
if they'd ruined everything? What if they broke up?

What if she was jumping to conclusions? *We can do this,*
she told herself. *We'll be a match made in heaven.* So what if
they were sort of an unlikely combination? So were her clothes
most of the time, and they still managed to work okay.

Chloe glanced down at herself, taking in the purple polka-
dotted boxer shorts she usually slept in, the bright orange bra
she'd substituted for her T-shirt in the name of maximum sex-
iness, and the way her fingers were shaking, and tried to
gather her courage. It was just Nick, for Pete's sake. *Her Nick.*
There was nothing to worry about.

Right. Before she could angst any further, she got busy
putting together breakfast: a pot of coffee, a box of chocolate
donuts, and a bowl of dried banana chips. Okay, so it wasn't
exactly health food, but it would have to do for now. Juggling
the wicker basket she'd put everything in, Chloe stopped at
the threshold of her bedroom and warily looked in.

Sunlight rushed between the slats of her bedroom's white window shutters and brightened the midnight blue walls, streaking glimmers of gold across plants and pictures and the man sprawled across her bed. Discarded clothes—his and hers—trailed across the carpet, making a path to the arched foot of her big wooden sleigh bed. Chloe tiptoed to it and set the breakfast basket on the bureau beside it, unable to wait any longer. It was time for Nick to wake up . . . and she was just the woman to make sure he did so in the nicest possible way.

A plaintive meow came from beside the bed. Moe, her fat orange tabby, arched against the footboard and meowed louder, the sound filled with feline reproach at not being first as usual on Chloe's morning agenda.

"Shhh," she told the cat, giving him a fond rub between the ears. "Just give me this one morning, and it's Fancy Feast for a week. I swear."

Praying for cooperation, Chloe lifted the bed covers and slid beneath them. Warmth surrounded her. Geez, Nick's body heat could power a whole city if they could find a way to harness it. She ought to ask him about that for his next invention. Smiling in the dark, Chloe took her own turn at inventiveness, sliding her palm over his hairy shin, his knee, his hard, muscular thigh . . . a game of blind man's bluff for grown-ups. He stirred and moaned, encouraging her without words to roam higher. She did.

Nick's fingers wandered to the nape of her neck, stroking and teasing. The feel of his hand against her skin called forth a million memories from last night. With a sigh, Chloe crawled higher. Morning breath be damned. She wanted to kiss the man she loved.

She raised the covers and poked her head out. Nick's linebacker-size shoulders, tousled honey-streaked hair, and adorably rumpled face filled her vision. Groggily, he opened his eyes and blinked his baby blues in her direction.

Her heart softened. Some part of her was obviously a sucker for the little-boy-lost look. If possible, she felt even more in love with him than before. Nick blinked again, and Chloe realized it wasn't tenderness that made him look that way: it was poor eyesight. His natty wire rims still lay on the bedside table where he'd left them last night.

"Nick?" she whispered, smoothing her hand across his chest. "Good morning."

His mouth opened. He blinked harder. "Chloe?"

The raspy, intimate sound of his voice thrilled her. "Mmmm hmmm, it's Chloe." She twirled her fingertips in a heated whorl of his chest hair and smiled in a way she hoped looked worldly and sophisticated. "Good morning . . . darling."

"Aaack!" Nick shot upward, his eyes widening. His head cracked into her sleigh bed.

"Oh!" She reached for him, crooning whatever comforting things came to mind as she tried to examine him for headboard-induced injuries. Yanking his head out of reach, grimacing at the movement, he scrambled higher on the pillows. Obviously, Nick wasn't an early riser.

Or at least his *whole* body wasn't.

"Are you all right?" How could she have known he'd wake up so grumpy? *She'd* never slept with him before.

Frowning, he pushed himself up on his elbows. Her gaze drifted to his bare chest and stomach. Grumpy or not, Nick did keep a surprisingly attention-getting body hidden beneath that stupid white lab coat he was always wearing. Who'd have guessed?

He saw her ogling and jerked the sheets higher. What was the matter with him? Why, a person would think he hadn't . . . that they hadn't . . . .

Oh, God.

His expression matched her thoughts.

"What the hell are you doing here?" Nick blinked harder. His mouth straightened, then gaped open again as Chloe crawled all the way out of the covers and sat up. His gaze went straight to her sheer orange bra. "You-you-you're not even dressed!" He glanced around, looking increasingly incredulous. "Is this your bedroom?"

Chloe handed him his eyeglasses.

"It *is* your bedroom!"

She wouldn't have thought things could get worse—until

they did. Shock made her nipples perk tight against her wispy bra, drawing his attention in the only way she had absolutely no control over. Feeling her face heat, Chloe drew up her knees and wrapped her arms around them.

Nick's gaze dropped to her snug purple-dotted silk boxers. Something akin to pain flashed across his face. "Aww, hell."

This time she recognized that gruffness in his tone for what it was: the remnants of a massive hangover from the Kahlúa, coffee, and sympathy she'd served him last night.

"Tell me this isn't what it looks like, Chloe."

Hurt stole her breath. His pleading glance finished her off. *He didn't remember.*

"Tell me I didn't take advantage of you last night."

Nick fisted his hand in the sheets. She imagined him caressing her cheek instead, pretended he'd smile and tell her he'd been kidding. Just a little morning-after humor, ha ha.

"I—" Her voice cracked and faltered. She frowned briefly and tried again. "Well, I, uhh—"

He must have sensed something was wrong, because he stopped her with a touch and curled his fingers beneath her chin. He tilted her face upward, looking at her carefully with that analytical scientist's expression of his. It wasn't a cheek caress, but it was near enough to tenderness that Chloe closed her eyes to savor it.

"I couldn't stand it if I thought I'd hurt you," Nick said. "I know how it feels to be used, remember?"

She remembered, all right. He meant what'shername. The one who'd decided her ticking biological clock couldn't handle Nick Steadman standard time any longer. The one who'd broken his heart and sent him straight to Chloe's door for solace.

"Chloe?"

There was nothing else to do. She loved him too much to tell him a truth he so obviously didn't want to hear. So she opened her eyes and gave him a choked little laugh.

"Who, me? And you?" She rolled her eyes at the notion. "Nah, don't flatter yourself, genius. Nothing happened here last night except too much Kahlúa, too much talking, and way too much sympathy." She put her hand to his forehead and tried out a wobbly feeling smile. "I think it's gone to your head."

"But—"

"Your virtue's safe with me." Chloe levered herself off the mattress and inadvertently treated him to a full-on cleavage shot. Geez. Maybe he'd think she always dressed this way to sleep. "Your virtue's safe, but your body," she added to distract him, "well . . . that's another story."

She bounced off the bed and shrugged into the lab coat he'd left on her bedroom doorknob last night, giving herself double bonus points for hiding the tears in her eyes and getting herself covered up all at the same time.

"My body?"

"Yeah, your hangover. Sorry about that."

The bed creaked. Chloe, busy swabbing surreptitiously at her burning eyelids, didn't dare look to see what Nick was doing.

"It's not your fault." His voice sounded muted, hoarse with hangover mouth and leftover sleepiness. "I brought it all on myself. I knew me and—"

"What'shername?"

"—weren't headed in the same direction. I wanted hot sex—"

"I'm not listening," she sang out, putting her hands over her ears.

"Yes, you are. I see your pinkies lifting. And anyway, you must have heard worse last night."

"You don't remember?" Her voice sounded as hoarse as his, but for different reasons. Funny that grief and Kahlúa would have the same disastrous side effects.

"After the fourth cup of your demon Kahlúa and coffee, it's all kind of a blur," Nick confessed.

The admission made her heart twist. The most life-changing night of her life, and he couldn't remember a minute of it.

She heard the sheets rustle and pretended to button the lab jacket she had on as an excuse not to face him. Why torture herself with ogling what she couldn't have?

He mumbled something about missing underwear. Then, "What was I saying?"

"Hot sex."

"Oh, yeah." The bed creaked again. "I wanted hot sex, and she wanted two-point-four kids and a dog. It just wasn't meant to be."

Not that he seemed too broken-up over it this morning. Chloe guessed the worst had passed.

Maybe he was getting used to it. Eventually, every relationship Nick had smashed to smithereens over the same issues: settling down, getting married, having kids. With him, his inventions and the work that subsidized them came first. To his credit, he was always perfectly upfront about it.

Unfortunately, most women he dated didn't believe him. They took one look at that smile, those shoulders, and the wit behind those baby blues . . . and decided they'd be the one to reform him.

Ha.

"Good thing I have you to pick up the pieces of my mangled love life, Chloe."

"What are friends for?" she choked out, giving him an offhanded wave.

"Drinking beer, watching football, and cruising for chicks."

The mattress groaned. The bedcovers rustled. Then came the sound of denim being dragged across the carpet. She pictured Nick naked, stepping into his jeans and snugging them up over his . . .

"Not necessarily in that order," he finished one zip later.

"Ha, ha. Chicks, huh?" How could he banter with her like this? If she didn't get away from him soon, she'd be a bawling mess of tears and confessions. "That's really evolved of you, Nick."

The familiar, beloved sound of his laughter made Chloe feel warm all over. No one could turn her to mush faster than Nick could. No one could . . . *stop it*! She took a deep breath and steeled her resolve. If he didn't want what had happened to have happened, then she'd be the last person to break the news. Nick might be a straight shooter at heart, but this was one little white lie she felt sure he'd forgive.

Besides, it hurt no one but herself. That she could deal with.

"Thanks for being there last night." He put his hand to her shoulder, turning her to face him. "You're a pal, Chloe."

He tousled her hair and grinned. Next thing she knew, he'd slug her on the arm and complete their resemblance to Wally and the Beaver. Chloe felt more miserable than ever.

"I'm the pal who gave you the hangover from hell, remember? You need my patented hangover cure." She pointed to the coffee and donuts, then edged to the doorway. "I'll just, umm, go grab the, uh, newspaper."

She escaped the bedroom on legs too wobbly to carry her all the way to the kitchen, then flattened against the striped wallpapered hallway. Clutching the ends of Nick's lab coat with trembling fingers—it was too big on her, but comforting all the same—Chloe peered toward her bedroom. She half expected Nick to follow her. He didn't.

Darn it.

It looked as if she'd pulled it off. She'd convinced him their platonic-ness remained intact as ever. He wouldn't suspect she loved him, wouldn't bolt with terror at the thought she might want his kids, his ring, his undying love and a white picket fence to match. Wouldn't consign her to the ex-girlfriend pile a month from now. Wouldn't think of her as anything more than his old pal Chloe, keeper of Kahlúa and bolsterer of bruised hearts.

What was she, crazy?

No, she answered herself. *Just a girl who wants to keep her best friend.*

In the bedroom, Moe issued a feline yowl.

"Uh, Chloe?" yelled Nick. "Can you call off your psychotic cat, please? I think he's trying to mate with my shoe."

Two

Six weeks later

He was almost there. He could feel it.

Frowning with concentration, Nick Steadman typed a few more variables in the inventor's journal he kept on his computer, then rolled his office chair across the pitted oak floor of his spare-bedroom-turned-laboratory. He examined the long table arrayed with precisely arranged test tubes and beakers, computer printouts and heat lamps, wires and solution bottles and the varying plants that were the focus of his current research.

God, what he wouldn't give to see the results of his research put in production. Just once to know that someone believed in him enough to invest cold cash in his ideas.

Just invent a pet rock, or something, his sisters said. *You'll make millions in no time.* They didn't understand it wasn't the money that mattered to him.

Still with the dreaming, Nicky? his mother always asked. *You've got a good job. Stick with that.* But she didn't understand, either. His engineering work at BrylCorp kept him busy and kept him in supplies for his inventions, but it wasn't security he was looking for.

You want to sell that thing? his brothers-in-law said.

Finance it yourself! You've got the cash. But they didn't understand that having the money wasn't the real goal. Interesting a bona fide investor was. Once Nick did that, once he'd set his work into production, then he'd know he'd really done it.

Somehow, he'd convince his old man that all those years of taking apart every appliance, every clock, every TV in the house had paid off. He'd prove himself, to himself, and finally make his dad proud of his only son.

Three generations of Steadman men had put their dreams last and their families first. They'd traded their hopes and plans, abandoned their talents, for the sake of mouths to feed and growing kids to clothe and mortgages to pay.

That particular family tradition was about to crumble. Nick meant to be the first to bring it down.

With one last glance at his computer screen, Nick picked up the next ingredient in the solution he was preparing and measured it in the nearest beaker. He had to get busy. One of the investors he'd approached for past projects was interested in his current research. He wanted a working prototype to present to his board of directors—in California—at their next meeting in December.

Just nine months away.

It wasn't much time to check the variables, to run tests, to re-formulate if necessary. Especially when Nick's inventing happened at night and on the weekends, sandwiched between cubicle-cramped stints at BrylCorp and what remained of his social life. But that didn't matter.

Come hell or high water, this time he meant to see one of his inventions in production. If he handled it right, this could be a very merry Christmas.

"Ho, ho, ho," he muttered, holding the beaker to the light.

"It's not even Easter yet, Uncle Nick."

"I know, Danny." He looked up at his houseguest for the day, his seven-year-old, sticky-fingered nephew. "I'm planning ahead."

"Oh. Is that how come you're not gonna hunt Easter eggs with us this year? 'Cause you're already starting on Christmas?"

A pang shot through Nick. He'd missed so many Easter egg hunts, so many birthdays and Halloween pumpkin-carvings and Fourth of July picnics. Danny was just a kid. Commitment was only a word on a second-grade spelling test to him.

Once this invention is off the ground, Nick promised himself, all that will change.

"Maybe I can make it this year." His own father, not to mention numerous Steadman uncles and aunts, had crowded into every track meet, school play, basketball game and science fair Nick had ever taken part in. Now, as an uncle himself, didn't he owe the same things to his nephew? "I can't promise anything, but I'll try."

"You can do it, Uncle Nick!" Danny grinned, all gap-toothed innocence and enthusiasm. "My mom says you're always trying to do stuff. Even totally impossible stuff."

Impossible stuff—like his inventions, he assumed. *Nice job, Naomi.* If she wasn't his sister, he'd invent a way to keep her opinions to herself.

On the other hand, he did have three other sisters waiting in the wings. . . .

Nick returned his nephew's smile. "Somebody's got to try the impossible stuff, Danny. It might as well be me."

"Or me!"

"When you're older, hotshot. For now, you probably ought to concentrate on not landing a permanent place on the Timeout Stool."

Danny made a face and squirmed atop his stool near the window. It was, his nephew had informed him, Uncle Nick's Timeout Stool.

Nick wasn't quite sure what that was. Until today, he hadn't even known he owned one. But his sister Naomi had apparently established them all over town, and Danny knew how to use one. He'd sent himself there after nearly singeing off his eyebrows with the Bunsen burner while conducting a melting experiment on one of Nick's Charlie Parker CDs.

Danny nodded at the beaker in Nick's hand. "So, what's that stuff?"

"It's my best shot at getting a big pile of moola for inventing stuff." Nick waved him closer to watch. "Wanna see?"

Danny took the bait and scuttled down from kiddie Siberia. He edged up to Nick's elbow and poked him. "You mean somebody's gonna give you money just for mixing up goop?" he asked, wide-eyed. "Cool!"

Nick grinned, feeling his uncle stock soar up a few points.

Danny frowned. "But Uncle Nick, my dad says your inventions never work."

His uncle stock plummeted.

"That's the nature of inventing." He swirled the solution and peered inside the beaker. "You keep trying out ideas until one of them works."

"Oh." Danny backed up, eyeballing the solution as though it might blow him out of his Converses any second. "Sure. Whatever you say, Uncle Nick."

"That's what I say." Nick held up the beaker and got ready to pour. "Cross your fingers, Danny. This is it."

Danny covered his ears and closed his eyes instead.

The element eased into the solution in a swirl of blue. Perfect. Not an explosion in sight.

"Booorring," Danny muttered. "I'm going outside."

"I'll be out in a couple of minutes. We can play catch or something."

"Cool."

After the back door closed behind Danny, Nick pulled a potted ivy closer and held the beaker of finished solution aloft. Time to test his theory.

Time to . . . duck! Something squawked and beat its way into the room on a blur of wings and a flash of green. *What the hell was that?*

Dodging reflexively, Nick almost spilled his solution. The winged creature shrieked like something straight out of a Hitchcock movie, then arrowed to the top of the fluorescent fixture he'd hung from the ceiling. It perched there, making the light sway and flash over his equipment.

A bird. A big, ugly, lab-destroying bird.

He had a pretty good idea which animal-loving, pet-store-managing softie next door it belonged to.

"Where's your keeper, Igor?" Nick asked it.

The bird cocked its head at him and shuffled with tiny click-clicks of its claws across the metal fixture. It looked at him the way it probably eyed a bowl of bird kibble. Great. A bird evil *and* stupid enough to think it might snack on something twenty times its size.

At least he'd saved the solution. Trying to ignore the bird, which seemed happy enough cha-cha-ing across his light fixture for the time being, Nick raised the beaker. He checked his calculations again, started to pour . . . and from the front of the house, his screen door slammed shut. His hand jerked sideways, nearly spilling his morning's work.

"Nick? You home?"

Chloe's warm, husky voice came toward him, followed by a clunk and slide down his hallway. A second later, her head popped in view around the doorjamb. Her green-gloved hands came next as she grabbed hold and arced into the room without letting go, dressed in short denim overalls, a very Chloe-worthy hot pink tank top, and enough silver bangle bracelets to make his eyes hurt.

If her pet store customers could see her now, they'd never recognize her as the same no-nonsense woman who dished out kibble and flea spray from nine to five. Nick couldn't understand having a Chloe-style dichotomy between professional and personal lives. But for her, somehow, it seemed to work.

"Hi! Sorry I couldn't get here quicker. I had a little trouble getting over the living room rug in these things."

She lifted her foot in explanation, showing him the in-line skates she'd used to zoom into his house and down the hall. His gaze traveled from her purple and turquoise skates to her green protective knee pads, slid upward past her shapely thighs and vibrant clothes, then settled on her head. Among her jumble of artfully cropped blond hair, she'd knotted a twisted headband of purple and turquoise bandanna.

Nick nodded toward it. "Nice bandage. Nobody would ever guess about the lobotomy."

She made a face. "Nice try, genius, but I don't have time to sling insults today. Have you seen—"

"Igor?" He jerked his chin toward the bird. A mistake, he realized as the bird interpreted the gesture as an invitation to dive toward his head like a miniature hawk on the prowl.

"That's not Igor." Chloe smiled, as though the little beast had done something especially bright and worth about a hundred points on the bird SATs. "It's Shemp."

"Sure." The bird landed on Nick's head. He held himself still, trying not to shudder as it dug its claws in his scalp and tromped around through his hair looking for the best spot to take a bite. Or a peck. Or worse.

"He's a lovebird."

"Literally?"

"Mmmm-hmmm." She gave the bird a fond look. "They make good pets, because they're very smart. Affectionate, too."

"Super." Nick put down his beaker for safekeeping and pointed toward Shemp. "Would you, uh, lasso him or something? I've got work to do."

"Spoilsport. When in this millennium *don't* you have work to do?" Grinning, Chloe raised her slender be-bangled arm and made kiss noises toward Shemp. Obediently, the bird flew to her forearm and walked placidly up to her shoulder.

"Nice work, Snow White."

"Thanks. You really ought to get over your fear of birds, Nick. They won't hurt any—"

"Fear?" He raised his eyebrows and gave her his best incredulous glance. "What's to be afraid of? I could squash the little bugger like a—"

Chloe sucked in a strangled breath. "You wouldn't!" she cried, cuddling Shemp to her cheek.

He thought he heard the damn thing actually coo at her.

She cooed back. "He's had a hard life already."

Nick examined Shemp more closely. "He looks okay to me," he said dubiously. "A little raggedy around the feathers, maybe. Sort of down in the beak—"

"Be serious. You'd be raggedy, too, if you'd been through what he has. Luckily, I was there to rescue him."

"Just what you need. Some other poor, defenseless creature depending on you."

With a smooth whoosh of her skate wheels, she rolled closer. She turned her hazel-eyed gaze on him. "Something you want to tell me, Nick? Feeling especially defenseless today? Or did one of your creations just go kaput on you?"

"My inventions never go kaput." What was she getting at, anyway? "And I'm not one of your . . . projects."

She shrugged. "Have it your way."

"Now wait a min—"

"Friends depend on each other, that's all." She petted the bird. "Anyhow, somebody brought Shemp in to work last night. They were moving away and couldn't keep him."

"Somebody brought a bird to Red's pet shop last night? I didn't know you took that kind of—"

"We don't. Especially now that Red's looking to sell the place and retire to Sun City with her husband. That's why I had to rescue him."

"You had to rescue Red's husband? From what?"

"Kibble overload, actually. Red thought a little Gravy Train might up Jerry's fiber intake, like the doctor suggested."

Nick grinned. Chloe rolled her eyes. "Be serious! I rescued Shemp, here, of course."

She raised her finger for a new perch and smiled like an approving mama as she watched Shemp walk onto it. She lifted him chest-high and petted him with her other hand. He cooed some more, giving Nick a beady stare that suggested some birds had all the luck.

And some human guys didn't know what they were missing.

Nick blinked and adjusted his eyeglasses at his temples, frowning at the wayward thought. Chloe smiled up at him, still smoothing her fingers over Shemp's feathers, and suddenly he imagined her fingers stroking over him. He could actually see her caress in his mind, gentle and crazymaking and accented with nails painted one of those wild nail polish colors she favored, like metallic blue or tangerine.

Dizziness walloped him. *This guy doesn't know what he's missing*, he thought.

She gazed over his array of test tubes and beakers. "So whatcha working on?"

Magically, she morphed into his old pal Chloe again. Good

old late-late-movie watching, Kahlúa-brewing, pour-out-your-troubles-to-me Chloe.

Whew. The last thing he needed was a distraction like dating the girl next door. Not after all this time, and not when he had his best chance in three years of licensing one of his inventions. Especially, particularly, *definitely* not when the clock was ticking on putting together the prototype and proposal he needed.

"I saw Danny outside, and he says you're not even blowing things up today," she went on with an air of mock disappointment. "What gives?"

"What gives? What gives is that four-foot, one-kid wrecking crew out there." Nick glanced through the window at his nephew. "I'm surprised *he's* not blowing things up."

"Come on." Rolling closer, Chloe looked out the window, too. "I'm sure you were the same way as a kid." Her shoulders straightened as she pinned him with a give-me-a-break expression. "Admit it. You weren't always Dudley Do-Right in disguise."

"Maybe not. But I've been a steady Steadman since birth."

"I think there's a cure for that now. An anti-boredom vaccine or—"

"Ha, ha. Anyway, it must skip a generation, because Danny's immune." Nick sighed and faced his beaker of solution again. "I like having him around, but the kid's a demolition expert in tennis shoes. So far he destroyed my Bunsen burner, erased my invention journal file—"

"You, being you, had a backup, of course."

"—sure, but that's not the point. Chloe, in the twenty minutes since his mother dropped him off—"

"Naomi, Nadine, Nancy, or Nora? I can't keep them all straight."

"—Naomi, and neither can anyone else except my mother."

"Nester, right?"

He grinned at her. "Having fun?"

"What? It's cute." She raised her arms, wobbling a little on her skates as she formed a TV-style frame around her head. "The Steadman family was brought to you today," she said with Sesame Street-style peppiness, "by the letter 'N' and the number seven."

"—and since Naomi dropped him off," Nick continued, returning to the subject of his destruction-happy nephew, "Danny's done all that, plus almost reformatted my hard drive, made a mud castle with the potting soil for my research, and—"

"—and, in general, acted like a perfectly normal, seven-year-old kid, right?" Chloe folded her arms, turning her gaze away from the window. "What did you expect when you agreed to spend Saturdays with Danny?"

Nick shook his head. "Aww, I don't know. Don't get me wrong. I love the little guy. With my schedule, spending weekends with my nieces and nephews is about as close as I'll ever get to having a family of my own."

"I dunno about that, Nick." She turned her back on him and gazed out the window again. "My dad's theory was leap-year parenting, and I turned out okay."

In spite of it, Nick added silently. If he ever did have a family, he'd want to devote more time and care to it than Chloe's multiply-divorced parents had. The way he saw it, a man could either be a good father and husband and provider—or he could be a great achiever and innovator and workman. Trying to be all those things simultaneously wasn't fair to anyone.

But the point was, "I'm telling you. I'm lucky as hell not to have kids yet, Chloe. I swear I'd never get anything done."

"Yeah. Lucky, lucky you."

"Nice sarcasm. What's gotten into you?"

She shrugged and trailed her fingertips along the tabletop beside them. "Maybe what'shername's ticking clock is contagious."

He shuddered. "I think there's a cure for that now."

"Har, har," Chloe snorted, her gaze falling on his filled beaker. "So, what's this great new invention of yours?"

Thoughts of nephews and destruction faded.

"It's a growth accelerator." He ran his fingers along the smooth glass beaker. The solution within winked blue and green, an ocean of possibilities. "This is a new version I came up with this morning. I was just about to test it." He waggled his eyebrows at her. "Want to watch?"

Chloe grinned. "That's not the kind of question a girl like me is asked very often."

"That's because that menagerie you keep next door scares off half your dates." He picked up the beaker and prepared to pour.

"Fun-ny. I'd hardly call a dog, a cat, a few fish, a hamster and"—she kiss-kissed at the bird on her shoulder—"Shemp here, a menagerie. I'd need to add at least a representative lizard or turtle to even *begin* to have that kind of variety."

She propped her hands on her hips, pushing her right skate forward and back, adding the imminent threat of wheeled lab destruction to her words.

"Besides, my so-called menagerie loves me. They don't snore, leave dirty socks lying around, *or* bail out on me when the going gets tough." She gave him a pointed glance. "That's not something you can say about just any old—oh—oh—oh!"

Her right skate shot out from under her. Flailing, she clamped her hands on his biceps, making his solution slosh against the sides of the beaker. If he didn't lose the whole thing between Danny, Chloe, and Chloe's winged avenger, it would be a miracle.

Gritting his teeth, Nick raised the beaker out of reach and inadvertently pulled Chloe halfway in the air, too. She shrieked and clutched his middle instead.

"Are you sure you know what you're doing with that?" She eyeballed the solution. "I think you spilled some of your magical Kool-Aid on Shemp."

The bird in question flapped to the light fixture and resumed his attempts to cast disco-ball mood lighting on them.

Chloe glanced upward worriedly. "Are you okay, Shemp? Do you feel anything yet?"

As if the bird planned to answer. Nick frowned and put down the beaker. "I'm at least as good with magical Kool-Aid as you are with roller skates," he pointed out, wrapping his arms around her so he could unclench her fists from the small of his back. It felt as if she was bending his vertebrae into new and interesting shapes.

Wait a minute ... he held her in his arms for a second, testing his reaction. No thoughts of stroking, kissing or anything else remotely erotic popped into his head. All clear. Double-whew! His earlier Chloe-induced fantasy had clearly been an aberration.

Maybe he'd been working too hard. Eight hours at the office and half as many more at home inventing each night would take its toll on any guy's libido, wouldn't it? It only made sense he'd fixate on the nearest woman within squeezing ... stroking ... kissing ... distance. Even if said woman happened to be his best platonic female friend.

He had to start getting out more.

Nick set her upright again and picked up his beaker. Chloe shot him a small, inexplicably disappointed glance, then bumped her hip on his lab table and stared at him.

"Okay. Let's have a look at what this joy juice of yours can do."

Momentarily discombobulated by the dispirited note in her voice, Nick stared back at her. Chloe had always been his most ardent supporter, even more than his family and close-packed clan of relatives. They'd known him all his life. None of them actually believed any of "Nicky's little inventions" would ever amount to anything. But to Chloe, his pal and confidant, he was Mr. Wizard and The Science Guy and the Absent-Minded Professor, all rolled into one big "you can do it!" package.

Nick rubbed the side of his nose, temporarily skidding his glasses askew. "What's the matter, Chloe?" he asked, setting them straight again. He tried to peek at the calendar hanging on the wall behind her without being too obvious about it. "Is it that time of—"

"Say it and die."

Her threat lacked punch, but he shut up anyway. He pulled the potted ivy close again.

She thumped her hip on the table, setting test tubes tinkling in their holders. A sheaf of Nick's notes trembled atop the computer monitor and scattered like cottonwood leaves over his chair and floor. Chloe gazed at them with a faintly morose expression and crossed her arms over her chest. Sigh.

He gently tipped up an ivy leaf and poured solution in the soil inside the plant's terra-cotta pot. Beside him, Chloe's next sigh trembled past his ear. The ivy's glossy leaves fluttered.

He quit pouring. "Spill."

"What?" She shouldered next to him and peered up at Shemp. "You did spill some? How much? Is Shemp going to be okay?"

"Aside from remaining a bird, yes." Nick pulled over the next test-group plant, being careful not to look at her. "I mean, spill. Whatever's bugging you."

Silence.

An instant later, she grabbed the beaker. "At this rate, no wonder your experiments take months. You need an assistant or something." She glanced around his lab, frowning at a stack of pizza delivery boxes in the corner. "You know, somebody to tend to the details of real life for you while you're off in La-La Land inventing stuff."

Nick folded his arms, looking at her carefully. "Now I know something's bothering you. You only turn mean when cornered."

Chloe's startled expression caught him unaware. So did the way she chewed her bottom lip, looking . . . vaguely guilty, if he didn't miss his guess.

She thrust her hands in her hair, loosening her bright bandanna by mistake and showing off the paler blond highlights she'd crowed about to him last week. The gesture was a dead giveaway. She'd never have messed up her hair for anything less than sex or a natural disaster.

Nick had a feeling this fell in the disaster category.

Chloe had a secret.

He wanted to know what it was.

"Well, I . . . ah . . ."

Good move. He gave her ten points for convincing hesitancy. Except Chloe was probably the least hesitant person he knew.

"Mmmm-hmmm?" he nudged.

"I-I—" She rolled her eyes, clearly conjuring up a whopper. The question was, a whopper to cover what?

"Good start," he coaxed, feeling close.

Her eyes brightened. "I'm worried about meeting Mr. Griggs at the bank tomorrow, that's what. That's it!" Her newly triumphant gaze shifted to him and lost a couple degrees of cockiness. "I mean, sure. That's it. That's what's bugging me."

"You're worried about your loan application." It wasn't a question.

"Umm, sure."

"Come on. What kind of a—"

"That's it." Now that the lie was out, she practically oozed relief. With a celebratory flourish worthy of game show hostesses everywhere, she raised the beaker.

Thoughts of her mysterious secret and whatever rebuttal he'd been about to make flew out of Nick's head. No. She couldn't. She wouldn't . . .

Gaily, Chloe poured every aquamarine drop of solution in the first ivy pot. "There! Now you can go on and do something fun with your day," she announced, whisking her palms together.

In the pot in front of them, the soil sizzled. The sound grew louder—loud enough to attract even Shemp's birdbrain onto the scene. He swooped on Chloe's shoulder and cocked his head. She did the same. So did Nick. He'd never heard anything quite like that sizzle.

An instant later, the lustrous green ivy plant drooped in its pot, looking about as growth-accelerated as a strip of overcooked bacon.

"Looks as if it's back to the old drawing board." Chloe peered sadly at the ivy. "But I know you can do it, Nick. Hey—can I watch?"

Three

Chloe couldn't believe it had come to this.

Bleary-eyed and yawning, she stared at the pregnancy test instructions in her hand. She blinked beneath the glaring seven a.m. lighting in her bathroom and read them again. Yup, it really did say she was supposed to pee on a stick. Gross.

She picked up the package. There, above several lines of fine-print medicalese, blazed the words that had lured her to this particular test. Ninety-nine percent sure. If it took bathroom acrobatics to come up with results like that, she guessed she'd better give it a whirl.

It took less time than she expected, more dexterity than she hoped, and miles more steadiness than her shaky hands could muster. Her stomach pitched as she set the tester on the vanity and turned her tomato-shaped kitchen timer to the three-minute mark.

Tick, tick, tick. The first minute passed about as quickly as hot weather in Arizona. Chloe paced across her black-and-white checkerboard-tiled floor, swiping microscopic dirt from the vanity and trying not to look at herself in the mirror.

Dumb. That's what she was, for not thinking of this possibility beforehand. When Nick found out . . .

He wasn't going to find out. She couldn't tell him about this.

She *had* to tell him about this, she argued with herself. She hadn't been with anyone else for more months than she cared to count. Her period was already two weeks late. Despite their fumbling, post-Kahlúa precautions, Nick might be a father in the making. He had a right to know, didn't he?

I'm lucky as hell not to have kids yet. I swear I'd never get anything done.

Oh, yeah. Nick didn't want kids. He'd told her that before. He wasn't ready for a family now, at least not until he'd gotten the inventing bug out of his system and gotten established in his career . . . and turned serious about settling down.

Ha! As if *that* would happen anytime soon.

But part of him already wanted to settle down, Chloe told herself as she straightened the already-neat bath mat and fluffed out the shower curtain. The wistful expression on Nick's face when he'd looked out the window at Danny yesterday had been proof enough of that.

With my schedule, spending weekends with my nieces and nephews is about as close as I'll ever get to having a family of my own.

Then again, he seemed pretty resigned to waiting for it.

Shoot.

And what about the little white lie she'd told him? Nick didn't even remember their night together. What if he never forgave her for lying to him in the first place?

What if he didn't believe her at all? She'd lose her best friend. End of story. *Finito.*

Aaack. The whole thing was too muddled to deal with. With a helpless groan, Chloe flipped down the toilet seat and sat on it. Chin in hand, she stared at the pregnancy test. It grew bigger in her imagination, pulsing on the vanity like an atomic experiment from one of Nick's Godzilla movies.

She was losing it.

Get a grip, she commanded herself. Then her front door swooshed open, Nick called to her from the living room, and Chloe nearly jumped out of her skin. The pregnancy test box clunked hollowly to the linoleum, punctuating the sound of the other shoe dropping in her life. Could she face Nick and still not tell him the truth?

She'd have to.

If necessary, she could always tell him the truth later. *If* the test was positive. No point worrying him for no reason, right?

"Chloe?"

His voice grew louder, echoing down the hallway. Coming closer. She leaped out of the bathroom and slammed the door shut behind her, just in time to collide with Nick.

"Ooof!"

"Hi!" She gave him an overly chipper smile, taking in his rumpled khaki shorts and Cardinals T-shirt with an appreciative glance born of knowing exactly what kind of fine-tuned body he kept beneath them. "You surprised me."

"Your front door was open." He straightened his glasses and gave her a quick once-over. "Oversleep again? Come on, Chloe. You're never going to convince that old coot Griggs to give you your loan if you can't even make it to your appointment on time. You know that. You—"

His gaze stopped on her purple-dotted boxers. "You, you, you've been in business long en. . . ." He stopped. "Do you always sleep in those?"

His eyebrows furrowed beneath his glasses rims. His fingertip raised to his lips, tapping in the way that always showed he was deep in thought about an experiment, or a new invention . . . or the night he thought they'd never spent together.

Chloe slapped her hands over her boxers and neon green T-shirt like an old-maid aunt. "These?" She tried to look horrified at being caught undressed. "Just got 'em yesterday. Big sale down at Bevick's department store. You know, the one down on Main Street with the, um, wedding dresses in the window and the cute little slingback crocodile shoes with the bows on the toes?"

Her monologue ran out of breath and she ran out of lies, but that was okay—Nick's eyes had already glazed over at the mention of shopping. Thank God he never paid attention to everyday details like clothes.

"I'd better go change," she muttered and made her escape.

At her entrance into her bedroom, Moe meowed, then tried slipping through the open door. It gave her an idea. She scooped him up, grazed her chin across his soft furred head, then leaned into the hallway.

"Moe's really missed you." Rapidly, she slipped her armful of orange tabby in Nick's hands before he could object. "He hates it when you work so much. We can't wait until your growth-accelerator proposal is done."

That ought to hold him for a while. Chloe snicked the door shut again, trying not to hear Nick's grumbling on the other side. It was beyond her why he didn't want pets of his own. All of hers obviously loved him.

Maybe he'd like something simple. Something small. A hamster like Curly, or a goldfish, or . . . no. The poor thing would probably keel over from neglect the next time Nick's inventing bug struck. A commitment-phobe like him was strictly the *faux* pet type. Maybe this Christmas she'd buy him one of those videotapes that made it look as if your television housed a whole aquarium of exotic fish. That was just about Nick's speed.

No commitment. No obligations.

No risk.

No change in plans.

Sighing, Chloe made herself quit mentally matchmaking Nick. She had an appointment to get ready for, and it didn't involve the wild kingdom—not unless Effram Griggs's toupee counted as a life form of its own. Whipping off her T-shirt, she whirled to fling it in the hamper, then slid open her mirrored closet doors.

Moe yowled outside. Her bedroom door opened. Nick's head emerged around the edge of it.

"Something's buzzing in your bathroom. Are you cooking up another batch of punk rock hair color, or what?"

Chloe flung her arms across her naked chest. Nick didn't even blink. She might as well have waved her arms in the air and tap danced, for as much attention as he paid to her appearance. Keeping her arms tight over her chest, she slowly turned to face him. His expression didn't change one iota.

Not even half an iota.

Her body felt as heated as a toaster glowing red, just before it turned the toast to a slab of coal. That would be her heart if she wasn't careful. Ruined and crumbly.

"Fun-ny. It was only that one time I tried those red stripes, and that was years ago. Now I'm sticking with my natural hair color."

Nick looked at her expensively streaked layered cut. "Uh-huh. That's you, nature girl," he deadpanned. "Do you want me to turn off the timer for you?"

He was utterly, completely, oblivious, Chloe realized with a sinking feeling. Even half-naked she couldn't dredge up any non-platonic interest from him.

Any child they might have created together deserved more than a lovestruck mama and an indifferent daddy. She'd already been around that block, wearing the diapers herself. She couldn't let history repeat itself.

Knowing Nick, he'd feel obligated to "do the right thing," no matter what his feelings were for her. She really *couldn't* tell him the truth.

"The timer?" he asked again.

"Timer?" She fought an insane urge to drop her arms and flash him, just to get some sort of reaction. "Oh! The timer! No, thanks. It'll turn off by itself in a minute."

He shrugged. "Okay. You'd better hurry up, or Mr. Griggs will reschedule you again. I don't know why you don't just go to one of the bigger banks in Phoenix or—"

"I'll be ready," Chloe interrupted, hoping to forestall the inevitable, familiar avalanche of financial advice. Turning, she concentrated on pulling one of the few suits she owned from her closet without giving Nick a thirty-four B-size eyeful in the process.

"Tucson for your loan." His gaze flicked over the red suit and matching pumps she threw on the bed. "You know, Red and Jerry would probably let you make payments directly to them for a while if that's what it takes. I'll bet—"

"No favors." She added a halter-cut, pale-colored bodysuit to the pile. Arizona in April, even early April, demanded the coolest clothes possible.

"Chloe—"

"And no help, either." She turned her back to Nick while

she sorted through the beads and bangles and multihued earrings jumbled together in her jewelry box. "I can do this on my own. There's no point involving Red and Jerry before I know I've got the bank behind me. I don't want to get their hopes up—"

"Then disappoint them," Nick finished. "I know, I know."

Holding a gold hoop to one ear and a *faux* ruby-and-pearl stud to the other, Chloe turned. "Which do you think looks best?"

His mouth dropped open.

Wowsers, that was some kind of reaction to a pair of earrings. *Note to myself: Ask Nick for jewelry opinions more often.*

Wait a minute . . . his gaze was focused a whole lot lower than her ears. In fact, now that she looked closer, she realized he wasn't even in the above-the-neck neighborhood. His dark-eyed gaze was aimed lower than that, closer to her . . . *omigod, her* naked *breasts!* Shrieking, Chloe hugged her arms over her chest, barely registering the cold kiss of the earrings still in her hands.

Nick whipped sideways, hiding his face by propping his arm on the door jamb. "Uh, they both look great to me."

Both what? Both breasts or both earrings?

Scratch that. She probably didn't really want to know the answer to that one.

"I meant the earrings," Nick added.

"I figured."

Sheesh! What had she been thinking? This pregnancy thing was turning her mind to mush. Her face burning, Chloe threw the earrings in her jewelry box and slammed the lid shut. She snatched her suit and clutched it, hanger and all, in front of her.

"But, uh, that's really a nice pair of umm, umm . . ." His arm churned, trying to crank something smart to his brain. "I mean, the rest of you is really—dammit, Chloe! Put some clothes on, will you?"

"You're blushing, Nick."

"Like hell."

"Your face is redder than my suit."

"Nothing's redder than that suit."

He ducked his head and chanced a look from beneath his elbow. She could almost pinpoint the exact moment he realized she'd safely covered her "nice pair" from view, because his grin returned.

"You might get faster action on your loan if you tried the earring trick on Mr. Griggs."

"Har, har."

He came closer. She must have imagined that blush on his face, because now Nick looked as composed as ever. Not to mention as miserably unaffected by her—as a woman—as he ever had.

"Anyway," she continued with a teasing smile, "I already tried that."

"And?"

"And the man has no taste when it comes to earrings. He actually picked a rhinestone pair."

She laughed at the look on his face, then met him halfway around the side of the bed, tucking her chin to her chest to secure the suit and hanger while she moved. "I'm kidding, you Neanderthal! What kind of woman do you think I am?"

"I think you're a big old softie, worrying over Red and Jerry the way you do."

He reached to help her hold up the curved metal hanger top, and his knuckle brushed warm against her chin. At the feel of his skin touching hers, Chloe's knees went weak. The hanger wobbled in her hand, making her suit flutter in front of her.

"I think you're going to get that loan of yours, or die trying." Nick smiled and fingered her suit jacket. "And I think you're going to be late if you don't hurry up and shimmy into this thing."

"Shimmy?"

He headed for the door, tapping a beat along the footboard of her sleigh bed.

"You think I 'shimmy'?"

Nick shrugged and stepped into the hallway.

He thought she shimmied!

Officially, of course, she was incredibly offended. But—he

thought she shimmied! Chloe grinned, just as Nick stuck his head around the doorjamb again.

"And one more thing."

She put on a straight face.

"If things don't work out with the bank today, you can always count on me."

Awww. "I can't ask you for help, Nick."

"Sure, you can. The rest of us deserve a chance to play hero sometimes, too, you know."

Sure. Chloe sighed and sank on her bed as he closed the door, leaving her alone. Would Nick really see instant unplanned fatherhood as an opportunity to be heroic? Or were those just so many words, words that were easy to say but hard to live up to?

There was only one way to find out.

She got dressed and ducked in the bathroom for one quick look at her destiny before leaving.

The blonde emerged from Saguaro Vista Cattleman's Bank just as Nick glanced up from his hydroponics research notes. Her long legs flashed beneath her thigh-high red skirt as she clicked toward him with the kind of hip-swaying, high-heeled strides that destroyed brain cells in men everywhere. Halfway across the city center's *saltillo*-tiled courtyard, she shrugged off her matching suit jacket and flipped it over her shoulder, trailing it by her fingertips over her back.

Her naked back. Her pert, perfect breasts bounced in the sunlight as she strolled through the mist given off by the tinkling courtyard fountain. *Whaaa. . . ?* his brain asked, but his body already had the upper hand. *Come on down*, it said.

He blinked. The vision in red transformed itself into Chloe. Fully clothed, *jacket-wearing*, non-bouncing, just-pals Chloe.

This had to stop. Chloe was his friend, his *best* friend, not a potential between-inventions playmate. The women he dated weren't like Chloe. She was e.e. cummings; they were Thoreau. She was mercury; they were iron. Chloe was bare feet and Ring Dings and touch football; they were designer shoes and *haute cuisine* and PTSO fundraisers. She was the sizzle; they were the steak.

And Nick was the overworked inventor who obviously needed to get out more.

No wonder Chloe's dual-earring nudist impression had affected him so strongly this morning. The sight of her standing there with jewels in her hands and nothing but bare, silky skin below had brought every part of him to attention. It didn't take a genius to realize he needed a break. His brain had obviously been forced to take drastic measures to shove the message through.

Cool it, he commanded himself. *Chloe is your friend, not your fantasy woman.*

His non-fantasy woman stopped in front of him, grabbed his sleeve, and thunked her forehead on his shoulder.

"Let's go," she mumbled into his chest.

Nick's other concerns vanished. When Chloe did the shoulder clunk, it meant she needed him. "Awww, Chloe. What happened?"

She mumbled something into his T-shirt. He got as far as, "Effram Griggs is a shirt-tidied, misery grist beanie outback," before interrupting.

"What was that part about his beanie?"

She beat her fist softly against his shoulder and made a frustrated sound. "I said," Chloe told him, turning her head just enough to make her words heard, "that Effram Griggs is a short-sighted, misogynist weenie-throwback with delusions of grandeur and cigar stubs for brains."

"He turned down your loan application again?"

"Again." Miserably, Chloe nodded against his shoulder, giving him a mouthful of jaggedly cut blond hair.

He blew it away and hugged her one-handed, careful to keep his notebook wedged between his chest and her . . . curvy parts. Not even three inches of his chicken-scratched notes could block the alluring tropical scents of her shampoo and perfume, though. Too bad.

"I thought I'd start to wear him down by now!" She wriggled against him as though her frustration just had to have an outlet. "You know. Third time's the charm, and all that?"

"There's always next month." After her second loan attempt, Griggs had refused to consider any applications she made with less than one month's time between them.

The arbitrary, power-hungry jerk.

"I can't wait another month!" she wailed.

"It looks as if you don't have much choice." Nick squeezed her a little closer. "In the meantime, it's my job to cheer you up. What you need is Kahlúa and coffee and sympathy."

Chloe stiffened in his arms. A sniffle sound came from somewhere near his collarbone, followed by something that sounded like, "Kahlúa hurts."

Which didn't make any sense at all. Taking over Red's pet shop must have meant more to her than she'd let on. Why else would Chloe reject their time-tested cheer-up remedy?

"Ice cream?" Nick suggested. "A movie? A retro-style racquetball game? You can pretend the ball is Effram Griggs's greasy gray toupee-wearing head."

Another sniffle, but hard on its heels came a choked laugh. "Now there's an idea."

"Wait. I take it back." He grinned. "With motivation like that, you'd probably cream me. I wouldn't be able to hold up my head in public."

At that, Chloe laughed outright. "It wouldn't be the first time, you welsher." She twisted her fingers in his T-shirt sleeve, then nestled closer and pressed her cheek against his chest, soaking up comfort as easily as she walloped a racquetball. "You still owe me a dinner from your last crushing defeat, remember?"

"I remember. One of these days, I swear I'm revoking that 'do-over' rule of yours."

"Bully."

"Cheater."

"Pushover."

Nailed, Nick admitted. If anyone could turn him into an easy mark, it was Chloe. "Maybe, but Effram Griggs isn't. Running the only bank in town went straight to his head fifteen years ago. It's only gotten worse since."

She sniffled and raised her head, staring over his shoulder

at the Cattleman's Bank. If looks could burn, hers would have set fire to the building's rustic southwestern façade.

"I guess the good-old-boy network still stands tough in Saguaro Vista," she croaked, swiping her hand across her eyes. "Since I'm not a man or, worse, not one of Griggs's poker buddies, it looks as if it's back to the old drawing board."

"Hey." Nick thumbed her chin higher and examined her face. "Are you crying?"

She jerked her head sideways. "Who, me?" She brushed intently at something on his shoulder—a smudge of her candy-apple red lipstick, probably. "You know me. I never cry."

"I know. That's why I—"

"And I'm not now." She frowned up at him, then slung her purse higher on her shoulder and took a deep breath. "Look, buying Red's pet shop was just an idea, okay? Nobody knows about it but you. Nobody knows, nobody's disappointed, and things go on the same way they did before." Her voice cracked. "It's no big deal."

"You're acting as if it's a big deal," he persisted.

Chloe wasn't the type to get worked up over nothing. She wanted that loan to buy Red's pet shop. It was important to her—mysteriously important. Nick wanted to know the reason why. There was definitely more going on here than met the eye.

"It doesn't add up." He examined her closely. "What's special about getting this loan, this time? About getting it now?"

"Please don't ask me that, Nick."

"Chloe—"

She said nothing, just closed her eyes. When she opened them again, her slanted hazel-eyed gaze looked bright with determination.

"It's just time I started acting like the responsible adult I am, that's all." She swiveled on a burst of new energy, her high heels clicking on the tiled courtyard. "I do a good job running Red's pet store, and I'd be an equally good pet store owner. I'm not going to let Effram Griggs and his old cronies stand in my way. I'll find a way to convince him yet."

"There's always a Phoenix bank."

"No."

"Or an assumable loan. Talk to Red and Jerry. What have you got to lose?"

"It's not what I have to lose. It's what *they* have to lose. I'm not telling them until everything's all set." On tiptoes, she stuck her face in his. "And *you're* keeping mum, too, mister. Not a word about this to anyone, okay?"

Nick held up two fingers. "Scout's honor."

She gave him a sassy grin and looked him up and down. "You're no boy scout, Steadman."

Not with the kind of thoughts he'd been having about her lately, he wasn't. And Chloe was no damned campfire girl, either—not with the secrets she'd been keeping.

He still wanted to know what they were.

"I still know how to light a fire." He grinned. "It's all in the way you lay the kindling."

She quirked her lips. "Save it for your breathless admirers, Smokey. I've got things to do."

Yeah. Mysterious things.

Turning, she headed for the parking area with a little less sizzle in her stride and a lot more secrets than he'd suspected whirling in that crazy blond head of hers. Suddenly, Chloe seemed something Nick had never imagined she could be: a woman of mystery.

He put his hand on her shoulder from behind, slowing her down to his speed. Beneath her sleek business-suit armor, her neck and shoulder muscles tensed like knotted steel. This particular loan denial had been especially hard for Chloe to take. He wanted to know why.

Hell, as her friend, it was practically his duty to find out why.

"Wait up." He tucked his notebook beneath his elbow and kneaded her shoulders with both hands, hoping to coax out some of the tension and all of the truth. Her secret was getting bigger, and it was driving him crazy. "I was serious back there. You've tried for this loan three times now, and struck out every time—"

"Thanks, Mr. Encouragement."

"You're welcome. Anyway, three strikes now, and you've never been this upset before. What's so special about this time?"

"You don't want to come with me, Nick?" Chloe whirled to face him just as they reached his motorcycle. "Is that what this is all about? You've got better things to do, I'll bet. Like work yourself to death, maybe, or—"

"Hold on—"

She flashed him a belligerent look. "You know it's true. Admit it."

"Like hell, I will!" She sounded just like the rest of his family, every one of them a proponent of shorter workdays, less ambition, and family, family, family . . . regardless of the cost.

She jutted her chin. "Have it your way. Live in denial. Live alone! It's none of my business."

"Aww, Chloe. Not you, too."

She shrugged. "I'm your friend, not your . . . whatever." Her voice cracked. "You don't owe me anything. Not even an explanation for why you don't want to drive me to the bank anymore."

"Wait a minute. I never said I wouldn't drive you to the bank anymore." *Chick logic.* He'd never understand it. "Where did that come from?"

Her eyes welled up with—he'd swear it—honest-to-God tears. That's how Nick knew it was a trick. Chloe never cried, especially not at advantageous moments like this one. But he still felt like hell anyway.

"Aww, come on. Just because I don't want to turn into Joe Family Man like every other Steadman doesn't mean I won't help you when you need it."

"I don't need it."

"Fine."

"Fine." She sniffed and held out her arms for her helmet.

Nick handed her the purple metallic one she used, feeling vaguely as though he'd been outmaneuvered. He couldn't pinpoint why . . . until he remembered what they'd been talking about before.

"Anyway, what's so important about *this one particular loan application*?"

She stopped midway through putting on her helmet. With trembling hands, she slowly pulled it the rest of the way over her head. Buying time to think up another sidetracking tactic, he'd bet. *What was her secret?*

When her face came in view again, she was grinning.

"Like a dog with a bone, aren't you?"

"Ruff."

"Ha, ha." Chloe hitched up her skirt and straddled his motorcycle, something he'd probably seen her do a million times—but never to this effect. Suddenly, the April sunshine took on a searing, dizzying quality.

"Am I driving, or you?"

She blinked up at him calmly, just as though most of her thighs weren't bared for the whole wide world to see. Didn't she realize what a sight like that could do to a guy who *wasn't* her best platonic male friend?

"I'm driving," Nick gritted out.

"Okay." Chloe unbuttoned her suit jacket and shrugged it off her shoulders. For real this time. Her bare skin gleamed in the reflected glare from his bike's hot chrome.

Her bare skin.

Nick thought he might pass out.

Then she tugged off her jacket the rest of the way, revealing the skintight, nude-toned top she had on beneath it. His breath left him in a whoosh.

Think science thoughts, he commanded himself. Chloe smiled, just as though she'd guessed what he'd been thinking before . . . and wanted him to know she approved.

No. That was nuts. She'd probably be appalled, Nick told himself as he watched her slide innocently from the back of his bike and wait for him to get on. He had to quit thinking of her this way.

"Look, you're being irrational." He hoped it wasn't contagious. Trying to look serious, he tucked his chin to his shoulder so he could glimpse her behind him. "What's the big deal with your loan, all of a sudden? *What's going on*?"

Her arms sagged around his middle, then tightened. She

sighed. He waited a second, then realized Chloe still wasn't going to tell him.

Damn. Foiled again.

"Well," she finally said. "As of this morning, I'm pretty sure I'm pregnant. Do you think that's it?"

Four

"Pregnant?"

"You can stop saying that now, Nick." Chloe whipped off her helmet and shoved it at him. "I'm pretty sure I understood the first twenty-two times you said it on the way home."

Thankfully, now they were parked on the paved driveway at his house. Free to make her getaway, she jumped off the back of his motorcycle. More than her ankles wobbled when she hit the ground. "Okay?" she asked, her voice breaking on the word.

"Okay." He hesitated . . . then swore instead. "Dammit, Chloe. This isn't the kind of secret I was expecting."

Ha. He didn't know the half of it.

"Umm, surprise! I guess," she said weakly.

He frowned.

Oh, geez—Nick was never going to buy this. She wasn't prepared at all. She needed a better strategy, one that would keep him off the trail of the truth. It was for his own good, after all. Who was she to wreck his life plans, to sidetrack his dreams, to saddle him with responsibilities he didn't want?

Nobody, that's who. Chloe decided to retreat.

It didn't work. Nick tailed her all the way across the side yard bordering their matching redbrick, white-trimmed houses, mumbling something about secrets and women of mystery.

Clearly, escape was futile.

Sidestepping a patch of blooming prickly pear cactus, Chloe reached her front porch and abandoned her hopes that Nick might actually let her get away without having this discussion. So far, he wasn't handling the news very well.

She hadn't even gotten to the good part yet.

All she wanted was to be alone. To postpone all the explanations and have some time to think. Her loan application had tanked, her so-called best friend was having a meltdown, and it wasn't even happy hour yet.

Not that a cocktail would have helped, or even been advisable, under the circumstances. Maybe a milkshake.

Or maybe a prenatal vitamin. Did those give you extra pep? She hoped so, because she was going to need it to deal with Nick. A trip to the doctor was definitely in order, and soon.

Until then, she had a secret to keep—or at least part of one. With elaborate casualness, Chloe fished her keys from her purse and unlocked her front door. The moment she finished, Nick's hand clamped on hers and twisted the knob. She could barely breathe as he barreled them both inside.

"Pregnant?" He slammed the door shut behind them. "You're actually pregnant."

"No, it's all a big joke. Get it?"

"*What?*"

The force of his yell backed her across the living room, stumbling over microscopic bumps in the carpet. Then his arms came up and trapped her between his chest and the living room wall. His body heat washed over her, as searing as his expression.

"Explain," Nick said, grinding the word through his teeth.

"Sheesh. I've never seen you like—"

"*Now.*"

Great. She'd reduced him to monosyllabic responses. This *was* serious.

He pressed forward, pinning her beneath a scary glare that did a lot to explain what probably went wrong between him and what'shername.

Chloe pressed her lips together and kept mum.

Nick saw straight through her. But then he'd always been able to before. What made her think she could deceive him now?

Desperation, that's what.

"*Please* explain," he growled.

Civility, however grudgingly given, counted toward progress, Chloe supposed. But something in his voice still made her shiver.

Under different circumstances and minus the Incredible Hulk routine, she might have enjoyed their nearness. As it was, she did her best not to think about wanting his arms holding her close instead of caging her in. She tilted her chin as defiantly as she could.

"The Neanderthal routine doesn't suit you, Nick."

He blinked, a perfect picture of disbelief. She'd have preferred a portrait of understanding or even cheer-me-up humor, but she wasn't going to get it. Not this time.

"Neander—" He stopped on a frown, straightened his specs with one hand, and tried again. "Never mind. You're not sidetracking me this time."

He stared straight in her eyes, looking analytical and determined and not half as tender as she'd hoped a prospective father might. Chloe realized she'd set a tough task for herself. How could she keep a secret she didn't want to keep? Especially from somebody as inquisitive as Nick?

She wasn't sure, but she had to try.

"Chloe," he began, sounding suspiciously patient, "exactly how did this happen?"

Good question. She should have been ready for it, but she wasn't. Behind her, Moe meowed and Larry barked to be let in the back door, but now wasn't the time to be distracted. The sooner she got this over with, the better.

She ducked beneath his arms to put some distance between them, then threw her suit jacket on the sofa and faced him with her hands on her hips. "Oh, I dunno, Nick. The usual way, I guess. *You know.*"

His gaze whipped over her, lingered in the neighborhood of her hips—gauging her suitability for childbearing, she supposed—then rose to her face. He swallowed.

She'd stunned him into silence. Maybe the idea of somebody finding his platonic pal Chloe sexy threw him for a loop. Ouch.

"*'You know'?*" Nick mimicked. "*'You know'?* What does that mean?"

"You're turning red in the face, Nick. Do you want some water? I'll get you some water." She headed for the kitchen. For sanctuary.

He grabbed her arm and hauled her back. "I want answers."

"Would you believe . . . immaculate conception?"

"Answers. Now."

"I didn't think so."

Okay. Be strong, she told herself. Stick as close to the truth as possible.

"The truth is, I met someone." Chloe kept her gaze trained on his T-shirt's football helmet logo. "We talked, we laughed, we. . . ." *We loved*, she wanted to say. But he didn't want to hear it, and she couldn't stand lingering over what she couldn't have. "We're over."

"Over."

"Yeah." She kicked off her heels and padded to the kitchen, wanting to maximize the distance between her and Nick before she started bawling over lost loves and best friends and second chances that couldn't be. Behind her, his breath whooshed out as he sank on the sofa and put his feet up.

"These things happen you know," Chloe called over the opened refrigerator door. "Over. As in you and what'shername."

"She has a name. I just . . . dammit, Chloe! You've been calling her what'shername for so long, I can't remember what it is."

Good. And good—he was sidetracked successfully. Maybe she could handle this secret stuff after all. She grinned despite everything and shoved the fridge shut with her toe, then carried two slippery cold soda cans to the living room with her.

She handed him one. "Serves you right for dating more women than you can count."

"I can count 'em. I just can't keep 'em."

"Maybe they can tell you're already wedded to your work. They know there's no future with a guy who kisses with one hand on his research notebook."

"Hmmph." He turned his gaze on her as she curled up on the other end of her vibrant red plaid sofa, then gave her a bad-boy's smile. "I use both hands when the situation warrants it."

I know.

"I'll bet." She turned her can of diet cola in her hand as she groped for the tab to crack it open. With one finger hooked beneath it, she conjured up a mock shudder. "But spare me the details, Casanova. I don't want to know."

I want to experience it again.

Too bad she never would.

"Then we're even." Nick sounded unexpectedly weary. "Because I'm not sure I'm ready for the nitty gritty details of your love life, either."

Good. Because she wasn't ready to tell him all the things he didn't really want to know. And bad—because that had to be the shortest sidetracking on record. He was already back on the case.

But silently. Beside her in his habitual spot, Nick let his head loll back along the sofa's cushions, eyes closed. Probably still absorbing her pregnancy news.

Well, so was she. Maybe for now it would be best to just leave Nick alone and give them both some breathing room. If she was lucky, maybe he'd take an impromptu nap or something, and grant her a half-hour's respite.

Fat chance. When Chloe opened her soda, slurping at the fizz that crackled out, Nick's head turned unerringly toward the sound. His eyes opened.

"You almost had me sidetracked again. You might as well give up, Chloe, because—" His gaze landed on her diet cola can, halfway to her lips, and whatever he'd been about to say sputtered beneath his next words. "Are you insane?" he yelled.

"What?"

He flung himself across the stretch of red plaid separating them and yanked her diet cola out of her hand. "This is bad for you," he said, plunking it on her scarred square coffee table. "You've got to start taking care of yourself better."

"I'm a grown woman, Nick. I—"

His thumb touched her lips and startled her into silence. "You're a woman with a . . . a baby. That means things are going to change for you."

Change? That sounded promising. Maybe he meant they'd. . . *No*. That was only wishful thinking. That was the first thing she'd have to change—by cutting it out of her life. She slumped against the sofa cushions and eyeballed her soda longingly while Nick went on talking.

"You'll have to watch what you eat, what you drink, what you do," he said, warming up to his expertise. "Things like that"—his gaze shifted to her banished diet soda can—"are off limits."

She rolled her eyes. "Who are you, Mister Spock?"

"That's Doctor Spock. And no, I'm not."

"Look. This is the twenty-first century. You're—"

"I'm just a guy who's been an uncle four times over, Miss Only Child," Nick interrupted, "and that's four times more experience with things baby and pregnancy-related than you."

Chloe saluted. "Yes, sir." His concern was touching, if a little overbearing. "Maybe you'd like to carry the baby yourself? I'm sure there've been supersecret scientific advances by now that would let you do it. You're connected with the science community, Nick. You should look into it."

"Fun-ny." He picked himself up off the sofa with a new aura of purpose, then paused to tousle her hair. "But ridiculous."

He was right. No man would submit to maternity clothes.

His fingers trailed away as he stepped over her legs and edged between the coffee table and sofa, headed for the kitchen.

Sighing, Chloe watched him leave. His brief caress left her temporarily crazy, wanting to drag his hand back to her head, thrust his fingers back in her hair, even demolish her entire hairstyle . . . just to feel him touch her again. But that was impossible, so she stuck both palms beneath her thighs and reminded herself that no price was too great to preserve their friendship.

Except maybe whatever . . . glop in a glass Nick handed her a few minutes later. He emerged from the kitchen carrying it, looking so triumphant that she forgave whatever mess he'd created with all the banging and slamming he'd been doing.

He beamed. "Drink up. It's my specialty."

She gazed into the Flintstones glass of foaming . . . stuff . . . he'd whipped up, not at all sure she could actually consume it. She sniffed.

"This smells like . . . I can't put my finger on it, but I'm thinking . . . Christmas time, punch bowls, rum." Chloe snapped her fingers. "Eggnog!"

"Sure. You could call it that." Nick ran his fingertip around the edge of the blender container. "It's got eggs in it."

He licked the tip of his finger, then held up the blender pitcher and lapped up a drip. She'd never envied a hunk of plastic before.

"Eggnog, huh?" she managed to say. "Okay."

She sipped. It tasted of cold frothy milk, a touch of banana . . . and the slimy glob of raw egg that slicked down her throat on the first gulp.

"Aaack!" Chloe thrust the glass at Nick and leaned toward the coffee table, shoving aside books and magazines and knocking a rental DVD of The Three Stooges to the floor in her quest for the tissue box. "Why didn't you tell me the egg was *raw*?"

She heard the muffled whump of tissues being pulled out of the box, then Nick pressed a wad in her hand. She used it to wipe away the last traces of his pseudo health drink. That horrible stuff had to be revenge for the way she'd sprung her pregnancy surprise on him.

"Of course it was raw," he said, exactly in the same way he might have said, "Of course I hate shopping."

"You've seen too many Rocky movies."

"Don't be a baby."

"Don't be a doofus." She aimed a shuddering glance at the Flintstones cup. "I'm not drinking that stuff. Don't you know raw eggs can carry salmonella? You're supposed to be the Science Guy, here."

"Sorry, Chloe." He looked disappointed. "I meant well."

Something told her she hadn't seen the last of his efforts to make sure she was a suitably healthy example of an expectant mother. The idea had a certain irony, but it wasn't anything Chloe could consider further with egg aftertaste in her mouth and Nick's steady gaze making her feel warm all over.

"I'll come up with a better drink next time."

"Thanks for the warning." She dreaded it already.

"You're welcome." He picked up the Flintstones cup, then peered thoughtfully into it. "Nadine's got some recipes for smoothies. I'll make some for you. Otherwise, you'll be missing out on some good stuff."

I know, Chloe thought, watching him carry the cup to the kitchen. *I'll be missing you.* The sink faucet rumbled, then water splashed. She imagined a future with Nick elbow-deep in soapsuds at her sink every day, a kitchen towel slung over his shoulder and a babbling baby at the table and her whipping up something gourmet at the stove . . . and knew her fantasy was only that.

She couldn't even cook.

She followed him to the kitchen anyway and found Nick head-and-shoulders deep inside her refrigerator, mumbling to himself. His backside faced her, every bit as cute as she remembered. His denim shorts stretched tight as he reached for something on the shelf in front of him.

Chloe stifled a sigh and leaned on the counter to watch. Fate was cruel to have delivered her a man like this next door, given her a taste of life in his arms . . . then dangled him just out of reach with Kahlúa-induced amnesia and the constraints of platonic friendship. It just wasn't fair.

Nick's hand emerged holding a box of Twinkies. He slapped it on the countertop beside the six-pack of diet cola he'd already removed from the refrigerator.

"Hey!" She was beside him in an instant. "Those will get all gooey if you leave them out like that."

He faced her, eyebrows raised. "They'll get even gooier in the trash can." He picked up the box and aimed it toward the plastic bin in the corner like a basketball player making a free throw. He paused. "Want to say goodbye?"

"What? No!" Chloe grabbed one end of the box and pulled. Nick pulled back.

The tug-of-war that ensued wasn't pretty.

"You can't eat this stuff," Nick said, wrenching his end of the box.

His tug sent her stockinged feet skidding across the linoleum. She added her other hand to the struggle and gained an inch or two. "Let go!"

"You let go." He tugged back, and she lost the ground she'd gained. His broad chest and grinning face forecast his victory, but she wasn't ready to call it quits yet.

Chloe Carmichal was no pushover. She never surrendered.

Instead she stuck her foot on top of Nick's ankle for leverage and tightened her grip on the Twinkie box. "It's mine. Give it up, you brute, before I have to manhandle you."

The idea had merit. She couldn't allow herself to dwell on it—but she couldn't deny herself a quick roving glance over his . . . manhandleables, either. The man could entice a nun to sin, and never know he was doing it. That was the trouble with brainiac types like Nick. He lived in a world of the mind, where a buffed-up body was just efficient packaging for the real goods.

She never knew efficiency could be so sexy.

"Grow up, Chloe," he said, interrupting her in mid-fantasy-flight. "Doing without junk food for a few months won't kill you."

"Oh, no?"

"No. Anyway, it's for your own good."

He pulled harder. She skidded and tried backpedaling against the slick waxed linoleum. The motion destroyed whatever balance she had left. Chloe tightened her hold on the Twinkies, felt herself falling . . . then Nick caught her. Cardboard crunched and cellophane crackled between them as their chests came together and squashed the Twinkie box.

"Oh!"

His arms held her close and his hands splayed across her shoulder blades to keep her steady. When she looked up from the flattened remains of her prize—he *had* let go of it, after all—somehow Nick's face hovered only inches from her own. Concern turned his eyes mesmerizing and blue. Chloe felt herself melting, easing into the warmth of his arms like Moe easing into a brilliant patch of sunlight. Suddenly she understood exactly what it was about the heat that made the cat purr.

"Whoops," she whispered.

His gaze dropped to her mouth. She wanted to say more, just to keep his attention there, but the feel of being in Nick's arms stole her breath and sent her wits walking. She licked her lips, drew in a deep breath, and couldn't release it to save her life when she felt her chest expand and press closer against him. Time spun slower.

"Are you all right?" he asked.

"Mmmm-hmmm." *Better than all right.* "Thanks."

And thank God he didn't let her go. Instead, he held her a little tighter. "You should have just given up the Twinkies peacefully. Now they're ruined."

As if she cared. She'd crush a million boxes if it would land her in his arms. Chloe didn't know how she'd lived without his warmth surrounding her these past weeks. Like a supplicant, like a woman in love wanting to be kissed, she tipped her head back.

Her eyes drifted closed. *Please, just give me this one moment,* she thought as she sensed Nick's face coming nearer. *I'll live on it forever and never ask for more.*

"Chloe . . . ?"

The wonder in his tone opened her eyes. The desire she glimpsed in his gaze made her heart spin into a happy dance of love lost and returned. He was going to kiss her! Even without knowing the truth of their baby, Nick really wanted her, just for herself. It was all she could have dreamed, happening before her eyes.

He lowered his head fractionally closer. His minty toothpaste breath drifted past her cheek. The lean, close-shaved caress of his jaw followed, making her twist her head to capture his mouth. *Kiss me.*

"Kiss me. Oh, Nick—"

His whole body went still. Slowly he drew back, and the heat in his eyes was from anger, not passion.

"*What*?"

"I-I-I-" *I said it out loud*! "I was kidding!" She raised her Twinkie box prize and tossed it on the kitchen table. "I win!"

"You win."

She nodded.

"You win . . . that." He cocked his head toward the Twinkies.

She nodded.

"You did all . . . that, just to win." He straightened his glasses and peered at her. "Ruthless competitor that you are, of course."

Was that irony in his voice? "Umm, sure."

"Like hell. You're not like that, Chloe, and we both know it."

In silent explanation, she gestured lamely toward the Twinkies.

"You were serious."

"All true Twinkie aficionados are serious about their—"

"Cut it out, Chloe. This is important. I have to think."

Don't think! *Don't think*! She grabbed his hand. "Later. Think later. I know! Let's go watch that Three Stooges DVD I rented."

She yanked his hand, trying to pull him toward the living room and away from further explorations of the disaster that had just happened between them. He didn't budge.

Now she knew how Larry felt when they played tug-of-war with his doggie toys on the slick kitchen linoleum. Lots of movement . . . no forward motion.

"You've never kissed me before," Nick said.

Her heart twisted. Chloe quit pulling and let go of his hand. "I didn't kiss you now, either."

"You . . ." Nick's gaze searched hers. Typically, he dismissed the facts and went straight for the truth. "You wanted to."

She was in so far over her head. But as long as they were speaking truths, Chloe figured she might as well play along.

"So did you."

He frowned. "I didn't. I can't. *I won't.*"

Her hopes rose. She couldn't help it. "Which is it?"

Nick slammed his hands on her bright Spanish-tiled countertop hard enough to make her wince. That had to hurt, but he didn't seem to notice.

He squeezed the edge hard enough to whiten his knuckles. "I won't."

Why not? part of her wailed.

"I won't come between you and"—he ducked his head and his gaze shifted to her non-pregnant looking belly—"and the father of your baby."

Openmouthed, Chloe stared at him. This was a wrinkle she hadn't anticipated.

"Who is it?" Nick asked.

Tell him the truth! part of her urged. But the Chicken Little side of her personality prevailed.

"I told you. It's over." Over because he didn't love her. Over because having a family now would ruin Nick's inventing career.

Most of all, *over* because she owed it to her baby to accept nothing less than a father who loved and wanted children. The kind of father she'd never known.

"Even now, it's over?" Nick turned to lean on the countertop instead of mangle it in his hands. "Even with the baby? Babies change things—"

"Not for him." Not if she could help it.

He frowned. "You're wrong. I know you haven't dated that many men lately, but—"

"Now you're the expert on the men I date?" she interrupted, crossing her arms over her chest. "Thanks, Mr. Dating Game, but—"

"—but I think," he continued patiently, holding her gaze with his own, "whoever he is, he deserves to know he's going to be a father."

"No!"

Chloe grabbed the mangled Twinkie box. If he wouldn't move on, then she would. She'd move right on to a gazillion calories worth of distraction, if that's what it took, and nobody had better try to stop her. Cellophane rustled as she touched the Twinkies-turned-pancakes inside the box. Then Nick's hand closed over the outside.

She snatched it out of his reach. "I'm hormonal," she snapped. "Cut me some slack, okay?"

He raised both hands and grinned. That grin alone was enough to break her heart. How had coming so close that night only wound up pulling them apart now?

"Okay . . . if you tell me who your baby's father is."

Chloe made a face at him. "Like a dog with a bone."

"Ruff." His grin widened. "Well?"

"No deal." She unwrapped a Twinkie and licked up some of the sweet, squished-out filling, trying not to show all the sidestepping going on in her brain. "Drop it, Nick. He's . . . gone, and he's not coming back."

"Gone? Gone where?" Nick spread his arms wide, turning a circle between her kitchen table and the sink as though looking for something. "He didn't just vanish."

"No, he-he-he-" Oh, great. Now he'd rendered her tongue-tied and stammering. She, who'd never been at a loss for words in her life. Frustrated, she cried, "I don't need him. I can do this on my own!"

"Like you do everything else?" He slammed his hand on the kitchen table. "Dammit, Chloe! You don't have to do everything all by yourself!"

Why not? She always had. "I'm doing this."

Nick touched her shoulders. Slowly, she looked up at him, then licked some filling from her fingertip. "I'll be okay."

He squeezed gently, his gaze stuck on her mouth, then blinked up at her. "Let someone help you. Let *him* help you. He has a responsibility to you."

She shook her head.

"Dammit, don't tell me he ran out on you!"

The sudden fury in his face caught her off guard. Chloe stepped back, stammering out a reply.

"He-he didn't run out on me."

Nick arched his eyebrows. *I'm waiting*, his expression said.

Oh, cripes. This just got worse and worse. She'd thought she could handle it at first, but. . . .

"That wasn't it at all. No, he-he-he-" Desperate, Chloe wheeled her arm in a circle as though that might kick-start her imagination. "He—"

"He. . . ?"

She looked around, seeking inspiration. Her gaze landed on the "Macho Men of the Military" pinup calendar hanging beside her refrigerator—Mr. April was dressed in a sailor's hat and boots and not much else besides a smile—and all at once, Chloe had the lie she needed.

"He's in the Marines," she blurted.

Nick's eyes narrowed suspiciously. "The Marines."

"Sure. He was, um, called back to duty suddenly."

"I don't remember you dating any Marines."

Aaack. He was right. Chloe crossed her fingers behind her back and gave Nick her sweetest smile. "I didn't tell you about him."

She spun a more elaborate story in her imagination. Love lost to duty, a brave soldier called back before his true love could tell him about their baby . . .

Maybe it was crazy, but she was committed now.

"I just couldn't tell you." She added a sigh for effect. "Bruno was too special to be shared."

Five

Bruno.

The name haunted Nick night and day all summer long. Even his work was affected. Who could concentrate with thoughts of Chloe's mystery Marine buzzing around in his head?

He could, dammit. Scowling at the printout in his hands, Nick tried to make sense of the scrawled notes he'd made past midnight last night—he'd resorted to working past dark most days, just to get something done—and finally gave up in disgust. Something had to give. It just couldn't be his work.

It couldn't be Chloe, either. She needed him, now more than ever.

Hell. What a mess. Nick threw the printout on his desk and swooshed his wheeled chair across his home office to gaze out the window. As it was, he'd been dividing his time between taking care of Chloe and working on a new version of his growth accelerator—and giving short shrift to both. He'd dreamed since he was a boy about making a name for himself by inventing miraculous things. Without a proposal and prototype, without an investor and licensing, his dream would be impossible to achieve.

Without Chloe, his achievements would be pointless.

He didn't buy her story about Bruno. Something about it

rang false, and Nick had operated on instinct and educated guesses long enough to trust his gut. So far he hadn't been able to find the mismatched element in her story, but he would. The more important question was, why would she keep the truth from him?

He had a feeling the answer hovered just on the edge of his memory, like a misremembered name on the tip of his tongue. All he needed to jog it to the forefront was the right stimulus. Whatever that was.

With a growl of frustration, Nick slapped his hand on the windowsill beside him, ready to whirl back to his computer and try to get something done. Instead, a flash of movement outside caught his eye and stilled his slide. A second later, he realized what he'd seen.

A bird bobbing past the window.

Not flying. Not soaring or swooping or gliding. Bobbing.

It could only be Shemp, Chloe's winged avenger. Where one of her animals was, she couldn't be far behind. Where Chloe went, trouble followed. Nick decided to investigate.

Outside, he spotted her halfway down the block, power walking through the shade of a feathery-leafed mesquite tree. Her orange shorts, yellow T-shirt, and floral baseball cap glowed as brightly as the Saguaro Vista summer sun overhead. Chloe added more vibrancy to their small-town block than all the surrounding Fifties-era redbrick houses and their water-thrifty desert landscaping put together. As he watched, she waved to an elderly neighbor lady who was outside gathering her newspaper, then crooked her elbows at her sides and picked up speed.

Just as he'd suspected, Shemp rode on her shoulder, which explained the bobbing he'd seen earlier, if not the rest of what he saw now. Her beagle, Larry, secured by an auto-winding leash attached makeshift-fashion at Chloe's waist, trotted along at her side with his tongue lolling. Moe the cat slinked through the yards bordering the sidewalk, safe prowling distance from the rest of the menagerie but keeping up, all the same. The only things their troupe lacked were Chloe's goldfish and her hamster, Curly.

Wait a minute . . . Nick peered closer. If he didn't miss his guess, that hunk of round hot-pink plastic spinning at Chloe's heels was Curly's exercise ball. Powered by furiously pumping rodent feet inside.

He blinked. They were all still there. Only Chloe would think to walk her hamster.

They turned the corner and disappeared from sight. He really ought to take advantage of her absence and get some work done, Nick told himself. Somehow, his feet started down the sidewalk anyway.

"Hiya, Nick!" Chloe yelled to him over her shoulder as he approached, almost as though she'd sensed him coming up behind her—or known he'd follow. Her breath panted out in measured whooshes, keeping pace with her strides. "Whatsa matter? Can't keep up with a girl with a bun in the oven?"

She didn't even slow down. In fact, she sped up a little, making her behind wiggle enticingly. Nick doubted she realized it—and wished *he* hadn't. What was the matter with him? He was ogling his best friend like one of her hapless lust-crazed Brunos.

Lucky lust-crazed Brunos was more like it, some aching part of him whispered.

Shut up, Nick told himself, putting thoughts of Chloe's wiggle firmly out of his mind. It wasn't easy. Somehow, since he'd learned about her pregnancy, those . . . fantasy episodes . . . about Chloe had become more and more frequent. It was becoming impossible to see his pal as just a pal, when every glance at her gently curved belly reminded him she was a sensual woman, too.

Frowning, Nick clamped the lid on his libido and caught up with her in few jogged steps—it wasn't for nothing he ran five miles around the Saguaro Vista High track every morning—and matched her pace.

"I can keep up with you." He couldn't help but grin at the exaggerated way she pumped her arms at Rock-Em-Sock-Em Robot angles. "It's Larry I'm worried about. He looks ready for a Milk-Bone and a doggie Gatorade."

She stopped and wiped a trickle of gleaming perspiration from her neck. "Do you think so? It is pretty hot out here."

Giving Larry a worried frown, Chloe crouched beside him

and stroked between his ears, working one-handed at the plastic squeeze bottle strapped to her waist. "I didn't mean to wear you out, boy. Maybe you do need a sports drink to keep up your strength, if we're going to keep up this exercise routine."

She aimed a squirt of bottled water between Larry's sharp canine teeth, then straightened while he licked his muzzle. "Doggie Gatorade is a good idea," she told Nick. "It would be better than plain water, at least for long walks. For replacing electrolytes and things."

"You'd be just crazy enough to try it."

She frowned and stuck out her tongue at him.

Larry, apparently feeling refreshed, wagged and walked circles around Chloe as they talked. The auto-wind leash spun out more and more line, creating a frayed purple web around her white pom-pommed sweat socks and sneakers.

"Crazy in a good way," Nick elaborated with a grin as she raised the bottle to her mouth and sucked down some water for herself. He watched her lips pucker around the bottle top, then made himself look away. He'd never envied a hunk of plastic before.

"I think you'd do almost anything to take care of your menagerie here," he said when she'd finished, mostly to distract himself from the surprisingly erotic sight of her tongue depressing the bottle's snap top. "Even tote along Gatorade for Larry."

"But a dog's physiology is completely different from a person's, Nick." Chloe stepped out of Larry's twisted leash with a grace that bespoke frequent practice. She straightened her flowery baseball cap, lassoed the dog, and started walking again. "I'm afraid a sports drink formulated for people wouldn't be good for him. Too bad, though."

Too bad he'd brought it up, that is. He hadn't expected a twenty-minute heart-to-heart about something that didn't even exist. "Actually, I was only kidding."

She blushed and darted a glance at him.

"Oh. Oh—oh—oh!"

She stumbled as Larry yapped and took off at a barking run more befitting a greyhound than a low-rider beagle, dragging Chloe behind him.

"Chloe!" Nick chased after her, cursing the stupid leash that kept her attached to her maniac dog. She yanked on it, fighting for control, but Larry just kept on running, tail low and claws clicking sharply on the sidewalk as he gained ground. The object of his frenzy was in sight. He scampered hard on his stubby legs to reach it.

The postal worker walking blithely toward them didn't know what was about to hit him, but Chloe did.

"Look out!" she screamed, pulling harder.

The carrier looked. His eyes bulged. His legs, bared and extra vulnerable in his summertime uniform of jacket and dark shorts, churned to get him on the nearest front porch. He scrambled on the porch rail, leaving his legs to dangle like two enormous doggie treats. He dug in his mail bag for something.

No letter delivery was that urgent. A sick feeling in Nick's stomach made him run faster, just as the mail carrier pulled a long slender canister from his bag.

"Nooo!" Chloe shouted, recognizing what it was.

Nick recognized it, too. Pepper spray. He'd seen it used once before, on a stray pit bull that had gone after the newspaper deliverer. The ferocious dog had run off whimpering with its tail between its legs after just one squirt. There was no telling what the stuff would do to poor runty Larry.

"Nick, help!" Chloe looked back at him, both hands pulling her rasping, choking dog away from the postman's perch. Larry might have been a two-foot beagle, but he had the heart and soul of a Doberman pinscher.

Nick left the sidewalk and headed for the house's walk where Chloe struggled with her dog. Landscape gravel crunched beneath his feet. At the same time, a curious whine reached him. It sounded like . . . the ping of a tuneless guitar string pulled and released, or a tight-stretched clothesline about to break.

Or a dog's leash about to snap.

A glance at Larry's frayed leash confirmed his guess. Another few seconds, and he'd be free to commit a doggie death leap. Chloe wouldn't be able to do a thing to stop him.

She stared with horror at something just behind Nick. She pointed. "No, wait! Get Curly!"

Nick looked where she pointed. Curly's exercise ball plunked off the sloped sidewalk into the street, spinning like mad. Inside, the hamster's furry shape was just distinguishable. Deprived of his focus on Chloe's heels, he'd steered himself right off their route—and straight into the path of an oncoming pickup truck.

Larry barked. Nick glanced his way and saw the beagle lunge forward. His leash, still intact, slithered through Chloe's hands. She jerked forward like a puppet, held by the leash holder attached to her waist.

The pickup truck revved closer, gaining ground on Curly's hot-pink exercise ball.

Nick lunged sideways. Gravel spewed beneath his feet. The world jogged up and down as he left the smooth sidewalk for the street below. Hot asphalt rose to meet him, smelling of tar and engine oil. A flash of pink rolled just past his fingertips: Curly's exercise ball. He'd be damned if the stupid hamster wasn't trying to get himself squished on purpose, just to avoid walking the equivalent of a million more hamster miles with Chloe.

"Niiiiiick," she cried. "Hurry!"

He scooped up the ball, cradling it like a running back going for the game-ending touchdown. The pickup truck rumbled past in a blast of hot air and exhaust fumes, then kept on down the road, its driver plainly oblivious to the man and hamster he'd almost flattened.

Heart pounding, Nick straightened. "Good thing I got you," he told Curly between breaths. "Next time you want to go AWOL, just roll in the bushes and hide, okay?"

Curly stuck his furry hamster snout to the air vents carved into his exercise ball and sniffed. Nick could almost understand the little runt's appeal . . . until Curly bit him.

"Ouch!"

"Niiiiiick! I can't hold on much longer!"

He turned. Chloe sprawled facedown, half across their neighbor's sidewalk and half across the artfully graveled yard. Her arm stretched forward, her hand maintaining a desperate, wobbly clench on Larry's leash as she tried to pull him back.

The mail carrier squinted down at them both, pepper spray

at the ready, poised to shoot from his porch railing if need be. It looked like a stand-off—unless Larry managed to break his leash.

And all of it with Chloe in the middle.

Nick didn't remember getting there, but the next thing he knew, he was hunkered down beside Larry's growling, stiff-spined body, trying to talk him down. Paying no heed, the dog went on staring at his postal quarry, his white- and black-spotted fur bristling straight up. It was enough to make the hair stand at the nape of Nick's neck, too. Stark, unreasoning terror made his gut clench. It didn't take a veterinary genius to spot the signs of a pissed-off, territorial doggie defender.

Only a lunatic would get in Cujo's way. *Guess what that makes me?* Nick thought as Larry's rumbling growl got louder. The dog's lip lifted to expose several pointy, vicious teeth. Nick's gaze met Chloe's—only briefly, but it was enough to tell him what he needed to know. She was depending on him.

He put Curly down in the gravel, where he couldn't roll far, and edged closer. "Don't try anything stupid," he warned Larry as he scooped up all fifty squirming pounds of him. "I'm way too tough to make a good doggie treat."

In his arms, Larry's body vibrated with a fresh growl. Luckily, it was still aimed at the postman, not at him.

"Go on," Nick yelled to the mail carrier. Groaning beneath the dog's weight, he stepped back to let some slack in the leash. He looked Mr. Pepper Spray in the eye. "I've got him. You can put that stuff away now."

The postman eyed him suspiciously. As though egged on by his blatant distrust, Larry morphed into Superdog in Nick's arms, lurching hard to get free. Then the postman got wise and put away his pepper spray, Chloe got to her feet, and everything turned right with the world.

"Oh, Nick!" She leaped toward him, enfolding both him and Larry in a bone-crushing hug. The dog squirmed, trying to lick her face. "Thank you! You saved us." Her gaze shifted to Curly, rolling his exercise ball uselessly atop a patch of vol-canic rock gravel, then upward again. "You saved us all."

Sure, Nick thought, gazing down into her shining eyes. The way she looked at him made him feel ten feet tall, the greatest hero ever conceived of. *I saved myself right into your arms.* What was he, nuts?

Chloe's flowered baseball cap was askew, her hair damp at the ends and clinging to her neck, her outrageous lipstick mostly melted away by the Arizona afternoon. Her fluttery eyelashes were devoid of mascara and whatever other girly gunk she usually used. She looked wrung out.

She looked gorgeous.

He was a goner.

Where the hell had that thought come from? Nick shook it out of his head. Clearly a case of testosterone talking. It had to be, because he was Chloe's platonic male friend and nothing else. Nothing else, because her romantic side belonged to a mysterious Marine named Bruno. The reminder snipped the last strand of his already wire-thin patience.

"Well, you damn well needed saving." Nick scowled. "What the hell were you thinking, anyway, taking your whole stupid menagerie out for a walk like that?"

Chloe backed up. The sunlight left her eyes, but he couldn't let that deter him. She'd get over being mad at him. She might not get over the next ditzy stunt she decided to pull.

"You could have broken your neck!"

"You're right. Curly could have gotten—" Her voice broke, forcing her to try again. "Larry might have been hurt, or—"

"*You* might have been hurt! What's it going to take to knock some sense into you? Because, God knows, your baby hasn't accomplished that miracle yet."

Her hands went to her belly, cradling the child within. He doubted she was even aware of the gesture, or of the tears that shimmered in her elfin eyes.

"That's not fair, Nick. You don't know—"

"Don't know what? Don't know why you don't get some help?"

Larry wriggled in his arms. Frustrated, Nick scanned the neighborhood and saw that the postman had already gotten in his vehicle. Larry would be safe on his own for the moment. Nick dumped his dog-breath burden on the gravel and went on talking.

"You're right, Chloe. I don't know why you insist on being so stubborn that you'd rather risk hurting yourself than ask for help."

"I don't need help."

"Ha! That's a laugh, after today. If I hadn't—" He glimpsed Larry nudging sideways, casting longing looks toward the sidewalk. "Larry, stay."

The dog cocked his head, seeming at a loss to understand the command. *Great*, Nick thought as Larry gave him a tentative tail wag. *Even her dog is featherbrained.*

"Stay," Nick growled.

"He responds better to kindness." *And so do I,* Chloe's expression said.

"Chloe—"

"Come on, Larry," she said, her voice quavery. "We've got a walk to finish. Doctor's orders."

The dog got up—Nick would have sworn the mutt rolled his eyes at his ignored "stay" command—then sneezed and sauntered away. A definite swagger propelled all four of his doggie legs.

At least one of the males present had managed to stay in Chloe's good graces. How could it *not* be Nick, when he'd done all he could to protect her? It didn't make sense. Nothing drove him crazy like things not making sense. But it wasn't illogic that made him call out to her. It was something far less defined and much more irresistible.

It was the sudden, crazy need to take care of Chloe. To keep her safe and happy. Him. Not one of her Brunos or anybody else. Just him.

If he'd stopped to think about it, the whole idea would have probably scared the hell out of him. But the sight of Chloe swaying down the street, leaving him behind, shook everything else from Nick's mind.

"Chloe, wait."

She turned. And waited, with a sad look in her eyes that hurt just to see it. It worried him to see her fighting spirit dampened, even if only for a block or two. Even if only for as long as she needed to power walk out of his sight.

Frowning, he reached her and drew her closer to him. She bumped along reluctantly, twisting Larry's leash from its dispenser between them until they stood toe to toe.

"Wait," he said again.

She gazed up at him, all sweetness and seduction without even knowing it . . . and frowned in confusion. "What's up?"

In her place, he'd be wondering exactly the same thing. But the combination of her nearness and the realization that his hand fit perfectly in the delicate curve at the small of her back waylaid his explanation. It was as though he'd been born to hold her this way. Damp heat rose through her bright T-shirt to tease his palm, and suddenly Nick wanted to slip his hand beneath the fabric and feel her bare skin on his instead.

Why hadn't he ever held her this way before? She felt better than he could have imagined.

"That was a rotten thing I said back there."

The tropical scent of her perfume wafted to him, muddling his thoughts. It was feminine and sweet and almost tantalizing enough to make him forget that the woman in his arms was Chloe, his best friend. She needed him now. Not as another one of her muscle-headed Brunos, but as the voice of reason.

Damn, but it was hard to be reasonable when her softness surrounded him and the curve of her hip melted into his forearm. It made him wonder how soft she'd be everywhere else . . . without eye-popping clothes and a layer of anger between them.

Only one of those barriers could be dealt with on a city sidewalk in broad daylight. "I'm sorry I said it."

"You meant it," Chloe said matter-of-factly. Her spine straightened against his hand. He felt her take in a deep breath. "Or else you wouldn't have said it. I'm a big girl, Nick. I can handle it."

"Oh, yeah?"

"Yeah!"

He tightened his hold on her waist. His other hand went to her front and captured the frayed line from Larry's leash.

"Well, you can't handle this." One sharp tug snapped the line in two.

Chloe gasped. At her feet, Larry plopped on the grass and

scratched his paw over his ear, not caring that he was technically free to roam wild through the neighborhood. He looked bored with the whole thing.

Chloe didn't. She stepped out of Nick's arms and propped her hands on her hips. The old Chloe was back, and she was mad.

"What's that supposed to prove? That you're some big he-man who can snap a couple inches of leash line? Sorry, not impressed."

She wheeled around. Nick grabbed her elbow and yanked her back. "It proves you can't handle things as well as you think you can." How could she be so stubborn? So blind to the facts?

"It's just a broken leash!"

"You're right. And this is just a baby." He put his hand to the curve of her belly, felt the warmth and life within her. "Your baby."

She went still. She paled and pressed her hand over his. "Don't do this, Nick. Please, I—"

"You need help. Have you told Brutus—"

"Bruno."

"—about the baby yet? Because he has a responsibility to fulfill. He should take care of you. Marry you. Do whatever it takes." At her mournful look, Nick rubbed his thumb gently over her belly. "I'm warning you, Chloe. If you won't make sure you're taken care of . . . I will."

Six

He'd take care of her? What in the world did he mean?

Chloe bit her lip, trying to hold in the surge of joy she felt. Then her elation wavered. The last thing she wanted was for Nick to take care of her out of some antiquated sense of responsibility. Their baby deserved more, and so did she.

Besides, if Nick really wanted her for himself, why did he have to keep bringing up Bruno? Why now, of all times? The two of them were near enough to tango, close enough to kiss. A million miles away from the love she'd touched so briefly.

Why, oh why, had she invented Bruno? He'd only complicated things better left simply heart-wrenching and insolvable.

"I don't want a man who'd only marry me out of duty. That's no kind of life for me." Chloe looked up at him, needing to make him understand. "Don't you get it yet, Einstein? I want the whole fairytale ending. White picket fence, a ring on my finger . . . and a man who loves me."

Nick caressed her belly again. "There's more than yourself to think about now."

She couldn't believe what she was hearing. Why wouldn't he understand?

"That's the whole point, you big idiot!"

Tears gathered in her eyes, blurring her vision until Nick didn't even look like someone she knew anymore. Blinking hard, Chloe bent to catch hold of Larry's collar and urge him to his feet. She had to leave, had to get out of there before she blurted the whole sordid truth to Nick and ruined everything.

"I'll see you around." She sniffled as she churned down the sidewalk. Power walking was almost impossible when you couldn't see anything, she was discovering. "I've got more indulgent and incredibly self-absorbed things to do with my time than be lectured to."

Behind her, Nick mumbled something about hormones and irrational women. Something stupid enough to make her blood boil, probably, if she'd stopped to listen. So she didn't.

Chloe was already at her front door, scrabbling around in the zebra-striped mailbox affixed beside her doorbell, by the time Nick caught up with her.

She held up her hands in frustration. "What do you want now?" she demanded.

The mailbox lid clinked shut, neatly hiding the wrapped package of books she'd left inside for her mail carrier—a secret romance novel reader. They were a payment of sorts, for his part in her stupid ploy to get Nick to play the hero for her. She had to admit, his pepper spray threat had been the most inspired touch in her otherwise ridiculous plan. He probably deserved an extra book for that one.

What had she been thinking? She should have known her ploy was doomed from the instant she perched Shemp on her shoulder and paraded past Nick's window. Just getting him to glance outside at them had taken four trips.

Now, ironically, she couldn't get rid of him.

"I said, what do you want? Maybe you've got a textbook on pregnancy for me? Or another earful of clueless, bachelor, non-father wisdom?" Getting angrier by the minute, Chloe pointed her finger at Nick and backed him against the porch rail. "What's it going to be, huh? I thought I'd had all the advice I'd ever need from my mother, but I guess there's always room for one more opinion."

She folded her arms across her chest, glaring at him.

He smiled at her.

"Arrgh!"

He laughed, the rat.

Chloe turned her back on him and whistled for Larry. She had the key in the lock before Nick finally came clean.

"I brought you this."

She looked over her shoulder. He held out Curly's scuffed exercise ball, offering it to her with the same attitude he might have used to lob over a grenade.

"You left poor Curly stranded back at Mrs. Marchen's yard."

When you left in a huff, his grin added.

Chloe reached for the ball. Her fingers touched the edge, dug in the grooves, and pulled with no effect at all. He wouldn't let go.

She tried to pry his fingers loose. "I'm not up for another tug-of-war."

"Are you up for a peace offering? I'll make you dinner tonight."

Her heart stopped. Dinner at his place was Nick's standard third-date maneuver with the what'shernames in his life. Was he actually asking her for a date?

Yes, yes! her heart shouted. *Say yes!*

"Tonight?" she asked, feeling breathless.

Their fingers touched across the exercise ball. Heat jolted from his to hers, and when Nick gave her a wide, eyelid-crinkling smile to go with it, Chloe knew she was a goner.

Maybe she was going about this all wrong. Maybe running away from Nick was a step in the wrong direction—so to speak.

"Tonight."

His voice sent a fresh shiver through her. How had she not noticed before how throaty, how thrilling, how all-out sexy his voice was?

"It's a date," she said happily, prying his index finger loose from Curly's ball. He winced. She looked closer. "Nick, you're bleeding!"

"It's nothing." He shrugged, flexing his finger and looking macho. "I guess Curly thought I might taste good."

*   *   *

So did Chloe, when she arrived at Nick's place that night. He opened the door against the orange and gold rays of the setting sun, wearing a pair of slouchy navy shorts, an open-necked white shirt, and a smile. His hair was still damp—from a recent shower, she guessed—and it looked as though he'd even shaved for the occasion.

Very tasty, indeed.

Smiling in appreciation, Chloe edged closer and considered taking a bite. Right at the intriguingly masculine-looking place where the side of his neck disappeared beneath the collar of his shirt. Or maybe she'd just nibble gently on his earlobe, finding the secret spot she now knew was ticklish.

Instead, she tamped down the impulse and settled for a simple, "Thanks for the invite."

His grin widened, probably because he'd caught her ogling him. "Thanks for coming."

She handed over the sparkling apple juice she'd brought, then froze as soon as the bottle hit Nick's hand. He looked at it, then at her, with something akin to confusion.

"It's non-alcoholic, if that's what you're wondering."

"I . . . okay." His voice told her he hadn't been wondering if the apple juice was forty proof. "I'll put this in the fridge. Dinner's almost ready."

He stepped back to let her in, holding aside the lush foliage of a potted palm—one of his growth-accelerated beauties, Chloe guessed—so she could pass. She shimmied between the plant and Nick's chest, wishing his hands would touch her as gently as they did those shiny leaves . . . but then, the plant was part of his dream. She wasn't.

Chloe ducked beneath an enormous spider plant in a hanging planter, gazing around her at the well-tended greenery that filled his living room. *I hate plants.*

The screen door slammed behind her. The aromas of tomato sauce, garlic, and roasted peppers wafted from his kitchen.

"Smells good."

"Thanks. If my research came together half as easily as my pasta puttanesca, I'd have had the growth accelerator finished a month ago." He hefted the tapered bottle of apple juice. "I'd better go put this in the fridge."

Chloe eyed the wine-shaped bottle. It practically screamed her hopes that this was going to be A Real Date. A new *romantic* beginning between them.

Idiot! she told herself as Nick disappeared around the corner. The refrigerator opened and shut. Next came the sound of something scraping in a pan to the accompaniment of Nick's humming.

This was definitely a Non-Date. His confused glance at the bottle had told her that much. She really had to start clamping down on that wishful-thinking routine of hers.

Chloe collapsed on Nick's sturdy tweed couch beside a pile of clean laundry and buried her face in a jumble of towels and jeans. *See? He hadn't even bothered to tidy up for her visit,* she thought morosely, hugging the pile closer. All she wanted was to disappear. Maybe Nick wouldn't notice if she slunk out the front door and went home?

His jovial, humming entrance into the living room wrecked her getaway plans. Moaning, she stuffed her face deeper in the pile and inhaled big lungfuls of fabric-softener-scented air, trying to get a grip on herself. The last thing she wanted was for Nick to guess how much she wanted to move things between them to a non-platonic level. How much she wanted him to do the moving . . . and the kissing, the touching, the lovemaking that they'd. . . .

His hand on her bare thigh sent her bolt upright.

"Wake up, Sleeping Beauty. Aren't you hungry?"

If he only knew. Chloe tilted sideways to straighten herself and wound up at eye-level with his groin. She eyed the fit of Nick's shorts, remembered what lay beneath, and had to fight an urge to lick her lips. The night they'd spent together had only been the appetizer, just enough to make her hungry for more.

"Appetizer?" Nick asked.

She whipped her head upward and almost brained herself on the tray of bruschetta in his hand. Her heart quit racing just as she recognized the toasted bread topped with tomatoes and herbs. She cleared her throat and selected one, hoping he hadn't caught her leering at him.

Sheesh. Hormones.

Who was she kidding? *Love.*

Grinning, Nick plucked something from her hair, making static electricity crackle above her head. Something white flashed past her field of vision. She recognized it as a pair of white briefs—*oh, God, she'd been wearing his underwear on her head!*—and wanted to crawl under the sofa.

"Cute." He dropped the tighty whities back in the laundry pile. "But I like your outfit better without the headgear."

His gaze skimmed over her clothes—electric blue shorts and a neon green loosely buttoned shirt—as though committing their smooth, washed silk textures to memory. His scrutiny did disturbing things to her ability to think or react, or even chew, apparently. A dollop of tomato slipped from her bruschetta and plunked down her chest.

He watched it slide beneath her vibrant green silk shirt with a starving man's look. It gave her an unreasonable amount of hope for their potential couplehood—far too much to pin on a half-inch piece of cold tomato. Then Nick shook his head and blinked, fingers on the temples of his eyeglasses.

"And preferably without tomato sauce, too," he added on a grin, grabbing a fluffy blue towel from the laundry pile. "Here, let me help you."

Chloe sat still, dying to suck in a gulp of air to bolster herself for his touch, but too filled with anticipation to move. Frowning, Nick scrubbed at the neckline of her shirt, lifted the corner of the towel to assess his efforts, then scrubbed some more.

The ends of the thick terrycloth towel flopped in her lap, tickling her bare thighs. It was nothing compared with the friction he'd set into motion with his clean-up efforts. Her shirt rubbed against her breasts, sensitizing them even through her layers of silken shirt and silkier bra.

Watching Nick's strong, capable hands at work, Chloe briefly considered dumping the rest of the bruschetta tray in her lap. Reluctantly, she abandoned the idea. She had all she could handle already.

"Wait." She caught hold of his wrist. "I think it's clean. Much more of that, and you'll rub me naked."

Which sounded pretty great, actually, no matter how much she wanted to groan at having blurted it out. But there was no way she could stand being touched like this for much longer and not reciprocate. Not with Nick and definitely not in the supersensitive state she was in. Biting her lip, she fished her other hand in her shirt to retrieve the tomato herself.

No dice. The little bugger must have slipped past her bra. Letting go of Nick's wrist, she lifted her shirt hem just enough to glimpse a plump bit of red just above her navel.

Before she could move, Nick ducked. His mouth fastened on the tomato, sucking gently against her skin as he nibbled it up. Too shocked to move, Chloe stared down at the incredible sight of his familiar, golden-haired head against her. His lips puckered on her tender flesh, igniting flickers of yearning, remembered passion in places lower than the rounded belly he kissed.

If she hadn't been sitting already, her knees would have surely buckled. Wowsers! Shivering, Chloe delved her hand in his hair, wanting to pull Nick closer, to draw him upward where she could properly kiss him back. His hair buzzed beneath her roving hands, spiky soft shafts that tickled her palms even more than the towel had tickled her thighs earlier. She thought of feeling those close-clipped shafts where the towel had been and was squirming in her seat even as Nick's mouth popped away from her belly.

"Got it." He winked at her, leaned over to gather up the pile of laundry, and straightened. "You're good as new."

Chloe boggled as he juggled the armful of clothes against his chest, smoothed her shirt in place again, and casually said, "I'd better get these out of the way before I find you wearing a pair of sweat socks or something."

Sweat socks? He could talk about sweat socks, after what had just happened? Shivering, she settled deeper in the couch's nubbly tweed and watched him disappear down the hallway with the clothes.

Nuzzling her bare belly was *not* the act of a platonic best male friend, no matter how Nick tried to pretend it was. Never mind that as friends they'd been swimming at the lake dressed in less than she had on now. Never mind that they'd nursed each other through colds, income taxes, and broken hearts. That wasn't TLC Nick had administered just now. At the least, it qualified as a pass. So what was she supposed to do about it?

Before she could decide, he returned, looking vaguely warm, rumpled, and so much like everything she'd ever wanted in a man that Chloe felt like sobbing with the unfairness of it all. He was as perfect for her as she was for him—except for his lack of interest in having children as soon as five months from now.

I'm lucky as hell not to have kids yet, Chloe, he'd said. *I swear I'd never get anything done.*

If there was one think Nick wanted, it was to get things done. To accomplish his dream of becoming a great inventor. How could she stand in the way of that?

She couldn't.

She couldn't forget her vow to give her baby a loving home with two loving parents, either. *Buck up,* she told herself. *He's just a man. You can resist him.*

Suddenly, Chloe found new sympathy for Nick's what's-hernames.

He reached out and tousled her hair. "Hungry? How 'bout some grub, Blondie?"

"Sure." She felt her spirits plummet even further as his hair-tousle turned into a brotherly shoulder punch. "Lead the way, Galloping Gourmet."

Poor Bruno, Nick thought later. *Poor, doomed, besotted Bruno.* How had he faced temptation like this and survived?

Maybe fortitude like that was what made a man a Marine.

He and Chloe had finished the pasta puttanesca, polished off the better half of the bruschetta, and moved the party onto his back patio. Out here beneath the clear dark skies and bright stars of summer, Nick could almost believe it was a night like any other they'd spent together. The pink bougainvillea bloomed along the backyard fence the same as they ever had. The cicadas chirped just as constantly beyond that fence, and the citronella candles burned just as lemony-sharp on the wrought iron table between them.

The difference was, this dark night felt intimate in a way it never had before. He'd never before been forced to watch Chloe savor a dish of vanilla ice cream with strawberries, bite by slow shivery bite, the way he'd been doing for the past ten minutes. It was enough to make a guy yearn to be a soup spoon.

"This is *so* good, Nick," she said for what had to be the fifth time, turning over the spoon to lick a strawberry remnant from the tip. "Yum, yum, yum."

Yeah . . . yum.

The piece of strawberry disappeared between her lips. Reminded of the tomato he'd nibbled up earlier, Nick shifted in his chair and tried not to think of what an insane move he'd made with *that*. "Glad you like it."

Curled up in a patio chair beside him, Chloe spooned up the last of the ice cream from the big plastic bowl on her lap. Licking her lips, she let her spoon clatter back in place.

"Every bit as delicious as the first bite," she announced, swabbing her finger leisurely around the bowl. When she popped her finger in her mouth and sucked off the creamy vanilla, Nick knew he couldn't take any more.

"Wanna watch a movie?" he blurted, taking the empty bowl from her lap as he stood. "I rented *Norgon's Revenge*."

"Another monster flick?" Grinning, Chloe shook her head. "I swear, Nick, you're a little boy trapped in a man's body."

Just as she got up from her chair, Nick passed in front of her with his arm outstretched, headed for the patio door. They wound up nose to nose. Or, more accurately, since Chloe was a few inches shorter than he was, forehead to chin.

"Oh! Whoops." She teetered. He put out his hand to steady her, then sidestepped out of the way. So did she—in the same direction.

"Sorry." Chloe laughed when they found themselves pressed even closer together than before. "I'm a little wobbly these days."

Her hand went to his upper arm, holding onto him as she explained something about hormones, pregnant ligaments, and other medical trivia items he didn't quite catch. Her fingers stroked up and down his arm, making it impossible to concentrate on anything except the feel of Chloe touching him. Nick had the stupid, nonsensical urge to flex his biceps, to sweep her off her feet . . . to show her he could be every bit as manly as the Bruno she was so enraptured with.

He ought to go inside, get away, leave things as they were between them. Chloe had Bruno now. To hear her talk of him, he'd been all she'd ever wanted in a man, even if things were temporarily off-kilter between them. She didn't need that mucked up with tomato nibbling and soup spoons and kissing. Not when she'd found herself a man "too special" to talk about, even with her best friend.

Friend, schmiend, the rebellious part of his soul prodded. Bruno was gone and Nick was here and this was a moment that might never come again.

"I don't mind," he said quietly.

She looked up at him. The amusement simmered out of her smile, replaced by something a little bit . . . wilder.

It was all the encouragement he needed.

Somehow, his hand went to the nape of her neck instead of the patio door. She tilted her head back, closing her eyes in the flickering candlelight, and although he meant to kiss her, all he could do was stare in wonder at how beautiful she seemed.

Her hair glowed like gold, bright as the candles. Moonlight and shadows chased across her face, highlighting the curve of her cheekbone, the delicate line of her nose, the lush fullness of her lips. He ached to taste her. Would she taste of strawberries, or the sweetness of vanilla?

In the darkness behind them, a warm breeze swirled dried bougainvillea leaves through the yard like whispers. On the same breath of air, Chloe's tropical perfume wafted toward him, making him groan at the impossibility of resisting her. Kissing her felt inevitable. It felt right. Nick leaned closer . . . and her eyes opened.

"Whew!" She fanned herself with her hand. "Thanks to

you, I'm as good as new. No more wobblies." She grinned broadly and stepped back. He actually thought he saw her wink at him as she released his arm and gave him a brotherly shoulder punch instead. "Thanks for helping me out, Nick. So, how 'bout that movie?"

Seven

Her guerrilla platonic-ness tactic backfired.

"How 'bout it?"

Nick lowered his voice as he backed her toward the patio door. He kept his head bent, his gaze on her lips, and Chloe couldn't have kept her feet from moving, or her heart from speeding into overdrive, if she'd tried.

So much for bravado. Or for turnabout being fair play. Her flippancy deserted her when she felt the glass door, smooth and cooled by the air conditioner inside, touch her back. She jerked involuntarily at the contact.

"Easy," Nick murmured. His big hand cupped her shoulder, keeping her exactly where she was. His thumb rubbed over her shirt, moving slowly as he watched the slide of silk over skin. He closed his eyes briefly, then opened them and tightened his hand on her shoulder. "We've got all the time in the world."

He meant it to reassure her, she knew. Somehow, his words sounded closer to a wish than anything else, though. Funny, because Nick was far too pragmatic a man to rely on starlit wishes or fate or anything else he couldn't hold in his hands and examine.

Through the patio door at her back, incandescent kitchen light spilled over his features, making him seem both familiar and achingly new. This new Nick, this man who'd touch her like this without even a broken heart and Kahlúa courage between them . . . he was a stranger to her. One Chloe wanted to get to know better.

"Time?" she asked, feeling breathless. "Time for what?"

"The movie, brainiac." His voice rumbled through her, teasing and arousing at the same time. "Can't you keep your mind on the conversation?"

No. She couldn't. Not with Nick's hard, muscular thigh wedged warm between her legs, not with his palm pinning her shoulder to the glass and her heart to the wall. Not with all his considerable attention concentrated only on her. He'd moved fast and moved hard, and the feel of his body pressed against hers made the whole world tilt.

"It takes a really long time," he murmured.

"The conversation?"

He shook his head, smiling for the first time since he'd tangoed her backwards. "No, the movie. At the end, of course, the climax comes quickly." He traced a path over her shoulder, then slipped his thumb just inside the neckline of her shirt. "But the rest of it moves pretty slowly."

She was sinking, sinking in this world turned tilted and hot. Amazingly, Nick was her only anchor. The warm pad of his thumb stroked along the side of her neck, sending shivers trembling from her collarbone to her heels. Talk of climaxes and moving slowly was only that—talk—but his touch spoke of more. Much more.

And she wanted it all.

Chloe's hands went to his chest, smoothing imaginary wrinkles out of his shirt as an excuse to touch him. Wrinkles— as if anything of Nick's would have dared misbehave. Letting her hands fall to her sides again, she felt an answering smile lift her lips. "But that can be a good thing, sometimes."

He raised his eyebrows.

"Moving slowly, I mean."

His smile was wicked. So was the forward nudge of his hips against hers. The hard, slow impact of his hips felt too wonderful for words. The heated meld of their bodies made everything else slide away. Her heartbeat pulsed faster, keeping time with the rhythm of his breathing.

"Mmmm, moving slowly. . . ." He trailed his fingers down her shirt buttons, pretending to consider the idea. "You mean, in a conversation?"

She shook her head. Her third and fourth buttons bumped beneath his fingertips as he made his way downward, edging between her breasts and lower.

"In a movie, then."

His voice teased her, taunted her . . . reminded her of the closeness their banter implied. Chloe bit her lip, holding in the answer he waited for.

"Hmmm. Won't talk?" Nick's smile flashed in the night. "Then I'll just have to guess how this slow-moving thing comes into play for you." He fingered the next button. The next. His fingers slipped between the buttons to caress her bare skin, then quickly slipped out and continued to the next button. The last one. "Maybe you like it when . . . everything moves really slowly?"

"No," she whispered as his hand followed the curve of her hip, then captured her wrist. He laced their fingers together and pushed her hand beneath his against the glass behind them. The rest of her answer emerged on a gasp. "No, I like that in a man."

"Mmmm." His fingertips tickled her wrist. "I thought so."

Quit talking, Chloe thought. *Just shut up and kiss me.* But instead Nick only raised his head and focused his gaze on her. For one long, breath-stealing moment, she thought he'd changed his mind. He studied her, seeing her in a way she thought he might never have before.

As a lover.

He drew in a deep breath and released her hand. Only his hips touched hers as, casually, he raised the plastic ice cream bowl he still held in his palm and examined it.

"You want a slow-moving man?"

She licked her lips and sucked in a breath for courage. "I—"
I want you.

She couldn't say it aloud. Apparently, the atmosphere in

Saguaro Vista didn't have the magical bravery-enhancing properties she needed. Maybe Nick could invent a solution to that.

"Yes," she whispered instead, trembling so hard the words emerged on a shiver. "I . . . I want that."

"Too bad. Because I'm not moving slowly anymore."

The ice cream bowl tumbled to the patio tiles. The spoon spun away, whirling silver like a child's top set into motion. Both his hands came up to cradle her face in his palms, to raise her gaze to his. Once there, she couldn't look away.

"This time," Nick said, "*I'm taking.*"

His mouth came down hard over hers. Just as he'd promised, just as he'd warned, Nick took everything. Her thoughts. Her fears. Every ounce of caution.

Her heart.

His hands delved in her hair, his fingertips rubbing soft against her scalp to hold her still for his kiss. Moaning, he captured her mouth again and again, now licking her lips with tiny, fiery strokes of his tongue, now sucking and retreating and making her crazy with the slanted pressure of his mouth on hers. Chloe kissed him back with all the love she'd kept hidden, twining her arms around his neck, burying her fingers in his hair, pressing hard against him.

Her breasts crushed against the solid warmth of his chest. Her legs wobbled, and she blessed the patio door that held her upright. The muted sounds of wind and burring cicadas and neighbors talking in the distance receded even further, pushed far beyond the spill of light where she and Nick came together. Between kisses, smiles burst between them like raindrops on a summer lake.

Half insane with wanting him, Chloe squeezed Nick's shoulders and burrowed closer. She couldn't get close enough, couldn't kiss him enough, couldn't do enough to show him how much she wanted this. *Wanted him.* Laughing, she hugged him close, pressing fervent fast kisses on his neck . . . made him laugh, too, when she nibbled the ticklish spot on his earlobe. She climbed him like a kitten with a new toy, tasted him like a gourmet with a delicious new dish. A connoisseur of men who'd found the one she'd always craved.

Groaning, Nick brought both hands to her waist. "Chloe, Chloe, you're killing me. Ahhh—" Grinning, he wrapped his arms around her and lifted her off her feet. "But what a way to go."

She laughed, then whooped louder when he swung her around. Within the darker shadows at the patio's edge, he backed to the heavy wrought iron patio table and sat on it, settling her on his lap with her knees pulled up around his hips. The table's warm woven metal surface pushed basket-weave dimples into her bare shins, but Chloe didn't care. She had Nick's lap to ease the pressure.

Or maybe to build it, she thought as she jiggled in his arms and settled more comfortably atop him. Thank God she was wearing silky shorts instead of a skirt.

Although a skirt suggested delicious possibilities, too.

"Yeah, what a way to go," she told him, keeping both hands on his shoulders for balance as she kissed him. "I can tell you're really hating this kissing stuff. Or maybe that really *is* a banana in your pocket?"

He laughed. The sound made her heart soar like a kid's helium balloon zooming skyward.

"Nah, that's no banana. And these"—he cupped her breasts, thumbing her nipples through her smooth silk shirt— "these are—"

Chloe clapped her hand over his mouth. "Are not a subject for discussion, mister. Is that all you can think to do with me? Talk?"

He shook his head. "Mmmmph."

Nick's eyes glinted turquoise at her through the lenses of his glasses. *Foggy lenses*, she noticed, leaning a little closer. Wowsers. Had she done that?

She removed her hand.

Nick didn't remove his. They stayed curved over her breasts, making conversation as difficult as breathing was, considering the way he touched her. Through her silk shirt, she felt her nipples nudge his palms. He looked at his hands covering her, then stroked his thumbs slowly over her again. Her nipples peaked even harder beneath the heat in his gaze.

"These," he finished, squeezing gently, "feel like heaven wrapped in silk."

Why in the world had she tried to stop him from saying something like that? "You big faker," Chloe managed to whisper. "I thought you were going to say something else."

He kissed her, rubbed his lips softly over hers, then kissed her again. Smiling, Nick looked into her eyes.

She quivered. Surely he could see all the hope and love and . . . *oh, God, but not the secrets* . . . reflected in her gaze. Chloe closed her eyes and squeezed him close.

"Trust me." He slipped his fingers around her top shirt button. "Don't be afraid, Chloe. We can take this as slowly as you want." He used his thumb to push her button through the buttonhole, then stroked the skin he'd revealed. "As slowly as you want."

She gasped, openmouthed as his lips came on hers again in a kiss hungry enough to rock them both backward. The table beneath them rocked, too, not that either of them cared.

"Awww, Nick. I've waited forever already." Chloe clung to his shoulders. "Don't make me wait anymore. Please."

His hands told her he wouldn't. *This time I'm taking.* Again she heard that abandoned bowl spinning on the tiles, remembered the feel of Nick pulling her close for that first, heart-shattering kiss. Giddy anticipation tightened her stomach, making her feel light-headed and tremblingly, achingly, ready for whatever came next.

Biting her lip, Chloe watched, transfixed, as he unfastened her next button, then slipped his fingers inside the gap he'd made. His knuckles brushed over her newly impressive, hormonally boosted cleavage—*thank you, pregnancy!*—and her whole body tingled at his touch.

"Beautiful," Nick murmured.

"Thanks. They're all-natural, too," she babbled, temporarily undone by the incredible, impossible feel of his hands on her. No wonder she hadn't been able to forget the night he thought they'd never spent together. Between his magical hands and that killer smile . . .

Waitaminute . . . that smile meant something.

"All-natural?" he asked.

Yup, that smile definitely meant something. It meant she'd blurted out a stupid something. Whoops. Well, what could you expect from a love-starved woman, finally in the arms of the man she loved after months and months and months of waiting?

"Sounds like a granola commercial," Nick added on a grin.

She felt a blush heat her face—and probably the rest of her, too. "Tastes great, too."

He grinned wider. "That's a beer commercial."

"Whatever. You can sample the merchandise later and decide for yourself." Chloe ground her hips against him for diversion's sake, then almost wished she hadn't. The man definitely had a banana in his pocket, and she wasn't sure how long she could wait to get reacquainted. "Just as long as *this* isn't less filling."

"Youch!" Nick clutched his heart, laughing. "You really know how to hurt a guy."

Nah, she thought, kissing him to soften her teasing. *But he really knew how to hurt a girl.* How long would it be before Nick came to his senses and realized the two of them were this close to passing the just-friends barrier forever?

She'd think about that later. Chloe couldn't end what was happening between them now, no matter how bittersweet her memories were of their night together. She didn't have the strength. Not now, and maybe not ever. Not when Nick was only beginning to see her as a woman.

A woman, she hoped, he might love.

"But I didn't mean just these." He cupped her breasts again, and she swayed against him. "Beautiful as they are."

His eyes twinkled at her, filled with humor and affection and—oh, God, was that passion? She really, really hoped it was passion.

He kept talking, looking somber and Nick-serious even as he stroked her through her silky shirt. "I meant the whole package. All of you. Inside. Outside. Everything." Nick stroked her cheek, and she felt his thumb tremble against her skin. "You're beautiful, Chloe."

Oh, she was done for. Finished. If he hadn't been holding her up, she might have keeled over right there on the patio table. Melted in his arms like the hot wax from the candles and oozed straight through the basket-weave wrought iron. No one had ever said anything so wonderful to her before. It felt so alien she couldn't stand it.

"It must be the pregnancy thing," she told him for an excuse. "You know, the way pregnant women are supposed to be all glowing and radiant and—"

"It's you." He kissed her. "Shut up and just believe it."

He went on unbuttoning her shirt, and fairly quickly, Chloe found herself believing it. Believing him. He really did want her. The proof was there in the tenderness of his touch, in the huskiness of his voice, in the warm, hard strength of his body beneath her.

"It's you," Nick said again. "Just you. And I've been an idiot not to realize it sooner."

Yes! *Yes, yes, yes.* Well, not yes, Nick was an idiot, but yes—oh, how she wished he'd taken a closer look at her sooner. Maybe he would have, if he'd ever been between what'shernames long enough. Or if she'd ever had the guts to make a move without Kahlúa courage and comfort-giving for an excuse.

She'd never know what it might have taken to bring them together. Right now, with her whole body pasted to Nick's and his fingers making magic, Chloe didn't much care to ponder the question.

She nuzzled his neck and kissed him again, happy and wanting and filled to bursting with love, and desperately needing to transmit every jumbled emotion through her kiss. *I love you*, she thought. *Love you, love you . . .*

Beneath her busy hands, Nick's body stilled. She felt his hands, motionless at the front clasp of her bra. She felt his breathing, harsh-sounding but gentle as a kiss against her collarbone. She felt him withdraw from her, lean back a little and spread the two halves of her unbuttoned shirt in his hands.

His forehead crinkled. Dread crept in her heart and set up shop. What was he waiting for?

Releasing one half of her shirt, Nick reached behind him and grabbed one of the citronella candles from the tabletop. Chloe couldn't move as he held its flickering light to her chest and looked closer. If he'd had another hand free to tap his lips in his patented thoughtful pose, she felt sure he would have.

"Haven't I seen that before?" He gestured to her chest. His gaze flashed to her face, then back to her . . . bra, she realized. Her sheer, orange push-up bra.

The same one she'd worn the morning after the night he thought they'd never spent together.

"Now, where would I have seen your bra?" he asked, still looking puzzled—for the moment.

Knowing Nick, it wouldn't last. He'd remember their night together . . . and realize her lie. Damn, damn, double damn! Given away by her weakness for fancy date lingerie. Chloe tugged her shirt out of his hand and wrapped it around her torso, hugging it over her belly. Maybe a joke would distract him? She decided to try sounding flippant, as though they weren't still halfway stuck together in a heated clinch.

"I dunno, Nick." Chloe hugged her clothes close as she slid down from his lap. "In your dreams, maybe?"

He didn't look convinced. In fact, he looked sort of . . . deflated. Exactly the way she felt. But thankfully, Nick didn't look that much closer to a solution, either, now that she'd safely hidden away the incriminating evidence.

The minute she got home, she was burning that damned bra.

Eight

"Oh, darling," Nick said, pacing across Chloe's living room almost a month later, "I just can't go on without you. Since you left, I've thought of nothing but you. Night and day, day and night—"

"Eastern time, Pacific time, Standard time!" Chloe added dramatically. Sighing, she bounced her pencil off of the notepad in her lap and crossed her arms over her chest. "This letter is killing me."

She watched her freshly sharpened number two ricochet off her paper on its eraser and spin end over end toward the opposite arm of her red plaid sofa.

Nick ducked. Her deadeye aim wasn't doing him any favors, either. How had she gotten so much loft on that thing? The pencil thumped into the wall behind him, then dropped harmlessly to her wildly colored, flower-splashed rug.

"I'm not writing something stupid and sappy, Nick. I'm not. It's just not me."

"You're right. You're very intelligent."

"Har, har."

"Too intelligent to let the father of your child get away. Now concentrate," he ordered, handing her the pencil.

She took it, smirked, and saluted him with it. Damn, he

hated it when Chloe turned flippant. Probably because it reminded him of the pat answer she'd handed him on his patio that night.

I dunno, Nick. In your dreams?

Ha. That sexy orange bra of hers—along with the curvy, Chloe-worthy rest of her—had haunted his stupid dreams ever since then, as sure as if she'd predicted it. Never mind that he didn't want them to. Never mind that he had other things to concentrate on: mainly his growth accelerator, which still hadn't come together properly. Never mind that becoming lovers would probably ruin their friendship and her chances with Bruno alike. All he'd been able to think about was her.

Somehow, Chloe had gotten under his skin that night and stayed there. Memories tortured him . . . of her soft, warm body curved against him, of her breathless whispers, of her dangerous roving hands. Memories of the cute way she'd wiggled when he'd kissed her and the husky way she'd moaned in the back of her throat when he'd slipped his hands inside her eye-popping, silky shirt. Memories of the shy surprise in her face when he'd told her she looked beautiful.

Yeah—beautiful. Another fella's beautiful girl.

Specifically, Bruno's.

Damn him.

And damn the last month Nick had spent being platonic with a capital "P." It was making him cranky.

He swiveled past a stack of cardboard boxes bearing the pictures and pastel-printed names of more baby paraphernalia than even he—a four time uncle—had known existed, and looked straight at Chloe.

"Look. You've put off writing this letter long enough."

"Hey, I—"

"Uh, uh, uh." Nick held up his hands and shook his head. "No more excuses. I've heard them all."

She pouted her perfectly lipsticked mouth. It was just his bad luck the motion made him want to kiss off all that glossy, shimmering pink. It was just his bad luck he had an overactive, out-of-practice libido aimed in her direction. It was just his bad, miserable, luck that just when Chloe had finally found someone she cared about enough to make babies with—he wasn't fooled for a minute by her "We talked, we laughed, we're over story"—he'd started falling for her, too.

Whoa. Falling for her? The hormonal soup surrounding Chloe must be getting to him, too. No way was he falling for her. Not with his invention's production dependent on this summer's work, and not with her Bruno-the-Marine waiting in the wings. Not with her future happiness, and her baby's, riding on patching together her temporarily off-track relationship.

Was he her friend or wasn't he? Friends wanted each other to be happy. They did not necessarily want to drag each other off to the big comfy sleigh bed that just happened to be right in the next room. They did not typically imagine ripping off each other's clothes, sinking on the pillow-piled mattress and . . . . Hell. It was past time to end this and get down to business.

Nick tried to look stern. "No more excuses," he repeated.

She gazed up at him with one hand on her rounded pregnant belly, as innocent as a newly minted angel. "But Shemp really did need some fresh air the other day. That wasn't an ex—"

"Right. And I suppose Curly needed those home-baked hamster treats last week."

"I—"

"And Larry was just dying to have his toenails—dog nails—claws!—painted purple yesterday?"

"It wasn't purple."

He raised his eyebrows, feeling his blood pressure approach the redline. "Oh, no?"

"No," she said, all earnestness and precision. A saint, doodling on a notepad. "It was fuchsia. And anyway—"

"Arrgh! Write. The. Letter!"

Flinching, Chloe flipped her notepad to a new page. "You don't have to yell," she grumbled, eyeballing the huge burbling aquarium separating her living room from the dining area.

"Quit looking for another excuse. Your fish don't need fresh air or a manicure, and don't even try to tell me they do. I won't believe it."

She mumbled something under her breath about stick-in-the-mud scientists who needed proof to find their own pants, then gave him a brilliant smile. "Okay. Dictate."

"You didn't like *my* letter."

Unimpressed by his resistance, she ignored him and doodled hearts along the top of her paper. For some reason Chloe's patience—her surety that he'd come through for her with a stupid Dear Bruno letter—annoyed the hell out of him. Nick would have shaved his head before admitting it.

Tapping her eraser against the paper, she looked up at him. "I'm waiting, oh professor of love."

He glared at her. She snickered.

He crossed his arms. "The professor of love has left the building."

"Aww, come on. I'm only kidding! Sheesh, what happened to your sense of humor?"

It got smothered beneath a month of wanting you.

"What happened to *your* sense of practicality?" he shot back, feeling out of control. And hating it. "You're what, four, five, six months—"

"Five and a half months."

"—pregnant now, and you still haven't told Bruno. You're more than halfway there, Chloe! Do you want to patch things up with the father of your baby or not?"

Her eyes widened. For an instant, she looked twice as vulnerable, twice as alone, and twice as tempting snuggled against the outrageously bright pillows littering her sofa. Then the old Chloe returned.

"I dunno, mister mind-meld. Do I? Do I really want to set things straight with junior's daddy?"

Beneath her notepad, she rubbed her palm over her belly, probably without even knowing she was doing it. It had become a habit as her pregnancy progressed, he'd noticed. Now, at the worst possible damned moment, Nick found himself wondering exactly what it would feel like to put his own hand there. To feel her baby growing and kicking and—

Something dangerous flashed in her eyes, burying his tender thoughts along with it. "Why don't you tell me? Do you think getting in touch with . . . with Bruno is the right thing to do?"

"Yes, dammit!"

She paused, staring at him, then flipped back to the page she'd been writing on. "Fine. *Oh, darling*," she started reading. "I just can't go on with—"

"Hold it."

Something niggled at the back of his mind. Some . . . hint, some clue, some . . . *thing* hovered just on the edge of his memory. Damn. What was it?

"Read that again."

"Oh, come on, Nick. A line-by-line critique? This isn't meant to be read aloud, you know."

"Humor me."

Chloe put the pencil in her mouth, gazing up at him thoughtfully while she ran the eraser back and forth over her bottom lip. Her eyebrows dipped, as though she were trying to remember something.

"The professor of love always gets his way," Nick said. "It's one of the perks of the position."

She shrugged. "Okay, okay." Clearing her throat, she raised the notepad like a Shakespearean preparing for a soliloquy. "Oh, darling!" Chloe intoned, flinging one arm wide. "I just can't go on without—"

Moe yowled and fled from beneath the coffee table. The drama of the moment vanished along with Nick's tip-of-the-tongue sensation. Whatever he'd almost remembered, it was gone now.

"Never mind. Let's start over."

"Good idea." Chloe ripped the letter they'd drafted out of her notepad. She crumpled the paper with a flash of her yellow-painted fingernails and added it to the wadded-up pyramid on the coffee table. "I never call anyone darling, anyway. Except maybe you, *darling*," she added with a wink.

There it was again. That niggling sense there was something he ought to have remembered, something . . . awww, the hell with it, Nick decided, setting his glasses straighter. It was probably just the strain of six months' worth of celibacy, finally getting to him. Ever since his heartbreak over what'shername—

dammit, what was her name, anyway?—he'd been spending too much time taking care of Chloe to date.

And not enough time working on his inventions. He had to get Chloe's love life squared away, so he could quit worrying about her and get down to business.

"Okay," he said in his most dog-determined voice. "Here goes. Dear Bruno—"

"Original opening."

He made a face at her. "As you so succinctly put it, har, har."

She laughed in earnest and threw a pink-fringed pillow at him. Nick ducked. In Chloe's house, they weren't called "throw pillows" for nothing.

"Pick up your pencil," he commanded, "and get busy."

Dutifully, she picked up her pencil again. And balanced it on the bridge of her nose. If he didn't know better, he'd swear she was trying to distract him from finishing the Bruno letter.

"Very nice," he deadpanned. "For a trained seal. Come on, Chloe. It's just a simple letter."

The pencil rolled off. She caught it. "Yeah. With a not-so-simple message."

So that was it. "Well, we'll make it simple then."

Nick paced to the window, thinking. Outside, Danny and Larry the Wonder Beagle played in the yard, tugging a battered blue Frisbee between them. For the past few Saturdays, Chloe had invited Danny to her place for half the day—ostensibly so his Uncle Nick could get some inventing done. Nick suspected their time together was more of a "life with kids" preview than anything else. Which was actually kind of endearing, when it came right down to it.

Danny glanced up and waved. Nick waved back, then turned his attention to the problem at hand. "A simple letter. Simple. Okay." Tapping his finger against his bottom lip, he said, "Dear Bruno. I'm writing to tell you that you're going to be a father. The baby is due around Christmastime, and—"

"Maybe I ought to tell him to sit first? That might come as kind of a shock."

Her voice came from the wrong direction. He looked for Chloe and found her, not on the sofa writing, but at the other end of the room, bent over Curly's hamster cage as she refilled his water container. She leaned a little closer, and her short stretchy sky blue skirt rode up her thighs. Her toned, shapely enough-to-drive-a-guy-crazy, half-naked thighs. *Thank God for power walking*, Nick thought.

I mean, get a hold of yourself, his conscience replied. So what if Chloe had on a miniskirt that left her legs almost completely bare? So what if he could just glimpse a peachy scrap of undoubtedly lacy underwear underneath it? So what if she was also wearing an oversize yellow and blue necktie-print silk shirt that was almost an exact duplicate of the one she'd worn . . . the one he'd unbuttoned . . . *that night*. So what?

He could handle it.

They were maternity clothes, he reminded himself as she put down the water and crossed the room. How sexy could they possibly be?

Except they were. Chloe picked up Moe and cuddled the mangy orange fur ball to her chest, and suddenly Nick felt almost . . . jealous.

Of a cat.

Ridiculous.

He had to get out of here before he lost it completely.

She frowned and nuzzled Moe's ears. "That's putting it a little too simply, don't you think so, Nick? I mean, what if poor Bruno reads it and drops dead with shock? What then, huh? I'm not trying to kill the guy, just inform him."

"You've got a point," Nick conceded. If someone was about to tell him *he* was going to be a father, he'd probably want it softened up a little, too. "All right, then. How about this—dear Bruno. I hope you remember me, because—"

"Nick!"

"What?"

"'I hope you remember me'?" she mimicked, raising her eyebrows. "I'll have you know, mister melodrama, that I am not *that* forgettable. Sheesh, what kind of girl do you take me for?"

The kind of girl I could love.

What the hell? There was something seriously wrong with him today. Nick wasn't sure what it was, but he was pretty sure Chloe was causing it somehow. Scowling, he removed Moe from her arms, dumped the hissing armful of cat on the cushy chair beside the sofa, then grabbed Chloe's arms.

"Look." He frog-marched her backward to the sofa again. "This is important. You've got to tell Bruno. Send him a letter. A fax, a postcard, a telegram, an e-mail. Rent a billboard or hire a blimp to broadcast it. I don't care how you do it." He sat her down and put the pencil in her hand and the paper on her lap. "Just do it!"

"You forgot skywriting."

"Arrgh!"

Chloe sighed. "You're right. It is important. Important to you! Why is that, Nick? You wanna tell me that?"

"Children should have two parents."

"Two loving parents," she specified, hugging her paper and pencil to her chest. "Not just two people brought together by . . . by . . . by biology!" She flung her arm sideways, and the pencil went flying again.

Nick ducked. "Is this your white picket fence thing again? Get over it, Chloe. Maybe this isn't happening in a picture-perfect way, but you're having a baby. Bruno has a responsibility to you. A responsibility he can't fulfill if he doesn't know about it."

He retrieved the pencil from the leaves of a potted philodendron near the window and handed it to her.

She tossed it aside along with her paper. "What about *my* responsibility?" She got up and stalked toward him. "What about my duty to provide a good home for this baby?"

"That's my whole point!"

With a muttered exclamation, Chloe shoved her fingers through her hair. She turned away from him. "No. Your whole point is doing the right thing, no matter what the cost."

"What cost?"

She wasn't making any sense, and he wasn't any closer to getting the damned letter written, either. He wasn't going to, not if she kept pacing around the living room instead of writing. Crossing his arms, Nick gave serious consideration to super-gluing Chloe's adorable mini-skirted butt to the chair and the pencil to her hand until she got the job done.

Again, he asked, "What cost?"

She paused in front of the battered antique cupboard she used for a TV stand and ran her fingertips over the framed photographs arranged on its hundred-year-old wood. It was the only area in Chloe's house that got dusted regularly, which was saying something for a woman who considered vacuuming hand-to-dust bunny combat.

"Nothing Nick 'Steady' Steadman would understand, I guess," she said without looking at him.

"Try me."

He saw her shoulders rise with the deep breath she took, then her fingers fluttered over the photograph frames again. "Duty at the cost of love. Partnership." She picked up an old photo of her father, a young man in John F. Kennedy clothes beside a Buick. Carefully, she rubbed away a spot on the glass. "A sense of being wanted."

He frowned. Before he could reply, though, she put the picture down and whirled into motion.

"Never mind, Nick." She breezed past him on her way to the kitchen. "I can't explain it, and you can't understand it, so let's just drop it, okay?"

Understand it? What the hell was he supposed to understand? That Chloe needed a stable family life for her child— soon—and all she could do was throw around pie-in-the-sky concepts like love and partnership and living happily ever after?

I want the whole fairytale ending, she'd said. *White picket fence, a ring on my finger . . . and a man who loves me.*

Maybe she was in denial. Maybe she was hormonally impaired. Or maybe she really *wasn't* crazy in love with Bruno, and that was what was behind her reluctance to contact him again. The idea perked Nick up. Fortunately, his conscience was there to keep him on the straight and narrow.

He followed Chloe to the kitchen and stood next to her beside the open refrigerator door. She rummaged inside, probably looking for her secret stash of diet cola, Nick figured. The one he kept taking out and hiding behind Chloe's unused ironing board. He leaned beside her, too, meaning to say something that might put them back on track to finding a solution.

Instead, what emerged from his mouth was, "I've known you, what . . . three years now? And I never, in all that time we spent together, knew you were this naïve."

"It's just orange juice!"

He took the carton from her hand and slammed it on the countertop. "Not the juice. You. This fairytale attitude you have about the way things should be."

Her mouth dropped open. But only for a nanosecond.

"Not 'things,' Nick." She shut the refrigerator and leaned on it with her arms crossed. "My life. My baby's life. But I guess you wouldn't understand that, with your Father Knows Best upbringing and all your big plans for inventing fame and fortune."

"It's not about me!"

Chloe's lips twisted, quivered faintly in the moment before she turned her face to the refrigerator and rested her forehead on its shiny surface. A muffled little sniff came from within the halo her arms made around her head.

"Awww, hell." Scrambling sideways, Nick opened a cupboard and took out a plastic Snoopy cup. He filled it with orange juice, racking his brain to figure out what he'd said to make her cry. Chloe never cried. Never.

Except when he was around lately, it seemed.

He took hold of her wrist, eased her arm downward, and shoved the juice in her hand. "How about if you just call up Bruno instead?" he suggested, straightening his glasses. "Maybe the letter isn't such a good idea."

It sure wasn't doing them any favors today.

She sniffed. "You're avoiding the issue."

Nick's head started to throb.

"No," he said with an excess of patience, "you're avoiding the—"

"Being pregnant," Chloe interrupted, turning toward him at last, "is not just some fairytale attitude of mine."

Though her cheeks looked blotchy and her eyes looked a little red-rimmed, her gaze met his steadily. She put down her juice and touched his clenched fist. She lifted it toward her, easing her fingers inside to open his hand.

"Neither is this baby." She smoothed his palm over her rounded belly. "This baby's real, Nick."

He felt her shirt's cool silk beneath his fingers, sensed the warmth of her skin penetrating the fabric. Chloe pressed his hand closer and closed her eyes. Her belly suddenly . . . *bumped* at him.

He jerked in surprise. She held his hand in place, smiling faintly.

"Real enough to kick." He felt ridiculously like laughing as he realized what that funny little bulge in her belly had been. A tiny head or foot. Hell, for all he knew, it was a miniature fist waving at the big bully who'd been pestering his mama. Nick grinned.

"Real enough to love," Chloe murmured.

By the time the next kick came, he knew she was right. All of a sudden, her baby was real to him, real enough to love, and there'd be no going back now.

Nick was a goner.

Nine

Power walking, Chloe discovered on Thanksgiving when her eighth month of pregnancy rolled around, was pretty near impossible when your belly preceded the rest of you by a good step or two.

Still, she and Larry kept it up—minus poor Curly, whose overexuberance kept rolling him into mud puddles, various cacti, and the occasional "doggie surprise." With Shemp perched on her shoulder and Moe slinking along beside her, she and Larry walked, rain or shine, every day that passed between the writing of the Bruno-gram and her eighth-month obstetrician appointment. If nothing else, it helped burn off her frustration from that nitwit Griggs's continued refusals to grant her the pet shop loan she needed.

Now, rounding the corner that led to her and Nick's side-by-side houses, Chloe thought of the Bruno letter they'd collaborated on. She sighed. She'd never mailed it, of course. There was no one to mail it to. Even if there had been . . . well, she wanted Nick and that was all there was to it. No other man would do.

She'd tried to give him space, to let him work on the inventions that were so important to him. But no matter what she did, there he was. At her doorstep with four "extra" cartons of milk that had somehow hopped in his shopping cart when he wasn't looking. In the baby's room assembling the new, brightly painted crib and hanging a fairytale wallpaper border to match. On her sofa with peppermint foot massage lotion at the ready and an open book of baby names to read while he massaged her poor pregnant feet at the end of the day.

You'd think he was the father or something.

Ha.

The way she longed for all that affection and extra close-ness to continue was scary. Especially considering that she'd done all she could to make sure it wouldn't continue. Why, oh why, had she ever invented Bruno?

"Hey!" Nick called from his front porch. "Hiya, Blondie." Grinning, he came down the steps with a handful of mail and stopped in front of her, then leaned down to pat Larry's head.

"Are you feeling all right?" Chloe asked, watching him murmur something in Larry's floppy beagle ears.

"Sure. Why?"

"You're actually being affectionate with one of my pets."

He smiled wider and went on patting, looking good enough to eat in a pair of perfectly fitted jeans and a knit sweater the color of the autumn Arizona sky. In defiance of the cooler weather, he'd pushed up his sleeves. His forearms flexed as he put his hands on his thighs and pushed upright again.

"They can't be all bad. *You* love 'em, right?"

At the teasing warmth in Nick's voice, Larry thumped his tail, then nosed his way beneath Nick's palm. His big brown eyes closed in doggie ecstasy as he was rewarded with more petting. By the time Moe crept up and started winding himself between Nick's legs and Shemp began to moonwalk on her shoulder, seeking an opening so he could join the fun, Chloe was feeling wildly left out.

Jealous of her pets, of all things. Geez, she was pathetic with a capital "P."

"Sure." She tugged at Larry's leash. "I'd love to get them home and get myself into a shower about now, too."

Nick examined her red extra-extra large Arizona Wildcats sweatshirt, blue yoga pants, and sneakers. "Nah. You look good sweaty. Must be that 'glow' thing you pregnant women are always going on about."

"Gee, thanks. Maybe I should skip showers altogether and really rack up the dates."

"Speaking of dates, have you heard from Bruno yet?"

Ugh. She should have seen that one coming.

"No." Chloe tried to dredge up an expression of disappointment. "I, ummm, guess I should have heard something by now."

"Especially with the videotape message we made." Nick ducked to peel Moe away from his legs, but the cat dug his claws in the denim and hung on. "And the—ouch! Let go, you big fur ball!—photos we put in the last letter."

He pulled a little harder. Moe didn't budge, only arched outward like a bow.

"Chloe, call off your cat, will ya'?"

Gladly. Anything to avoid discussing their various Bruno contact methods. None of which she'd actually followed through with.

All of which had only buried her deeper in the lie.

Much to her regret.

Stupid, *stupid* Kahlúa and coffee and sympathy.

"Come on, Moe." She slipped her hands under Moe's silky belly and caught hold. The cat yowled and reluctantly came free. At the same moment, Larry abandoned the ecstasy of being petted in favor of trying to lick the indigo dye out of Nick's jeans.

"Hey!" Nick squirmed out of the way. Larry, licking his chops with a sort of "giant Milk-Bone" gleam in his eyes, pursued him.

Shemp, apparently spotting the perfect moment to strike, flapped toward Nick's head.

"Shemp! Come back!" Chloe yelled.

Nick backed up, holding his mail on top of his head. It formed sort of an envelope runway just as Shemp swooped in for a landing. Moe jumped gracefully from her arms and slipped between the tangled length of Larry's new leash to rub against Nick's legs again. The cat-hair coating he'd begun laying down earlier glommed on extra well, Chloe noticed, now that Larry had been at work on the jeans, too.

"Larry, come *on*!" Grunting with effort, she managed to drag her dog away from the love-in. She reeled in the leash and locked it in place. "What's the matter with you?"

"I think I know." Nick lifted his mail—and Shemp—from his head. "They probably smell the ingredients I've been using for my latest invention."

"Eau de pet chow?"

"Something like that. It's a sports drink. Beef- and tuna-flavored—"

"Pet Gatorade!" Chloe interrupted. "You really made it!" She couldn't believe he'd remembered. And taken time away from his growth accelerator work to do it. "Can I put some in Red's shop? It'll be a mega-seller. You'll see."

"Before you come up with a multilevel marketing scheme, maybe you'd better come check it out for yourself." He grinned and aimed her bird toward her, letting Shemp click-click his way across a sweepstakes envelope and onto her shoulder again. "You want to?"

"Hmmm."

"Hmmm?"

"Hmmm, I hope you weren't planning to enter that." Chloe leaned forward to examine the Shemp surprise on the envelope.

Nick leaned forward, too. "But I'm already a winner!"

She grinned and batted her eyelashes at him. "You were always a winner with us, Nick."

"Cute. Anyway, come on inside. I'll show you what's got your menagerie all riled up."

"I'd better take these guys home first." Chloe lifted Moe from his new perch around Nick's shoulders. "Next thing you know, Shemp will decide you're his new lovebird companion and things will get really interesting."

Nick shuddered. "I don't even want to know what you mean by that."

"Nope, you probably don't. See you in a few minutes!"

* * *

Chloe's "few minutes" stretched into a half hour before Nick heard her coming up his front walk. *Female standard time*, he mused as he opened his front door and watched her approach. *It was a whole other dimension.*

She waved, hurrying with surprising pregnant-bellied grace between the white oleander bushes bordering his walk and front porch. Her sneakered feet clomped quickly over the porch floorboards.

"Look!" She waved a huge, ripped-open express mail package. "This was waiting on my doorstep when I got home."

She bounded inside, powered by excitement and something else Nick couldn't define. He shut the door and turned to find her jiving across his living room, hugging the package to her chest. This time, that "glow" of hers was no joke, and this time it didn't come from a workout or her pregnancy. It came from whatever was in that package.

Hell.

It could only be one thing, Nick figured. Even though he'd known it would come someday, the reality still felt like a sucker punch to the gut.

"So, when's Bruno coming back?"

Chloe's head came up. Her fingers froze on the package. Somehow, he'd liked it better when she'd been hugging the damned thing. At least then she'd looked happy.

Well, he'd be damned if he'd make her miserable now. Wasn't this what they'd both worked toward for so many weeks? Bruno was coming back. Nick would be able to concentrate full-time on work again for a change. They should both be ecstatic, dammit!

Or at least one of them could be.

"I mean," he went on, forcing the words past his suddenly aching throat, "you must be wanting to go get things ready for him. You know, to meet him at the airport." Why wasn't she moving? "Or the harbor, I guess. What's the preferred Marine mode of travel anyway?"

His voice cracked on the joke. Swearing under his breath, Nick stared at the test tubes he'd arrayed in their holders on the coffee table, all set up to show Chloe the different varieties of pet sports drinks he'd come up with. For some reason, the samples looked smaller than he'd remembered.

"Oh, you mean this!" She waved the package. "Nick, it's the—"

"Yeah. Good news, huh?"

She beamed. Hell. Next she'd probably want to read him the damned thing.

"Let me put these back in my office and we'll—"

"Nick, wait." Her voice came hesitantly from across the room. "I'm sorry. Your invention. . . . Awww, Nick. I'm sorry. I was too excited to think straight. I should have—"

"No apologies necessary." Striding toward the table, he swept the tubes in his arms. They clinked against each other, sounding as hollow as his heart felt. "I can show you these another time."

"No, wait! It's just been so long since I've heard from my dad that I couldn't wait to—"

She kept on talking, but Nick's brain stuttered on the word "dad," and refused to catch up. The package wasn't from Bruno?

She touched his shoulder. "Why don't you show me what's got Larry and Moe all crazy over you today? Then we'll do this." She nodded at the envelope and shook it in her excitement. "Okay?"

Only one thought zinged through his head, replaying itself like an ancient vinyl LP stuck on one really well-played groove: *The Package Wasn't From Bruno* song.

"Okay?" she prompted.

Nick shook his head to clear it. He focused on Chloe. It wasn't an easy task, considering the way she was bouncing in place.

"Are you kidding?" he asked. "I'll show you this later. It's not every day you get a supersize express mail from your father."

"It's never, actually," she admitted, raising the package. She flipped it over to read the addresses on the front. "He's very busy." She frowned briefly, then her gaze zipped to Nick. "Are you sure?"

Nodding, he arranged the test tubes on the coffee table. As

long as it wasn't a letter from Bruno in that package, he'd listen to just about anything.

"Okay!" She jigged toward him, all excitement restored. Her smile brightened as she put her hand in the envelope. The flexible waterproof packaging bulged as she rummaged inside, talking non-stop. "He must have gotten my letter about the baby," she said breathlessly. "I wasn't sure whether I should send it to his vacation house in Florida or his new apartment in Manhattan. You know, he's always, ummm, on the move."

She withdrew a small bubble-wrapped bundle and an embossed ivory card. For an instant, she hugged the items to her chest. She all but threw them toward him in her excitement. "Look!"

"Okay!" he squealed, mimicking her high-octane delivery. He grinned despite himself as he caught everything. Her enthusiasm was impossible to resist.

The bubble wrap crinkled as Nick juggled everything to get the card on top. He rubbed his thumb over the monogrammed initials on the front of the card. Ritzy. But then, if he remembered correctly, Chloe's father was a corporate executive for an international consulting firm. He could undoubtedly afford something nicer than a drugstore note card, especially for his own daughter.

Beside him, Chloe hugged his arm excitedly. She gave his biceps a vise-grip squeeze. "Go ahead. Read what it says!"

Resisting the urge to flex, Nick flipped open the folded note card. A business card fluttered out. He caught it with his thumb just before it slipped to the floor, and read the words beside the tasteful logo. *Sloan, Hinkle, Hinkle-Sloan, and Carmichal: Consultants.*

"Whoa. Consultants too exclusive to reveal what they're supposed to be consulted about. Swanky."

"I guess so." She shrugged as she read over his shoulder. "I've never visited his company, but it keeps him pretty busy."

Not too busy to advertise for more business from his own daughter, Nick noticed. What kind of guy slipped a business card in his family mail?

Chloe tapped it. "Hinkle-Sloan is my father's second wife," she explained. "Remember? The one I told you about?"

"The wedding where you wore your Brownie uniform instead of the flower girl dress they gave you and staged a sit-down strike in the middle of the church aisle?"

She gave him a mischievous grin. "I was seven years old." She made a show of examining her manicure with inch-thick innocence. "What did I know about weddings?"

"Enough to know you didn't want your dad to remarry, I guess."

"Hmmph. They managed to squeeze past me and do it anyway." Chloe rested her hand on her middle and stroked gently. "Anyway, it wasn't just me. The ring bearer helped, too."

"See? Even then you could wrap a guy around your little finger."

"Fun-ny."

"He wasn't wearing a Brownie uniform, I take it."

"No. He thought his knees looked too knobby in the little skirt."

Nick laughed as she snuggled nearer. Her belly nestled companionably against his hip, familiarly warm and round beneath her sweatshirt. Chloe hadn't been this close to him since their patio-table encounter, Nick realized. Over the intervening weeks, she'd kept her distance from him. Now, if he hadn't had his hands full already, he'd have pulled her even closer.

"Since the wedding, it's really been Hinkle-Sloan-Carmichal," she went on, wrinkling her nose, "but Tabitha doesn't think that looks nice on a business card."

"Aww. Poor Tabitha." He grinned. "I hate it when multi-marriages wreck my business cards. Sooo inconvenient."

"Be nice," she ordered. And pinched him.

"Youch!" he yelped, rubbing his elbow against his side. "Be nice yourself, you big bully."

"Sorry." She jabbed him in the ribs. "Hurry up and look at everything!"

Nick gave her a sideways glance and realized she was probably oblivious to all the Three Stooges poking and jabbing she was doing. In fact, she wasn't even looking at him anymore. Instead, she squished up closer to him and stared at the things in his hands, twirling her hair against her cheek.

Insecurity clue number one. Messing up that immaculate

hairstyle of hers. He wondered what was bugging her. Maybe she'd thought the package was from Bruno, too, and was disappointed it wasn't.

Grrr. He resisted the urge to rip open the bubble wrap, and scanned the message on the card instead. Congratulations, Chloe, it read in neat laser-printed type. Tabitha and I—

He quit reading and looked up. "Chloe, this message is printed. As in computer-generated and printed."

Her forehead wrinkled as she glanced at the card. *Yup, it's still the same one*, her expression said. "Of course it is. Catch up, Nick! This is the twenty-first century. Secretaries don't handwrite things these days."

"Secretaries?"

Another shrug. "My dad suggested I route my correspondence through one of his secretaries. It's more expedient."

His jaw dropped.

Then snapped shut when Chloe laughed.

"I know, I know." She gave him an ignore-those-pesky-concerns kind of wave. "You're thinking my dad must be some big old stuffy corporate muckety-muck, having secretaries at his beck and call like he does, right? But—"

"No, that wasn't precisely what I was thinking, but—"

"—but not even four secretaries would have that effect on him. He's a regular guy, really."

"Four. Four secretaries?" And the guy still couldn't find the time to handwrite a note to his only daughter, a month before his first grandchild was due?

"No, he only has three secretaries. Sheesh, Nick, you're not listening. All I'm saying is, my dad's just an ordinary Joe who happens to be in big business." She stared expectantly at him for a minute, then prodded his shin with her sneakered foot. "Keep reading!"

Nick looked at the note card and seriously considered shredding the thing. That was about the nicest treatment it deserved. But Chloe seemed thrilled to have it, so he only raised it higher and went on reading.

Tabitha and I are delighted with your news. We'll be thinking of you during our annual Christmas

cruise next month! Give the newest Carmichal a
kiss for grandpa, and call me if you need anything.
Love, your father, Newton Carmichal.

At least the signature was handwritten.

Beside him, Chloe sighed. "Isn't that sweet? Did you see
how he put 'grandpa' in there? How he said to call him if I
needed anything?" She hugged herself and beamed up at him.
"Thank God for Lucinda."

"Lucinda?"

"Secretary number two."

"Of course."

"If not for her, my letter might never have reached him."

"Right."

How had Nick never noticed how outrageously . . . absent
her father was? How thoughtless?

"You know, this really gives me hope, Nick. I think this
might be a new beginning for us."

"You and Lucinda?"

"Me and my dad, silly." Chloe poked him again and gazed
fondly at the card. "Sweet, huh?"

Nick gazed down at her smiling, sunlit expression, and realized there was nothing else to do. He didn't have the heart to
tell Chloe a truth she so obviously didn't want to hear. So he
smiled right back and lifted the bubble-wrapped package still
waiting to be opened.

"It's really nice, Chloe." *You're really a liar, Steadman.* He
rattled the package in his hand, then winked. "What's this, do
you think? Gold-plated mutual funds? Baby bootie bonds?"

"He's not a stockbroker." She took away the note card and
hugged it close while Nick unwrapped the bubble wrap. "Just
look, will you? I can't wait for you to see!"

The last of the clear cushioned coating came away. Nick
looked inside. Nestled inside the wrap, nestled inside a fancy
white box, nestled inside a pillow of tissue paper, was a shiny
silver thing wrapped with a white ribbon. Monogrammed
with a set of three script letters too fancy to make out on the
curved surface and polished to a high-gloss, it looked sort of
like a miniature silver dumbbell.

For a newborn baby? The fitness craze was getting way out of hand.

Never mind, Nick commanded himself. *Say something nice.*

"Umm, I can see my teeth in it." He made a goofy face at his reflection. "What do you know about that?"

"I know!" Chloe burbled, dancing up on tiptoes. "Isn't it great?"

"It's—it's—" He turned it over and experimentally hefted it like a tiny barbell. "What the hell is it, Chloe?"

She quit dancing. "It's a baby rattle. From one of those exclusive department stores back east."

"A baby rattle?" Nick looked at the cold, hard thing in his hands. Even wrapped in a bow and soft paper it looked bleak, somehow. He clapped on the lid. "Not for your baby, it's not."

"Nick!"

He raised the box overhead, trailing bubble wrap and ribbon like pastel tears. "He'll knock his teeth out with it."

Chloe put her hands on her hips and glared at him. "Babies are born without teeth."

"He'll knock himself unconscious the first time he lifts that thing. It's not safe."

"Babies have hard heads." She reached for the box. "It's a built-in safety mechanism to reassure overprotective fathers." Struggling on tiptoes, she bumped her belly into him and all but climbed his feet to get higher. "Give it to me!"

"No. He'll put his eye out with it."

"You're being ridiculous." She reached higher, grabbing his upraised arm to steady herself. "You don't know anything about babies."

"I know more than you do."

Her body went rigid. Chloe shoved his elbow to push herself away. Far away.

"That's a low blow, Nick."

"It's the truth." Pretty irrefutable logic, as far as he was concerned. Obviously she disagreed, if her fire-breathing expression was anything to go by. "Nobody's born knowing this stuff, you know."

He reached to pull her close again, but she stepped back

before he could touch her. Threading her fingers through her hair, Chloe looked out the window, at the floor . . . anywhere but at him.

"It's not the truth," she said in a voice like ice. Clipped. Precise. Totally Un-Chloe-like. "I've been taking classes, reading books. . . ."

Practicing on Danny, grilling my sisters for baby tips, he thought, but couldn't say it.

"I know. Inexperience isn't a crime. I only meant that I'm already an uncle and you're—"

"Leaving." Stiffly, she held out her hand for the box. "What I am is leaving, before this gets ugly. You're the king of botched explanations, Nick. Good intentions with disastrous results. So why don't you just quit, okay? This time at least, quit while you're ahead."

This time? What was she talking about? Anyway, he couldn't. Not without one last stab at making her see reason.

"This isn't a baby gift, it's a-a—" He shook the box, trying to think up something suitably pretentious, then flung his arms wide. "—it's a damned paperweight, Chloe! What's the matter with you?"

Her hand fisted, then dropped to her side. Carefully, coldly, she stuffed the note from her father back in the envelope, then snatched the few scraps of wrapping they'd scattered.

"This is an implement of baby destruction," Nick protested. "If you want a rattle, I'll get you a rattle. A nice, safe, well-padded one with something friendly on it. Like bunnies. Not a stupid designer logo."

"It's a family monogram."

"Whatever."

Biting her lip, she raised her hand toward him, palm upward. "Give it to me, please."

Maybe a small concession was called for. Nick tried out a smile. "Okay. What do I know, right? I'm just an uncle. I—"

"Please, Nick," she whispered, blinking hard. A suspicious sheen brightened her eyes. Her lower lip wobbled with the beginnings of what he could tell was a gigantic, stifled sob.

This, from a woman who never cried.

"Awww, hell." How had he done it to her again? The tears in her eyes had him pressing the stupid box in her hand even before he realized he'd decided to do it.

"Thanks." Sniffling, Chloe pushed the box back in the envelope again, then went to the door. "Talk to you later," she mumbled in a choked voice.

"Wait."

Somehow, he'd botched things big-time. How had it all gone from jumpy-jivey happiness to tears so fast? Judging by the way she clutched her damned envelope, he suspected it had as much to do with his reaction to her father's gift as it did with what he'd said to her. But why?

A few steps took him to the door, close enough to smell the coconut shampoo in her hair. Frowning, Nick slapped his hand on the thick wood to keep the door closed a little longer.

To keep her with him a little longer.

"I don't get it. What's so special about this, Chloe?"

She swiped her hand across her eyes, then sniffed and squared her shoulders. "You can't tell, genius?"

Her voice was softer than he'd expected, but the anguish behind it wasn't. He smoothed his hand over her shoulder. "Nah. Maybe your feminine mystique has got me all confused."

Her mood swings sure as hell did. So did the way her father treated her. How, in three years, had he not noticed it?

Chloe smiled faintly. "It's simple. I'm having a baby in a few weeks, and the idea of screwing up has got me scared to death."

Good going, Steadman, his conscience poked at him. *Jump right on her big fears, tough guy.* But how could he have known? She always seemed so . . . certain about everything.

"Chloe, I didn't mean—"

Her choked little laugh cut him off. "Awww, don't worry, Nick. My mom's been giving me lots of advice over the phone. I'll be ready."

"There's always Bruno," he added, hoping to reassure her. "That package could just as easily have been from him."

"Yeah." Thoughtfully, Chloe squeezed the package in question. "Actually, you know something? It's funny—I figured the odds of hearing from my dad were about on par with the odds of hearing from Bruno."

"Looks as if the odds are on your side, then."

She gave him a funny look. "I guess that's one way of looking at it."

Taking a deep breath, she twisted the knob and opened the door. Sunlight and flower-scented air rushed inside, but all that sweetness and shine held no warmth. Nick rubbed his arms, fighting the urge to drag her against him and do whatever he could to make up for the stupid insensitivity of her family. The proud tilt of her head warned him to stay where he was.

So did her voice, falsely cheerful enough to make his heart ache.

"Anyway, I told my mom not to mess up her schedule, but she said she might even be able to drop by the hospital when the baby's born." Chloe paused on the threshold. "If there's time between beauty shop appointments and husband-hunting down at the bingo parlor."

"At least there she's guaranteed a man who can count."

She smiled at his joke, quite possibly the lamest he'd made all year, and touched his face. "I knew you'd understand."

Her fingers stroked across his temple, warm and feather-light, then whisked away. "See ya'."

Nick captured her wrist before she could leave. Briefly, he pressed his cheek in her cupped hand and closed his eyes.

"*I'll* be there," he promised.

She made a garbled sound of surprise and pulled her hand away. "At the hospital?"

"Sure."

He opened his eyes to see her shaking her head.

"Are you kidding me? I'm not that mad at you, Nick. I'm not about to inflict that kind of obligation on you. No way."

He leaned closer, raised her chin with his fingertips, and stopped her protest with a kiss. Just a small kiss . . . fast, soft, and sweet enough to widen her eyes when it was over. Nick put his hands around her waist and tugged her a little closer.

"What if I insist?"

Her eyes darkened with something only a blind man would

mistake for passion. Chloe shoved his chest and stepped out of his arms.

"Thanks for the pity party. But no thanks. You'll have to find another gal to play knight in shining armor with."

"Dammit, Chloe! That's not what this is, and you know it. You—"

"Anyway," she interrupted, preparing to leave, "it's not as though I'll be all alone. Now that it's certain my dad and Tabitha won't be there, my mom probably will be." She smiled thinly over her shoulder as she headed for the steps, hugging her package as closely as he wished she'd hold him. "I think the beauty parlor bingo-rama was just an excuse to avoid running into them."

Nick couldn't think of a damn thing to say to that. A bitter divorce he could understand. But not neglecting their own daughter because of it. No wonder Chloe was so hung up on having two happily ever-after, crazy in love parents for her baby.

No wonder.

It would have been hell growing up with that bunch of marital miscreants around.

"Listen, I'd better run, Sir Galahad." Waving, she clomped down the steps in her sneakers. "I've got childbirth class in an hour or so. I've got to start getting ready."

So do I, Nick thought, waving good-bye as he watched her cross from his yard to her flower-bordered one. Ready for big important things.

Big important *surprising* things.

This time, he had more in mind than inventing beef- and tuna-flavored Gatorade for Chloe's pets.

Ten

Chloe spent the entire holiday season—aka her ninth month of pregnancy—in a constant state of red alert. Every kick, every contraction, sent her diving for the phone and the overnight bag she kept packed for the trip to the hospital.

She'd stand there beside her scrawny, gaily decorated Christmas tree, clutching the birthday bag handle in both hands, gauging the chances that *this time* it might be the real thing, keeping one eye on the clock's sweeping second hand . . . and the other eye on the view outside her bedroom window.

The window that faced Nick's house.

And his bedroom.

She never saw him. Although light usually filtered between his mini-blinds, showing he was home, his shadow never darkened those tasteful beige slats. His big hand never reached up to nudge one down, allowing him to look past their adjoined yards and into her room. He never sneaked a glance from the edge of those blinds, wondering how she was doing.

But Chloe did.

She shouldn't. It was stupid and pointless. After all he'd said about her father's gift—after all he'd said about her!—she should have been able to quit caring. *I know more than you do.*

Ha. *Not anymore*, she told herself, plunking the birthday

bag on the carpet for the thousandth time. She'd prepped and planned, grilled Naomi every time she brought over Danny, befriended all the women in her childbearing class. She was as ready as a woman could be to bring a new little person into the world.

"Except for providing the father," she muttered.

"What?" Red asked on the other end of the phone.

Chloe had red-alerted her ten minutes earlier for a Braxton-Hicks contraction. Between peeks at Nick's window, they'd been talking since then. Not everyone had a boss, a surrogate mother, and a birth coach all rolled into the same big-hearted, redheaded pet shop owner.

"You've been provoking the father?" Red went on. "Well, hon, no wonder you need me to drive you to the hospital, if you're badgering the fella."

Make that redheaded pet shop owner busybody, Chloe thought grumpily. If Red poked much deeper, she just might confess everything. Lying to herself was bad enough. Lying to everyone she loved was even worse.

She rebalanced the phone on her shoulder and paced through her living room. Absently, she fingered the ribbons and bows on the gifts piled beneath her Christmas tree. "That's not why I need you, Red. I'd drive myself, but—"

"But nothing. I'm driving you and that's that." Red's cigarette-roughened voice lowered. "If you'd tell me where to find that Bruno of yours, I'd bring him, too. He should be there, hon. Nothing makes a man a daddy like seeing his own child born."

That's what I'm afraid of. Chloe patted one very special gift: the one for Nick, wrapped in a big red bow. She swiveled toward the armoire to select another Christmas-music CD, trying not to think about Nick's assurance that he'd be at the hospital, even if no one else was. If he did, would he realize the truth?

She'd never find out.

Because she, like a dummy, had told him not to come.

Anyway, at the rate he seemed to be working, her baby might be toddling over to pick petunias from Nick's yard by the time he emerged from the invention-induced haze he was in. Since Thanksgiving, their contact had been mostly limited to waving as they strung their individual Christmas lights and decorations, waving as Chloe power-walked with Larry and Moe and Shemp, and waving as Nick scribbled invention brainstorms on his mail before carrying it inside.

"Anything from Bruno?" he'd ask when he saw her carrying hers in.

"Not yet," she'd always answer—just as though a letter might actually arrive someday. In truth, she was about as likely to hear from her make-believe Marine as she was to fall in love with anyone other than Nick.

On the phone, Red made an exasperated sound. "Hon, it's hard to raise a child alone. Ease up on that pride of yours and call the man!"

Pride? Was that what it was?

No. It was not being really, truly loved that was the danger here, to her and her baby both. Chloe paced down the hallway toward the cordless phone stand in the kitchen, pausing to adjust the Christmas stockings—one regular size and one baby size—she'd hung by the fireplace.

"I'm sorry about the false alarm, Red," she broke in. *I'm sorry to tell you only half the truth.* She dragged in a breath to ease the ache in her chest. "Listen, I've got to run. See you at the shop tomorrow?"

"You bet, Sweets."

Red inhaled. The faint crackling of her ever-present burning cigarette came over the line. *I've got to get that loan, get Red retired, and get her a truckload of stop-smoking gum.* Maybe Nick could invent something, some kind of nonsmoking . . .

Stop it, Chloe ordered herself. She had to quit depending on Nick. Starting yesterday.

Red exhaled. "I'll be there. You open up shop, though, okay? I'm meeting with another one of those buyers at the Downtown Grill. Nine o'clock. Maybe this one won't be itching to tear down the place and build one of those godawful tourist traps with sooouvenirs and pink suede cowboy boots."

Chloe grimaced. "Red . . . I've got a pair of those boots."

"You would, darlin'. You would."

Her friend's raucous laughter crackled over the line before

they said their good-byes. Chloe hung up the phone. The thought of bulldozers rumbling over her beloved pet shop made her fingers turn to ice. What if she never persuaded Griggs to give her the loan? What if Red got desperate and sold out to a developer before she could make any headway with her plans?

It was time to settle her future, once and for all.

Or at least part of it.

The same left-hand turn that brought Nick onto Main Street brought him his first view of the crowd. From the looks of it, a third of the town had turned out. Men, women and children clumped around the town plaza's Christmas-decorated courtyard in bunches, talking, pointing, and peering in the artificially snow-frosted windows of Saguaro Vista Cattleman's Bank. Police cars blocked the street, lights flashing. The town's sole newspaper photographer ducked behind one, aiming for a *Territorial*-worthy shot of the fracas.

It's Chloe, his sister Naomi had told him on the phone. *Chloe needs you at the bank.*

That's all he'd heard before dropping the phone and sprinting to his motorcycle. Now, steering between a woman wearing pink sponge curlers and a sheriff's deputy directing traffic, Nick wished he'd waited to hear more. Was Chloe being arrested? Had she finally had a hormonal breakdown, snapped, and assaulted Effram Griggs?

The town's fire engine careened around the corner. Suited-up firefighters piled out. Nick's heart slammed harder. He wrenched his bike to a stop at the curb and ran through the crowd. They surged along with him all the way to the bank's front door, where the first-comers spilled out along with incongruously cheerful Christmas music.

Nick elbowed his way inside.

He spotted Chloe's blond head first. She was near the wagon-wheel table in the middle of the bank, the same one used to hold deposit slips and pens on chains and——he looked closer——today, one very pregnant woman wearing wild hot pink clothes and an expression he'd never seen before. While

Nick edged closer, Effram Griggs came in view, flapping a sheaf of paper toward Chloe like a human ceiling fan. She bent forward in the breeze. Her head disappeared from view.

Dear God, Nick thought, realizing what all the paramedic-packed fuss was about. *Chloe was in labor.*

Right on top of the glossy home-banking brochures.

She'd probably come to the bank to confront Griggs about her loan—minus Nick, because he'd been too busy working on his growth accelerator to help her, dammit—and his latest refusal had sent her over the edge. Those lunatic hormones of hers could probably cause just about anything to happen.

"Chloe!" he yelled.

"Nick?"

He reached her and held her face in his hands, keeping her still so he could make sure she was all right. She *felt* all right, silky and warm beneath his palms. She looked okay, sort of pink and glowing . . . but then again, that could have been the reflected glare from her clothes. Her hot pink mini-dress looked vivid enough to peel paint.

"Hiya, brainiac," Chloe said. "What are you doing here?"

"Naomi called me. Danny's bus driver was late because she had to detour around the bank. The street's completely blocked outside. You're the talk of the town, Chloe."

Looking pleased, she sat up straighter. "The street's blocked?"

"The *Territorial's* outside, too. You'll probably make the evening edition."

She beamed. "That's great!"

It was worse than he'd thought. She'd gone temporarily crazy. Who knew pregnancy could do this to a person?

Nick rubbed his thumbs gently over her cheeks. This didn't look like the writhing, screaming childbirth they showed on TV—or the grueling forty-eight hour laborathons his mother and sisters had moaned about—but he couldn't be sure. Chloe's method of having babies was bound to be a hundred-and-eighty degrees different than anyone else's.

"Are you all right? Is the pain bad? Is the baby—"

"The baby's fine." She smiled against his hands, making him realize how much he'd missed the feel of her. Then she slipped her fingers around his wrists and tugged downward.

"So am I. You're acting as if I'm going to pop out the kid right here, or something."

If she was, she was being pretty blasé about it. Nick frowned, casting his arm toward the noisy crowd. "You're not? But there are paramedics outside, police and firefighters and—" Something else occurred to him. He gave her a stern look. "Are you still mad about our argument? Because if you're just saying this to make me go away, I—"

"No, I'm not. Not mad, not in labor, and not fibbing. The crowd's here because of the sit-down strike, the police are probably here for crowd control, and the firefighters are probably here in case Griggs locks me in the bank vault after all." She peered closely at him. "You're looking a little woozy, Nick. You want to sit?"

"Uhhh—"

Scooting over the table's thick wagon-wheel rungs, Chloe flashed her knee-high boots and made room for him. "Come on. Hop aboard. You probably need some of the Christmas-blend coffee they're serving today, too. Griggs?" She put her hand on Nick's shoulder and gazed through the murmuring crowd like a queen calling her court jester. "Oh, Griggs!"

She *had* snapped. "Another sit-down strike? Chloe, come down from there. I'll take you home."

"Don't be ridiculous, I—oh, there you are."

Effram Griggs appeared beside Nick, looking as though he'd just emerged from a sauna. His forehead looked shiny with sweat, and his western shirt had twin wet spots under the arms. Clearly, having Chloe hold court in the middle of his bank wasn't his usual Monday afternoon routine.

She inclined her head regally toward him. "Would you bring Mr. Steadman a cup of your complimentary Ho Ho Ho blend, please? I think the crowd's too much for him."

"Right away. Have you finished the, ahh—"

"When you bring the check." Chloe tucked a pen in the top of one boot. The motion called attention to the rolled-up sheaf of papers stuck partway beneath her thigh. They looked like the ones Griggs had been waving around earlier. "And the coffee."

"I don't want any coffee," Nick put in.

Too late. Griggs had already left.

He swiveled toward Chloe, who, having dispensed with both her pen and the pesky Mr. Griggs, cheerfully tapped the papers against her boot.

"The check?" Nick asked. "A payoff for not causing a bigger riot?"

"For my loan." She rubbed her other hand over her round, round belly and smiled at him. "My loan for my pet shop."

"You got it?"

"*Yes!*" She patted the table. "Come on up. Celebrate my victory, Nick."

"I can't believe you got it."

Griggs returned, a Styrofoam cup of coffee in one hand and a slip of paper in the other. Solicitously, Chloe set the Ho Ho Ho blend on the table within Nick's reach, then snatched the paper. She held it up for the crowd to see.

"The check!"

Bedlam erupted. Shouts of "Hurray!" mixed with clapping and whistling, then mellowed into a chant. It sounded like . . .

"No more Neanderthals?" Nick asked.

She laughed and flipped over a homemade poster from the table beside her. It showed a club-toting caveman's body encircled by an "O" with a diagonal slash through it. Effram Griggs's head, sour-faced in an old newspaper photo, was pasted on the caveman above the words: *No More Neanderthals. Say Yes to Loans for Ladies.*

"Turns out," Chloe said, shoving the poster through the wagon-wheel slats, "that Griggs has a policy of refusing loans to women. He's turned down half the ladies in my childbirth class. Most of whom were forced to get loans in their husbands' names."

She frowned at the injustice of it all. Nick tried not to wonder if she'd have married him for her loan's sake, if he'd asked.

"So," she went on, reaching behind her for the fuzzy white jacket she'd left there and smoothing it over her lap, "I came in and told him I wasn't leaving until he changed his stupid throwback policy. I can't believe the old protest ploy worked! I didn't exactly have a good track record with that one, you know."

"The only thing you're missing is that Brownie uniform of yours." Nick put his arms around her waist. "Now there's something I'd like to see."

"Actually, hot pink is more attention-getting."

"I'll say." He waggled his eyebrows as he looked her over.

"But it was probably the baby. An extra sympathy measure I didn't have when I was seven."

"Maybe." *Or maybe Mrs. Griggs had been pregnant once, too, and her husband had learned his lesson.* It was better to roll with the lunacy than to fight it.

Or maybe that just described life with women in hot pink and triumphant grins. Nick smiled back amid the chants and stomping feet and draped Chloe's puffy jacket over her shoulders, then tugged her into his arms. The crowd cheered.

"Let's go home and celebrate." God, she felt good against him. "I know just the kind of party you need."

She hugged him closer and raised on tiptoes to whisper in his ear. "A party of two?"

"Something like that."

The crowd bumped and jostled them, milling toward the exit now that the excitement was over with. Effram Griggs, muttering and wringing the loan papers he'd taken from Chloe in exchange for the check, passed by on his way to the vault, probably planning to lock *himself* in until his personal nightmare had passed. Police officers loomed closer, probably wanting to make sure the poor pregnant women in Nick's arms was all right.

Or not. A sound at the back of Nick's head, where Chloe had her arms wrapped around his neck, killed his poor pregnant woman theory in a hurry. Nothing else sounded quite like the metallic snick of handcuffs closing.

"Chloe Carmichal?" one of the officers asked.

"Hey!" She snared Nick as she tried to tug her bound wrists over his head. "Hey! I'm-I'm—"

Stuck. Gently, Nick lifted her forearms past his nose. He hugged her against his side, turning them both to face a pair of Saguaro Vista's finest.

The men in blue smirked. "You're in trouble, is what you

are," one said. "Disturbing the peace, harassment, destruction of property—"

"Unlawful assembly, fire code violation," the other officer continued, going on with a description of her rights.

"But-but—" Chloe protested. "But I'm—"

"Under arrest," they finished in unison.

"I still can't believe you staged a sit-down strike to make Griggs give you your loan," Nick said, squinting into the sun as it set over downtown plaza.

"You can't argue with success." Smiling, Chloe slipped the loan check the police had returned to her in her white pillbox handbag and struggled to fasten the vintage latch. The stubborn old thing never had operated properly—just like Effram Griggs. "It worked, didn't it?"

"To the tune of five hundred dollars in fines and bail. It would have been cheaper to marry for the money, like your friends in Baby Birthing 101 did."

"They didn't! They just couldn't get credit in their own names, that's all, and-and you're teasing me, aren't you?"

His sparkling eyes told her he was. The rat.

"I would have helped you, you know," Nick said. "Red and Jerry would have, too. You only had to ask."

"I know." Chloe snuggled deeper in her warm, fuzzy jacket. "I just . . . thought I had time. I thought my way would work, if I only stuck with it long enough."

The town's annual Christmas banners, red and green and gold, sparkled overhead as she and Nick headed for the curb where his motorcycle was parked. She took his arm as they passed the courtyard fountain. Its wintery spray misted them both, making Chloe shiver—but not with cold. Losing her pet store dream had come too close. All because she'd refused to try getting her loan another way.

If I only stuck with it long enough.

Maybe sometimes it was smarter to recognize what wasn't working. Maybe dogged dedication to a plan *wasn't* always a surefire tactic.

Maybe not telling Nick the truth was exactly the same

problem in different clothes, Chloe decided later as they zipped into Nick's driveway. Maybe her Bruno alibi had outlived its usefulness. Maybe Nick *could* handle the truth.

He'd been interested enough to critique her father and Tabitha's choice of baby gifts, interested enough to set up the nursery and pack her refrigerator with milk for a crowd, interested enough to hound her about Twinkies and volunteer for hospital duty on junior's birthday.

She eased off his motorcycle—no easy task, now that she couldn't see her toes anymore—and handed her purple helmet to Nick, still thinking. What if she'd been wrong about him all along? The evidence, when viewed in a certain light, pointed to a different Nick than the no-kids, none-of-the-time, marriage-as-obligation type she'd pegged him as.

He blinked at her and straightened his glasses. "What's the matter? All protested out? You look like I do when I've been working on an invention all day and it won't quite come together. Like that damned growth accelerator . . ."

Or maybe that yes-kids thing was only wishful thinking. Nick went on talking, telling her something about his invention and the meeting he'd set up for Wednesday with an interested investor in California, but Chloe could only listen with half an ear.

His inventions will always come first, she realized. She watched his eyes light up as he described the prototype he'd come up with for the licensing meeting with the investor's board of directors, and her heart sank. *Always.*

"Come in and check it out," he was saying.

In encouragement, Nick's fingers touched hers, warm in the twilight. Smiling that devastating, you'll-like-it smile of his, he tugged her gently past the staked-out Christmas decorations in his yard.

Her feet hit the porch floorboards at the same time her conscience made up its mind once and for all.

"Nick, wait!" Chloe blurted.

He squeezed her hand. "For what? If you're worried about Larry, Moe and Curly—"

"It's not that."

"—and Shemp, I'm sure they're okay."

"I, I, ummm . . ." Oh, God. When had telling the truth become so difficult?

When you started lying for a living, Carmichal.

Chloe twisted her handbag's short straps and stared up at him, trying to dredge up some courage. Surely she had some beneath the layers of well-meant lies she'd told. She was the same woman who'd just staged a showdown at the bank, wasn't she?

Except looking at Nick's tender expression and lopsided, familiar grin made everything twice as hard. Biting her lip, Chloe pulled her gaze from his face and looked at the soft-lit windows behind him instead.

Just say it! she ordered herself. *Nick, this is your baby. Sorry I've lied to you about it for the past nine months. Ha, ha!*

Right. That would go over like Curly's exercise ball sinking in the fish tank.

"Chloe?"

She tried again. "Remember how you said you'd go to the hospital when the baby's born, if I needed you?"

"Yes."

Something in the way he said it drew her gaze back to him. He'd put on that analytical scientist's expression of his—the one she'd dreaded all these months. Was she giving off lie-detector signals, or what?

"I meant it, and I will." Nick bent to speak to her navel. "Wouldn't miss your debut for anything, big guy."

Tenderness washed over her. He loved the baby already, and he didn't even know the truth.

The truth. *Get back on track,* she ordered herself.

"What if it's a girl?" she asked instead. *Where had that come from?*

"A girl?"

"You said, 'big guy.' What if it's a girl?"

He straightened and gave her a quizzical look. "Then I'll teach her to play football anyway."

Behind him, something bumped inside his house. Chloe thought she glimpsed something dart past his half-opened blinds.

"What was that?"

"Nothing." He took her hand again. "Look, let's talk about this inside."

"No. I've got to tell you this now." Sheesh, she sounded like a spoiled brat. Next she'd be stomping her foot. "It's . . ." Her breath caught in her throat, making her gulp for air. ". . . about Bruno."

Another noise inside made her jerk. And breathe harder. Suddenly, Chloe couldn't get enough air. Beside her, Nick's image wavered like the Day-Glo castle inside her aquarium.

His voice yanked her back to the land of the listening, but that didn't help her breathing any. Probably a panic attack, she figured, brought on by the stress of actually telling Nick the truth.

Not to mention risking the loss of the man she loved. Forever. Dear God, he'd never forgive her for this.

"Huh, huh," she gasped, grabbing his arm for support. *Help. I've become physically incapable of honesty.*

He mistook her grappling for something else. Insistence that he listen to another Bruno story, probably.

"We can't do this now." Abruptly, Nick hauled her inside his front door.

"Wait, I'm-I'm—"

Lights burst on in a blinding flash. No wait. Those were flashbulbs popping all around her. Noisemakers screamed. What looked like a hundred people surged up from their hiding places in the tropical rainforest that Nick's living room had become.

"Surprise!" they yelled.

". . . hyperventilating," Chloe finished weakly.

Then the world turned black.

Eleven

Surprise parties were underrated, Chloe decided once she'd come to and been ensconced in the chair of honor—in this case, Nick's weathered Barcalounger, specially decorated with pink and blue balloons and pastel stick-on bows. Because this party, this surprise, had saved her from making a potentially disastrous mistake.

Telling Nick the truth.

Maybe she wouldn't have to, some cowardly part of her thought. To look at him now, surrounded by all their friends and most of his family, it was easy to believe they could go on the way they had been . . . partners in parenthood, just like they'd been partners in pregnancy. Even without the white picket fence and the ring and the happily ever after. Any guy who'd stage a surprise baby shower couldn't be all work and no baby, could he?

From across the room, Nick's voice drifted toward her. "That's right," he was telling Red's husband, Jerry. "A growth accelerator. I've been working on it night and day."

Then again, she might be wrong.

Beside her, Nick's mother patted Chloe's hand. "Poor dear. You still look a little pale. But I guess a day like the one you had would make anyone feel a bit peaked, wouldn't it?" Heads nodded all around their little Barcalounger ladies' group. "Are you feeling better now?"

Chloe gazed fondly at Mama Steadman. *Except for wanting to leap in your warm, hugging arms and never let go? Sure*! She'd never envied Nick his close-knit family as much as she did at this moment, when they were all around her.

Just as though she were part of a real family.

"I'm fine." *Your son is going to be a daddy*. No, she couldn't say that.

"Nick told us about your showdown with Griggs," Red said, speaking around her *faux*-cigarette carrot stick. It was her latest concession to a smoke-free, baby-ready environment. "Congratulations, hon. I was starting to wonder how many of those developers I'd have to trot in front of you before you got the hint."

"You knew?"

"'Course, I did. But I also knew you wouldn't accept my help if I offered it, so I decided to give you a nudge in the right direction instead."

The five Steadman "N" women murmured to each other, heads together. Nancy leaned over the coffee table to cut the Italian cream cake she'd made, and Naomi handed out thick slabs of it.

"Nicky says Chloe's stubborn as a mule," she told Red as she handed over a tottering, white-iced slice. "That's why we had to surprise her with the party. He said she'd never agree to it otherwise."

"As if Nick doesn't have a monopoly on stubbornness himself," Nora said with a snort. She ducked beneath a towering rubber tree plant and sat on the sofa opposite Chloe, then waved her arm toward the rest of the plants cluttering the living room. "Just look at this place! All these plants around— it's like a greenhouse in here."

"This latest invention is the worst," Nancy agreed. The Steadman women nodded, looking concerned. "He acts as though he'll actually make money from this one!"

"With that investor of his in California," Nadine put in. She forked up some cake and gave her brother a pitying glance.

"Can you imagine, embarrassing yourself in front of an entire board of directors? This hobby of his has gone too far."

"He's going to get hurt," Naomi murmured. "Danny says he blows things up pretty regularly."

Nancy put down the beribboned silver cake server and shook her head toward Nick. "Someone really ought to speak to him."

Nadine nodded. "I don't see why he can't just find a nice girl, settle down, and have kids, like the rest of us." She paused to wipe her toddler son Nigel's nose with a tissue. "What's so wrong with that? That's what I want to know!"

"He's got a perfectly good job at BrylCorp, too." Mrs. Steadman sighed. "Exactly the type of thing to support a growing family, the same way his father and grandfather did. I wish he'd stick with that and stop all this inventing nonsense."

Chloe couldn't stand it any longer. "It's his dream! How can he give that up? He's worked so hard, for so long, and—"

"—and maybe that ought to tell him something," Nadine interrupted gently. "Like maybe he's not cut out to be an inventor. Like maybe life's passing him by while he chases some impossible dream."

Chloe stared at her. *No wonder Nick works so hard*, she thought. *He's trying to make them all believe in him.*

Suddenly she was glad she hadn't added one more expectation, one more obligation, to the ones he already shouldered. Suddenly she was glad she hadn't confessed out on the porch and given him another reason to give up.

"How can you say that? Don't any of you have dreams?"

"Shhh." Nancy cast a furtive glance toward Nick. "He'll hear you!"

"Maybe he should hear me!" Chloe cried. "Nick's brilliant. And creative. If working night and day will let him share all that with the world, I think he ought to do it."

The room had gone silent, she realized. Even the CD player had stopped between Christmas carols. Nick's head turned toward the ladies, and the troubled expression on his face was one Chloe had never hoped to see. Had he heard what they'd said?

"What's all the fuss about?" he asked.

"Now look what you've done," Nadine moaned beneath her breath. "We never meant to hurt him. Now he's on to us."

"He was already on to you," Chloe told her.

She waved cheerily at Nick, just in case he *didn't* know what they'd been talking about. It was possible, between the Jingle Bells music and the crowd—and the sound-muffling qualities of his Amazonian plants—that he hadn't heard all of it. She plastered on a big, bright smile.

"We're just fighting over the last piece of cake," she called. "You know us women. Calorie deprived."

He bought it, thank God. United in their common, be-nice-to-Nick cause, the women clustered together. In mutual, unspoken solidarity, they started discussing something else.

"Oh, look!" Nadine said. "Nick's brought out the baby shower gifts we dropped off earlier."

He had. Nick emerged from the hallway with an armload of them. With Jerry's help, he piled them on a ratty bachelor chair beside the TV and started going through them.

"Uh-oh," Naomi murmured.

"What?"

"That. Watch. You'll see."

As instructed, Chloe watched in amazement as Nick picked up one of the oddly shaped, gaily wrapped gifts and bashed himself in the forehead with it. Grinning, he nodded and put it in a separate pile.

"I didn't have time to check all these earlier," he told Jerry.

"He's been doing that with every one of them," Nora whispered. "He said nobody got into the party with a . . . a . . . shoot, what did he call it, Nadine?"

"A baby basher."

Nora snapped her fingers. "Yup, that was it."

"He wouldn't let us put anything in boxes before wrapping it, either," Nadine added.

Chloe flashed on the monogrammed silver rattle from her father and had to smile. This time, Steady Steadman was taking no chances.

"No boxes, huh? I guess that might have interfered with his

bash-detection device." She tried hard not to giggle as Nick picked up anther gift and, looking intensely serious, bonked himself on the side of the head with it.

"My husband Rikk got kind of crazy like that, too, right before our youngest was born," Nadine confided. "I thought it was kind of cute."

All four sisters smiled fondly.

Behind them, Nick frowned at a purple-wrapped package and walloped it over his head for a second time. *Must be a tough case*, Chloe thought.

Nancy, the eldest sister, plunked her chin in her hand and rolled her eyes. "He's so protective of you and the baby. You'd almost think Nick was the father, wouldn't you?"

For the second time, silence descended. Dammit, did the CD player have a Social Mortification detector, or what?

"Almost. Ha, ha," Chloe choked out, strangling on a bite of Nancy's Italian cream cake. She managed to get her napkin to her mouth seconds before causing a mascarpone cheese disaster.

"So!" Naomi slapped Chloe's knee cheerfully. "Why don't you tell us all about your guy?"

"My guy?" she wheezed.

"Yes, tell us!" Nora urged. "We'd love to know all about your mystery Marine, uhh . . . B-something . . . shoot, what was it again, Nadine?"

Chloe devoutly hoped memory loss wasn't an inescapable consequence of motherhood. Poor Nora only had three children, but she couldn't remember her way out of a paper bag.

"Bruno," Nadine supplied. She smiled at Chloe. "Yes, do tell us all about him."

"Arrgh!" In the kitchen, Nick slammed his forehead on the refrigerator, gripping both sides hard enough to wobble the appliance. "I can't take it anymore, Red. It's 'Bruno this,' and 'Bruno that.' 'Bruno's sooo wonderful.'"

"I heard." Red grabbed another carrot stick. "So what are you going to do about it?"

"What am I going to do about it?"

"Yeah."

Pound a new head-shaped dent in my Frigidaire.

Nah, that wouldn't help. *Pound a new dent in Bruno.*

"The Nick Steadman I know wouldn't just stand by and let some other guy steal his girl." Blithely, Red propped her hands on her bony hips as she rolled her carrot around her mouth. "The Nick Steadman I know would fight for her."

Nick cast her a miserable glance. "How can I?"

He thought of the conversation he'd heard earlier, thought of his sisters listening openmouthed and teary-eyed as Chloe described her mysterious, romantic Bruno, and knew he couldn't destroy her chance at happiness. Not if that was what she wanted.

Even if the bastard still hadn't managed to get in touch with her. For some reason, she obviously wanted him anyway.

"If you could only see her eyes when she talks about him," he told Red. "It's like-like—"

"Like she's in love with him."

He nodded. "And the crazy thing is, I have this feeling . . ."

"Go on."

"I've been remembering things . . ." He rammed his hands in his hair, realized what he was doing, and straightened his glasses instead. "Things . . . awww, hell. They can't be true, Red. Otherwise—"

"Otherwise?" She edged closer. The carrot stick disappeared between her lips.

"Otherwise Chloe's been—"

A movement in the kitchen doorway stopped his words. Nick clamped his mouth shut as Chloe stepped inside.

"Been what?" she asked, her gaze darting from Nick to Red and back again. "Besides surprised, revived, and treated like royalty?" Grinning, she lifted the full coffee pot and assessed its contents, then flipped open the cupboard above it. "This guest of honor stuff is great," she went on in a muffled voice as she rooted around inside. "Thanks so much for the party, Nick. It was really sweet of you."

Consider it my send-off, Nick thought, watching her hot-pink-clad backside sway as she searched. *Straight into Bruno's arms.*

"You're welcome. I think even Larry, Moe, Shemp and Curly had a good time."

"Thanks to your sports drinks. That was a brilliant idea. Did you see them lap up that stuff, Red?"

"Sure did. Looks as if you're fixing to help us lap up some of your special coffee, too."

"Nick's sisters asked me to." Bright-faced and happy, Chloe plunked a half-full bottle of Kahlúa on the countertop and started arranging cups beside it. She glanced over her shoulder at Nick. "Since alcohol's off-limits right now, your mother said she'll drink an extra cup for me."

"That's my mom. Generous to a fault."

"I know." Chloe sighed and lifted the bottle. "Hey, I'll make some for you, too, if you want. Interested in Kahlúa and coffee?"

And sympathy? his brain added, half on autopilot.

He looked at her standing there, swinging the Kahlúa bottle between her fingertips and waiting expectantly for his answer. Suddenly, answers for all the half-formed questions he'd had for months clicked in place. *Kahlúa and coffee and sympathy.* Chloe's never-fail remedy for disastrous job interviews, bad hair days . . . and Nick's months-old heartbreak over what's-hername.

The night they'd spent together crystallized in his mind, clear for the first time in months and heartrendingly remembered too late. An image of Chloe's comfy sleigh bed—and waking up in it—the morning after. Her sheer orange bra, those sexy purple-dotted silk boxers she'd had on . . . the way she'd called him *darling* and smiled at him sleepily from beneath the sheets. He'd held her in his arms and in his heart that night, and wakened denying everything.

What was that he'd said? *Tell me this isn't what it looks like, Chloe. Tell me I didn't take advantage of you last night.*

So she had. *Nothing happened here last night except too much Kahlúa, too much talking, and way too much sympathy.* Damn, damn, damn.

But Chloe was wrong. Everything had happened between them that night, including love.

Including a baby.

How could he have been so blind? So ready to believe her, despite all evidence to the contrary?

The same way he'd been blind to missing Danny's birthday party, the family Thanksgiving dinner, the annual tree-trimming preholiday brunch with his sisters and their husbands and his nieces and nephews. The same way he'd turned into an invention-obsessed workaholic without realizing it.

The whole truth hit him like a whap on the head.

Chloe's baby was his baby, too.

He was going to be a father.

Nick's knees buckled. He slammed his hand on the table-top just as Red jabbed her elbow in his ribs. Luckily, the motion helped keep him upright.

"Well, sonny?" she asked.

"Huh?"

He was going to have a baby.

"Are you having some of this or not?" Chloe elaborated, swirling the liquor around inside the bottle. "I think there's just enough for everyone to try a little."

Nick, Jr., maybe.

"Nick?"

Holy cow!

"Should I fix you some Kahlúa and coffee, or not?"

He looked up at her. "Are you dishing out the truth along with that Kahlúa? Because that's what I'm really interested in."

She went white, down to her fingertips wrapped around the bottle. It wobbled in her hand as Chloe stared at him.

He stepped forward and grabbed it. The cool, dark glass slipped from her hand as easily as the lies had come from her mouth, month after month after month.

"We can start with Bruno."

"B-Bruno?"

"Yes."

She licked her lips and gave him a wary look. "What do you want to know?"

Sticking with her alibi, all the way down the line. Nick's heart twisted.

"I want to know why you didn't trust me with the truth."

Chloe backed into the counter behind her, twisting her hair like a hairdresser on fast-forward. Nick followed.

"I want to know why you didn't tell me *I'm Bruno*," he said, his voice rising. "I want to know why you hid my baby from me and—"

"*You're Bruno?*" Red shrieked, staring, dumbfounded, at them both.

He kept his focus on Chloe. "I want to know why the *hell* you didn't come to me first and let me help you!"

"Maybe because I thought you'd react just like this," Chloe yelled back, rising on tiptoes to face him better. "Just like a . . . a . . . a *man*!"

Nick planted both hands on the countertop, fencing her in. "I am a man," he said quietly. "As it turns out, I'm going to be a father, too."

"*You're Bruno?*" Red asked again. She shook her head and tapped out a cigarette from the case in her hand. "My, my, my—"

"I had a right to know!" he shouted.

"Why? So you could abandon your dreams, just like every other steady Steadman has for generations?" Chloe asked. *Twist, twist,* went her hair. "So you could 'do the right thing'? So you could jump in and take over and—"

"Yes, dammit! We could have already been married by now. Had all this settled! Not be doing—"

"Doing something that's totally wrong for us?" She shoved at his arms caging her in. "You don't have any obligation to me, Nick."

"—doing *this*, a week before your due date! I damn well *do* have an obligation to you. I—"

"Four days." Red puffed furiously on the cigarette she'd lit. "Her due date's in four days, not a week."

Gritting his teeth, Nick squinted through the haze of cigarette smoke. "Could you do that someplace else?"

She looked at her Lucky Strike as though it had sprouted, fully lit and smoking, from her fingertips. "Sorry. I crumple under pressure."

"Let me go!" Chloe demanded with another shove, this one at his chest. "I've got a party to finish."

"*A party?*" Was she in denial? Or just too stubborn to realize how she'd shut him out . . . how she was still shutting him out? "You want to get back to your party, in the middle of all this?"

"Uncle Nick?" Danny stuck his head around the corner. "My mom wants to know if you're coming to our house on Christmas Eve. We're making a gingerbread village, remember?"

"Never mind," Red said. *Puff, puff.* "Looks as if the party's come to us."

"She said you should bring some toothpicks. Lot and lots of toothpicks," Danny went on, "if we're going to make that fancy design you told me about. Look, I drew a picture of it."

His nephew held out a folded piece of paper. The hopeful expression on his little face was like a knife to Nick's heart. How much time had he missed with Danny while trying to make his mark as an inventor?

How many chances to watch his baby grow had he missed, thanks to Chloe's deception?

Hell.

Nick took the paper from Danny's hand just as Naomi's head appeared above her son's. "Honey, I told you to ask Uncle Nick another time. He's, umm, busy right now."

"You mean fighting with Chloe?" Danny squinted at the adults. He shook his head with the supreme confidence of a seven-year-old. "Nah. She's his best friend. Best friends always make up."

"Don't bet on it." Nick glared at Chloe.

"I tried to tell you!" she cried, waving her arm. "Out on the porch, remember?" She stepped closer to the kitchen doorway, moving farther and farther away from Nick. "You wouldn't listen. You-you-you—"

Were thinking about getting her to the surprise baby shower before somebody gave it away.

"Wouldn't listen," he said, and it was hideously, unarguably true. He'd been absorbed in his own thing, concentrating on nothing except the goal to be reached.

The same way he'd focused on his inventions, even at the expense of everything else.

Your whole point is doing the right thing, Chloe had said. *No matter what the cost.* Nick hadn't known then what she meant. Now he did.

"Awww, Chloe." He reached for her. "This is never going to work between us. Not this way."

Her eyes misted. Her lips wobbled, setting off all the tell-tale, weepy signs. Dammit, somehow he'd done it again . . . except this time Nick felt like bawling right along with her.

Chloe lifted her chin. Her fingertips brushed his jaw like a fluttery, warm kiss good-bye. Her voice sounded husky when she spoke.

"Didn't you know, Einstein? That's what I've been trying to tell you all along."

With one last, sorrowful glance, she put her hand to her rounded belly. She slipped away between Danny and Naomi. An instant later, the front door opened and closed, as quiet as the whole crowd of partygoers had become.

Danny's hand nudged Nick's. His small arm wrapped around his uncle's waist, then his voice broke the silence Chloe's departure had left.

"Look at it this way, Uncle Nick," he said, giving him a man-to-man squeeze. "You know all that nice stuff Chloe was sayin' about Bruno? It was really about you!"

"Yeah," Nick mumbled, feeling forlorn. "That's really great."

"Can we go blow up some stuff now?"

Twelve

"I knew Nick would never forgive me," Chloe said.

"He's just mad, hon," Red replied with a knowing shake of her head. She settled sideways on Chloe's cushy plaid sofa and reached for the bottle of red nail polish Chloe held out to her. "That was a real whopper you kept from him. It's only been two days. Give the man some time! He'll get over it."

"Get over me, you mean." Feeling morose, Chloe leaned against the sofa pillows and extended her bare foot.

There was no worse time to be heartbroken than Christmas, she'd discovered. Every carol, every twinkling light, every ribbon and bow and sprig of mistletoe only made her feel worse. As long as she'd known Nick, they'd spent the holidays together. Tomorrow was Christmas Eve . . . and they'd never been farther apart.

"If you'd give Nick half a chance, he'd forgive you." Red twisted open the nail polish and dunked the brush a few times. She squinted up at Chloe. "Are you sure you want to take time for this beauty rigmarole?"

"You bet. It's my last chance to look glamorous."

"Raising a child is not a lifetime sentence of frumpery. Besides, glamour comes from within." Grinning, Red waggled her fingertips over her head like a cowboy-boot-wearing, red-pompadoured fairy godmother awakening Chloe's Inner Glamour-puss.

"Beauty comes from within. Glamour comes from the Estée Lauder counter."

"You're turning into a real cynic, Chloe Carmichal. I just might be having second thoughts about selling my pet store to someone like you."

"Too late . . . ouch! You already used the money for the down payment on that retirement place in Sun City."

Red laughed. She examined Chloe, then frowned. "Was that another contraction?"

Chloe nodded, panting as she clicked on the stopwatch in her hand and set it on the coffee table beside the plate of Christmas cookies—with sprinkles—Red had brought to cheer her up. "They're coming about fifteen minutes apart now."

At the onset of the contractions earlier this morning, Chloe had been excited. Finally! It was almost time for her baby to be born. Now the excitement had mixed with fear, and both emotions were roller-coastering through her insides. She wasn't ready yet.

Not without Nick.

"Look, the fancy pedicure can wait." Shaking her head, Red got to her feet. She started toward the bathroom to put the polish away. "We're going to the hospital."

She made it almost to the fireplace, where the Bruno letters and the "Macho Men of the Military" pinup calendar that had started the whole stupid mess crackled merrily, before Chloe grabbed her hand and eased her back beside her.

"No! I'm not ready to go yet, anyway. Not until I finish this." She tapped the fabric-covered notebook in her lap and gave Red a beseeching look. "Please?"

"Oh . . ." Red made a reluctant face, rolled the crimson polish bottle between her palms, then sighed. "All right, hon. But I make no guarantees if those contractions speed up."

"It's a deal."

Almost an hour later, Chloe had ten perfectly polished toenails, one updated and gift-wrapped pregnancy journal, and one very antsy soon-to-be-ex-boss.

"I'm the labor coach!" Red cried, dogging Chloe's heels all

the way to her bedroom as she pulled on her winter coat and took one last look around to make sure she hadn't forgotten anything. "I can't be late!"

"*You* can't be late?" Between contractions, Chloe grinned. Red snatched the packed birthday bag right out from under her fingertips and hustled out of the room. "What about me?"

On the front porch, Chloe carefully locked the door behind them, feeling strangely calm now that the time to head to the hospital had arrived. She hugged her finished pregnancy journal to her chest, gazing across the yard at Nick's house.

The journal, detailing her thoughts and dreams for their baby, described her pregnancy all the way from the contortionist pregnancy test she'd taken to the contractions she'd been having this morning. It was only one of the concessions she wanted to make—just one way to share what he'd missed with Nick. What would he say when he read it?

Red stopped halfway down the front walk. "What are you dilly dallyin' for?" she hollered, jangling her car keys. "That baby's not waiting all day."

She turned, saw Chloe's desperate clutch on the pregnancy journal and her equally desperate watch on Nick's house, and her expression softened. She clomped up the walk.

"Giving him that is the right thing to do, hon. I know it." Affectionately, she draped her arm over Chloe's shoulders and squeezed. "He was madder over your keeping the baby a secret than over fathering him, you know."

"Or her." *Then I'll teach her to play football anyway.*

"Sure." Red held out her hand for the journal. "I'll make sure he gets that."

Red pulled. Involuntarily, Chloe's fingers clamped harder on the vibrant fabric-covered book.

"I can't!" she wailed. "Oh, Red. What if I'm making a big mistake?"

"You're just scared, 'cause taking a chance on that man wasn't something you planned on doing." Gently, Red pried Chloe's whitened fingers from the book, one by one. "But hon . . . love never is something you plan."

Fear clutched at Chloe's belly. Or maybe that was another contraction. Either way, it hurt like crazy. But sticking with her Bruno alibi hadn't worked. Keeping the truth from Nick hadn't worked. And fooling herself any longer was impossible.

She had to give Nick the chance to love them . . . her and the baby both. She had to trust him to be the best friend he'd always been.

And more.

"Okay." She gave the journal one last squeeze for luck. Then she gave Red her sternest look. "But he doesn't get this until tomorrow. Not until *after* his investor meeting."

"Now hold on—"

"Not until tomorrow afternoon, Red. Not until Christmas Eve. I mean it." She was willing to be flexible about things for a change, all except for this *one* thing. "I won't wreck Nick's shot at making his invention a success."

Red rolled her eyes.

"I'm not changing my mind."

She rolled her eyes again and clucked her tongue, too. Disagreement personified.

Chloe wavered and grabbed the porch railing. "Ohh," she moaned. "I think I feel a sit-down strike coming on. You'd better alert the media and call up the—"

"All right, all right!" Red yelled, throwing up her hands. She yanked the journal the rest of the way out of Chloe's grasp, grabbed her arm, and hauled her to the car. "I heard ya' the first time. I won't give the dang thing to him until Christmas Eve."

"I'll look forward to receiving the agreements." Nick smiled at the man who, upon signing those agreements, would become his growth accelerator's first investor. "Thank you for meeting with me, especially right before the holidays."

The man, who looked about as patrician and big-business as he imagined Chloe's absentee father did, smiled too. "It's our pleasure, Mr. Steadman." His nod indicated the video camera and remote conferencing setup Nick had arranged. "This is nothing less than we'd expect from an innovator like yourself."

Nick was just glad it had worked. The video conference,

his first step toward cutting back his work hours and putting some balance back in his life, had linked him with his California investor in less than a quarter of the time it would have taken him to attend the meeting in person.

Chloe and Danny would have been so proud. Nick glanced at the six boxes of toothpicks he'd bought. Out of camera range, he smoothed his fingers over the drawing of the ginger-bread monolith he planned to construct with his nephew after he'd wrapped up the meeting. *I'm finally doing the right thing.*

By doing less of the right thing. It had all the makings of a new Steadman family tradition.

On his computer monitor, his new investor's image beamed with satisfaction at a job well done. "That just about wraps it up. Have a merry Christmas."

"Merry Christmas to you," Nick said. "I'll be in touch."

He signed off and shut down the equipment, then looked around the empty room. He slapped his hands on his thighs, grinning like an idiot. *He'd done it!*

News this momentous was meant to be shared. Still smiling, Nick tromped down the hallway to his bedroom and lifted the mini-blind slats with one hand. He'd never spotted Chloe gazing across their adjoining yards the way he did, but it was the fastest way to find out if she was at home.

Also the fastest way to make a good mood plummet, he realized when he saw her lights were out and no curvy, Chloe-shaped shadows moved behind her dusky windows.

Should he go over anyway? He'd been waiting—since she'd been the one to walk out on him at the baby shower—for her to let him know she was ready to talk things over. It had seemed the best way to make sure he didn't make her, the woman who never cried . . . cry.

Again.

Nick waited a few minutes, then looked again. Okay, mixing business with pleasure he could take. Maintaining a balance in his life he could handle. Waiting for Chloe to make her move was another story altogether.

He was going in.

He opened his front door and stepped onto the porch, nearly squashing the gift-wrapped package waiting there for him. The name and address written on it in green ink confirmed it was for him, whatever it was, and the minute Nick recognized Chloe's squat, round handwriting, he knew his make-up mission was going to have to wait a little longer.

He ripped open the wrapping and pulled out the heavy notebook inside. Slowly, Nick sank to a seated position on his front porch steps. He started to read.

He was hooked from page one.

But it was the final entry, dated earlier today, that made him thrust the journal in his coat pocket and sprint to his motorcycle. He just hoped he wasn't too late.

Thirteen

"Try to get some rest," the nurse told Chloe, reaching beside her shoulder to affix the call button more securely to the hospital bed's mattress. She pulled up the crisp white sheet and tucked it in snugly, then smiled and squeaked to the door in her cushioned shoes. "We'll let you know just as soon as baby Carmichal wakes up."

"Thank you." Chloe watched as the nurse pulled the thick hospital room door halfway closed, then left. "I'll try."

She'd never felt more deeply tired, more utterly relieved, more proud of herself then she did right now. Looking around her flower-bedecked, private room—arranged for, somehow, by her father's number-two secretary Lucinda—Chloe had also never felt more lonely.

Because Nick wasn't coming.

Naturally, the baby looked just like him. Except a little more squashed. Also smaller, pinker, and slightly more adorable. But otherwise, their child looked exactly like his father.

Sighing, Chloe gazed out her window at the velvety, starless night . . . until suddenly the view blurred and she had to look away. Funny how tears made everything look soft-focused and a little more sparkly.

She sniffed and blinked. Her hospital room came back into focus. It would have looked just like home, if home was a really, really antiseptic log cabin. *Okay, concentrating on ambiance isn't helping.* Chloe closed her eyes and thought about the baby instead. She felt pretty sure no one else in history had ever had a more perfect child.

A ghost of a smile quirked her lips. If only Nick were here, everything would be wonderful. Maybe it had been a mistake not to call him. She reached for the phone.

Before she could dial, someone knocked on the door. "Ms. Carmichal?"

Hallelujah! The baby must have woken up, and one of the nurses was bringing him in. Chloe bunched the pillows at the small of her back and sat up higher so she could hold him again.

"Come in," she called, fiddling with the neck of her gown.

A hospital worker entered, carrying . . . something that *wasn't* the baby. It looked like . . .

A length of white picket fence, about as high and as wide as her hospital bed, and just as dazzlingly bright. The hospital worker unfolded it, magically erecting a three-sided white picket fence beside her bed.

She blinked. It was still there. Chloe whipped her gown closed again. *This* situation definitely didn't call for the football hold the nurse had suggested for breast-feeding.

"What's this?"

"I'm just delivering it like the fella asked." The hospital worker jerked his thumb toward the doorway. He shrugged. "I guess some folks don't think flowers are enough. You got plenty of those, though."

She had, thanks to her father and Tabitha—and her mother and her new bingo partner. They'd all sent gorgeous bouquets. Her mother had even phoned. Twice. At length. With advice. Clearly, grandparenthood hadn't effected any drastic changes in her family yet. Certainly none that would call for delivery of a white picket fence.

In amazement, Chloe stared at it. Was it from Nick? But Nick was probably in California for his meeting by now. Maybe Red had thought the fence would make a kooky gag gift for Christmas?

"Ms. Carmichal?"

"Yes?"

A tall, thin man entered, carrying a black velvet box on a silver platter. Without a word, but with a grin wider than his waistband, he took up a position beside the bed, just inside the fence.

"Chloe?"

"*Red*? Do you know what's—"

"Hang on. You're about to find out," Red interrupted, speaking louder to be heard over the sudden murmur of voices coming from the hospital corridor.

Visitors? Chloe pulled up the covers and patted her rat's-nest of a hairdo. How could she have enough visitors to create an audible *murmur*?

Red came nearer, followed closely by Jerry. "Don't kill me over delivering that journal early, neither," she added.

Chloe was too busy staring at the paper banner they carried between them to question what she meant.

As they neared the bed, Sun City's newest retirees-to-be unfurled the paper. AND HERE HE IS, it said in fancy foot-high block letters. A MAN WHO LOVES YOU!

Chloe gasped. It couldn't be . . .

"Hiya, Blondie."

Nick.

He came in her room carrying a white-wrapped bundle of snoozing baby. His face was luminous. If joy wore faded blue jeans, it would have looked just like Nick. As he neared the bed and slipped inside the white picket fence, Chloe knew she must look exactly the same way. That radiant feeling shimmered all through her, leaving her trembling beneath his smile.

"I got here as fast as I could," he said. "I had some things to arrange first."

A silly, nervous giggle burst from her lips as she looked at the fence, the banner, the man with the silver platter. "I-I—so I see."

Nick folded back a portion of the blanket and gazed down at the child in his arms. His child. *Their child*. His smile could have lit the midnight outside her window.

"He's as beautiful as his mother." Nick stroked the baby's pudgy cheek. "Only a little less well-coiffed."

Laughing, Chloe swept her palm over their baby's sweet-scented swirls of fine blond hair. "Give him time. He's just getting started."

"So am I."

Nick nodded to the platter-bearer, who opened the hinged black box and displayed its contents to Chloe with a flourish of silver. Glittering back at her was a gold and diamond engagement ring.

"Oh, my!"

Carefully holding the baby against his chest, Nick bent to one knee beside the bed. He reached for her hand. His fingers quivered as they touched hers, then squeezed.

"Chloe, I brought you the white picket fence, the ring, and the man who loves you . . . that's me, by the way—"

"I know." Tears prickled her eyes. Suddenly Nick was all soft-focused and sparkly, but Chloe didn't care, just as long as he was with her. "Oh, Nick! I love you, too."

His hand clasped hers tighter. "There's only one thing left, and the fairytale ending will be complete." He smiled, kissed the baby's forehead, and hugged him close. "And that's you. I need you, Chloe. I love you so much I'm crazy with it."

"You're not crazy. You're brilliant."

"You're beautiful."

"Brainiac."

"Blondie."

"Beloved," she murmured, and the tenderness in his gaze sent her smile into overdrive all over again.

"Aww, Chloe. Please say you'll marry me."

She looked at him, just long enough to really let his words sink in. *Nick wanted to marry her*! Then Chloe raised her hand and spread her fingers to get ready for the ring.

"Just try and stop me."

"Is that a yes?"

"Yes, yes, yes, yes, yes!" Laughing, she put her arms around his neck and held on tight, careful not to jostle the baby. "Yes," she peeped, just in case he hadn't gotten it yet.